PENGUIN BOO[...]

PATRIOTS

Sousa Jamba was born in Angola, fled at the time of the civil war to Zambia and later returned to join UNITA against the MPLA government (an experience on which he has drawn in writing *Patriots*).

He now lives in London. He has been a winner of the *Spectator*'s Shiva Naipaul Prize for travel writing and is a regular contributor to that journal. He also writes a column for the American literary magazine *Wig-Wag*.

SOUSA JAMBA

PATRIOTS

PENGUIN BOOKS

PENGUIN BOOKS

Published by the Penguin Group
Penguin Books Ltd, 27 Wrights Lane, London W8 5TZ, England
Penguin Books USA Inc., 375 Hudson Street, New York, New York 10014, USA
Penguin Books Australia Ltd, Ringwood, Victoria, Australia
Penguin Books Canada Ltd, 10 Alcorn Avenue, Toronto, Ontario, Canada M4V 3B2
Penguin Books (NZ) Ltd, 182–190 Wairau Road, Auckland 10, New Zealand

Penguin Books Ltd, Registered Offices: Harmondsworth, Middlesex, England

First published by Viking 1990
Published in Penguin Books 1992
1 3 5 7 9 10 8 6 4 2

Printed in England by Clays Ltd, St Ives plc

In loving memory of my sister,
Altina Flora Jamba

Glossary

assimillados	Black Angolans who had the status of Portuguese conferred on them
CADIS	Centre for the Defence of Internal Security – UNITA's secret police
chisangua	an Umbundu beverage
DEP	the branch of UNITA which decided where its fighters were assigned
DISA	Centre for Information and Security of Angola – the MPLA's secret police
manu	a word used when addressing an older person
PIDE	International Police for the Defence of the State – the Portuguese secret police

Main tribes in Angola

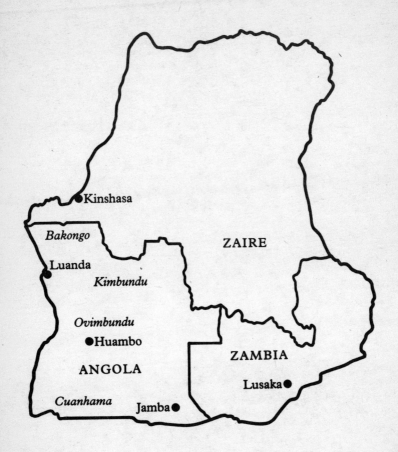

BOOK I

1

Hosi Mbueti decided to return to Angola one morning while he was lying in bed. He had been a refugee in Zambia for ten years now, having fled from Angola during the 1975 civil war. He summoned all the energy he had and got out of his single bed, the springs screeching as he moved. He rented a small room from Mrs Banda. It was so small that his few belongings – three pots, a basin, a brazier, a box containing cups, three pairs of trousers and two shirts – hardly seemed to fit. He groaned loudly as he stretched, picked up the basin and went out to fetch some water to wash himself. It was ten o'clock in the morning and the sun was shining hard.

The first thing Hosi saw as he opened the door was Mrs Banda's grandchild, John, who was squatting beside the water pipe with a piece of bread in one hand. Tears falling from the child's eyes showed that he was trying hard to relieve himself of the maize he had had the previous night. Hosi could not help noticing that the grains were the same consistency as when the child had eaten them. As soon as he finished he called out to his mother to come and clean the mess. As Hosi stood beside the water pipe, watching the basin fill, he thought of the child's nauseating habits. He had complained to Mrs Banda on several occasions, but she had merely told him that the child was free to relieve himself wherever he wanted; the house was hers and she was not going to bend to anyone else's rules. Hosi could not leave because Mrs Banda's room was all he could afford.

He went back into the house and washed himself. The sight of the child beside the water pipe kept coming back into his mind. It reinforced the feeling he had that there was nothing left for him in Zambia. In fact, he had had this feeling from

3

the very day that he and the other Angolans had passed through the Shinkongo border post into Zambia. At that time the Angolan refugees had believed that they would stay for a few weeks and return when the MPLA government had been overthrown or when a government which included UNITA had been formed. The weeks had turned into years and still people were hoping. Some had decided to return to Angola – that is, to the UNITA-controlled territory.

The elders among the Angolan refugees kept telling Hosi and his contemporaries not to adopt the ways of the Zambians, which left much to be desired. Hosi felt that there was a tiny part of him which was now Zambian, but he never admitted this to any other Angolan. He tried to speak Portuguese as fluently as those who had come from Angola as adults and he also took to listening to the conversations of elderly men to improve his Umbundu, his mother tongue.

The sun beat down on the corrugated-iron roof. As Hosi was getting dressed he decided that before leaving for Angola he would get new clothes. He was due to receive some money from the office of the United Nations High Commission for Refugees, along the Great North Road. He hated going there: the place made him feel like some kind of invalid and the bureaucrats who manned the office behaved like small gods – when you needed their assistance most, that was when it was their tea-break.

Hosi walked to the bus stop to catch a minibus to the city centre. From there he would change to another bus, which would drop him near the UNHCR's office. As he walked he saw Mable and his heart missed a beat, but there was no need to worry any more – the trouble he had feared was now past. Mable was one of the girls in Mtendere all the young men who thought highly of themselves hoped to go out with. She was at secondary school and she was beautiful. Whenever she went past a group of young men, they would whistle and some would gasp, saying: 'Ah, she is so beautiful. If I married her, I'd give up eating for a year.' Mable had dark, shy eyes, her skin was smooth and she had the shapeliest bottom around. Her parents were very protective of her and she was under strict orders not to talk to any young men who approached her. People had thought that she was a virgin – a rare thing in an age when fourteen-year-olds were said to make men old enough to be their grandfathers dribble with pleasure. Hosi had won Mable's love with several poems and letters, but then she became pregnant. All sorts of rumours flew about. Some said it was Daniel, her choir master; others blamed Solomon, a cousin who lived with the family. The most bizarre speculation of all was that Mable's father had made her pregnant. Hosi was terrified. Mable was a Tonga and the Tonga charged a lot for their daughters, especially when they had attended secondary school. Mable stayed inside and had no contact with anyone. Hosi was waiting for the bombshell, but when she had the baby, to his relief it turned out to be a half-caste. Some said that an Indian shop-owner was the father; others that the Catholic priest was the man. Whatever, Hosi leapt for joy and decided never to have anything to do with Mable again.

Before reaching the bus stop, he decided to walk through the market, a large enclosure made of bricks. Inside, there were small rooms with windows, the front of which served as grocery stores. They sold anything from skin-lightening creams to petromax lamps. There was one section with nothing but chickens, which were kept in box-like frames covered by wire. As there were no customers, the chicken vendors snored in the shade. In the middle of the market there was a huge building. As Hosi entered it he was greeted with the smell of dried fish. He wanted *chikanda* – a soft, spongy cake made from roots, sometimes jokingly referred to as 'African ham'. Hosi bought three chunks and walked over to a woman selling *mukoyo*, a drink made from mealie-meal porridge and roots. He felt squeamish as the woman handed him a cup. As a child in Angola, his mother had warned him never to drink *chisangua*, as it is called there. It was said that the women vendors used witchcraft to get as many customers as possible. However, after the *chikanda* and the *mukoyo* Hosi felt better. He belched and walked to the bus stop.

The minibus came, loudspeakers blaring out the latest disco number. It was Shalamar's 'Second Time Around'. People crowded in. Where the Japanese manufacturers had intended two people to sit, the minibus conductors fitted three. In rare instances a person could have a chair to himself, if he could pay the price of three. This happened quite often with girls, who, it was said, felt that travelling crammed like caterpillars in a basket diluted their perfume. The minibus set off. Then, halfway through the journey, the driver stopped. A heated argument between an obese woman and the conductor was taking place.

'I have paid for two. What more do you want?' asked the woman with a desperate expression on her face.

The conductor, a short tough-looking man who had shaved his head and had a ring on his left ear, was shouting at the top of his voice: 'You are very fat. Three people can fit in that seat. Either you pay or you leave.'

'Listen, son,' pleaded the woman, 'if I had the money, I would pay you. I have children as old as you are. Please, son.'

The conductor shook his head. The driver, a dark man with pimples all over his face, strained his neck, contorted his face and said: 'I have enough problems in this bloody life. Who is trying to make this wretched world more of a mess?'

With the expansiveness of one who thinks he can never be wrong, the conductor said: 'It is this mama. You see the chair she is on? Usually we have three, sometimes four, people there. I have told her to pay for three. She has refused. She has only paid for two.'

'I always pay for two,' cried the woman.

'Liar!' the conductor burst out. 'They usually charge you for four. Now, get out!'

The woman was about to leave her chair when a man dressed in a three-piece suit who had been poring over the pages of the *Times of Zambia* turned to her and began to speak in English. 'What is your plight, mama?' he asked. The woman told him. He took a brand-new ten-kwacha note from his wallet and gave it to the conductor.

'Deduct your due, young man,' he said as he handed over the money to the conductor and bade the woman stay. Everybody looked on with admiration. 'At least there is one true humanist in Zambia,' someone shouted from the back.

6

The benefactor nodded, appreciating the comment, and returned to his newspaper. The minibus resumed its journey. Meanwhile, the conductor turned to the fat woman and said: 'You are too fat. You should do something about it. It is you fat people who are finishing our bags of mealie meal. A visit to Ethiopia will do you some good.' The woman did not reply. Instead, tears began to fall from her eyes. The other women on the bus were incensed by the conductor's remarks. One, who was so thin she looked ill, turned to the conductor and began to shout: 'Some people talk as though they came out through their mother's arseholes. Yes, as if they were shitted. Where I come from older people are respected. What is the world coming to if people with mouths in which frogs have rotted can yap at will?'

The conductor remained silent. He knew that the woman was an expert at insults. The minibus screeched to a halt and Hosi got off to wait for the next bus, which would drop him in front of the UNHCR's office.

It was almost twelve o'clock – not a very good time, Hosi realized, for the officers were now preparing to go to lunch. But that was not going to matter too much because he also wanted to meet other Angolan refugees.

The UNHCR reception room was full. South African, Namibian, Ugandan, Zairean, Malawian and Sudanese refugees were chatting with each other. The office was in a huge three-storey building. The reception room was always dirty – desperate people have little concern for hygiene. Among the refugees, the South Africans and the Namibians enjoyed the greatest prestige and always appeared to be jovial. They seemed to have genuine reasons for being there. Next in the hierarchy came the Ugandans. They had a war in their country, so it was acceptable to ask for handouts from the UN. The presence of a Ugandan filled Hosi with awe. He wondered whether the person before him had just escaped from one of their carnivorous dictators. Then came the Angolans. Rarely a day passed without the papers carrying an item from the Angolan official news agency saying that a hundred more people had been killed in the war.

7

Hosi soon spotted a group of Angolans. They smiled when they saw him. They were Lindo, Pinto, Jaime and Ze. Like Hosi, they had all come to Zambia as children. They avoided the older refugees, because they were always made to shut up whenever they wanted to say something about Angola. 'You left Angola as a baby. What do you know?' they would be asked. The younger refugees, like Hosi, had all completed secondary school and were now trying to get the UN to give them scholarships. Pinto wanted to go to America and study engineering. Lindo dreamed of Lisbon, where he hoped to train as a solicitor. Ze was crazy about Australia. They would talk for hours about the merits of this or that country. Hosi wanted to go to England. If there was one group he admired, it was the English. He believed that they were the most civilized people on earth, drinking tea in the afternoon and spending the evening reading Shakespeare.

Hosi often went to the British Council in Cairo Road to read the thick British Sunday papers. He found it hard to relate to some of the features but he always read on. He would read anything and after an hour or two of trying to make sense of the wrangles in the British Cabinet, he would leave with the feeling that a very tiny part of him had become British. He had also joined the library at the British Council and read George Orwell. Hosi concluded that a lot of what this Englishman had said was relevant to Africa and, as he had once said to himself, only a great society could produce such a man.

Lindo was tall, so tall that the only shoes he could fit into were the military boots which a soldier friend of his had sold to him. He was very popular with girls because he was such a good dancer. Some of them said he was as handsome as a *umunigga*, a black American. Pinto was short, so short that he was nicknamed 'Penguin'. He was an inveterate liar, to the extent that he even came to be admired for it. None of his contemporaries had the imagination to concoct the stories he did. A typical one went like this.

'Now, this witch doctor had some roots which, when thrown into the Cuanza river, it was said, would bring the Angolan war to an end. But he said he needed a pig from Zambia as a fee. So these two chaps decided to walk to Angola with the pig. One carried a sack full of popcorn and the other carried the pig itself. They reached this village, where they decided to spend the night. Now, the man with the pig seduced one of the women in the village. Just when he was about to get into the chorus of the first round, the woman's husband came in with a machete, ready to chop this chap into pieces. Serious negotiations took place. Finally they were made to leave the pig as a fine.'

The others would listen attentively. 'Penguin could make a fine novelist,' someone would say. Penguin would screw up his face and say: 'Now listen to this. This is absolutely true.' Another story would be told. Few were surprised when Penguin became an inmate of Chainama Hills mental hospital.

Jaime was asthmatic and said little. It was rumoured that he was going to die soon. Ze was interested only in football. He knew by name most of the players of the leading national teams in the world.

When they saw Hosi, they stopped talking. 'Now, you little devil,' Ze began, 'what the hell have you been up to? Gloating over pictures of white girls in magazines at the British Council, eh?'

'Nothing of the kind, you bastard. There are far more important things in the world than girls.'

'Such as rich men!' Ze interjected.

This was met with laughter. Penguin, who never let such an opportunity pass, came in quickly: 'There are some white men, I am told they are Greek, who get these boys who line up at night along Ridgeway Road. They take them to their houses, wash them properly and then spray them with perfume before they do it. If they find them attractive enough, they marry them. True. Men marrying men. It happens. Now, in Europe I am told that . . .'

Penguin did not finish what he was saying for Jaime, who had a you-know-what-he-is-like expression on his face, raised his voice and said: 'What is the latest from Angola? We have heard that Cangonga has fallen.'

'We have been hearing this and that for so long. You see,

Angola is rich, so rich that there are many people prepared to see us fight for ever,' said Hosi.

Penguin interrupted him: 'If it was not for this bloody war we would now be competing with Japan.'

'Now, you shut up,' bellowed Jaime. 'This is a serious matter. No more of your fantasies. I think the Cubans are about to leave. They must be fed up with the war.'

'I don't think that they will leave so soon,' said Hosi. 'I have decided to go and fight them. I am going to Angola to fight with UNITA. I am prepared to die. I don't want no mother-fucking Cuban to have a say in Angola.' Hosi was thumping his chest. The others looked on admiringly. There was silence, broken by Lindo.

'We have to be careful. We came to Zambia as children and we don't know Angola that well. In fact, I think we are Zambians, not Angolans. Wait a year or more, Hosi. These people will sooner or later have to find some kind of solution. And then we will all go back.'

Ze, who had been listening attentively throughout, joined in: 'I don't agree with you, Lindo. We are Angolans and we shall always remain Angolans. Look at the way people treat us. How many times have you guys heard these Zambians say that it's we Angolans who are finishing their bags of maize?'

'That is not fair,' said Lindo. 'We are enjoying the same health and educational facilities as the Zambians. We belong to this land whether you want it or not. Don't the elders laugh at us? They say we can't speak proper Portuguese. They say we prefer to eat with our hands, like the Zambians, and not with spoons and forks, like them. They say we are as uncivilized as the Zambians. They say the English never gave the Zambians any culture, which is why they drink too much, whereas Angolans are so civilized that they don't make much fuss about alcohol. When they have a bottle of wine with lunch, it just washes down the meal.' Even Penguin was now serious.

'I think these older Angolans are foolish,' said Hosi. 'They worship the Portuguese and praise their civilization as if it is superior to the British. The Portuguese have never produced a Shakespeare. This is the truth.'

10

The others nodded in approval. Hosi continued: 'I am fed up of hearing them say that the Portuguese have the best food and that the Portuguese have the best manners. That is crap. The French produced Descartes, Maupassant and I don't know who. The Russians produced Tolstoy. The Germans produced some chap – I don't remember his name. Even the Italians produced somebody. Was Galileo an Italian?' Hosi looked at Jaime, who quickly replied: 'I don't know!'

'Yes, as I was saying,' Hosi continued, 'the Portuguese have produced no one. No one really. I can't think of a famous Portuguese, apart from Vasco da Gama, of course.'

Salomao Kachiungo, a tall, middle-aged man, had been listening behind them. He was incensed and went to look for two of his companions – also middle-aged – who were outside. They came back together, walking with the fury of men going to battle. Uncle Salomao, as he was known, began: 'Hosi, my son, have you ever heard of Luis de Camões? The Portuguese discovered the world. My history teacher, Senhor Joao Alfonso de Carvalho Albuquerque, would rather have committed suicide than hear you talking this nonsense. You see, when there was an earthquake in Lisbon, people asked Camões: "Now, Senhor Poeta, what are we going to do?" He said: "Let's bury the dead and take care of the living." He was a great man, Camões.'

The argument went on. The two elders decided to give up when Hosi said they were still reeling from their colonial hangover. They said that they couldn't stand to hear Portuguese spoken so badly. Uncle Salomao said that Camões would be turning in his grave and that the three of them would come back as ghosts to torment anyone making mistakes like Hosi and his colleagues.

As the elders walked away, derogatory remarks were made about them by Hosi and his friends before they resumed their conversation. Jaime said, 'There must be a solution. If Angola remains the way it is, Namibia will never become independent. Those Boers are as thick as adobes. As long as they perceive a threat from the north they will stay put.'

Penguin could not keep silent. 'Hell! Am I fed up with

politics! Years ago, when you guys were still eating mucus, I was already into politics. I used to listen to Radio Kudibangela when I was seven. You might not believe this but I tell you that I knew of Che Guevara as soon as I was able to talk.'

Ze pushed Penguin aside and said: 'The problem with lying is that you start believing your own lies. Now shut up! Let's hear some sense.' Penguin protested that Ze was not being democratic. It was agreed that he could speak, but only if he was going to be sensible.

'I don't believe you black men,' Penguin began. 'I know I am black, too, but just see this. Here I am, a man who has gone through the shit that Angola is and you think that I am lying.' Several voices were raised at once. They called Penguin a son of a bitch and told him to buy skin-bleaching creams and leave for Europe.

'Fuck it,' he began. 'Look at the way you blacks ... I mean we blacks, treat each other. The whites are mother-fuckers but they would never let one of their own down. The British, the Israelis, even the Boers in South Africa, value their own people. Just you kill one Israeli or Boer today. They will turn the earth upside-down. You great pan-Africanists, what are you doing when your brothers are starving in Ethiopia? Reading Nkrumah?' They all remained silent, trying to think of an answer.

'I mean, Africans are lost. Look at Angola. The MPLA is out defending socialism and UNITA says it is fighting for democracy or whatever it is. So people kill each other. Some of them become one-legged heroes with imported crutches. Why the hell can't we tell the bloody foreigners to buzz off?'

Hosi burst in. 'There are no easier political solutions than those thought up in exile. The answer is to go back and help change things. When these people get back from lunch I will ask for some money and then leave tomorrow. I will be going home. There is nothing I can do about it. I just have to go.'

'So you are going to join UNITA?' asked Lindo.

'Yeah, I am an Ovimbundu,' Hosi said. 'There is no place for me in the MPLA. I am proud to be an Ovimbundu.'

'True,' Penguin shouted. 'We are the majority and yet we

12

don't have power. There will be no peace in Angola for the next century if it is not ruled by a man from the south. This is the truth.'

'No, no, no, no, no,' shouted Hosi. 'I don't believe in Umbundu supremacy or the supremacy of any other tribe. Angola can be ruled by a mulatto, Ngangela, Chokue, whatever, as long as he has the guts,' he said seriously.

At this Penguin left, talking to himself.

The UNHCR official responsible for finance came back at about three o'clock in the afternoon. He saw Hosi quickly. Fifty-two kwacha wasn't much money, but it was enough to buy a pair of trousers and a shirt. Hosi got a minibus and then walked to the city centre.

Nearly all the shops in Lusaka were owned by Indians and the locals hated them for this reason. Hosi was no exception. Someone had once told him that Hitler wasn't wrong after all for killing the Jews, who, like the Indians here, had come to possess most of the money in Germany. It was Jimmy who had said that, Jimmy who was now serving a long prison sentence for several armed robberies on Indian-owned shops.

Hosi's mind flitted back to Jimmy. He imagined him in his white prison uniform, now stained to a nauseating brown. He went into the restaurant and ordered a cup of coffee and a cake. As he drank his coffee he thought of Jimmy's remark. If only he could meet him now he would show him how mistaken he was. Hitler, he had now learned, thanks to the books and magazines in the British Council library, had been a killer, a heartless man. The saddest thing of all, thought Hosi, was that since his death Hitler kept being reincarnated, especially in Africa. There had been Amin, Bokassa, Nguema and several other dictators. Hosi thought of ways he could reach out to Jimmy. He decided to write him a letter before he left. Now, he thought of their past together.

In 1979 Hosi and Jimmy had been in the same class at Kamba Valley primary school. They often played truant, for the school work was boring and the teacher was often drunk. The school was right in the middle of the valley, with a military camp nearby. Some of the officers' daughters attended the school, but Hosi avoided talking to them because he thought his English was not good enough. He lived for the day when he would have a house with a television set; then he'd be able to speak like white people, as those girls did.

There were several maize fields in the valley. Hosi and Jimmy used to steal maize, then go and roast it at the Foxdale bricks furnace nearby. There hundreds of tiny bricks were packed into huge granary-like enclosures, beneath which were a few openings for the coal to fire the bricks. Stealing frightened Hosi but the temptation was too great to be resisted, even though it was said that most people planted special charms in their fields to catch thieves. He had suspected that one day his stomach would swell, but it never did.

Hosi liked Jimmy; they were best friends. Jimmy, who was about sixteen – three years older – regarded himself as being very wise and had this feeling reinforced whenever he told Hosi something Hosi had not known before. Once there was an incident that both embarrassed and fascinated Hosi. Jimmy had said that he was a real man and Hosi only a baby. To prove his point Jimmy had ordered Hosi to masturbate. Jimmy also began to masturbate and after a while his hands were filled with a mucus-like liquid; Hosi's hands were empty. Looking at the liquid, Jimmy said: 'This is life. Do you realize that what I am holding here could be the man who will save the world?' Then Jimmy had taken some soil and mixed it with the liquid. He made a hole in the ground and buried the mixture. As he did so he said: 'Dust to dust, ashes to ashes!' Then they went to steal maize, as usual. As the two had sat eating the cobs later, Jimmy said to Hosi: 'I will be rich, no doubt about it. I will not live in poverty like my father. I will have a beautiful house in Kabulonga, where the rich live.'

'How are you going to manage that?' Hosi had asked.

'You see, you are really young, a kid. System, my friend, system. You think all these people who have Mercedes sweated for them? No way! They know the deals.'

'What deals?'

'The world is a machine. Those who know how to use it get

14

the best; fools get crumbs. You see those Indians? You think that they are rich because they work hard? Not at all. They are bloody thieves. Now, I have some guy who intends to fix these chaps. I will join him. You wait and see. Next time you see in the newspapers, "Police are looking for Jimmy McStrangler," don't be surprised. It will be me.'

It had seemed like a joke then, a teenage fantasy. But now it was real. Hosi ordered another cup of coffee. He would have followed Jimmy had it not been for Ester, the woman who had looked after him since the day she had found him, alone and afraid in Angola.

Hosi needed to say goodbye to Ester and that was not going to be easy. She would rebuke him for having decided to return to Angola. She had always wanted the best for him. When he did well at school she was as pleased as if he was her own child. But like most people living in Chaisa Compound, Hosi had hoped to get away from the poverty as soon as possible. There were two ways this could be done: crime and education. The latter was not easy; the former was tempting and profitable. But there was a part of Hosi that told him he was destined to be great. It was a part that kept reminding him that he should fulfil what his father would have wished for him, come what may.

After three cups of coffee he left the restaurant to go shopping. Two state-owned shops – ZCBC and Mwaiseni – stocked relatively cheap clothes, but neither Hosi nor his contemporaries wanted them, preferring instead to be fashion-conscious. They were interested in the latest styles from New York, London, Rome and Paris. The trends in the town were set by pilots and air stewards – the people who were always going abroad and knew what was in vogue. Hosi wanted a pair of baggy satin trousers. He knew this was an unsuitable thing for someone going to fight in the bush, but he still wanted the trousers. As long as the money was there, he had no need to worry.

He went into Patel and V.J., the shop frequented by people who thought highly of themselves. There were not only French but also Italian shoes available there and it was the favourite shop of *abasungu abashala*, or the remaining whites, as wealthy Zambians were called.

15

The Indian girl behind the counter told him to wait. She was serving two Zambian girls who had had their hair permed, a sure sign of affluence. Hosi could tell that the girls had not been to a school like his because they spoke as if they had marbles in their mouths in an attempt to affect an American accent. One of the girls was tall; the other short.

'I am afraid we don't have that,' said the Indian girl.

'You are behind,' the short Zambian girl said. 'Nobody wants knickerbockers now. What people are wearing in New York now are those skirts.' Turning to her sister, she asked: 'Liz, what do they call them, the skirts that are now in fashion?' Liz shook her head. She didn't know.

The Indian girl directed Hosi to the Zambian guard standing sheepishly nearby. 'Tembo,' she cried, 'attend to this customer.' The man approached Hosi. As Hosi was telling him that he wanted some cheap baggy trousers, the man bent over, speaking almost in a whisper: 'You see those girls over there? All your father's cattle would not be enough to buy them a dress. They are really rich. These are the people getting fat on the spoils of independence.' Hosi smiled.

2

Before going to say goodbye to Ester, Hosi decided to go to Plaza 1 to watch a film. He knew that this could be the last one he saw – the thought that he might die in Angola had occurred to him more than once.

There were not many people in the auditorium and the film would not start until it had filled. There was the usual noisy lot in there. For them, films were not meant to be watched. Few people could understand the accents of the American actors and none could refrain from voicing his own opinion while the film was running. When, for instance, there was an intimate love scene, lewd comments would be heard coming from all sides and the actress would be called a prostitute. Hosi hated this, but there was nothing he could do. Perhaps people enjoyed coming to the cinema for the comments that were made throughout.

At last the film began. It was a kung-fu film and the audience immediately became restive, as if they too were about to have a fight. Kung-fu films had once been banned, because people could not help getting into fights after watching them. Hosi remembered Joshua, a classmate of his, who had been in favour of a total ban on any film that portrayed the least violence. 'What we need,' Hosi remembered Joshua saying, 'is more sex. In the States they say: "Make love, not war." You see!' Joshua was rumoured to be a frustrated man now. He had contracted an incurable form of syphilis!

Hosi was not concentrating on the film. The knowledge that he was about to return to Angola overwhelmed him. He looked at the screen. The leading actor was about to have a fight with a snake. The audience was hissing.

Then, as if some electrical charge was passing through him,

he began thinking of his childhood. He shook himself. He had always considered his past a sacred thing. To think of it now, while he was in the auditorium with noisy people and wafts of marijuana up above, was simply doing himself an injustice. The auditorium, he decided, was very similar to hell. But he couldn't help it, he simply had to think of his childhood. He sat quietly and let all the events unroll before him, like a film.

Cuando mission, where Hosi had been born, was on the banks of the Cuando river. Hosi thought it was the most beautiful place in the world. Someone had once told him that Venice was the most beautiful place in the world; someone else had argued for San Francisco. Neither had been to America or Italy, but they thought that because all the magazines and books said so, it must be true.

A great bridge had been built across the Cuando river. Standing at the Catholic mission on one side, two huge mountains could be seen. It was rumoured that there was a man-eating snake which could be seen whenever there was a rainbow. His mother had often told him not to stray far, and although she had never said why, he now knew that she had wanted him to keep away from the dangerous snake. It wasn't just the snake. There was a time all his playmates had stayed locked in their mothers' bedrooms for most of the day. That was when a local tribal chief had died. Tradition demanded that the chief be buried with several boys and girls. Hosi once overheard his father say that some of the chief's advisers had been sent to prison for having attempted to sacrifice two boys and a girl. As for the snake, Father Adao, the Catholic priest, was said to have thrown holy water into the river and made it disappear.

Hosi's father, Nataniel Mbueti, a tall, corpulent man, was then a clerk in the police station that administered the area surrounding the Cuando mission. Hosi recalled that in the years preceding their departure, the Portuguese had become very edgy. Any Angolan who disputed the fact that his country was a province of Portugal was promptly sent to prison. The prison was called Sao Nicolau. Hosi knew the name for he had heard it spoken many times by his parents, who lamented

18

privately that yet another person had been sent there. Before people were sent to Sao Nicolau they were interviewed by Senhor Miguel dos Vasconcelhos, the PIDE (Portuguese secret police) officer. He was so fat, claimed his servant, Artur, because he ate a whole pig in a week and drank cooking oil by the gallon.

Although he had been born in Angola, Senhor dos Vasconcelhos did not know a word of Umbundu. Most people who appeared before him were so scared all their Portuguese simply vanished. Hosi's father served as an interpreter. When the people who were brought before Senhor dos Vasconcelhos went free, they would remember Hosi's father with gratitude.

Hosi's parents had been devout Catholics. Now, whenever Hosi tried to compare his conduct with that of his father he felt very ashamed. He was so deep in sin, he thought, that there was no way he would be forgiven. Hosi could not remember when he had last had holy communion. His guardian angel had rejected him. He was not, however, completely without faith and he still hoped for a return of the days when he would feel holy, as he had after his father had taken him to the chapel for mass.

Hosi remembered the chapel. It was huge and filled with portraits of Jesus Christ and the Virgin Mary. Christ had struck him as resembling Father Adao: both were white, had brownish, short beards and both looked kind. Father Adao went one better because he used to give Hosi sweets when they met. Nataniel Mbueti had told his son that it had taken many years to build the church. Hosi now remembered overhearing the elders talk of a man who had died during its construction: he had fallen from the roof. This fact seemed to make Hosi feel that the place was actually holier.

On Sundays his mother would come along to church too. These moments, Hosi now thought, were the best of his life. She would wake him up early and send him to buy bread from the market, which was near the mission's hospital. Hosi was then eight. After getting the bread he would treat himself to two buns; he said to himself that these served as fuel. One day, just after Sunday mass, he fell from a branch of a guava tree

19

he was playing in and hit the ground. The pain was so great that he believed this was punishment from God.

He rushed to his mother, wanting to confess.

'Mama, Mama,' he cried out aloud.

His mother, who had been sweeping outside, stopped and looked up at him, mouth agape. 'What is it, Papa?' she asked.

'Mama, I have sinned,' Hosi cried out, 'I have lied to you.'

'Tell me, Papa. God has already forgiven you. Tell your mama your sin. Come on, my dear Papa.'

'Mama, I always eat two buns without telling you. I have just fallen from a guava tree. God has punished me.'

'Who told you that?'

'Minguito. Last week he also fell from a tree. He had been stealing sugar.'

'Too bad. Have you got other sins to confess?'

'Yes.'

'What?'

'Well, Mama, you remember when Auntie Laura came with that man?'

'Don't say that man. He is Uncle Adolfo. He has now married Laura. What happened?'

Hosi screwed up his face and said: 'Well, Mama, please forgive me. Whenever that uncle woke up in the morning I used to go and wee on his bed. Then Aunt Laura would go to wash the bedsheets. She thought it was him who pissed every night.'

By the time Hosi had finished, his mother's eyes were filled with tears. He too started crying. His mother decided at once to take him to the priest. Father Adao was having a siesta and had instructed his servant, Cesar, a self-proclaimed church elder (he was instantly fired when Father Adao discovered this), to wake him only if it was a matter of life and death.

'We need to see the priest,' Hosi's mother said to Cesar.

'What for?' asked Cesar.

'It is to do with my son. Please, I need to see him.'

'If you need medicine for worms you might as well deal with me. How many did he shit?'

'It is more serious than that. Is the priest in?'

'You are not telling me that he is coughing blood? Strange things are happening nowadays. First it was Tiago's wife. Did you know that she had swallowed a needle?'

'Of course. Everyone knows about that! It is very sad. The priest, please.'

Cesar coughed and continued: 'Swallowing a needle? They say this woman was sweeping and found a needle on the floor. She is very forgetful, just like her husband and her uncle Jeremias. So she put the needle in her mouth for a while; she thought if she put it somewhere else she would forget about it. Then she thought of something funny, chuckled and swallowed the needle. Stupid woman. Me, I couldn't marry a woman from Camudongo; they are idiots.'

'Please, brother Cesar,' pleaded Hosi's mother. 'I need to see the priest urgently.'

Cesar had now become listless. 'What is that you want? Are you ill?'

'No. It is my son.'

'I already asked whether he has worms.'

'No. He has a spiritual problem.'

Cesar turned towards Hosi, his eyes bulging, as if he was expecting to see a miracle. Hosi felt important. Cesar left at once to go and call the priest.

Hosi's mother told the priest the whole story, without leaving out a detail. The priest held Hosi's head and started praying at once. He then said: 'He is a fine boy. He will grow up to be a good man. I can see him going to a seminary and becoming a priest.' Hosi's mother beamed with pleasure.

That night Hosi got the severest beating of his life, after his mother had told his father the whole story. Unlike the priest, Nataniel Mbueti reached for his belt. After several lashes, during which Hosi confessed all the bad deeds he had ever done in his life, his mother came to his rescue.

'Papa, it is enough!' she cried.

His father pushed his mother aside. 'He'll be a thief. He'll be a liar. Not my own son. What is the point of raising a thief, a liar and a sinner?'

Immediately after the beating, Hosi went to his room and

began to read the only book he liked. *Anita vai ao colegio*. He heard his father bang the front door and shout that he would be back later. Soon his mother came into the room and sat beside him. She smiled at him but he refused to smile back. Then she began to sing. He liked the song and soon started to laugh.

Hosi was woken from his reverie by the tumult in the auditorium: on the screen a couple were in bed, kissing passionately.

'Let her go. She's had enough. Her mouth will be swollen,' a voice cried from the back.

'But the Chinese style is useless. What is he waiting for?' cried another voice.

Hosi fell back into his reverie. He had been an only child. He knew that his parents were very proud of him. His mother had had three sisters, all of them barren, and Hosi often thought that the reason she loved him so much was that he was the only child in her family.

Nataniel Mbueti had once been a troubled man, for he had no child of his own. He had been godfather to many, yet he could not reciprocate the honour that had been conferred upon him. His wife consulted several witch doctors, even one unscrupulous man who said that all her problems would cease if she allowed him to make love to her at least once. The fact that she was seeing a doctor in itself was already a sin; to sleep with him would be fatal, she thought.

Nataniel Mbueti's relatives were very concerned. His father, Evaristo Mbueti, an old man who, despite his advanced age, was said to have fought barehanded a he-goat that had gone wild, was the most vocal. One day he called his son to the banks of the Cuando river for a serious talk. He sat on a stone and bade his son sit down on another stone next to him.

'Nataniel, my son,' the old man began, 'I had a dream. A serious dream. You know very well that I will be leaving soon. So be it, anyway. I did not come to this world to stay. Even the greatest witch or the Pope in Rome has to go, not so?'

'Indeed, Papa!' answered the son.

22

'Now, there was this dream. My dreams are never wrong. What was the last dream that I had?'

'That your dog was speaking Portuguese.'

'And then what happened?'

'I got my first salary increase.'

'You see, I am never wrong. Now, I was talking about something. Oh yes . . . children . . . I mean, the dream. Now, Kasesa. Who is Kasesa?'

The son scratched his head. Shaking his head, the father said in a mournful tone: 'Where is the world going to? You don't know who Kasesa is?'

'Oh, he is the cousin of grandmother's second husband, not so?'

'No! Kasesa is my brother – same father, same mother, understand? Now, he came in a dream. He says he wants to have a baby named after him, otherwise there will be no peace in the clan.'

'But, Papa, you know that we have been having this problem for so long.'

'Don't worry. That is why I am here. They say what a crocodile catches leads to the boatman. They are now pointing fingers at me. They say you are not having children because I have been cursed. Cursed? Me? They will see. Anyway, so I have this plan that will help you have a child.'

'But, Papa, I am married and the Church won't allow me to have a child by any woman other than my wife.'

The father shook his head furiously and then said: 'Don't fool yourself. Even those priests have children. You get a child and then go to confess. God will understand. Just think of the many sins you have committed and how he has forgiven you.'

'What, then, is your plan, Papa?'

The old man looked to the sky and puffed at his pipe. 'You know Julio's daughter, Minga?'

'Oh, no, Papa. She is a baby. I held her in my arms only a while ago.'

The old man screwed up his face. Then he began talking fast, making it obvious to his son that he was indignant.

'Cursed? Me? Never! It is that woman of yours who can't have a child. I don't know her background well enough.'

'But, Papa, when I married her you said you knew her family very well.'

'Now, I want you to have a child. Minga has just come of age.'

'But she might not want to have a baby with me. Girls today have changed. They are not like the girls of your time, Papa.'

The old man shook his head. 'Not if she's Julio's daughter. When Chief Mbaka died, it was Julio and I who carried out the funeral rites. I know so much about Julio that he would never let me down. You know that he has been angling for the post of church elder? If I revealed some of the things that are under his bed he would have to go to Sao Nicolau. By the way, are wizards sent to Sao Nicolau too?'

'No, Papa. They are not a danger to the state.'

'Stupid whites. They don't know some of the things we can do. Anyway, everything will be under my control. Now, you have this child and Kasesa will leave me in peace. He says the child should be called after him.'

Nataniel Mbueti nodded. His father smiled, then began to puff at his pipe and walked away. Nataniel Mbueti was so troubled that he decided to go to the nearest shop for a few drinks to drown his sorrows. He went into Senhor Ventura's. When he got there several men were already gathered, including Almirante, a man who was much talked about because he had just fathered triplets. Several men were taking turns at buying Almirante glasses of wine because they thought he was a superman. As soon as they saw Nataniel Mbueti coming one of the men who was drunk said: 'There you are. Here, two cups for the man who has put us all to shame.' Nataniel Mbueti smiled and walked over to the counter to buy the wine.

3

Ester lived with her two children in Kalingalinga, one of the many shanty towns that had sprouted around Lusaka. Hosi alighted at the main bus stop and wandered about a bit. He had forgotten the way to Ester's house. It was hard to tell which direction it was in from where he stood, because all the tiny houses looked the same. He finally saw something he recognized – the huge wall surrounding the tavern nearby. Ester's house, it turned out, was a ten-minute walk from there. As Hosi passed in front of the bar, he saw the men inside wriggling their bodies in blissful ecstasy. 'Banamayo', a song by the Mulemena Boys about women who went to the morgue to get water used to wash the dead for a love potion, was blaring out loud. Hosi said to himself: 'Now, those are happy people. When are we Angolans going to be as happy as they are?'

Ester was sleeping on a mat in front of her house. The house, like several others nearby, was made of adobes. It was short and one had to bend down at the door to enter. Ester was sleeping deeply, her breath coming in what sounded to Hosi like snores. He stood before her, wondering whether to wake her or not. He was discomforted by the smells from the pit latrine nearby. True, Mrs Banda's place was not the cleanest on earth, but he found this stench unbearable. He bent down and shook Ester, hoping to wake her. She turned over but didn't wake up. 'Mana Ester!' he cried out.

Ester opened her eyes, gasped for air and then, as if chewing some exotic fruit, went back to sleep. Hosi decided to sit on an oil drum nearby and wait for her to wake up. Ester was soon snoring loudly again. Hosi walked up to her and shook her gently. This time she sprang from her sleep and in an instant her leaden eyes brightened. She beamed at Hosi.

25

'Hosi! My God! When are you going to stop growing?' Ester cried out.

'When Angola is free.'

'Well, we will see a lot before this Angola is finally free. People will be marrying, dying and having fun and Angola won't yet be free.'

Ester sat down on another oil drum. She acted as if she hadn't seen Hosi for ages.

'Where are the kids?' Hosi asked.

'They have gone to the bar. They have to sell eggs and fritters. That is how we survive. Hard life, not so?' Ester flashed her teeth. Hosi recalled that they had once been very white, but now they were brown because of cigarettes; toothpaste was a luxury.

'I don't think it is that hard. I mean, look at Ethiopia. People there are dying from starvation. At least here we have food. I am sure, Mana Ester, many people in this world dream of having a shelter like yours and of having something to fill their stomachs.'

Ester smiled and then said lugubriously: 'I have been through so much. Hosi, you don't know how it feels when someone you have learned to trust and love leaves you. I am not worried about the children – I can look after them – but Julio just walked out like that. I cried and almost went down on my knees for him to stay. I really wanted him to stay, but he simply carried on and left me.'

Hosi remained silent. There was nothing to say.

Ester continued: 'When I was growing up in Angola, we were never taught about love potions and the like. We were Christians and any marriage that had gone through the Church – like my marriage to Julio – was seen as sacred. Nothing was going to put it asunder. And yet when we came here we found that love potions were being sold at the market, like tomatoes.'

Hosi laughed and Ester laughed too. 'It all began like a joke. Julio kept saying that he had this interesting friend. And then he said he loved her and wanted to move into her house. I protested. I said, "You stupid man, think of the children and me." He said: "Nothing will stop me from going to marry Pamela."'

26

Shaking his head, Hosi said: 'I am really sorry. I am sure you will be happy someday.'

'Don't be sorry. They say he who laughs last laughs better. I am really laughing my lungs dry. Now listen to this. This girl, Pamela, won him, but his love for her was like wax: it started to melt in the heat of living together. What did she do? No need to guess. She went to the same witch doctor who had given her a love potion before. The witch doctor gave her a special one this time. He told her to cut Julio's toe nails and cook them with some roots he had given her. She went home and did so. Now I am coming to the crunch. The evil girl comes home and starts cooking the concoction. She then tries to look into the pot. What does she see? Julio's face: eyes, nose, teeth, everything.' Ester clapped her hands and looked at Hosi seriously. She could tell that Hosi was startled by her story.

'Where is the woman now?' he asked.

'Mad at the Chainama Hills mental hospital. Julio is nowhere to be seen. Now, some of her relatives are saying that I must have done something. I know nothing. Although I often drink a bit to drown my sorrows, I am still a Christian. I believe in Jehovah. Nothing will make me change that. Witchcraft belongs to the devil.'

Hosi wanted to change the subject so he said: 'I am sure you have a lot of fun being with the kids, don't you?'

Ester seemed a bit displeased by this shift in the conversation. She was happy to go on about Julio's misadventures. 'I enjoy the kids. But they are both boys, unfortunately. I am sure that someday when I am old and wretched they will leave. Let me go and get some *chibuku*. They call it German beer over here. Are you going to join me?'

'Thank you, but I have stopped drinking – at least for the time being.'

'Come on, have some! Are you afraid of having a *chibuku* tummy? You can't escape from it. Not if you are going to be an important man. Sooner or later, the tummy will appear. They say it symbolizes authority – and wisdom.'

Ester came back with a plastic can filled with a clear liquid –

kachasu. This was known as 'African gin'. She was visibly happy. She was whistling a tune that had been popular in what she called her younger days and went on until she brought out two cups and told Hosi to join her in the *kachasu*.

'Sorry, Mana, I really can't take this stuff.'

'Why?'

'Several reasons. But the first is that I am told that it kills. It is illegal to distil it, not so?'

'Yes. They got it wrong. Remember, this is Africa. Today they say *kachasu* kills. Tomorrow they will say that *kasolo* kills too. Yet they will never say that lager kills. Why? Because the bigwigs like it. Hundreds of people die in their cars each year from accidents caused by drunkenness. How many of these had been drunk on *kachasu*? None. Now, you join me in this stuff. You won't be the same after a few gulps, you will feel better.'

Hosi refused again and said: 'This stuff is poison.'

Ester was now getting drunk, and she returned to Julio's marriage to the Zambian girl. But Hosi interrupted her. He cleared his throat and said: 'Mana Ester, I have to tell you this: I am leaving for Angola tomorrow.'

'Which Angola?'

'Where else but the bush?'

'I have known it all along. OK, leave me. Maybe I should be left alone, then I will grow up. Julio and you were once my pillars here. I'll manage by myself. Right, go on.'

Tears trickled from Ester's eyes but her face was serene. She had the expression of one coming to terms with a hard fact. This gave way to a wistful smile. She held her nose between her forefinger and thumb and blew it. She then wiped away the tears from her eyes and took a swig from the can of *kachasu*.

Ester's two sons, Dilio and Jaime, came into view. Jaime was about ten. He wore a khaki shirt and shorts, which also served as his school uniform. His legs looked brownish with dust. Dilio, who was six, was dressed like his brother. As they walked towards Hosi and Ester, Dilio was sucking his thumb and had inserted his other hand into his shorts, twiddling his willy. This habit had earned him several beatings. His mother had once smeared chillis on his fingers and thumb. It had had the opposite effect: Dilio seemed to like the itching. His mother later discovered that the chillis had not been hot enough.

'Now, there you go, sucking your thumb and touching your John,' Ester bellowed to Dilio. 'What did I say will happen to you if you don't stop doing this?'

'It will rot,' Dilio answered lugubriously.

Hosi smiled at the boys, who walked over to him and started grinning.

'Will you buy me a ball?' said Dilio.

'Wait till I get myself a job,' Hosi answered. A voice in him said he was lying. The boys deserved to know that they would not see him for quite a while. Shaking his head, Hosi said: 'I will be going away. I will be going to Angola. I might not come back for a while.'

'Mama says people die in Angola. You will die. Why don't you buy us a ball first and then go to die?' asked Dilio.

Hosi started thinking about the two boys. Unlike him they knew nothing of Angola for they were complete Zambians. Unlike him they were not laughed at when they spoke Nyanja, for they did not have a foreign accent. Unlike him they did not feel that there was a land that belonged to them for which they had to fight.

Ester told the boys to start cooking dinner. Jaime gave some money to Dilio, who was soon back with a plastic bag full of charcoal. The charcoal was placed in a brazier. Jaime added paraffin to it and set it alight with matches. A metal pipe was then put on top; it was said to help the charcoal burn faster.

All along Ester had been drinking from the can. Hosi turned to her and said: 'Mana Ester, I know you might think it rude of me to ask, but why don't you find yourself another man? You are young and er . . . er . . .'

'What do you want to say? Come on, get it out. I have heard so much in my life. Nothing pains me any more.'

'I think you ought to find yourself a man. Think of your children. They need a father.'

Ester sobered suddenly, and spoke clearly. 'I made a mistake, a serious mistake. My mother told me, but girls of twenty never take their mothers' advice. My mother said Julio was not the man for me because he came of a family whose men were horrible womanizers. My mother had known Julio's father. She once told me this strange story about Julio's father. Now, promise never to tell anyone!'

'I promise,' said Hosi.

'Well, my mother tells me that in those days when most people still lived in their villages, Julio's father and several of his friends had gone to a party and taken up with several women of the night. They went and slept in a cemetery. In the morning it was found that rats had eaten the nipples off the women's breasts.'

Ester then started humming gibberish. The drink was getting the better of her again. She started to go to the latrine nearby but fell down with a stupendous thud. Her mouth began to dribble. Soon after she wet herself. Jaime and Dilio lifted her into the house and laid her on the bed. Hosi could tell from the expression on their faces that they had done this many times before. Jaime lit the kerosene lamp, then came back to continue cooking. Hosi walked into the house and kissed Ester on the cheeks. She chuckled. He bade farewell to the two boys. They said dinner – nshima with roasted fish – would be ready soon and asked whether he wanted any, but Hosi shook his head. Giving them a ten-kwacha note, which made them leap with joy, Hosi walked towards the bus stop.

4

When Hosi was seven his parents were transferred from Cuando to Capingala. Soon after his father was sacked from his job and suspended from the Church. Hosi was thinking now of the possible reasons for his father's dismissal. Several things came to his mind, but he did not want to dwell on them. He felt that the reasons would simply make him adopt a censorious attitude towards his father, and the dead, he said to himself, were supposed to be thought of tenderly and confined to the pleasant parts of the memory.

Capingala was what the Portuguese authorities called a *posto*, a settlement. The administrative centre comprised a couple of whitewashed buildings separated by a dusty road that led to Sambo, another settlement.

Near the administrative centre there were several shops owned by Portuguese merchants. Hosi remembered in particular a shop owned by a Senhor Alvaro, who had a wife called Dona Palmira. He was said to be an expert at making pork crackling. His wine was rumoured to be the choicest; he was said to add some special ingredient to it that the other Portuguese merchants nearby did not know of.

Nataniel Mbueti, Hosi's father, worked as a clerk for the administrative officer, a diminutive Portuguese man who was referred to by the Africans as Kadinguilinha, or the cub. He was always seen with a newspaper or a book under his arm. Hosi's father was given a large whitewashed adobe house which, to Hosi's horror, was near a cemetery. He often imagined that ghosts would one day come to take him.

The cub was said to be demented, primarily because it was widely believed that Susana, his African ex-wife, had cursed him. It was said that when the cub had first arrived from

31

Portugal he had been so poor that he could not afford a razor blade and had wandered about with a grotesque beard which had sent little babies screaming and toddlers running to hide under their parents' beds. Then he had married Susana, who served him wholeheartedly.

She had helped him set up a small shop and this began to grow. Then there was a vacancy at the administrative centre for some senior post. The cub was the only white who could read and write, so he got it. As soon as he smelt success, Susana meant nothing to him. He told her to leave. They had had a son, Junior, who was now in Portugal, training to become a doctor. The cub told Susana that she was not civilized, that he needed a woman who would speak proper Portuguese, be presentable and charming – qualities Susana would never possess.

Susana had gone to her home village, Kalomba, sobbing. Privately some people believed she deserved what she had got. They said Susana had thought of herself as a cut above the rest of the girls and had gone for a pig of a man who just happened to have a white skin. Most of the relatives who had claimed to miss her so much when she was still with the cub running the little shop now disowned her. She lived unhappily by herself.

The cub had a habit of wandering into the forest to listen to the sound of the birds. 'Good afternoon, boss,' a villager would say upon finding him in the forest, staring at a mulemba tree. The cub would turn around slowly and smile.

'Ah, there you are, my dear fellow,' the cub would gasp. 'I am trying to feel a part of nature. The trees and everything inspire me like nothing else does.'

The cub would then hold his heart and tell the villager to walk on. The villager would saunter to his village and say to the others as soon as they met in the evening: 'I was passing through Chiva pool this afternoon. Who did I see? The cub, talking to the plants as usual. He is a complete nutter.'

The others would chip in and say: 'Ah, these whites. They can easily get mad. Kamgombe, Mario's cook, told me that Kadinguilinha wants to marry Mario's daughter. He spent a whole day beside Kulimahala pond writing a letter to her and then spent the other day with his servant looking for a special flower to send with the letter. He then settled for those red flowers we used to throw into the river to make a fish drowsy before catching it. The girl accepted and they will marry soon.' The villagers burst out laughing.

One of them stood up, wanting to make a point: 'Never forget this. The whites are brainy. Not only did they make an aeroplane to fly with; they have also been to the moon.'

Hosi remembered the cub, whose real name was Joaquim dos Remos da Costa, because he had once given him a long lesson that had led to another beating from his father and tears from his mother.

It had all begun with Dona Palmira, who was immensely fat and who, Hosi remembered, always had a plate of pork crackling by her side. She would sit at one corner of the shop and chat with the Africans who were drinking. Hosi's father had once taken him there and she liked Hosi at once. Every time Hosi's mother sent him to the shops, he went straight to Alvaro's, for Dona Palmira would not only kiss him but also ask him to partake of the crackling.

There were always men drinking in the shop and Dona Palmira never missed the chance to talk. Sometimes she would bring the basin containing the duck she was preparing for the night to the shop and continue stuffing it with garlic and other herbs while talking with the men.

'None of you could stand seeing that fight,' Dona Palmira would begin, as the conversation turned to the use of knives in brawls, 'that terrible fight. I was sixteen and sneaked with my elder sister to a party in Luanda. We thought it was going to be a respectable party. By the way, I danced with the governor. If none of you believes me ask Alvaro. The governor! He held me like this, and then tararararararara . . . ha, heaven!'

The Africans stopped drinking, their eyes fixed on Dona Palmira as if they were about to devour her. She took a swig from a bottle of wine nearby and continued: 'Where was I? Ah, the governor. Yes, it was mainly for whites and a few respectable blacks – you know, the *assimillados*. Gosh, some of the blacks there were more white than myself. They spoke proper Portuguese and had civilized manners. Then, after four hours, a fight broke out. Chairs were tossed here and there. Several blacks came in. Now, you know that the Luanda blacks are not as stupid as you southerners. When they use knives they mean to kill. A man was stabbed. I saw the knife being inserted into his heart and come out reddened with blood.'

One of the Africans was so carried away by the story that he began to dribble. When Dona Palmira paused, he shook his head and took a long swig from his bottle of wine. Then Senhor Alvaro came in and said all that his wife had been telling them was a product of her imagination. Now he was going to tell them about a really frightening fight that he had witnessed in Portugal.

Hosi would often wander about the store and listen to the elders conversing. Voices were raised and tempers lost as more empty bottles amassed near the sacks of beans. Dona Palmira would call Hosi to her and say: 'Ah, now here is my husband.' She would hug him and kiss him on the cheeks. She reeked of garlic, but Hosi liked the smell.

Dona Palmira would then squeeze Hosi affectionately against her body. He remembered the feeling. It was as if folds of fat deflated to let him get closer to her. One day he had felt so close that his willy suddenly rose. When she let him go, he quickly put his hands into the pockets of his shorts and trotted out, embarrassed.

That night he dreamed he was lying with Dona Palmira in bed. Senhor Alvaro stormed into the room with a shot gun and aimed at him. Hosi simply pointed his finger at him and shouted: 'Look back.' Senhor Alvaro looked back and was instantly turned into a heap of salt. Then Hosi turned to Dona Palmira and she squeezed him tight again. But there was a problem – his willy was not big enough. So he called Dona Palmira's cook, Salomao, and shouted: 'Salomao, bring a pump. I want to make my thing big so I can do this woman. Fast man. Fast.' Salamoa brought the pump, fixed it into Hosi's mouth and began to pump. Hosi's willy began to

34

inflate, like a huge balloon. He began to scream: 'Please, Salomao, it is too big. My willy is too big.' Then Hosi woke up. He opened his eyes and saw his father and mother looking at him with worried expressions on their faces.

'What is wrong with you?' Hosi's father asked.

'I was dreaming,' Hosi answered.

His mother frowned and said: 'Horrible dream. It must have been a horrible dream. You were shouting some horrible things. I will leave the lamp here and hope that you do not have such a horrible dream again.'

Hosi covered his head and fell asleep at once. In the morning he decided that he was in love with Dona Palmira. He went to her shop and found her seated in her usual corner, knitting. As soon as she saw him she gave out a loud chortle. 'My darling, come here. Tell me some nice things.'

He walked to her and screwed up his face. Dona Palmira was startled. 'What is it, my love?' she asked.

'I love you,' said Hosi.

Dona Palmira burst out laughing. 'Of course, dear. I know that you love me. I also love you very much. Now where is this chap? I want him to give you some sweets. Nice sweets, dear.'

Hosi stood there, indifferent to what Dona Palmira had been telling him. He wanted to get his message across. 'I love you and I want to go to bed with you.'

Dona Palmira grimaced, as if something very bitter had found its way into her mouth. She held Hosi by the ears and started pulling him out of the shop and all the way to the administrative headquarters, in full view of everyone. There she handed him over to the cub and said that he had been rude to her. The cub said he would take care of the matter and told Dona Palmira to go back home. As she left, Hosi could hear her swearing.

The cub's office was huge. Hosi sat on a big chair in front of a mahogany desk, trembling. When Dona Palmira had brought him in the cub had been busy poring over the pages of a newspaper. As soon as Dona Palmira left, he turned back to the newspaper. Hosi could see through the curtain that a group of people had gathered outside, anxious to know what was going to happen to him. The cub continued with his newspaper. When he came across an item that aroused his anger, he thumped the table. One of the African guards was near the door and concluded that things were getting very bad for Hosi when he heard the thumpings.

At last the cub turned to Hosi. 'Now, my boy, what have you done?'

'I told Dona Palmira that I loved her.'

'Is that all?'

'And that I wanted to sleep with her.'

The cub giggled. He pulled out a felt pen and a sheet of paper from one of the drawers of his desk. Smiling, he said to Hosi: 'Now, you should not love that fat old woman. You should love someone your own age. How old are you?'

'Nine.'

'Still a baby. You have a long way to go. Now, when you are sixteen you will find youself a beautiful girl who won't smell of garlic. Horrible woman, that Dona Palmira, not so?'

Hosi nodded. The cub handed the paper and pen to Hosi and told him to draw any shape. Hosi did so. Then the cub worked the line into the shape of a elephant with dazzling speed. Hosi was impressed and drew another line. The cub drew a lion. Hosi burst out laughing. The African guard who was eavesdropping by the door wondered whether it was his head or his ears that were playing tricks on him.

That night Hosi received another beating. His father said he had to go and apologize to Dona Palmira and that he felt very ashamed that his son had such a dirty mind. His mother called him aside and told him never to think of going to bed with women.

Aunt Laura and her husband, Adolfo, had once come to spend their holidays with his family at Capingala. Hosi was then in the third grade at the primary school, a few blocks away from the administrative centre.

Hosi came home from school one day and found that Aunt Laura and her husband had arrived. They were in the sitting

36

room with his father and mother, eating chicken and rice. Uncle Adolfo pulled Hosi towards him and put him on his lap. As Hosi made himself comfortable, he heard the chink of coins in his uncle's pockets and decided that he was going to ask for some money when they were alone.

Uncle Adolfo gave a loud laugh and said: 'Now, this man has been growing really fast. Was it not only yesterday that he was eating mucus and weeing in his shorts? Really, children nowadays are growing so fast, like banana trees.'

Hosi's father, proud of the compliments that had been given to his son, said: 'It is fertilizer, Adolfo. Everything now seems to be wanting to grow only when fertilizer is applied. Do you know that there are now some chickens which refuse to hatch unless they are given special pills?'

'What class is he in?' asked Aunt Laura.

'Third,' replied Hosi's mother. 'He'll soon be going to do the fourth class. He can recite poems.'

'Really?' asked Uncle Adolfo. All along, Aunt Laura had been staring at a stain on Hosi's shirt that had been caused by a mango.

'Not only can he recite poetry, but he can also say prayers in Latin,' Hosi's father said.

'In Latin? My God. You told me once that you had once dreamt that he had wings,' said Uncle Adolfo.

'That he had wings and was actually flying,' concluded Hosi's father. 'Now let him pray in Latin. Come on, sonny, show your aunt and uncle. Say that Latin prayer you learned. Come on.' Hosi felt tongue-tied. His mother beckoned him and whispered in his ears: 'Now, you say the prayer and you will have a big chunk of chicken. Come on, please do it.'

Hosi cleared his throat and said the prayer. Everybody clapped.

'Now there you have a real priest. He has hardly been weaned and he already prays in Latin. What will become of him when he is thirty?' asked Uncle Adolfo.

Hosi's father smiled. His mother frowned and said: 'Did you say a priest? My son a priest? Never. I want him to have children.'

37

At this point Aunt Laura excused herself and left.

When lunch was over, Hosi's father said to Uncle Adolfo: 'Now, either we drink the wine or the wine will have us. My throat is as dry as a desert; I need to water it a bit.'

Uncle Adolfo laughed loudly and said: 'There is this stupid doctor who says I should reduce on my drinking, yet he himself always reeks of wine. When he said that to me I nodded, but in my heart I kept saying: "Why do you sons of bitches want to keep all the good things of life to yourselves? Today, it is no wine, tomorrow no salt, no cooking oil, and no what? Hell!"'

Hosi's father said: 'Now hurry. We have to get there quickly. You know, the wine of nowadays is so bad that you have almost to finish a whole bottle to notice that your speech has improved.'

Hosi's mother looked on, her face puffed up, as if she was about to explode. She was appalled by her husband's fondness for wine which had developed since he had been sacked in Cuando. Yet her tirades had little or no effect on him.

Hosi remembered Aunt Laura as an inveterate letter writer. While other people spat arrows – as it was said – when roused, Aunt Laura took to her pen. Anyone who was at loggerheads with her would be the recipient of an acidic letter, and the less literate the person, the longer the letter. Hosi recalled hearing his mother say on several occasions that Aunt Laura had not known how to read or write until very late in life. She had decided to learn after she had mistaken a prescription for a laxative from a medical assistant for a proposal. The medical assistant, went the story, was a man from Luanda, so people called him Kaluanda. His Portuguese was said to be perfect. Aunt Laura frequented the surgery regularly, dressed up to the nines. Wigs were then in vogue and she took the trouble of borrowing a blonde one to impress Kaluanda, who gave her a note and told her to go to the mission hospital for the medicine. Aunt Laura took the note to her friend, Ceciliana, who, as it later turned out, could hardly read a word herself. Ceciliana told Aunt Laura that Kaluanda was madly in love with her and from then on, Aunt Laura kept going to the hospital, giving suggestive titters whenever she saw Kaluanda. Then one day Kaluanda lost his temper. 'What you need,' he burst out, 'is a laxative, not my love.' Aunt Laura then discovered that Ceciliana had lied to her; Kaluanda did not, after all, love her. She decided there and then to learn to read and write.

In the evening, Hosi's mother ordered him to go and call Aunt Laura, who had been asleep for most of the afternoon. Hosi knocked on the door and was told to come in.

'Mama says supper is ready, Aunt.'

Aunt Laura pulled out her writing pad and began to write.

To the owners of this house

Just because I have no child does not mean that I am worthless. This afternoon when the lady of the house said her son was supposed to have children, I saw her look at me and I could tell what she was thinking. She was thinking that I am jealous. She was mistaken. It took ages for her to get pregnant. I too hope to have some luck. So stop thinking that I am useless.

Yours sincerely
Laura

Hosi took the letter to his mother, who wrote a reply promptly. In her letter she pleaded with Aunt Laura to feel free in the house because she should regard it as hers. Aunt Laura wrote back saying that if this was her house and she could do as she wanted, then her refusal to eat should be taken seriously.

Hosi's mother sat on the sofa with a sad expression on her face. When Hosi's father and Uncle Adolfo came back they were both completely drunk. Uncle Adolfo walked over to the portrait of Jesus Christ that hung from the sitting-room wall and said: 'Jesus, you understand this. You know very well why we love wine. If it is so bad, why don't you answer the prayers of so many people and deliver us from it?'

Uncle Adolfo staggered a bit, but he managed to light a cigarette and began to puff the smoke on to the portrait, saying: 'Let it not be said that when I was having my share of the enjoyable things of life I forgot you. Come on, Jesus, smoke with me.'

5

It was soon after Uncle Adolfo and Aunt Laura had left that Osvaldo came to join the Mbueti family. Hosi remembered it vividly. He was brought on a Sunday afternoon in a Land-Rover. Hosi could tell that Osvaldo had been crying because of the whitish patches on his cheeks. Everything seemed to frighten him.

Hosi's mother took Osvaldo's belongings, which had been tied in a bundle, into Hosi's room, while Hosi's father said: 'This is your brother. You will be sleeping with him. Be good.'

'My brother?' Hosi retorted loudly.

'Yes, your brother. No more questions. Go and help your mother make his bed.'

Hosi went into his room and found Osvaldo seated on his bed. The two boys glared at each other like two wild goats sizing each other up before locking horns.

'Who are you?' Hosi asked Osvaldo. Osvaldo was silent.

'Where are you from?' Hosi asked. Still, Osvaldo was silent.

'Are you deaf?' Osvaldo bit his lower lip. Hosi lost his temper. He held Osvaldo by the ears, screwed up his face and muttered through his teeth: 'Either you talk or you will have this till you open your mouth.'

Osvaldo freed himself and pushed Hosi, who ended up banging his head against the wall. The two boys pounced on each other. Hosi kicked Osvaldo hard on the leg, but Osvaldo managed to get Hosi's neck between his thighs and pressed as hard as he could.

'Leave me or I will scream and tell my mother,' Hosi cried out. Osvaldo let him go and smiled. He had won. Hosi was never to forget this fight. But, as the days went on and the two boys came to know each other better, Hosi realized that although Osvaldo was more powerful than him, there was an area in which he, Hosi, was the undisputed king – the multiplication table. This made Hosi feel immeasurably superior.

Hosi often imagined himself in a huge office with hundreds of papers awaiting his signature. Glowing with importance, he would pull out a fountain pen and write with a great flourish. Osvaldo, on the other hand, would be sweating in the blistering heat, breaking rocks. Osvaldo would end up wearing rags and eating the food that men who worked on roads ate. Hosi was intrepid enough to let Osvaldo know of these reveries.

'Do you know that I will never have to work with my hands?' Hosi asked Osvaldo.

'No, are you going to become lame?' Osvaldo asked.

'Of course not. I will be using this stuff.' Hosi tapped his forehead. 'People who know the multiplication table never end up using their hands; they use their heads.'

Osvaldo looked embarrassed. He had tried very hard to master the multiplication table, but after six times seven his mind would simply go blank. Anger would well up in him, he would scratch his head and bite his nails, but the answer would still not come to him. Hosi, who was eager to make the fact that he was better than Osvaldo apparent at every opportunity, would say: 'Let's go, Osvaldo, two times two.'

'Four,' Osvaldo answered firmly.

'OK. Eight times nine.'

Osvaldo started scratching his head. Hosi started to laugh. Osvaldo mustered all the energy he could and slapped Hosi hard on the face. Hosi turned round sobbing and left.

Osvaldo was brave. His bed was near the wall. Hosi feared that bogeymen would come at night, make an opening in the wall and take him away, so he tried to sleep as far away from the wall as possible. In the middle of the night any little sound from the straw mattress would make Hosi shiver. He often imagined that ghosts from the nearby cemetery were out trying to get him. He had heard many ghost stories. One day, while helping Old Pedro in his wheat field, he began to count his teeth, just for the sake of counting. As soon as Old Pedro saw him he shouted: 'Don't count your teeth!'

'Why?' Hosi asked.

'Because you will invite ghosts.'

From that day on, Hosi never did as much as touch his teeth.

Hosi and Osvaldo went to the same school, the only school in the area. There was one teacher, Senhor Xavier, a tall, partially bald man. Hosi overheard his mother comment to other women that the little hair that Senhor Xavier had had cost him a lot. This was because whenever Dona Palmira or somebody else went to Huambo, Senhor Xavier would give them money to buy him expensive hair products.

Xavier Ramos was said to be the smartest man around. His black shoes shone in the sun; whenever dust settled on them he would pull out a handkerchief from his pocket and wipe them clean. This was done with a great flourish, which impressed his pupils. His trousers were thoroughly pressed. The local joke was that any fly unfortunate enough to bump into his trousers' crease would be split in two.

School began at seven in the morning. The pupils would all stream into the class, their teeth chattering in the morning cold. The dew that had gathered on the grass in the night was so cold that it felt like several tiny needles piercing their bare feet. Some naughty pupils would come with cooked sweet potatoes or pumpkins, taking several bites whenever the teacher was facing the blackboard, to the amusement of the others. The teacher's moistened hands and hair showed that he had had a cold bath that morning. The pupils were simply awed by such bravery.

One day Xavier Ramos had come into the class with a toothbrush and toothpaste to demonstrate to his pupils how to take proper care of their teeth. That day all the pupils went about mimicking their teacher. Since then Xavier Ramos had taken to inspecting his pupils' teeth. After this he would pace about the classroom and shout: 'Dictation!' The pupils would reach for their exercise books and start writing.

'Joaquim is a good boy. He stands up and takes off his hat whenever he sees the teacher. Mario is a bad boy. He does not stand up when he sees the teacher . . . does not stand up. It is good to stand up when you see the teacher.'

42

Then Xavier Ramos would mark all the exercise books. Pupils who had made a certain number of mistakes would be called to the front. Osvaldo was always among them. People had become so used to his being among the turnips, as they were called, that one day when he did well the teacher asked the class to sing a special song to congratulate him.

School ended at midday. Hosi and Osvaldo would go home eagerly, for lunch awaited them. After lunch it was playtime and all the boys would come together to play football. A sock stuffed with papers would be kicked about furiously. Hosi was often forced to be the goalie.

'Why do I have to be in goal most of the time?' he would ask.

'Because you are a turnip. Really useless. You even miss penalties.'

Looking sad, Hosi would say: 'It is not my fault. When I kick the ball it does not want to go where I want it to go.'

They would burst out laughing and tell him to get back into goal, which was represented by two stones placed some distance apart.

Sometimes the boys would play mothers and fathers with the girls. The children would all go out, gather grass to build little huts and then break into families. Toddlers would be taken off their mothers' bosoms and made to play the part of babies. The boys would go out to work and the girls would remain behind, cooking. The girls would usually pinch onions, mealie meal, chunks of meat and the like from their mothers' kitchens. Powdered milk was very popular.

After, the boys would come back from work and find their meals ready. They would eat and it was then said that it was night and everybody was supposed to sleep. Here the toddlers would be taken back to their mothers since they usually refused to feign sleep. The most unpopular role to play was that of the cock, whose duty it was to crow and shout that it was morning. His crowing was often disputed.

'Come on, cock,' someone would shout, 'how can it be morning so early, eh?'

The cock, eager to have his turn at playing father, would all

43

but lose his temper and say: 'It is morning or I give up playing.' Nobody would answer him. Then he would threaten: 'It is morning or I will go and tell the elders.'

'Right, cock,' someone would shout eventually. 'I will be the cock now. You can be the father.'

6

Natalia, Old Pedro's wife, was tall, fat and serious. Children hated her: they said she was stingy and short-tempered. It was also rumoured that she was often seized by evil spirits which could be cast away only by her husband.

On this day Natalia was happy and kept smiling, for the boys had been doing the planting properly. There were many wheat fields and the boys would wander off to any one of them. The owner would ask them to give a hand at planting the seeds and then reward them with sweets or biscuits.

The children liked working in the fields not only because they would be rewarded but also because they enjoyed getting closer to the bulls pulling the ploughs. Hosi in particular enjoyed the smell of the soil being ploughed.

Old Pedro was singing a Zulu song. He said he had learned it in the South African goldmines he had worked in as a contract worker. Hosi liked him because he told many stories about the mines and the strange ways of other Africans who came to work there. His stories often set Hosi thinking. He wondered what gold was like.

'Tell me, Old Pedro,' Hosi began. 'What is gold really like?'

'It is like dust, brown dust,' Old Pedro answered.

'What is it for?'

'Many things. White women like necklaces made from gold.'

The clouds were gathered and it was getting dark. It was about to start raining. Old Pedro invited the boys into a little hut beneath a huge tree. Hosi walked to it feeling uneasy; he had been told that it was not safe to shelter under a tree when it was raining because trees were likely to be struck by lightning.

The boys entered the hut and sat on little wooden chairs. Natalia had lit a fire and was cooking some sweet potatoes, which were duly offered to the boys. There was a light drizzle but it soon abated. Paolo asked Old Pedro to tell them another story about the goldmines. He was about to begin when they heard a voice outside calling for him. It was Senhor Xavier Ramos, the school teacher. Old Pedro told the teacher to come into the hut.

As soon as Xavier Ramos entered the boys stood up. He looked at them like a general inspecting a guard of honour, then smiled and said: 'Have you all done your homework?' The boys were silent for a while and then Hosi said: 'Yes.'

'Good,' the teacher said, pressing his palms as if some dangerous stuff that needed to be crushed was between them. Then his face took on an expression which Old Pedro read as meaning that he did not want the boys around. So Old Pedro pulled out some groundnuts from a sack, handed them to the boys and told them to go and play outside. The boys scampered out of the hut, giggling with joy.

Xavier Ramos was a Bakongo from Maquela do Zombo in the north. He had come to Capingala to teach and had stayed on. At first people were hostile to him and kept asking whether he was not yet another cheeky northerner, but they soon began to think of him as one of them. Then he decided to marry Celestina, Chief Kabenji's daughter. This led to several murmurs. 'How can a northerner come and have the chief's daughter just like that?' it was asked. But several people sided with Xavier Ramos. 'This is no ordinary northerner,' they said to his critics. 'He is not only civilized but also rich and smart. His clothes make the Portuguese traders look like pigs in need of a bath.'

Xavier Ramos had two things in his favour: he had money and carried weight with the Portuguese. It was said – especially by the drunks who constantly met at Julio's shop – that he had once written to Salazar himself to complain about the glasses used to serve people with wine in Julio's bar. Julio lost his potbelly as he awaited the summons from the Governor-General in Luanda. It never came. However, from then on Dona Palmira, Julio's wife, made a show of washing the cups.

Lately, Xavier Ramos had been meeting Old Pedro constantly. This had led to all sorts of speculation from the ever vigilant public. Some said Xavier Ramos was impotent and needed a cure from Old Pedro. Others said that the two were involved in the diamond-trafficking business. The truth, however, was entirely different.

While in South Africa Old Pedro had worked as a lorry boy and had gone all the way up to the Congo. There, as he kept saying, he lost hope in both white and black men.

Outside, it was drizzling again. Old Pedro added some more twigs to the fire. Speaking in a whisper, he said to Xavier Ramos: 'Lumumba, Lumumba, he was a man! White men trembled before him. His black brothers sold him off and had him butchered like a dog.' Old Pedro shook his head. Pointing at his hand he said lugubriously: 'This skin. It is a cursed skin.' And then: 'They all say things will change soon. The Portuguese will go and we blacks will rule. We'll see.'

Xavier Ramos listened attentively. He knew a lot about Portuguese historical figures: Diego Cao, Albuquerque, Bartolomeu Diaz, and other hallowed men in the textbooks. But whenever he came before Old Pedro he felt like an ignoramus: he knew next to nothing about African history. He admired Old Pedro, but was appalled by his pessimism. As he kept telling him, Rome was not built in a day, so why did Old Pedro have to expect so much from the newly independent African states?

Old Pedro was still speaking when Xavier Ramos said: 'Let me tell you the reason I am here. It is about Susana.'

'You mean the woman who was ditched by the Portuguese?'

'Right.'

'What about her?'

'Well, her son, Junior, was in Lisbon studying medicine. He has written me a letter from somewhere in Africa. I taught the boy and he is certainly a bright fellow. In the letter he says he's had to escape from Lisbon.'

Old Pedro's eyes bulged as he said: 'Why?'

Xavier Ramos tiptoed to the hut's entrance, stuck his head out to make sure that no one was listening and came back. He bent closer to Old Pedro and said: 'Politics!'

Old Pedro's eyes brightened. He shook his head and said: 'Politics for a mulatto? Waste of time. He is not black. He does not know the white man's whip. He is a nobody. He was made in a hurry on top of maize bags in a shop. A product of the Portuguese master's desire to relieve himself. Beware. This might bring about your death, Ramos. They might be using one of theirs to trap you. They say a good friend is one who is present when drinking blood but also present when drinking *chisangua*. The mulatto is a friend during the *chisangua* time, but when it comes to drinking blood he flees and seeks shelter with his own – the whites.'

Xavier Ramos had heard Old Pedro's prejudices time and again before – against northerners, mulattos, Catholics and women. Xavier Ramos was also prejudiced to a degree – he hated some mulatto administrators – but when he received Junior's letter he no longer thought of him as a mulatto but as an Angolan.

But that was not all. After all, he had taught the boy to read, write and chant the multiplication table. He felt that Junior was an extension of himself. He had not forgotten that initially he had had a few problems with his pupil: he had not been able to master the multiplication table and was a bad speller. That had been overcome by the careful administering of the *sjambok*. Junior had then excelled in his work and Xavier Ramos had marvelled at his pupil's mastery of Portuguese grammar, history and arithmetic.

There was complete silence while Xavier Ramos was thinking. He told Old Pedro that he wanted to read Junior's letter to him. Old Pedro nodded. Xavier Ramos began:

Dear teacher and friend

Due to reasons I hope to tell you someday, I have had to leave the university. I am somewhere in Africa. I am preparing to come back home to join those fighting for the freedom of the Angolan people. The fire of freedom has spread throughout Africa, scorching all which stood for the exploitation and humiliation of our people.

Comrade teacher, you should spread the word among the trustworthy; not among those who, like the African chiefs of centuries ago, sold our land in exchange for beads and liquor . . .

At this point, Old Pedro intervened and said: 'What right has he got to mention the weakness of our ancestors?'

'Let me finish, please.'

'This mulatto's ancestors, the whites, they stole our land because they had guns. What could our forefathers have done?'

'Old Pedro, please listen,' Xavier Ramos begged.

Old Pedro shook his head and continued: 'I have always suspected it. Soon, we blacks will be blamed for our own colonization. The whites are clever. I know it. They will use all possible ways to maintain their hold over our land. What better way of doing it than by using their own sons?'

'He says there will be a democratic government in independent Angola. This government will serve the people.'

'Wait a minute, please,' said Old Pedro. 'Who will be at the top of this government?'

'The question should not arise now. Our prime concern is to get the Portuguese out. Junior belongs to the MPLA – the Movement for the Popular Liberation of Angola. He is a communist, a Marxist.'

'What is a Marxist?' Old Pedro asked.

Xavier Ramos cleared his throat and said: 'I will tell you. Communists and Marxists believe that there should be total equality. No one should have more than the other.'

Old Pedro laughed and said: 'I am sure that even with the angels in hell – where everyone is in pain – there are those closer to the devil. We can't all be equal.'

'You should have allowed me to finish reading the letter from Junior. He says that nearly half of the world is communist. He mentioned Russia. He says that the workers there took up arms and overthrew their exploiters. He mentions several other countries in Africa that are communist. It can be done.'

49

Old Pedro's eyes bulged. The idea of so many countries in which there was total equality fascinated him. 'I don't know much about communism. Everything I have read says that it is evil and godless, but this was all written by the Portuguese. Trust them to tell the truth!'

Xavier Ramos smiled. He had won his first convert to the cause. But he was apprehensive too. He wondered how he was going to ensure that Old Pedro behaved responsibly? He had a strong suspicion that Old Pedro would let something slip and it would soon become known that Xavier Ramos was exchanging letters with an MPLA militant.

On the other hand, Xavier Ramos felt that he had to trust people to be engaged in the cause that would set the people free. And there was always the possibility that he – Xavier Ramos – might gain office in a new government: a minister, for instance, or a secretary in some important ministry. The thought of becoming an important man excited him. He would be known all over the world, his name would be mentioned in the news bulletins and he would make trips abroad. There, he would meet other foreign dignitaries. Then there were the political speeches. In them, he would make pronouncements that would make headlines. And the history books. All the Portuguese heroes would vanish. Exit Albuquerque, enter Xavier Ramos!

Xavier Ramos, Angola's would-be hero, looked at Old Pedro and smiled. He held the old man's hand and shook it firmly. The old man smiled back and said: 'Viva Angola!'

Hosi started going to Dona Palmira's. By now, she had forgotten their quarrel. Whenever he went to Alvaro's shop he found her drunk, telling the customers stories she must have told many times before.

One day when Hosi entered the shop he found a number of Portuguese men conversing. They were looking sad and serious. He heard one of them say: 'What will happen to us now? This is our country.' Another man, with a bulging stomach, thumped the table and said: 'The people who have taken power in Portugal are a bunch of semi-literate buffoons.

They will get nowhere. Salazar kept them in their place. Now that he is gone they have all gone mad. Bastards!'

Hosi understood what Dona Palmira and her fellow Portuguese were discussing months later. It was then that he came to know that there had been a coup and that a repressive regime had been overthrown. People talked of nothing but politics. The winds of independence were in the air. After 500 years of Portuguese rule, Angola was finally going to be free. People began to celebrate. Drums were played all night. The literate dreamt of government posts and big cars, the illiterate of ploughs, seeds and fertilizers.

7

Hosi and his contemporaries were now reminded daily of how lucky they were. They were enjoined never to forget the humiliations their ancestors had suffered at the hands of the Portuguese. There was one story about a man who had been forced to eat his private parts by the Portuguese, another about the tribal chief who had been forced to clap his hands and dance while his wife was raped by Portuguese soldiers.

Hosi shared in the enthusiasm that was in the air. But there were several things that amazed him still: what now happened at dinner times, for instance. His father had taken to inviting several of his friends over to discuss politics. They would stay on to dinner, which meant that there were fewer chunks of meat on the table to go round. Hosi expressed his displeasure at the numbers of visitors his father had. He had by now mastered a number of political terms gleaned from conversations that he had overheard.

'Papa,' Hosi said one night after dinner, 'why is it that when there are visitors and we have chicken, they take the thighs while I get the wings?'

His father, who had been busy picking his teeth with a matchstick, spat on the floor and said: 'They get the thighs because they are visitors. When I go to their houses, I do not expect to be given the wings or some small chunk.'

Hosi frowned and said: 'There is neo-colonialism in this house. There should be a total revolution and a fair distribution of meat.'

His father laughed out loud and said: 'Angola, where are we heading? Soon dogs will be barking slogans.'

The other problem Hosi had concerned his love life. He was now deeply in love with Monica, a girl with whom he had played mothers and fathers many times. Monica was ten and Hosi was twelve. One day, while they were playing, they had kissed; it was a tongue-to-tongue kiss and Hosi had felt a rippling sensation down his spine. He had declared his love for her and she had responded. All was fine until Senhor Morais, Monica's father, had found them holding hands behind the banana trees. Senhor Morais had called to Hosi, who decided to run. Although Senhor Morais had chased Hosi, he did not catch him. That evening he had come to Hosi's house, fuming. He said that the day he saw Hosi near his daughter he would skin him alive, so Hosi kept away.

But now that Angola was going to be independent, Hosi felt that he was entitled to see whomever he wanted. He decided to write Senhor Morais a long letter. In it he called him a fascist and a neo-colonialist bent on exploiting the toiling masses of Angola.

Senhor Morais brought the letter to Hosi's father and said that such abuse was disgraceful. Nataniel Mbueti boxed his son's ears in Senhor Morais's presence and promised that this was merely a prelude to a better beating. Gleaming, Senhor Morais left. Nataniel Mbueti turned to his son and said: 'Hosi, my son, independence does not mean writing letters to adults. You should respect people. If you want to write, then you should just write for yourself.'

Hosi rubbed the tears from his eyes and said: 'I have been beaten many times. I don't want to be beaten any more. If you can't stand me, just tell me and I will leave.'

Nataniel Mbueti frowned and looked at his son sternly. It was then that his wife, who had been in the kitchen outside, entered the room. Hosi was frowning too. Shaking his head, Nataniel Mbueti said: 'I have given you some good beatings. They seem not to have worked. What you need is the beating of your life. I don't care whether you die.'

Hosi's mother protested that she *did* care whether he died.

His father turned to her and said: 'Mama, this is between men. He thinks he's now a man and can tell me what to do with him. The pity is that he does not know who he is dealing with.'

Sobbing, Hosi said: 'Why do you always have to threaten me? I fear your beatings, yes. But I also have a mind. You never listen to what I have to say.'

Nataniel Mbueti breathed heavily and said: 'I've not had the misfortune of killing a person yet, but I might have to do it someday.'

Valeriana Mbueti said: 'Papa, please. There should be no question of who will live or who will die here.'

'I really can't understood you, Mama. Here we have a boy about to become useless. What does he know? He says I never listen to him. What can he tell me?'

He turned to Hosi and said: 'There is something called prison. There, men have a beating and salt for breakfast. Who are the men there? Well, they are people that have argued with their parents. If you continue this way you'll end up there. You'll be having a beating and salt for breakfast. Now off to your bed or my belt will be on you.'

Hosi stood up and went to his bedroom. That was the night that Hosi did his first serious piece of writing. He wrote with a red crayon in an old exercise book that he had once used for sums.

I love Papa. And I love Mama. But I hate him sometimes. I hate Senhor Morais. I like Monica very much. When I grow up I am going to live with Monica. I am going to sleep with her the whole night. If Senhor Morais comes and talks too much we will run away to Portugal. We shall eat chocolates, ice creams and cakes. I will drive a fast red car like Antonio Peixinho.

Then Hosi began to dribble on the page and fell asleep.

8

He was a tall mulatto clad in combat fatigues – not like the ones in the Portuguese army but one the people of Capingala had never seen before. He seemed a bit outlandish when he stepped out of his Land-Rover. His name was Junior. His father was Kadinguilinha, the Portuguese administrator; his mother was Susana, an Angolan woman.

Junior had just come from the Congo and had been named district Political Secretary of the MPLA. It was 1975 and the transitional government was in power. This, it was said, would rule the country for a while and then there would be national elections from which the winning party would form a government. All the movements were campaigning hard. Each and every one thought of himself as a politician and had a burning urge to put his point across. There were heated debates everywhere: some argued over the merits of communism over capitalism; others held forth on the importance of Chairman Mao's teachings for nation-building; and others went on about the importance of a capitalist economy.

Junior was a staunch Marxist and was often impatient with people who held views that went counter to his own, especially some of the members of the FNLA, who had grown up in Zaire and had been led to believe that Mercedes cars, champagne, and eau de cologne were the hallmarks of progress. Junior had great ambitions for Angola. Deep within him he felt that the communist millennium was at hand. He could visualize the green fields of the central plateau filled with happy peasants singing the Internationale. He felt that once the MPLA came to power – and he did not doubt the fact that it would – people would be mobilized and the construction of socialism would begin at once. And it would not be African

55

socialism or any such distortion dreamt up by African intellectuals, but it would be socialism in its purest form, as envisaged by Marx and Lenin.

Junior was very popular in Capingala. He was, in fact, the star of the area and people never stopped talking about him. The cub had left Junior's mother for a Portuguese woman and it was said that Junior had never forgiven him. Now that he had returned he disowned his father and lavished gifts upon his mother. Indeed, Susana, who until recently had been going round wearing dresses made from cheap material bought in Alvaro's shop, was now seen in expensive clothes that made her look like the wife of some important Portuguese official. Women hoped that their sons would grow up and be like Junior. There were a few men, however, who were not very keen on him, complaining that he was an MPLA supporter and that the MPLA was not only the party of the mulattos but also the party of the cheeky northerners. They said that the ultimate aim of the MPLA was the subjugation of all southerners. These men soon found several eager ears.

Hosi and Osvaldo took to Junior. Whenever he came to see his mother they would go near his Land-Rover and ask for a ride. He would also give them lessons in Marxism. Only Marxism and the MPLA, he would tell them, stood for the interests of the Angolan people.

'How?' Osvaldo would ask with a sheepish grin on his face.

'Because Marxism will eventually bring about communism. It will be like paradise. There will be no government, no police and people will share everything.'

'I don't quite understand Marxism, socialism, capitalism, and imperialism. Tell me, why they should matter to me?' Hosi would ask.

Junior would smile and say: 'Right. I will tell you the difference between the Marxist and the capitalist by giving you an example. Take sweets. The capitalist believes that he should work to keep all the sweets for himself and his friends. A communist believes that the sweets should be shared equally.'

Hosi would say: 'I am a communist from now onwards.'

Osvaldo would say the same. Junior would clap and tell the boys that he would tell them more about Marxism in the future.

Nataniel Mbueti, on the other hand, was by a now a staunch UNITA supporter. He often said at dinner that this was the true party of the Angolans: Catholics, Protestants and southerners were all welcome to join. Nataniel Mbueti even said that UNITA was the best party on earth to join on the way to heaven. His eyes would bulge and his thick neck seemed to become slightly bulkier when he spoke of UNITA. To support his point he said that prayers were said before and after every UNITA rally.

Major Kalutemo, a man who had just come out of the bush, where he had been a guerrilla for years, was the UNITA representative in the area. He ordered the formation of a cell of the UNITA youth league, Jura, and of the women's league, Lima.

Nataniel Mbueti was appointed head of the local party's disciplinary committee. He marvelled at this appointment. Certainly, power was not new to him. As interpreter to the PIDE officer, he had been highly revered and few had dared to do anything to incur his wrath. Yet he felt that the power UNITA had just bestowed upon him was somehow illegitimate: he felt that he had sold out. He felt remorse at having served the PIDE officer, who was now, no doubt, somewhere safe in Europe while he was having to face people that had just been freed from prison.

At home there were heated exchanges between Osvaldo and Nataniel Mbueti. It was then that Hosi realized that what he suspected all along was true: that Osvaldo was his half-brother. Later, he was to discover the whole truth.

One night Nataniel Mbueti, his wife, Hosi and Osvaldo were seated at the dinner table after a hearty meal of rice and meat – a meal usually associated with festive seasons. Independence was about to come and every day had a ring of Christmas about it. Grimacing as he tried to pick out a thread of meat that had stuck between his molars, Nataniel Mbueti said:

'Osvaldo, things are getting serious. The movements are not getting on well. I doubt whether any of them will stick to the agreement that has just been signed in Alvor. Power is an aphrodisiac: once you taste it you can never do without it.'

Any visitor present would have concluded that Nataniel Mbueti was not quite sane. No one in a normal state of mind would talk to a thirteen-year-old boy like that. Those present, however, were not surprised. Nataniel Mbueti had the habit of calling someone's name and saying out loud whatever he was thinking. He turned to Osvaldo again and, looking straight at him, said: 'I don't want you to continue fraternizing with that mulatto and the teacher, Xavier Ramos. They are our enemies. I have been told that this country will soon see the bloodiest battle Africa has ever had.'

Valeriana Mbueti fidgeted, groaned and said: 'I knew it. This year we are in for it.'

'Mama, please. You have this habit of disturbing my discourse. It is very annoying. Where was I? Yes, the war. It will be hell. I am told it will be worse than the Congo. Dogs and humans will be decomposing by each other's sides on the roads and there will be no life left. By the way, there is this bomb which is said to kill any living thing once it is dropped. I am sure that those evil northerners would not hesitate to drop it here.'

There was complete silence. Nataniel Mbueti continued: 'They say that an egg cannot be broken by a visitor unless his host gives it to him or shows him the room where it is hidden. That teacher, Xavier Ramos, and Junior are both visitors: they do not belong to our party, UNITA. This house belongs to God and UNITA.'

Valeriana Mbueti, who had been listening to her husband with an increasingly serious expression, turned to Osvaldo and said: 'What do you see that is so special in the mulatto?'

Osvaldo cleared his throat and said: 'He is a revolutionary. He believes in the people.'

Nataniel Mbueti frowned so Osvaldo stopped talking and started scratching his head. Pointing his finger at Osvaldo Nataniel Mbueti said: 'No more Junior. This is an order. Disobey and you will be duly punished. Revolutionary, revolu-

58

tionary! Do you people understand what you've been going about saying? When a bullet rips through that thick head of yours, do you think any of these terms will help you?'

Although Hosi admired Osvaldo's ever-increasing political vocabulary, he was also beginning to feel hostile towards him. In the past six months he had come to believe in his father, the more so after his prediction of decomposing dogs in the streets. Hosi also visualized several limbless corpses lying in the streets. If this was what Junior and Xavier Ramos were trying to bring to Capingala, then his father was right, Hosi felt, to insist that Osvaldo stop seeing them.

That night he decided to take Osvaldo to task. As they were about to get into bed Hosi said: 'Osvaldo, why can't you be like everybody else and join UNITA?'

'They have no future.'

'What do you mean?'

'History is like a magnet. Whether people like it or not, they will have to obey its rules. The MPLA is for the people and everybody is going to join it. That was what Junior was telling me the other day.'

Hosi shook his head and said: 'Don't let these people pump all sorts of rubbish into you. Why do you want to hurt Mama and Papa? Be sensible.'

'Sensible? I will tell you this: that woman, your mother, is not my mother. I know that you know it. And that man, your father, is also my father. But he refused me because he feared for his job. He lost it anyway. He wanted to keep it secret because my mama was very young and still at school. But it was found out and he was sacked.'

Hosi was staring at him with bulging eyes. Osvaldo began to seem frightening. Hosi wondered what else lay hidden in Osvaldo's head and awaited more revelations. Osvaldo continued: 'When the MPLA come to power, people won't reject their sons or daughters. Children will have a very good father, the state. Comrade Junior told me that his father left his mother. He understands me. The MPLA is my father now. They will send me to Cuba and I might become a pilot or a commander. Do you see the point, Hosi?'

Hosi shook his head and said: 'No.'

'You, your mama and our papa laugh at me. I know it. I know that you are better than me at school; I am stupid. In the MPLA there are no stupid and clever people – we are all the same. That is what Comrade Junior told me.' Patting his shoulders, Osvaldo said: 'I will have stars here. I will have bodyguards. You will tremble before me, Hosi, I know it.'

9

Xavier Ramos was disappointed by Old Pedro. For some time now he had been trying to get him to recruit more supporters to attend MPLA rallies. Old Pedro had declined, saying he had more important things than politics to think about, such as ploughing his fields. He also said that he had to travel long distances into the forest to collect honey.

'What are you going to give your country, then?' Xavier Ramos asked him.

'What do you mean?'

'Your country needs your help, your contribution. This can come about only if you participate in the people's party, the MPLA. All these parties springing up from nowhere do not defend the people.'

Old Pedro smiled. Patting Xavier Ramos on the back he said: 'Son, I was not born yesterday. I have also travelled a bit. The Luvale say, "*Jipolitiki makuli*", which means "Politicians are liars."'

'How do you mean?' asked Xavier Ramos.

'I mean exactly that: politicians are liars. All politicians, that is.'

'Now wait a minute. You are comparing our party, the MPLA, with other African parties. That is a mistake. Ours is a communist party – the people's party.'

The argument went on, and took in Junior. Old Pedro said he was not very keen on him. 'That mulatto behaves at times as if he is a governor.'

Xavier Ramos was incensed. He frowned and said: 'Don't refer to him as that mulatto. He is Comrade Political Commissar. It is time we began to see people by their political duties and roles and not by the colour of their skins or by their tribe.'

Old Pedro patted Xavier Ramos on the back and said: 'Oh, teacher. Now people can't talk freely without committing this or that political mistake. I will shut up. Listen, come and help me write a letter to my nephew.'

'Who?'

'Julino. I am told that he has just joined UNITA. I am very happy. He had been in Huambo for a long time doing nothing apart from gambling and spreading babies. Now they will make a man of him.'

Shaking his head Xavier Ramos said: 'He's lost. A UNITA soldier? He has no future.'

'I know that you are a teacher and that you have read many books. But the truth is that there is no better place for my nephew than UNITA. He was as lazy as a pregnant boa constrictor that had gorged itself on a goat. Now he'll be a proper man. I don't care who will do it; all I want is that he should be a proper man. Now, give me something for a bottle.'

Xavier Ramos reached for his pocket, pulled out a bank note and handed it over to Old Pedro, who received it with a gleeful expression on his face. He even forgot about the letter he had just asked Xavier Ramos to write for him. Looking at the bank note and nodding, Old Pedro said: 'Now I understand your language; not the usual big words. Now that the Portuguese have left why should we hurt our jaws by trying to pronounce big words?'

Xavier Ramos cleared his throat, patted Old Pedro on the back and said: 'It is sad but I have to tell you this. Sometimes you sound like a reactionary. Yet the party and the people have much trust in you.'

Old Pedro dismissed Xavier Ramos and walked into his house to get his tobacco tin. As Xavier Ramos said goodbye Old Pedro replied: 'A pleasant day must always come to an end and that which is painful is often forgotten. God bless you for having given a wretched creature like me some money for a bottle. God bless you.'

Xavier Ramos walked away, trying to puzzle out where the old man stood.

★

Xavier Ramos was sitting on a wooden chair reading *The Communist Manifesto* and smiling to himself. Everything in his life seemed to be going well except for Old Pedro, who had chosen the reactionary road and become a UNITA supporter. He looked around his sitting room. The walls were covered with MPLA posters. One showed a peasant woman wielding a Kalashnikov whilst working away in her field; another was of the leader himself, benign yet severe, staring out at him. Often, Xavier Ramos felt that the eyes from the poster could plumb the emotions swirling within him: ambition laced with a good dose of avarice and a profound hatred of illiterate peasants. Xavier Ramos had always tried to suppress these ideas, but they kept emerging in his mind. Whenever he thought of his ambitions he would say to himself: 'Why worry? Surely even the president himself somewhere deep in his heart is moved by the prospect of big cars, a palace and good food. Horrible thoughts? Well, inside every revolutionary there must be some reactionary thoughts.'

As thought after thought hovered in his mind, he fell asleep on the chair. It was a sweet afternoon sleep. He was awoken by a gentle rap on the door. Looking startled he sidled to the door.

'Who is it?' he asked.

'Bastard. Open the door!'

Xavier Ramos swung the door open and all but leapt with joy when he saw the person standing before him. It was a tall, dark man dressed in a military uniform – Mingo, a distant cousin he had not seen for a long time. They embraced and slapped each other on the back for a while. Then they stood apart and looked at each other like lovers.

'I knew I was right,' said Xavier Ramos.

'What?'

'That you would be bald.'

'I am not yet bald. This patch over here is a sign of wisdom. Where is the madam?'

'Gone to fetch firewood.'

'Teacher's wife fetching firewood? Don't you at least have a brazier?'

63

'We have something like that but my wife is rather fond of firewood. She is the mission-educated type, not a town girl. Where have you been? I heard that you were somewhere in Europe.'

'Not Europe. I was somewhere in Africa – the Republic of Zaire.'

As they went inside, Xavier Ramos looked at Mingo's epaulettes and said: 'What on earth are those?'

Mingo shrugged and said: 'I am a captain in the FNLA. Actually I am the Regional Military Commander. I know that you have taken up with the communists.'

Shaking his head, Xavier Ramos said: 'Truly Mingo. I never thought you'd sink so low. What is your party's philosophy? Screwing the masses, eh? Your party licks the boots of American imperialism and your leaders are on the payroll of the CIA. It is a known fact. No one can deny it.'

Mingo laughed out loud and said: 'Pure lies. I am sure that the person who crammed that stuff into your head had just received his monthly payment of roubles from the KGB.'

Xavier Ramos crossed his hands and frowned. Mingo threw both arms into the air and said: 'Come on, we are brothers, not enemies. Why can't we have some good laughs before we start quoting irrelevant philosophers?'

Xavier Ramos fell back and stared at Mingo intently. Mingo fidgeted and leant towards Xavier Ramos. He cleared his throat and said: 'I have to tell you the reason I am here. It seems that there will be no peace. We are heading for a showdown. There will be bloodshed in this country, but we shall win, whatever the circumstances.'

Xavier Ramos said: 'You must be getting weapons from your imperialist godfathers. Tell me the truth!'

'Call them what you want, but they will be there. I just want you to know how powerful we are. All these gun-toting nobodies that you see trotting about will vanish at the sound of the first bullet.'

Xavier Ramos shook his head: 'Nonsense. We believe in the people's cause. If you look carefully around the world you will see that there has been a steady expansion in communism.

More and more people in Africa have come to realize the road to true freedom and prosperity. Indeed, the whole of Africa is ripe for a revolution. We are the people's party.' By now Xavier Ramos was worked up. He spoke as though he had an audience in front of him.

Mingo clasped his hands, licked his lips and said: 'I did not think that you were that far gone. Let me tell you the truth. I left this country seven years ago for the Congo to join the liberation movement. I had military training and came back to Angola to fight the Portuguese. I know that history is not fair. People like you who were gorging themselves on chickens while we were being hounded like antelopes by the Portuguese are now calling us traitors. That, however, is beside the point.'

Xavier Ramos thumped the coffee table and said: 'Don't think that I am new to the liberation war. One of the leading MPLA commanders, Comrade Junior, was my pupil.'

'I am not accusing you. Neither am I trying to judge you. They say that the sins committed before the coming of Christ will not count when people are considered for admission into heaven. The truth, my brother, is that in this war brothers – and I mean blood brothers – ought to stick to each other.'

'You are also a tribalist. Let the people hear you say that and you'll probably be beheaded at once. I would certainly not blame them.'

'I am not a tribalist, whatever you might think. I like southerners, especially their women. I am living with one right now. She is as obedient as a proper woman should be. I am a realist, my brother. If you look at all independent African countries today you will find that power is in the hands of the most powerful tribe. This is a fact. In the case of Angola, which tribe deserves the political power? Tell me?'

Xavier Ramos chuckled and said: 'The people.'

'The people? That is nonsense. Which people? The Bakongo? The Ovimbundu? Or the Kimbundu?'

Xavier Ramos chuckled again and said: 'We are not on the same wavelength.'

'We don't have to be.'

'Why?'

'Do you know how our kingdom came to an end?'

'No.'

'I will tell you. The Portuguese king – I think it was Pedro VI – sent our king a chair. Our king wrote back a letter thanking the Portuguese king. The Portuguese later claimed that this letter was a testimony proving that we had ceded our land to them. You see what I mean?'

Xavier Ramos said: 'That may be history. What we now have at stake is Angola, not the Congo kingdom.'

Mingo frowned and began to shake his head. He hit his forehead with his palm and said: 'I think the greatest lie going around is that we are all the same. That is a pure lie. Ours was an autonomous kingdom in which we, the Bakongo, were the absolute masters. History, brother, history. We should never forget our past. When southerners were running naked in the wilderness, we had a kingdom. We sent an ambassador to Lisbon and we were highly respected. We are not a tribe of house servants, like the Kimbundu; we are kings. History is a witness to this fact.'

'What you've said is completely true, but it is counter-productive. We should aim to build this nation, break down all barriers. But I quite agree with you that we are special. I was reading a book the other day about Manikongo, our king. There is nobody else like him. He was great.'

'That is why I said that we are great,' said Mingo. 'Do you think that everything I am saying is without foundation? I know the Angolan situation better than anything else. The MPLA was founded in 1956 by a bunch of mulattos, and UNITA in 1966 by semi-literate Maoists. Our party came into existence because we wanted to revive the glories of our kingdom that had been lost. Either we have what rightly belongs to us or there will be no peace in this country.'

Xavier Ramos shifted in his chair, frowning as he listened to Mingo. Mingo pulled out a handkerchief from his pocket, wiped his brow and said: 'I am in a brother's house and yet I feel as if I am trying to convince some old, incredulous widow that I love her. Bring something to tickle this goddam throat!'

Xavier Ramos went out and brought a bottle of wine.

66

Mingo poured out two glasses, drank them quickly and said: 'Dear cousin, I am on a mission. The Central Committee has appointed you as Party Provincial Secretary.'

Xavier Ramos laughed and said: 'I don't even belong to the FNLA. How can I be appointed Provincial Secretary?'

Mingo leant towards him and said seriously: 'The red you have in your blood, my brother, is not the same as the red that runs in the brotherly feelings that you and your fellow Marxists have for each other. The red that is flowing in your veins is far more important; it is the red that also flows through my veins. We, the Bakongo, are one and the same. That is a fact. A brand-new jeep and a house await you in Huambo.'

Xavier Ramos looked straight at Mingo. Their eyes met. They embraced and shook hands fervently. It was done. Xavier Ramos had moved to his brother's party, the FNLA. As Mingo was about to leave, Xavier Ramos said: 'I think we'll win. We are great.'

'Not only that,' Mingo replied. 'We also believe in democracy and freedom. The people have faith in us.'

The two shook hands and congratulated each other.

10

Junior ordered the driver of the Land-Rover, a stocky man called Saul, to halt. He jumped out of the jeep and beckoned to Osvaldo, who was at the back, to follow him. They walked till they came to a stream, where they began to talk.

'This,' said Junior, 'is a very important moment of your life. You will have to choose between your wretched father, who – I should tell you – is a complete reactionary, and the party. I have said this to you on several occasions: the party will never let you down; it will always be on your side, come what may. You must choose the party.'

Osvaldo said: 'I understand everything you've been telling me, Comrade. But I need to know whether I am really going to Cuba to be trained as a pilot?'

'An astronaut! You'll be the first African to step on the moon. Imagine that. Your father and step-mother will be jealous; the progressive people of the world will be very proud of you.'

Osvaldo smiled and nodded.

'So we are agreed?' said Junior. 'You are now an MPLA party militant, right?'

'Right!' Osvaldo answered.

'Now, I don't want you to be like Xavier Ramos. He is a traitor. Just because he is a Bakongo he has switched over to the FNLA.'

'I had always thought that Xavier Ramos was a good man.'

'Good men don't necessarily make good revolutionaries,' said Junior. 'I will be leaving for Luanda tomorrow, because I have been promoted.'

Osvaldo gave a little yelp. Junior shrugged and said: 'It does not mean much to me. It is the people that matter. It is time you got mentally ready. I am taking you away to Luanda with me. The party will take care of you. You will be famous some-day.'

The two shook hands. Osvaldo's stomach lurched. His heart began to beat fast. He had made up his mind: he was definitely going to go with Junior to Luanda.

After dinner Nataniel Mbueti subjected Osvaldo to yet another tirade for fraternizing with Junior and Xavier Ramos. In a fit of rage, he said: 'If you continue seeing that man I will kill you. I really mean it.'

Hosi and Osvaldo were then sent to bed. Unable to sleep, Osvaldo said to Hosi almost in a whisper: 'Can I tell you a secret?'

'Yes.'

'Promise not to tell anyone.'

'I promise.'

'Swear!'

'OK. I swear.'

'Upon what?'

'Upon God.'

'No. There is no God. Swear upon the people of Angola.'

'What will happen if I tell the secret to somebody?'

'You'll be a reactionary, a traitor, a worthless person.'

'I promise not to tell. Please tell me the secret.'

'I am going to Cuba. I will be leaving tomorrow. I will be a pilot. I might even go to the moon.'

Hosi's heart was beating fast. He did not believe what Osvaldo had just told him. He said: 'Never play with me like this again. You are not going anywhere. Papa is not going to let you go.'

Osvaldo said: 'Believe it or not, I am leaving. Don't tell anyone or you'll be shot. This is a revolution and, as Comrade Junior says, reactionaries are fit only for one place – the grave.'

Hosi felt then that even though Osvaldo was less intelligent than he was, he would become an important man.

*

The following night Nataniel Mbueti came to the dinner table looking very upset. Nothing could mollify him.

'Hosi,' Nataniel Mbueti thundered from the table.

'Yes, Papa.'

'Tell me the truth. What do you know about Osvaldo?'

'Nothing.'

'Liar. I am sure you know a lot.'

'I don't.'

Nataniel Mbueti's voice assumed the tone of an interrogator trying to worm vital information out of a criminal. He was trying to make Hosi feel like an accomplice to a crime.

Nataniel Mbueti slapped his son. Hosi was startled for a while but soon regained his composure. In the past such a slap would have been followed with pleas for mercy. Not this time. Now Hosi looked straight at his father and recalled the many times that he had been beaten. In all these he had believed that his father had been right; now he felt his father was wrong.

Valeriana Mbueti sat still on her chair, twitching occasionally, awaiting the most appropriate moment in which to say something to ease the tension between her husband and her son. Finally she plucked up courage and said: 'Hosi darling, say what you know. I hate seeing you being beaten.'

Nataniel Mbueti said agitatedly: 'Look here, woman. Keep silent. If your mouth is itching, just keep silent. I don't enjoy beating my son. What I want is to make sure that he is honest and tells the truth.' He then turned to Hosi and said: 'I know about your brother. You will have to tell me everything you know or I will give you a good thrashing. You don't want to have salt and a beating for breakfast.'

Hosi cleared his voice and said: 'Osvaldo has gone with Junior. He might go to Cuba. That is all I know.'

'I already know that,' said Nataniel Mbueti.

'What do you want to know, then?'

'I want to know more. Why did he leave for Cuba?'

'Because he wants to become a pilot. That is what Junior has told him will happen.'

'And he believed him?'

70

'Yes.'

'Fool. He does not know that they are sending him to work in the sugar cane plantation as a slave.'

Hosi immediately saw Osvaldo in a snake-ridden plantation, sweating profusely while a bearded Cuban with a whip watched him closely from behind. Nataniel Mbueti turned to his wife and said: 'Valeriana, you don't seem to be concerned.'

'I am. How can I not be?' she answered.

Natanial Mbueti patted his forehead. 'Well, he is not your son.'

Valeriana Mbueti shrugged and said: 'There you go again.'

Nataniel Mbueti turned to Hosi and said: 'Son, times are bad. Believe me. There will soon be a bloody war. All the radio stations in the world are saying the same thing: that Angola will soon be plunged into a civil war. The leaders of the political parties have been meeting everywhere, but they just can't agree on anything.'

All the hatred that Hosi had been feeling previously for his father vanished. For the first time he noticed a tinge of fear in his father's voice.

Nataniel Mbueti continued: 'I'd rather die than live under the MPLA or the FNLA.'

'Why, Papa?' asked Valeriana Mbueti. 'If it comes to it we might as well live under any of them as long as we aren't killed.'

'Various reasons,' Nataniel Mbueti snapped. 'Take the MPLA. It is for the northerners; it is for the Kimbundu, especially those from Luanda and Catete. They think we southerners are stupid. Everybody knows that is what they think. They've lived with the whites so long, they feel that they are better than us. But let's face it, they are crooks and house servants. It is only the mulattos who are better than us: on the whole, they are very well educated. What have the northerners contributed to Angola? Coffee? Not at all. The coffee and sugar cane plantations were a result of our labour. They are all lazy. We made Angola! Every year truck upon truck left for the north with contract workers. We were all over – Gabela, Cabinda, Novo Rendondo, all over.'

71

Nataniel Mbueti was fuming. He stood up, paced about for a while, then said, punching his chest: 'We built this country. We, the Ovimbundu. Not the mulattos, not the Bakongos, but we, the Ovimbundu. They find it hard to swallow the fact but there it is! Angola without us is like the sea without fishes – completely worthless. We built the bridges, the roads, the airports. If the northerners come to power, they will be at the top, enjoying themselves, while we will be at the bottom, breaking our poor necks. I'd rather die than see that day. And then there is the FNLA. A complete bunch of thieves. If this country falls into their hands, we are doomed too. All the money will be stolen. I know it! The Bakongo does not like to work and nothing pleases him more than living in comfort from ill-gotten wealth. Only UNITA can save us.'

Hosi and his mother listened dumbfounded. Till now Hosi had known little about the different tribes in Angola. After his father had spoken, he began to hate those that were not Ovimbundu. He believed immediately that his father was right when he said that their tribe was superior to the others.

That night Hosi had a dream in which dark clouds hung in the sky, proclaiming that there was soon going to be a torrential downpour. Then the wind began to blow hard. People fled into their homes. Hosi wanted to do the same but he couldn't. His legs felt heavy. Then he saw three dark birds coming in his direction. He tried as hard as he could to run from them but he was unable to move. The birds came closer; they were as big as helicopters. Hosi began to scream.

11

When it was heard that Aunt Laura had left Senhor Adolfo, Nataniel Mbueti and his wife spoke of nothing else. To make matters worse, as Nataniel Mbueti kept saying, Aunt Laura had moved in with Kaluanda, a man said to be of ill repute. But that was not the main thing that aggrieved Nataniel Mbueti. Kaluanda, whose real name was Noberto da Conceisão, was a northerner and it was widely rumoured that he would be appointed as the MPLA Provincial Coordinator. This was the worst betrayal possible on the part of Aunt Laura.

Valeriana Mbueti, however, was adamant in her sister's defence. 'Come on, Papa,' she said during yet another attack by her husband, 'you have to understand that she was not happy with Adolfo. What was she supposed to do?'

Nataniel Mbueti banged the table and burst out: 'What was she supposed to do? Go for a man from Luanda, as if there weren't enough bachelors in the south? Take Tomas Chipundo. Since his wife died, he has been looking for someone to look after his children. There is also Benjamin. All these are fine, respectable, fellows. She overlooked them and went for the northerner.'

'I will tell you the truth, Papa. Laura is pregnant and she says the father is Kaluanda.'

Nataniel Mbueti looked like a man who had received the worst insult of his life. He banged the table and said: 'That man deserves a bullet through his head. How can he make Laura pregnant?'

Valeriana Mbueti shifted. In an almost mournful tone she said: 'Papa, you have to understand. You know how desperate we once were when I was not conceiving.'

'But you wouldn't have gone with another man.' He banged the table again and said through clenched teeth: 'Southern women are quick to part their legs whenever a northerner comes along with his half-baked Portuguese.'

'Papa, sometimes you talk too much. Laura has been having problems with her in-laws. Adolfo's relatives have been making much fuss. They want a child. They have been threatening to kick her out for the past two years. That is why she left and went to live with Kaluanda.'

Nataniel Mbueti bit his lower lip and said: 'So you've known all this for a while?'

'In a way, yes.'

'And wouldn't tell me?'

'Well, it was you who said your mind was too busy with the future of Angola to be bothered with simple matters.'

'This is not simple. Wars are sparked off by such matters. Poor Adolfo. I will be meeting him at the party headquarters in Huambo soon.'

Valeriana Mbueti said: 'Please, Papa, don't make a fuss over this. Laura has always wanted a baby. Kaluanda has made her pregnant. Why can't she be left alone?'

'Be left alone? There are times when I think you are going mad, Mama. Someone hurts her husband and you expect her to be left alone? It can't be tolerated, not among us. This issue will take much saliva – and blood, if necessary. It is time that they stopped taking us for a ride. Just because we used to work in coffee plantations in their lands, doesn't mean we are the fools they make us out to be.'

Valeriana Mbueti was now in tears. She said: 'Please, Papa, be reasonable.'

'Reasonable? This is a war. Only fools are reasonable in time of war.'

The following morning Nataniel Mbueti got a lift to Huambo. The UNITA headquarters were next to a tall building under construction near a pool that had been built in front of the Estufa botanical gardens. There were many people hanging about the headquarters. Some just wanted to be spotted be-

74

cause they had political ambitions; others wanted to see those that had already carved themselves a niche in politics. All of them marvelled at the sight of people who until recently had been nobodies and who had now become district political secretaries.

Nataniel Mbueti was quickly ushered in by a guard. There was a girl with flawless Portuguese at the reception desk. She was engaged in deep conversation with a tall youth who was dressed in bell-bottomed trousers. He also had a belt tied above his navel and a shirt which looked as if it was going to burst open at any moment. The girl was saying: 'Tell me, Arcadio, what are they saying in the world? I mean, the radios you listen to.'

The young man stretched himself as if posing for a photograph and said: 'Well, there is a lot of talk about the transitional government. They all say that it might not last long. There are all sorts of problems. Anyway, if these blokes won't accept the ballot box, we gonna give them a taste of hell.'

As the youth spoke, the girl's eyes bulged. Nataniel Mbueti suspected that she was more interested in the young man than in what he was saying. Shaking his head, Nataniel Mbueti said: 'People on the other side, I mean on the MPLA side, are working hard. Here we are spending time admiring each other. How can we win the war? I want to get to the office of the provincial delegate.'

The youth stared at Nataniel Mbueti hard, and said: 'I know you old people – especially those of you that went to mission schools. You don't know how to mind your tongues. If you can't grasp internal and international affairs, then you're better off with your beak shut.'

Nataniel Mbueti glared at the youth, like a wrestler about to seize his opponent. He pointed his finger at him and said: 'I will not have babies talk to me like that. You don't know who I am. If you knew, you would not be talking to me like that.'

The girl smiled and then said in a mocking tone: 'Surely, colonialism has left many people dizzy. This is independence. To hell with that crap of kowtowing before people. We are all now equals.'

75

'Right on,' said the youth. 'We are going to build an egalitarian society. In China, for instance, all men and women wear the same. When our party finally gets to power, the same will happen. The youth will bring it about.'

Once he'd decided that the two young people were too far gone in their rudeness, Nataniel Mbueti wanted to get away as soon as he could. He turned to the girl and said: 'Please show me the way.'

Just as he was about to reach the door, the young man said: 'Old man, get it clear. I was not being rude to you. It is you who thought that it was improper for us to discuss serious issues affecting our country.'

Nataniel Mbueti walked on. As he strode through the building, he saw faces staring from behind thick metal grilles – the last Portuguese owner of the house had kept dogs in there – looking worried.

'What is your problem, brothers?' Nataniel Mbueti shouted.

'We are in prison,' one of them responded. 'I mean, this woman reported me. It all began when my bitch gave birth to triplets. I decided to name each dog after the leaders of the three political parties. Anything wrong in that?'

'I think you should be in a psychiatric ward,' said Nataniel Mbueti. 'How can any sane man name dogs after important people?'

Later Nataniel Mbueti decided to go to the Balcao, where he knew he would meet several friends. The Balcao was situated at the Bairro Academico and stood opposite the three main secondary schools in Huambo. Just as he was about to cross the road near the Liceu Nacional, he heard a voice behind him. He turned around and saw Adolfo. The two embraced.

Adolfo smiled and said: 'My God, you look as though you've just acquired a new mistress. You look so healthy. Somebody must be taking good care of you.'

'Not at all. I wish it was so!' Nataniel Mbueti laughed. 'We've heard about what Laura has done. There are times when I feel God must regret ever having created women. Look at the problems they cause! Do you realize what we men have to undergo for the sake of these ungrateful creatures?'

'Let's go to the Balcao and I will tell you everything,' said Adolfo. 'The blood in my heart is foaming with anger. Thank God I do not have a gun, otherwise someone would be in purgatory by now.'

'Who?' Nataniel Mbueti asked, pretending not to know who Adolfo was referring to.

Adolfo grunted and said: 'Wait till we sit down. You try to be civilized in this world and every son of a bitch takes you for granted.'

The two of them entered the Balcao bar, which was full of other middle-aged men. Soon, they were all exchanging pleasantries. Nataniel Mbueti and Adolfo ordered a bottle of wine and were then joined by Bernabe Gangu and Ze Maria. Ze Maria had once been an outstanding mathematician. To everyone's dismay, he had taken to drinking so much that he had become an alcoholic.

They all showed interest in Adolfo's plight. 'As you all know,' Adolfo said, 'Laura was not conceiving. But I knew that she would one day conceive. It had been the same problem with Nataniel over here.'

Nataniel Mbueti nodded.

'After so many years, I suddenly began to notice a change in our relationship. I began to love my wife more than before. True, we had tiffs and once in a while I would give her a few slaps – one of those slaps women love, the ones meant to keep the rage of love aglow.'

Bernabe interrupted him: 'They are also important to maintain discipline. A marriage without discipline is like a Chevrolet without a handbrake. It can never be secure. Please continue, my brother.'

Adolfo coughed and went on: 'Yes, as I was saying, I came to love her more than anything else. I said to myself: "Man, what on earth is making you want this woman so much?" At some point, I even began to suspect that she had given me this tea – what do they call it?'

Nataniel Mbueti replied quickly: '*Cha me gosta* [love me tea]. Do you know that even Portuguese women give it to their husbands? And then they say that they are civilized!'

Adolfo took a sip from his glass and continued with his story: 'Yes, I really loved her. Indeed, as they say, our relationship soon became like that between the belt and the waist. I just could not do without her. I noticed that her cheeks began to bulge, and her temper became shorter and shorter. Her skin became lighter. Now and then she would spit, and then she would say that she was feeling dizzy. At last she became pregnant. I thanked God and said to Him: "Please, say your wish to me here on earth and it shall be done." I heard a voice within myself say: "Stick to your woman and love her as much as you can." I complied.'

Adolf shook his head and continued: 'Laura's temper went from bad to worse. I accepted it. I knew all along that there was nothing as complicated as a pregnant woman.'

'A pregnant woman is like a quadratic equation,' put in Ze Maria, coughing and spluttering over his wine.

Adolfo continued: 'I asked Laura why she was behaving in that way. She refused to talk. No, I did not beat her; I would have never forgiven myself. I threatened her. I said, if she was going to continue treating me that way, then I would bring her back into line. Lord, it was almost as though I had given her the beating of her life. She began to insult my great-grandmother and all my family. I swallowed that; which woman in Angola gets on well with her in-laws?'

They all shook their heads. Adolfo resumed: 'I said to her that I knew she was pregnant. Of course I am, she answered. I said she should count herself lucky or I would discipline her. Then she said something that shocked me. She said the child was not mine and that she knew that my relatives were trying to get rid of her in order to find me a younger wife. Not my child? I felt like I was shit, like I was diarrhoea or even worse than that.'

Adolfo took a cigarette from his pocket and lit it. He puffed it once, threw it to the floor, and crushed it with the heel of his shoe. He went on with his story: 'She said the baby was not mine. I said, no way, this pregnancy is 100 per cent mine even if you've been sleeping with other men. She said she had slept with one other man. Who does it turn out to be?

78

Kaluanda. I know that he is a medical assistant and sometimes fancies himself a doctor. Whatever I am, the truth is that he is no match for me.'

The others nodded thoughtfully. 'When she told me this I almost exploded. I had never felt so hurt before in my life, and I am not a child. I have been through some hard bits. I felt something gather on my throat. I tried to swallow it but it would neither go up or down. However hard I tried to swallow it, it remained there. I just could not say a word. Thanks to God, I fell asleep at once. Yes, I am blessed in a way. Whenever I have problems, I seem to fall asleep easily. When I woke up Laura was gone. A day later I found out that she have moved in with Kaluanda. Brothers, this is my story.'

After a shocked silence Nataniel Mbueti spoke: 'I was just telling Valeriana that he deserves to be shot dead.'

'Shot dead?' Ze Maria asked, knitting his brows. 'He deserves to be burnt and buried alive. No physical pain is enough retribution for this most heinous crime. This is indeed what in politics is known as a crime against humanity.'

'I agree,' Bernabe said, nodding.

'I have done nothing wrong,' Adolfo argued. 'Laura and her man have wronged me. It does not matter. I am bitter, but what can I do?'

'Revenge,' said Nataniel Mbueti. 'I have said time and again that if we don't show the northerners that we are tough and that they can never get away with doing us wrong, then they will continue feeling superior.'

'What revenge?' Adolfo asked calmly.

Nataniel Mbueti frowned and said: 'Well, I cannot tell you exactly what to do, but I think something must be done.'

'Time will be the final judge. There is no question that the baby is mine.'

Just then, they were all disturbed by a commotion in the bar. Kaluanda walked in proudly with the smile of a very important man on his face. Everyone turned to greet him. 'Good afternoon, senhor,' someone called out.

'I prefer to be called comrade,' Kaluanda replied, waving his right hand. He nodded complacently.

The transitional government in Luanda was still intact and Kaluanda, who had until a month ago been a mere medical assistant, was now a high-ranking man in the MPLA hierarchy in the province. He told his friends that he frequented the Balcao to gather support, but his main aim was to show people that he had risen in the world. He was a firm believer in the principle that power needed to be visible and could be measured only by the number of people who kowtowed before you.

Kaluanda walked over to the counter and ordered champagne. As he popped the bottle open, someone said out loud that the bottle he was holding was one of the last three left in Angola. Kaluanda shrugged and said: 'Things will soon get better, my friend.'

There was complete silence. The men in the bar wanted to hear what else Kaluanda had to say. He cleared his throat and said: 'Angola is now in our hands – that is, we the Africans. Whatever they say, the country is ours. I have been listening to foreign stations lately. All of them, from the BBC to the Voice of America, are saying that our country will soon be in chaos. That is complete nonsense. I will tell you one thing – whites think that we are fools. We are not. We will resolve our problems and make this country prosper. We will have to beware, though. The imperialists are sophisticated. They will try and divide us in various ways. When an African commits a crime and is sent to prison for the sake of peace, the whites will stand up and cry that human rights are yet again being violated. They will produce pamphlets saying that people in Africa are being imprisoned. Do not be deceived. They want to persuade the world that we are savages and that we are unable to have any form of civilized government.'

By now Kaluanda had become livid. There were shouts of, 'Indeed', 'That is very true', 'Carry on, brother, man!' He noticed Adolfo standing beside Nataniel Mbueti and walked over to him, extending his hand. Adolfo, in typical southern Angolan style, greeted him with a smile. It was as if the two men were the best of friends. Kaluanda patted Adolfo on the back and said: 'Angolans, to tell the truth, are a very civilized people. Go anywhere in the world where they've heard that there are such people as Angolans and you'll hear them praise us. This is a fact. I mean, in other African countries people don't have the slightest notion of civilized behaviour. Say two men, as the case might be, have an argument.' Here Bernabe grunted. 'Yes, two men have an argument. Angolans will let reason prevail. Other Africans, or other blacks, will turn to knives or guns.' They all nodded in agreement.

Ze Maria coughed out loud to attract attention and said: 'I am sure that you're following what they're saying on the radio. British, South African, American – it's all stuff from the same bag. They think that we blacks are thick and can never do anything. Racists! There will be elections in this country and the winner will rule for a given period and we shall see that black men can practise democracy too. We do have our differences, that is normal. Just because I belong to the MPLA does not mean that I should try and kill all of you. No way. It is against our African traditions.'

'Just one thing,' said Nataniel Mbueti. 'I know this old man who has travelled a bit through Africa. He says at the beginning there is always talk of democracy but in the end dictatorships take over.'

'I have heard that before,' replied Kaluanda wearily. 'True, there have been instances when democracy has been betrayed. What really makes me sick is that foreigners dictate to us the political system that we should have. We don't tell the imperialists that they should look after their poor. In America, for instance, blacks live worse than dogs. They are really poor. And yet only the other day the BBC reported that the Americans are concerned that communism will spread to this part of Africa. They are afraid of communism – these whites!'

Kaluanda frowned and his face assumed a fierce expression. The others looked on intently as he continued: 'They are afraid of communism because it will free us blacks. Let's face it. For years upon years whites have been inculcating us with ideas. First, Christianity. I know some of you are staunch Catholics or Protestants, but can any one of you tell me which black man is at the top of either the Catholic or the Protestant Church? There will never be a black Pope – that is it.'

An old man who had been listening attentively came forward and asked Kaluanda to calm down. His voice was hoarse and he spoke with difficulty: 'I have known it all along. The world is coming to an end. From the way you are talking, I have the feeling that you do not believe in God, or do you?'

Kaluanda cleared his throat, smiled and said: 'Papa, it is not easy to explain my philosophical tenets. I am afraid that they might simply be beyond your grasp. I am a revolutionary; I believe in dialectical materialism. Years of colonialism have fossilized our mental faculties.'

The old man replied in Umbundu: 'Tell me, son, are you sure that the devil is not speaking inside you?'

Kaluanda answered him in Portuguese: 'Papa, I really understand your predicament. But times have changed. Your philosophy would have done for another era, but the positive and the negative have clashed and now we have the hypothesis of the phenomenon of Angola. There is no question about that.'

The old man walked away, shaking his head. Kaluanda continued with his speech. 'We are all one, whatever the world might think. That is the truth.' They nodded in agreement. Kaluanda turned to Adolfo and said almost in a whisper: 'I know that you are not happy with your wife. Or should I say with me? We should come together and clear this thing up.'

Adolfo was tongue-tied, and was unable to reply. As soon as Kaluanda left he excused himself, saying he had some urgent matters to attend to.

Nataniel Mbueti shrugged, turned to the others and said: 'Have you seen how a southern man behaves? Here was Judas himself and yet Adolfo did not do as much as point a finger at him. He was intimidated by his Portuguese. If I were Adolfo, Kaluanda would be preparing to get into his coffin by now!'

'I blame all this on the missionaries,' said Ze Maria. 'Personally, I believe in the Old Testament philosophy of a tooth for a tooth and a nail for a nail: in fact, that is a very African philosophy, too. The missionaries taught us to turn the other cheek once we had been slapped. That is why, when we were looking at a man who had stolen another man's wife, we were looking at him as if he were an angel.'

82

They all left saying they would do everything to ensure that Kaluanda was duly punished.

Days went by. The tension in Luanda was mounting. There were countless stories of shoot-outs between armed men belonging to the three different political parties. It was then that Kaluanda was told that he was not very safe in Huambo, a UNITA stronghold. There would soon be confrontations between UNITA and MPLA soldiers. But this was not the only thing that kept Kaluanda worrying. He was still living with Aunt Laura and he believed that Adolfo was planning something evil. A voice in him kept saying that southerners were the very dregs of humanity and that Adolfo was up to no good. No southerner could be offended without taking the most cruel form of revenge.

Soon Kaluanda began to feel unwell. He developed terrible backache. At first he thought it was rheumatism but he soon began to suspect witchcraft. This was the thought whirling in his mind as he lay with Aunt Laura. She was fast asleep, snoring in a sweet, low, feminine way. He shook her.

'What?' she asked, yawning.

'Our relationship. I am afraid. I think your husband is up to something.'

'Please, doctor, never call that pig of a man my husband again. When are we leaving for Luanda? If we leave as we planned, then everything will be fine.'

'Fine? I think I will have to swallow my words. I must tell you this. My wife in Luanda is making a lot of fuss . . . I don't know. I might have to go on my own.'

Aunt Laura turned to Kaluanda, looked him straight in the eye and said: 'I knew it. I am not surprised.'

'Surprised at what?'

Aunt Laura sounded mournful: 'I knew that every word you said was false. I have always loved you, you know that very well. I have always been prepared to do anything for you. When things were not going well with your wife, you came to me. And I gave myself to you. After your wife left, you said you'd marry me as soon as we got to Luanda. You said I would have a house in Marginal and that you'd put me through school because you could not stand living with a woman who was not educated. I knew you were lying.' Laura began to sob.

Kaluanda patted her on the forehead, shushing her as he did so. He said: 'I received a letter from my relatives in Luanda last week. They say there is only one proper thing to do – go back to Ana. There is no way out.'

'When should I leave?' Aunt Laura asked.

'Now.'

'I will wait till the sun comes up.'

'You better do so.'

There was a lengthy silence, then Kaluanda said: 'I think I should tell you the truth. I am leaving because I fear for my life. You southerners can be vicious. I don't know what Adolfo is up to.'

'That is not it. You are leaving because your wife comes from Catete and she has ties with the most powerful families in the country.'

'If she sets out to destroy me, she will manage it very easily. I need to keep my peace with her. I am giving all my life to Angola. I want to contribute as much as I can to make this country great. I am a communist; I believe in the international proletariat. All these and other factors mean that my life as such does not count. What I have to do is whatever will further the interests of this country.'

'And what about the baby?' Aunt Laura asked.

Kaluanda frowned and said: 'He'll be the son or daughter of the People's Republic of Angola. There will be no illegitimate children in the nation that we are going to build.'

Kaluanda was silent for a while.

'Please talk,' Laura said.

Kaluanda continued: 'These are hard times. The question now is whether we choose our country or our selfish needs. I will be very honest with you. I have to stick to Ana because she has access to those who have power so that I can help further the interests of my country. That is the truth.'

★

The drizzle outside was interspersed with a few light thunderstorms. Nataniel Mbueti, his wife and Hosi were having dinner – rice, beans and pork. The shortwave radio was tuned to the BBC Portuguese service. There was a rap on the door. Nataniel Mbueti rose and walked over to open it.

'Who's that?' he shouted out.

'Me. Laura.'

He frowned and opened the door. Aunt Laura stepped in with a large suitcase. Her hair was ruffled and her dress crumpled. Aunt Laura said: 'I look horrible. I travelled on the back of a lorry. The driver was driving as if he was possessed by some speed-crazy demon. The journey to hell must be more comfortable.'

Nataniel Mbueti pretended not to listen and kept his eyes fixed on the radio, where the news was being read.

Valeriana Mbueti rushed off to the kitchen to get her sister some food. Aunt Laura turned to Hosi and said: 'It has come at last, Hosi.'

'What, Auntie?'

'The war.'

'What did I hear you say, Laura?' said Nataniel Mbueti.

'The war. In Huambo people are killing each other. There was a time when we thought it would all end in Luanda. We were mistaken. It is now here.'

Nataniel Mbueti ordered Hosi to go to bed. Hosi stalled for a while but a few fierce looks convinced him that his father meant business.

That night Hosi wondered what would happen next. There was talk of war everywhere. There were armed men everywhere. Children who until recently had been playing mothers and fathers were now playing soldiers. They would divide themselves into three movements – UNITA, the MPLA and the FNLA – and then throw stones at each other. Hosi himself was a bit old for the game, and though the other children had tried to persuade him to play, he hadn't done so.

Hosi was worried, but not very worried. He knew there was nothing he could do to prevent the war, so at some point he began to enjoy the feeling that was spreading among other

85

children. Everyone wanted to have a uniform and a wooden AK47. Still, now and then he did wonder whether there would be a time when there were humans and dogs rotting in the streets.

12

There were soldiers everywhere. Some belonged to the MPLA, others to the FNLA and others to UNITA. Young men who until recently had been waiting to go to Gabela as contract workers were now enrolling in the different armies. Most of the Portuguese had already left for Portugal. There were countless stories of people who had had dozens of servants in Angola finding themselves homeless in Lisbon and having to sleep in gardens.

There was, however, one Portuguese who had not left. He was called Venancio and he had come to Angola as a very poor man. Some said he had been a convict in Portugal, others that he had been insane. Venancio lived in a tiny house in the middle of an orchard. He was very old, had a wrinkled face and walked with a stoop. He spoke very little but was obsessed with his orchard. He lived by himself now. There had been a time when he lived with Damiao, his servant, but the two had fallen out – it was rumoured that Venancio suspected Damiao of intending to poison him and take over the orchard. Now and then Venancio could be seen walking around the orchard as he tried to make sure that no one stole his oranges and bananas.

Hosi and his friends often went into Venancio's yard to steal fruit. It was not that they couldn't afford to buy the fruit; bananas, for instance, were sold very cheaply in Dona Palmira's shop. What Hosi and his friends were after was the excitement, the feeling that they were committing an evil deed. At one time Venancio hired a guard with two fierce dogs. It was said that the dogs had once been able to tear a hare to pieces with great ease. Fortunately for Hosi and his friends, the dogs had become lazy because they were overfed, so they had never been able to catch the boys.

One day a group of armed men went into Venancio's orchard and treated themselves to some fruit. The guard was terrified of them and fled into the house to tell Venancio, who came out panting furiously. Venancio charged at the armed men, pointed his index finger straight at them and said: 'Who the hell do you think you are? You just come here and eat as though this is your mother's orchard, eh?'

One of the men, a tall fellow with a thin voice, stepped forward and said: 'Your orchard belongs to the Angolan people. Leave or you will be given a proper beating.'

Undaunted, Venancio said: 'Beating? You are bluffing. If you have the balls, throw that machine gun away and I will teach you that I was not born yesterday. Come on, throw that gun away.'

The men laughed, concluding that Venancio was not normal. Venancio paced about, fuming, and then said: 'I sweated blood for this orchard. Ask the people around here. They will tell you. It is mine, completely mine.'

The tall, armed man walked forward and said: 'Shut up. You are talking too much, old man.'

Venancio screwed up his face and hit him on the head with his walking stick. The armed men began to jostle Venancio. By now people had rushed to the orchard to witness the spectacle. Some, especially the elderly, were saddened to see Venancio being tossed about. They respected him and admired him for having worked hard to cultivate such a plantation. The young were more enthusiastic: a white man was being beaten and this confirmed the fact that their time had come to an end.

Just as the argument between Venancio and the armed men was getting heated, Kaluanda arrived on the scene. He was soon hemmed in by the armed men, who took turns at explaining what had happened. Kaluanda slapped his forehead and said: 'I will not accept anything of this kind. Independence means that we, the people of Angola, must control everything. We'll take no more capitalist trash.' He turned to the people who were gathered and said: 'I am a high-ranking member of the MPLA. From now on this orchard will be divided among you people. Now, follow me and I will give you each a portion of the orchard.' Hosi trotted behind Kaluanda, admiring his authority. He felt that Kaluanda was a man who feared nothing.

That night Kaluanda was the main topic at the dinner table. Nataniel Mbueti said repeatedly that the northerner was a brute and a shame to the black race. Hosi was to remember this dinner for ever. It was beans, rice and boiled cabbage. It had tasted so good that at some point his father had had to warn him not to eat too much or he would get an upset stomach during the night.

Hosi was woken in the middle of the night by what sounded like fireworks. It was drizzling outside and he thought he might have heard a thunderstorm. He tried to go back to sleep but couldn't, and it occurred to him then that the noise might have been an explosion. Suddenly, as he was about to fall asleep he had the feeling that something had gone terribly wrong. He sat on the bed and reached out for a matchbox to light the kerosene lamp, but he could not find it. Groping, he sidled towards his parents' bedroom. He knocked hard on the door but there was no reply.

'Papa, it's me,' Hosi cried out. Still there was no reply. He peered through the keyhole and noted that there was light in the room. He knocked on the door harder. Now he did not mind if this was going to earn him a beating, he just needed to get to his parents. He stood still, feeling very confused and frightened. The floor felt very cold. He felt his stomach moving. He tried to take courage, but still there was this tragic feeling about. He returned to his room and tried once more to sleep. He could not and now he even thought that he could hear cries – yes, some loud wailings. Maybe it was just his imagination. No, it was real – two loud groans like those of people on fire. He sat on the bed and realized that there were tears on his cheeks. Maybe this was just his mind playing tricks on him and in the morning it would all be fine; then he would be too shy to tell anyone what he had been thinking.

There was another explosion, followed by silence. This time

Hosi made up his mind. He was definitely going to see whether his parents were well or not. He stood up and walked to the sitting room. It was like passing through a jungle full of lions. At last he came to his parents' door. He remained silent for a while, listening for any sounds coming from inside. He opened the door and peeped inside. He closed it at once, unable to believe what he had seen. The window was shattered. His father lay beside his mother, splattered in blood. Hosi knelt down. His bones creaked as he did so, making it clear to him that he was not dreaming. He knocked at the door again, this time a little more violently. 'Papa,' he cried out, 'it is cold here. Please open for me. I am dying. Please, Papa. Mama, can you hear me? I am sure you can hear me. Please come and open.'

There was still no reply. He opened the door again. His parents' bodies were still there. He closed the door quickly, he cleared his throat, took courage and said: 'This is Hosi. I have to talk to you, Papa and Mama. Please open this door. Open the door.' He knelt down again. It was obvious that his parents were dead, but he simply could not accept the fact and kept pushing it to the back of his mind. He felt helpless. As he knelt in front of the door he realized that he was supposed to be crying, but he was too frightened to cry.

It was now almost morning. The rays of the sun were coming through the windows. Somewhere deep in him Hosi was still hoping that what he had seen was not real and that as soon as it was clear enough he would go back into the room and find his parents alive. Then he would laugh at himself for the rest of his life.

Soon there was a very loud explosion, which was followed by machine-gun fire. It went on so long that it sounded like rain. There were single shots too. The exchange of fire was finally interrupted by an explosion that made Hosi feel he had died. The roof of the house shook. Dogs that had been barking outside stopped at once. Even the drizzle seemed to have come to an abrupt end and there was an eerie silence. Hosi's teeth chattered. He felt something slide down his face slowly. It passed by the side of his nose and stopped near his mouth. It was a tear. He felt slightly better; at least he was crying.

Hosi knew from that moment that his life would be hard. He had heard his mother tell him time and again that he would one day come to miss her, but he had not believed her then; he had felt that she was just talking too much again. But he knew now that nobody would love him as much as his parents had. Still, there was nothing he could do about it. He wished he could change everything and make this another nightmare, but he couldn't. It was done; his parents were dead.

The exchange of fire began again. By now it was morning and a clear day. Hosi opened the bedroom door again. His parents were still lying there. He took a few steps in to have a closer look. His mother looked as if she was smiling; his father seemed more serious. He shook them both. There was no response. He bent down and put his head on his father's chest. There was no sound of a beating heart. He did the same with his mother; her heart, too, was silent.

Hosi left the house with the intention of finding Aunt Laura, who had now moved to Old Pedro's. Outside, armed men were shooting. Later, Hosi wondered who had been exchanging fire with whom, but that was the problem: when men had guns they just had to use them.

As Hosi walked towards Old Pedro's house, he was not afraid of the bullets. By now he felt very bad, and he also felt very confused. Emotions were swirling around in him. He was upset not only by the actual loss of his parents but also by the fact that from now on he would be haunted by the way they had died.

Just as he was about to cross the road a van stopped in front of him. The driver, a corpulent man with a husky voice, told him to get in. Hosi hesitated. The driver said: 'Don't be a fool. Get in the back or you'll die.' Hosi climbed into the back of the van, where he found several other people looking, as he recalled later, exactly like zombies. The van sped towards Huambo. After two hours, they got to the main market in Baixa, the city centre.

Hosi was sad but not worried. He knew that because he was an orphan people would take pity on him and tend to his needs.

Huambo was strange to him. He had made several trips there before and he was confident that he would find his way about. But in all these trips he had been accompanied by his mother or father and they had never allowed him to stray far. During the different trips they had made, he had been taken to various family friends and relatives. He could have gone to them now, but he wanted to be alone.

Many people from all over southern Angola were converging on Huambo as refugees. There were many other young boys in the main market, some of them gambling with cards. Hosi walked towards one who was sitting by himself. He was short, and dressed in a white T-shirt, blue shorts and brown canvas shoes, and was whistling a popular song. Hosi said nervously: 'I am Hosi Mbueti. What is your name?'

'Raul.'

'Where are you from?'

'Ndondo.'

'Where is that?'

'In the north.'

'Where?'

'Don't ask me too many questions. I don't want to know where you're from.'

Hosi had the feeling that although Raul was acting fierce, he was really friendly. Hosi smiled. Raul looked at him sharply. Pointing his finger at Hosi, he said: 'Don't play with me. I can beat you to death.'

'Sorry, then,' Hosi answered, taken aback.

Raul said: 'Say what you want.'

'No, I don't want to offend you,' Hosi replied.

Raul screwed up his face and said: 'Talk or I will beat you.'

Hosi bent over and whispered into Raul's ear: 'My parents are dead.'

Raul stared at him and said: 'Is that all you were going to say?'

'Yes,' Hosi replied.

'Stupid. OK, your mama and papa are dead, so what? Give me twenty *escudos* or I will beat you for telling me a boring thing.'

Frightened, Hosi dipped into his pocket. All he could find was a five-*escudo* coin. He handed it over to Raul, who stared at him fiercely and said: 'Fool. I said twenty *escudos* and you give me five. I said twenty.'

'But I don't have twenty.'

'Come over here!'

Hosi stepped forward. Raul searched his pockets and found nothing. He held Hosi by the ears and began to pull them hard. Hosi began to cry. 'Leave me alone,' he pleaded.

'Fool. You will know who I am. I am horrible. When I say twenty, it must be twenty!'

The other boys were now interested in what was going on. They came forward and began to cheer Raul on. 'Teach him a lesson. Give him a good one, kung-fu style!' one of the boys cried out.

'No. This chap is a pawpaw. You will smash him to pieces. Just give him a few whacks on the head.'

Raul whacked Hosi on the head. Hosi grunted and slapped Raul hard. The other boys were clapping by now. Hosi began to fume, ready to fight. Raul was smiling slyly. One of the boys extended his arm between the two and said: 'Let's see it now. He who does not fuck his mother and wants to fight should hit my hand now.' Raul hit the hand furiously. Hosi hesitated. He did not want to fight. Holding both hands high, he said: 'I don't want to fight, please.'

The boy who had extended his hand said: 'Come on, man. You surely do fuck your mama. Hit my hand and fight to show that you're no coward.'

Hosi hit his hand. The boys cheered wildly. Raul was pacing about, like a boxer about to pounce on his opponent. Hosi said: 'I have hit your hand and I still don't want to fight.'

The other boys booed him. Raul trotted a bit and gave him one powerful punch on the cheek. Hosi staggered to the floor. The others clapped. 'Come on,' one of the boys said, 'flex your muscles.'

Hosi began to cry. Raul came and punched him again. Hosi found that the second punch was not as painful as the first. Then Raul flung himself at Hosi and the two fell. Raul was on top and held Hosi by the throat. Hosi struggled hard and managed to stand up. Raul slapped him hard again. Hosi's eyes were now clouded with tears. He flung himself at Raul and fell on top of him. Enraged, he began biting at Raul's penis. Raul screamed. The other boys came forward and began hitting him on the head saying: 'Coward! Never touch that place when fighting.'

Hosi somehow managed to stand up and fled as fast as his legs would take him. The other boys tried to follow but failed to catch him. Hosi ran towards the railway station, where most of the refugees were gathered. There Hosi found other boys on their own, but he did not want to talk to them, feeling that they would be as unfriendly as the boys he had just met. He went to sit under a huge tree and began to cry. Pain is an obstinate tutor. Unlike joy, it often refuses to water down its lessons. Hosi wanted to face the facts. He was now alone and would have to face the world on his own. He would have to learn to fight and to make sure that other people feared him. He promised himself that he was crying for the last time in his life. Just then he heard footsteps behind him. He turned round and was surprised to see Raul, who said: 'You almost killed me.'

'Please leave me alone,' Hosi muttered.

Raul paced about and said: 'I don't want to fight you any more. We are now going to be friends. You are lucky, you know, that your parents are dead. I am not that lucky. I don't know whether my parents are dead or not. I don't know whether my mother and young sister are alive. I was chased from home.'

'Why were you chased?' Hosi asked.

'I used to pinch coins that were left about in the house. Mama said I would die in prison. Rubbish. I used to steal small money. Mama tried to do everything to make me stop stealing money. She put my feet in hot water and she made me go without food for days. But I still kept on stealing. Well, not stealing – I kept taking the money away. You don't steal your mother's money, you take it away.'

Hosi and Raul both smiled. Then Raul sat by Hosi's side

and told him several stories. Hosi told his story too. Just then, a lean, attractive woman approached the boys and said: 'Hey, boys, would you like to make some money? I have some boxes over here. If you help me carry them to my home, I will pay you something.'

The two boys stood up at once and the woman gave them the boxes to carry. Hosi found that his box was not that heavy. At last they got to the woman's house. It was big and had previously belonged to a Portuguese family. Many people had moved from the quarters that had been reserved for Angolans to the houses the Portuguese had left. The woman told Hosi and Raul to go in. Hosi noted that the frames on the wall still had photographs of bearded white men – relatives of previous occupants.

The woman brought the boys orange juice and said: 'Stay a bit longer and I will cook some food for you.' She went into the kitchen and some time later emerged once the food had begun to cook. She said: 'My name is Ester. My husband is Julio. He'll be coming soon. We've just married. Where are you from? Yes, you, the short one.'

Raul told his story first, then Hosi told his. As Hosi was talking, Ester shook her head. Then Julio, her husband, a tall, thin man, entered the room. He looked at the boys and said to Ester: 'Shit. Is this a centre of the International Red Cross or what?'

Ester frowned, and signalled Julio to follow her into the kitchen. Hosi and Raul could hear their argument. Julio said: 'Ester, you have to understand that this is a war. First, you took the little sugar we had to that baby. Then you brought that stinking old man and gave him one of my best shirts. And now you have these boys. Why don't you tell them to leave?'

'Calm down. Just because we are in a war does not mean that we have to lose our hearts. People are suffering, they need someone who can help them.'

Julio slapped his chest and said: 'But why should it be you or me? Nobody will thank you. Angola is in a mess. Why should an innocent person like myself bear the burden?'

The argument went on. Ester brought some food – boiled

pumpkin and maize cobs – which Hosi and Raul gobbled down at once. As they were about to leave they heard Ester say to Julio: 'Remember that you'll be a father some day soon. Imagine that your son is in difficulty. How would you expect other people to treat him?'

'The fact is, I don't have a son or daughter. It would be very nice if every being on earth believed in the do-unto-others-as-they-do-unto-you philosophy. But people are realistic – each of them is pulling the fire to his pot, as the saying goes.'

Raul stood up and walked out. Hosi went to the kitchen and said to Ester: 'Thank you very much for the meal. I am leaving now.'

It was then that his eyes met Julio's. Julio smiled and said: 'You can stay with us. Ester has told me your story. Where is the other boy?'

'He's gone,' Hosi replied.

More people kept coming to Huambo. They all told stories of confrontations in different parts of southern Angola, from where they had fled. The situation in Huambo was becoming tense too. Armed men exchanged fire all night. Then the MPLA and the FNLA were flushed out and the city became a UNITA enclave. Some spoke of Cubans in hushed tones. The UNITA officials declared that rumour-mongering was counter-productive and that those who went around talking about Cubans would be locked up.

Many years on Hosi was to realize how much tension and fear had been mounting in Huambo. There was a prison at Acmol and people were being sent to it daily. Hosi was to reflect later on whether a UNITA victory would have meant complete freedom. From what he remembered of Huambo at the time, he felt this would have been unlikely. Like the MPLA and the FNLA, UNITA had by now created an effective secret police that kept tabs on political aberrants.

Julio and Ester kept saying that things would soon clear up and that Hosi could go back to Aunt Laura, but the situation in fact deteriorated. People became very nervous. The Cubans were said to be near Alto Alma, a town that was 100 kilometres from Huambo. Hosi wondered what the Cubans would be like. Some said they were like mulattos with very long hair; others said they were black men with the noses of whites. There was also talk of Stalin's organ, a rocket launcher which was named *monakashitu*. It was very frightening.

One day Raul came to Hosi and asked him to go and see the tanks and armoured cars. Hosi agreed and followed Raul timidly. They went to a clearing near the central hospital and the police station where they found many other people gathered to look at the armoured cars. Tall white men were getting in and out of the cars. Their faces were red and they spoke a language Hosi could not understand. They were South African soldiers. These were said to be the soldiers that would save Angola from the Cubans.

One fact was clear, though: the Cubans were closing in on Huambo. Hosi did not completely share the fear this aroused. He felt he had lost everything already, so what else could he lose.

Then one day Cuban tanks were heard in Acmol. UNITA, it was said, was now finished; the Cubans had finally won the war for the MPLA. Most southerners felt that there was nothing left for them: the MPLA was the party of the northerners and they would come to oppress the southerners.

The whole of Huambo seemed to be on the move. Hosi left with Julio and Ester for Zambia, where they thought they would stay for a few weeks, until UNITA defeated the MPLA. In fact they were destined to stay there for years.

BOOK II

13

Jamba, the headquarters of the Freeland of Angola Movement, was referred to by many names. Some called it the Bastion of the Resistance; others the Last Hope of the Black Race. At the time when the UNITA soldiers were wandering around southern Angola, trying to survive, it had been nothing but a village by the side of a swamp. Angola was now a divided country. The north was under the control of the MPLA; the south belonged to UNITA.

On a hot September morning in 1984 Hosi Mbueti and three other young men who had gone to Zambia ten years earlier arrived in Jamba. They had been driven from Likua in a Ural truck that had been captured in battle by the UNITA soldiers. No one in Jamba paid any particular attention to them and no one could have imagined how pleased they all were to be back in the motherland.

While in Zambia Hosi had imagined that the day he returned to Angola would be the greatest in his life. People would come out cheering and would rush to pat him on the back. Hosi had once tried writing poetry. Now, as they waited for the officer in charge of accommodation to come and attend to them, he recalled a poem in which he had said that his feet would crumble upon his return to Angola. They had been in Angola for a week now and nothing like this had happened. People seemed to be too involved with themselves, or with the war – he could not tell exactly which. Later Hosi learned that convention demanded that people did not talk to those who had just arrived, because they could be prisoners, spies or just people whose 'political health' was not sound.

Everyone was proud of Jamba. It was a symbol of the fact that victory was at hand. It reminded people that their suffering had not been in vain and that those who had died had not done so for nothing. Most of the houses in Jamba were made of reeds and had grass roofs. The reeds were cut by gangs of elderly MPLA prisoners who worked on the banks of the Luenge river. Younger MPLA prisoners were quickly drafted into the UNITA army.

Hosi and other 'returnees', as they were called, were lodged in a huge reed edifice called a *pousada* or guesthouse. It was near the telephone exchange and the pavilion where dances and other public functions were held. The telephone system had been captured from one of the towns that had come under UNITA control. Next to the exchange was a clearing that led to an area of trees with very broad branches. This was called the *presidencia* and was where the president lived. It was surrounded by special commandos, who were as fierce as men could be. It was rumoured that they had a special diet which made them ruthless. Two guards stood to attention at the entrance that led to the president's residence. Next to them was a tall pole on which the UNITA flag flew during the day. People were expected to salute it or stand to attention whenever they came close to it. Those who forgot to do so were dealt with severely.

As Hosi settled down to lunch with the others, he concluded that life was not going to be easy. When he had read about the UNITA-liberated territory in newspapers, he had imagined a land akin to paradise, a land where people wandered about freely, thought freely and said what they wanted without fear of being upbraided by some party hack. He began to wonder whether he would regret returning to Angola – that is, to the UNITA-controlled area. True, Zambia was not the freest place on earth – people were stopped at road blocks and roughed up by policemen; refugees were referred to as sycophants, and were treated with great suspicion and were often imprisoned – but it was certainly better than this part of Angola.

After the meal Hosi decided to take a siesta. As he lay on the metal bed he noticed that the floor of the guesthouse was made of dried clay which was emitting a pleasant smell. Like the rest of south-eastern Angola, Jamba was built on sand.

In charge of the guesthouse and the guests was a portly man with dozy eyes called Sergeant Herculano. He stormed into the room in which Hosi was lying and said: 'Good. You are here. I was wondering where you had gone to.'

'I am entitled to go whichever place I want to, not so? It's my country.'

'Yes,' the Sergeant replied, smiling sheepishly and backing out of the room.

Hosi dozed off again and was awoken by a hard tap on his back. He turned over and saw a tall man in uniform. He rubbed his eyes and took a closer look at the man. He could tell from the stripes on the man's shoulder – three bars and a black cock – that he was a captain. The captain said: 'Wake up, man. Beds were made to rest on, not to sleep in. There is a difference between the two.'

Hosi cleared his throat and said: 'I was having a little siesta.'

The captain chuckled and said: 'Siesta? You've really come from abroad. We did away with siesta long ago. Are you Hosi Mbueti?'

'Indeed I am,' Hosi replied.

'I am your uncle,' said the captain.

Hosi smiled and said: 'How?'

'We'll talk later. Anyway, I will come for you around six. I am having a birthday party and I will be glad to have you around. By the way, I have heard that you are an artist.'

'I wouldn't describe myself as such,' Hosi said. 'I have had a couple of stories and articles published in the school magazine, but nothing serious.'

The captain snapped his fingers and said: 'A true artist, indeed. Never exalting his work. Anyway, at six o'clock sharp I'll be here.'

Hosi nodded. He felt very happy. Coming back home was not, after all, that bad, especially if uncles kept popping up from nowhere and inviting you to their birthday parties. What would the birthday party be like? Would there be any girls and would any of them be attracted to him? He wondered whether people were going to think of him as a foreigner or as a son of the land who had merely been away for a while.

At six o'clock the captain arrived, and Hosi followed him into the Land-Rover that was waiting outside. Hosi sat between the driver and the captain. He decided to have a closer look at the man who claimed to be his uncle. Wondering whether he was related to him through his mother or father, Hosi decided to be bold and said: 'Tell me more. I have no clues as to how we are related.'

The captain pulled out a cigarette, lit it and said to the driver: 'Chiquinho, stop driving as though we are corpses. Accelerate, man! Get the fucking thing moving!' The driver increased the speed at once. The captain turned to Hosi and said: 'Now, what did you say?'

'Our relationship. How are we related?'

The captain puffed on his cigarette and said: 'Relationships and relatives: all that crap counts no more in the Angola that we are constructing. We are all brothers and sisters, that is the truth. I am your uncle. It does not matter how I came to be your uncle. Just remember that the blood in your veins is the same as the blood in my veins, or indeed the blood in every other Angolan's veins.'

At last the car came to a halt. The captain jumped out and Hosi followed. The captain lived in a huge tent. The floor was covered with large canvases on which someone had been painting. The captain turned to Hosi and said: 'I am the head of the Visual Propaganda Department of the Secretariat of Information. That is what they call me, but in actual fact I am an artist. When you were abroad, did you see paintings of the Elder and other progressive black leaders such as Nkrumah and Senghor?'

'Yes,' Hosi replied.

The captain frowned and said: 'I painted them. But it doesn't matter. I did it for Angola and my people.' The captain slapped his chest and corrected himself: 'I mean, I did it for the people. Who am I to call them my people?'

The captain asked Hosi to follow him into a small grass enclosure that had been erected at the end of the tent. There was a small bed at one end which was the captain's bedroom. There were several paintings hanging on the wall. Hosi found some of them too cryptic. He wondered whether the captain was dabbling in surrealism (Hosi had come across this word in a book in the British Council library). Hosi turned to the captain and said: 'Are you an abstract painter?'

The captain sat on the bed, shook his head and said: 'That is crap for European artists. They don't have better things to do. Here we are fighting a war. While brave Angolans are grappling with their Kalashnikovs, here we are holding on to our brushes and paint.' The captain stood and asked Hosi to follow him into another enclosure that was connected to his bedroom. He turned the switch on and the large enclosure was lit. Fastened to the wall were large and small posters of the Elder. Some just showed his face, some his whole body. What fascinated Hosi was that the figure in all the posters was in uniform. He was impressed and smiled. The captain smiled too and said: 'You see what we've been doing? This is a real revolution.'

'What are these paintings for?'

The captain slapped his forehead, grunted and said: 'Sorry to ask this question, but how far did you go at school?'

'I have seven O levels,' Hosi replied. 'My certificate is a joint one – that is, one given by the Zambia Examinations Council and Cambridge University.'

Looking at Hosi with some admiration, the captain said: 'Another intellectual. Intellectuals are really useless in a revolution like ours.'

'I think intellectuals are crucial in the development of any country.'

Shaking his head the captain said: 'That is not true. I have a theory. Never tell it to anyone. You see, I am an intellectual, but of a different kind. Anyway, we'll get into that later. Remember, this is just between the two of us. Never tell it to anyone, especially a peasant – that is another problem we have. There are two dangerous species in Angola, intellectuals and peasants. I will come to them later. Here is my theory. An intellectual in a revolution is like a child: he has to be nurtured. Give him too much importance and he'll be spoilt; ignore him and he'll be spoilt too. If you give intellectuals too much

105

importance in a revolution, they will want to debate every-thing, and no creature on earth enjoys debating for debating's sake more than a man or woman who thinks their head is full of valuable ideas. That is why I say that it is important to nurture intellectuals. To discipline them and make them have proper manners. Now, as far as I can tell, you are still raw. I can understand that. You've missed a great gap in Angolan history. While you were abroad, we were building a nation. But it would have been impossible had it not been for the Elder's wisdom. That is why each and every portrait of him should hang in every corner of Angola where there are humans. My dream is to ensure that each tree in Angola can have his portrait. Do you understand that?'

Hosi nodded and said: 'I do. I am not against having posters of the Elder, not at all. My only fear is that if his posters are all over, people will become bored by his face. It would be like having honey for dinner every night.'

The captain groaned and said: 'You don't understand. The fact is that we are fighting and need inspiration. This can only be brought about if you look at the Elder's portrait. I will tell you an indisputable fact: no other living person has the ability to inspire Angolans like the Elder. That is the truth, my brother.'

'I thought you were my uncle,' Hosi said.

'In a revolution we are all brothers. Nepotism is eating the soul of Africa away,' the captain replied. 'What Angola needs are smart idiots. I know you must be wondering what they are. I will tell you. But before that I should finish the point I made earlier, that the problem with Angola is the intellectuals and peasants. These two have one thing in common – lack of discipline. Peasants are undisciplined because they are not used to abstract ideas and intellectuals are undisciplined be-cause they are obsessed with abstract ideas. What Africa needs, or rather what we need, are concrete ideas. If the party says Cubans are to be killed because they are the enemies of the people, that is it, everyone is supposed to pick up a rifle and fight. Peasants will fight for a while but at some point will start asking what they are fighting for. You tell them that they are fighting for the freedom and dignity of the black man. A peasant will simply shake his head and wonder what you are talking about. An intellectual, like a peasant, will also fight but will stop at some point and say: "What really do you mean by the black man's dignity?" And then you will waste precious time debating that question. That is not all. The intellectual will stop fighting at some other point and say again: "What guarantee have we got that the blood being split will ensure the creation of a society in which there will be a free flow of ideas?" Meanwhile the enemy is making advances. That is where the smart idiot comes in to save the situation.'

Hosi slapped his thigh hard to attract the captain's attention. The captain was by now heated up and spoke as if to an imaginary audience. Hosi said: 'But what exactly do you mean by a smart idiot? It's a contradiction.'

The captain smiled and said: 'There you are. That is another habit of intellectuals – they see contradictions where there are none. A smart idiot is what Angola, or maybe I should say Africa, needs. These are men and women who wear masks of idiots and yet deep in them they are very smart. A smart idiot is never tired of working hard and is dedicated to the cause. If, for instance, a smart idiot is accused of committing an offence he has not committed, he will not be taken by a fit of rage. A peasant will go to witchcraft straightaway for revenge and an intellectual will moan and whinge or write poems on the backside of his underpants. I am not joking. A few days ago a very good friend of mine showed me two sonnets written on the backside of his underpants. He had been accused of having said that Agostinho Neto was, warts and all, the best poet the world had ever seen. He was told that the time was not yet right for literary discussions. He swore upon the party's flag that he had never uttered such words. So he took to writing a line or two about the injustice of existence whenever he went to the latrine.'

Hosi burst out laughing and said: 'But why the toilet?'

The captain sighed and said: 'He told me that – and I was not meant to tell anyone this – that the revolution had thwarted creativity to such a point that the only time people were

107

inspired was when they were relieving themselves. Back to the smart idiot. When he is accused of committing an offence he did not commit, he will take his punishment willingly – even if it is death. This is so because he believes that he'll serve as an example to the others and thus prevent them from committing similar offences. If the punishment is not death, he'll still take it willingly, believing that sooner or later the truth will come out. It can even take ten or twenty years – he won't mind.'

The captain paused for a while and then said: 'Why do I call him a smart idiot? I call him an idiot because, as far as intellectuals like myself are concerned, he may seem like one, or rather, he *is* one, but in actual fact he is not stupid. He has understood the revolution. He knows that in order to get things done a dosage of stupidity is important. That is why he is smart. He knows that if the whole nation was to adopt the habits of intellectuals, then it would be ripe for enslavement. The smart idiot is very important. Because he is the individual who gets the peasant working and ensures that he does not stray from the right path.'

Hosi, who was getting a bit bored, said: 'But tell me more about yourself, captain. I admire artists, poets and the like.'

'I am not very popular around here. I have been to jail several times, but that has to do with my mouth. It often succumbs to the artist in me.'

There were noises in the other room. Hosi concluded that people were coming to the birthday party. He was anxious to see the girls, but the captain kept talking. 'You see,' he began, 'I am the only guy around here who has admitted in public to having smoked marijuana in his life. They all laugh at me and think that my ideas are produced by marijuana. But they do worse things than that. If God was to come down – I don't believe in his existence, that is another question – but let's pretend that he exists and that he came down one day to say in public what each of us does in private. They say I am not normal because I once smoked marijuana but I will tell you something that's really not normal. Most of these people will only have sexual intercourse to make children; otherwise they prefer to remain celibate. This is a fact. It will come out on the BBC Portuguese service someday.'

108

'Why is that so?' Hosi asked, dumbfounded.

The captain shook his head and said: 'They believe that those that have anal intercourse are bullet-proof and less likely to die. Madness. I am sure that this was started by a pseudo-intellectual.'

The captain called out to his bodyguard, who answered promptly. The bodyguard was ordered to bring a large Sony cassette player. The captain began to play a Bob Marley cassette, *So Much Trouble in the World*. He pulled out several paintings from under his bed. He came to one and said: 'This is my inspiration. If someone sees this, I will be dead.' The painting showed Jimi Hendrix and Bob Marley smoking marijuana.

Hosi smiled and said: 'I don't see anything harmful in this. I think people should be more receptive to ideas.'

The captain showed him his other paintings. Most of them were of a woman. The captain laughed and said: 'I am crazy about this woman. And yet I can't marry her.'

'Why?' Hosi asked.

'I will tell you. Her name is Debora. I knew this woman while we were still at school in Huambo. She was a beauty; the Angolan answer to Marilyn Monroe. She had the kind of smile that makes toothache and diarrhoea stop at once. I was not able to shower her with gifts such as Roberto Carlos's records or perfume; I could not afford them then. Though she was only sixteen, she knew the art of keeping men on the leash. She gave me the impression that if I tried a little harder, I could win her. So I kept giving her my paintings. I remember telling her one night after a dance – yeah, we had just finished dancing to Teta Landu's "Tata Nkendo". That was a song, my friend, that could make the earth tremble; not the trash that passes for music nowadays. Anyway, that is beside the point. I said, "Debora, say that you love me and I won't mind dying at this very moment because I will have been given what my heart has long been craving for – your heart." Debora said: "Stop being comical and take me home. Oh," she said, "I have a little pain right here." And I saw her fingers press her breasts. I closed my eyes and imagined myself pressing them while she lay on a quilt made of purple feathers.

'Then came the civil war. I fled, along with other young people, to the bush. I know that you must be thinking of yourself as immensely clever because you've just come from school. But we are not as thick as you think we are. Anyway, back to Debora. As we went through the hard bits – Cubans, offensives, tanks and all that was after our fragile lives – I kept praying that I would survive and come to see my sweet Debora again. Praying is not the word: I kept hoping. Hoping, for a revolutionary, is more powerful than praying is for the Christian. That is a fact.

'I survived and as soon as people came from the towns I rushed to ask about Debora. They all said she was alive and in full blossom. I had a secret plan of capturing her to bring her here to the bush. It was a very well-planned operation. I would have gone secretly to Huambo, disguised as a mad prophet of some cranky cult, and then brought her into the bush.

'Sometimes I feel as though I am not very sane. Back to Debora. Then I heard that she was having an affair with some MPLA bigwig. It was very painful. There was only one way I could erase my anger – go out with an illiterate peasant. I went for a Chokue girl. I tell you, those girls are trained to please men. They don't believe in foreplay or any of the nonsense our girls are now learning from those silly magazines coming in from Brazil. From the word go, it is double quick for them. People said: "How can you, an artist, sleep with an illiterate girl?" They asked me in private, of course. Officially, there is no distinction among Angolan women: they are all beautiful and desirable. In reality, however, it is different.

'At some point I could stand the illiterate girl no more. I wanted a woman who could fire the intellectual in me, a woman with whom I could discuss the purpose of existence after making love. Do you know what she did?'

Hosi shook his head. The captain sighed and said: 'She started having an affair with my own bodyguard, who, like herself, was illiterate. Well, like poles attract each other, that is what they say. It was very humiliating and I think this was the reason women avoided me after I told the Chokue girl to go. I

110

became a marked man. They thought there was something seriously wrong with me. They asked themselves what had made a peasant leave me and came to one conclusion: that I was impotent. But I wasn't.

'Then I heard that Debora and several other women had been captured. They had been travelling in a military convoy that had been attacked. I leapt with joy. Life was going to be different. Debora would soon bring sunshine to my clouded life, I said to myself. After several months, Debora came. She had grown a bit older, but there was still a trace of beauty about her. I should say, however, that I no longer found it maddening. It was said that Debora had had an affair with a chap from DISA, the secret police, a mulatto called Junior. I know him, I also knew his father. He was a Portuguese administrator called Kadinguilinha.'

'Junior, son of Kadinguilinha?' Hosi asked. 'I know him. He took my brother Osvaldo to Cuba.'

The captain waved his hands and said: 'Let me finish, please! You have a very bad habit. It is typical of Angolan intellectuals. They are poor listeners. Yes, Junior. He was not the only impediment to my union with Debora. She was said to have been a DISA officer herself. Somewhere in her body, it was said, were wires transmitting to Moscow each and every word that was said near her.

'When she arrived in Jamba she and her colleagues who had also been captured lived at a place called Coordenation. Few people were allowed to talk to her: she was still being interrogated. She then became free and I went to see her. Soon after seeing me she said she had been waiting for my arrival all along and that she loved me. I have another theory. This too is not supposed to be told to anyone. My theory is that there can only be romance if there is affluence, or, to be more concrete, there can only be a proper, poetic romance if there is enough bread, sugar, mealie meal, bathing soap and other essentials. I suspected that Debora was not in love with me but that she wanted corned beef, South African cheese and to wear chiffon dresses, like most officers' wives. I suspected that she was not in love with my heart but with my rank. She wanted to survive

111

on the little clout that I had. I said to myself: "No man, you have dignity. Do not fall for this famished woman." I went back home that night and thought of the little girls whose breasts had just come out and were soon going to deflowered by an Angolan with honour like myself.

'Two days later, I received a letter from Debora. Halfway through the letter, my eyes filled with tears of love. Now, I am no sissy, that is a fact. I have seen men die like flies and yet my heart has remained as hard as a diamond. I told myself it was life and one had to accept it as such. But this letter struck parts of me that had not been struck before. In the letter Debora said she had tremendous admiration for me. She said when I had accosted her in the colonial times I was very handsome. Now all that had vanished; I looked old and haggard. The revolution had taken away the moistness of my skin and the whiteness of my teeth. She even noticed that I walked with a little stoop. Now, here comes the crunch of her letter. She said she still adored me because she was perhaps the only person in the world who knew the good looks that lay beneath my war-beaten face. What reasoning? I concluded that she was a genius.

'One night I invited Debora for dinner. My cook, or rather my bodyguard, prepared one of his best dishes – rice, corned beef and vegetables. We ate and talked at length. After the meal, I invited her into my bedroom. We sat on the bed and . . . well, I kissed her. God, her tongue started to vacuum my mouth. She managed to provoke my manhood. Soon we were doing it. Just as we were about to reach fever pitch I heard her say: "Hernandez, Hernandez, *suavemente por favor*", Hernandez, Hernandez, gently please! I said to her: "What the hell are you saying in Spanish?" She said: "Oh, sorry. Hernandez was my last boyfriend. He was a Cuban." Brother, I turned over, leaving her open-mouthed. Since I had already attained the critical stage, I did what no Angolan man should ever do beside a woman. I hate to think what would have happened to me at that moment had both of my hands been blown off in a landmine or an accident. They helped me retain my dignity. I was not going to let my revolutionary Angolan seeds reside

112

beside those of a Cuban. I had to maintain my dignity; that was it.'

Just then a voice was heard from behind the door calling for the captain. It was Debora. Hosi suspected that she had indeed been very beautiful in her youth and he concluded that any man would have been as infatuated with her as the captain had been. The captain introduced them. She extended her hand and greeted Hosi with a coquettish smile – the kind that drives Angolan men to write poetry.

The captain asked Hosi and Debora to follow him into the room where the others had gathered. A table was laid out. Chunks of cheese and brownish, hard biscuits were placed beside the plates. Hosi noticed the girls in particular. They all looked shy and kept giggling among themselves. A cake was brought in.

The captain asked everyone to pay attention and said: 'Comrades, I have to introduce to you a very important person, Hosi Mbueti. After years abroad, he has finally decided to return to his fatherland, or motherland, as you may wish. Today, as you all know, is my birthday.'

'How old are you?' a short, stout girl murmured from behind him.

The captain chuckled and said: 'I am very proud to be thirty. As I ask you to join me in celebrating the great day . . . it is not a great day. As far as birthdays are concerned, we Angolan patriots know which is the greatest in Angolan history. Well, as I ask you to join me on this day, I want you all to think of Angola and ask yourselves what you can give to it.'

The captain's speech was greeted with applause. Debora was seated between Hosi and the captain. 'So you are from Zambia?' she said.

'Yes,' Hosi replied.

'Speak English, eh?'

'Yes.'

'Speak well?'

'I do not only speak well, I also write in it. I write short stories, poems and the like. I'd actually like to be a writer, a journalist or a poet.'

Debora thought for a while and then said: 'There are too many poets in Angola. That is why we have problems. We just need one leading poet, or one leading thinker, and the rest of us should follow. Then there will be peace. As it is now, you just have to switch on the radio to see the confusion. The people in Luanda are going on about this and the people at Jamba are going on about that.'

'So who do you think should be the sole poet?'

'What I really meant was that there should be only one political poet. There is a difference between love poetry and political poetry, not so?'

Hosi nodded. Debora continued: 'Yes, we should have one political poet – say, the president. Only he should write poems about the country, patriotism and the like, and then you can have battalion upon battalion of love poets. Oh, I would love to learn English someday.'

'Why do you want to learn English?' Hosi asked.

'Because I'd like to understand the songs of Lionel Richie. When I listen to him, I can tell that the man is saying something profound, something that resonates in the deeper confines of my heart. But I can't actually understand what he is saying because I don't know English. After English I will learn French. I am told that it is the most romantic language in the world. A Cuban friend told me that most Europeans moan in French when they are making love. Is that true?'

Hosi smiled and said: 'I don't think that is true.'

Debora bent closer and whispered into Hosi's ear: 'Can I tell you a secret?' Hosi nodded. 'There is no peace in this bloody country. I want to go to Brazil. Yes, I want to go to Recife, Sao Paolo or Rio de Janeiro, fall in love with a very tall North American white man and forget about Africa.'

The captain had now stopped talking and was looking at Debora, who was whispering into Hosi's ear. He tapped Debora on the shoulder and said: 'What are you two plotting? No secret schemes!'

Debora said: 'There you go again. I am just telling him that I have tried all along to learn English and yet I seem to be getting nowhere.'

The captain grinned and said: 'That is a pity. On the whole Angolans are polyglots – that is, they learn languages with great ease.'

Debora banged the table and said: 'I can't understand Angolans. Sorry, but that is how I feel. I am fed up with them up to my throat. Wherever they are they cannot help boasting about this or that. It does not matter whether they are in Luanda, Huambo or Jamba. They are all the same.'

The captain said: 'One of the symptons of neo-colonialism is self-hate. I am proud to be Angolan. We should all be proud to be Angolans. We should all be patriots.'

Debora said: 'There is nothing special in being an Angolan.' She turned to Hosi and said: 'Never take what I say seriously because I am mad, really mad.'

'I don't think so,' Hosi replied. The cassette player was now playing a number by Kachiungo. A girl came forward and asked the captain to dance with her. As he got up, Debora said to Hosi: 'I knew that guy years ago. Now he's a captain and highly respected. He was once after me; that was long ago. He's a bit mad, but I wouldn't mind getting involved with him because I am also mad, as I told you. The problem is that he is afraid. I was practically captured from the other side and people think that I am a spy. But I think the reason he does not want me is that he thinks I am too good for him. He feels that if he was to marry me the brigadiers would die of jealousy. But I don't want these brigadiers. I want a man of my own. Life is too short to share such a precious thing as love.'

Hosi smiled and said: 'I like that. Life is too short to share love. I will remember that for a long time.'

'Never mind. I talk a lot of rubbish. I mean, I love this guy and I know that he loves me, but he just can't make a move. Instead, he satisfies himself by painting portraits of me. Nothing wrong in that. You should see them, I mean the portraits. They are lovely. The problem is that here everything is political – including love. I have heard it time and again that love is political. Rubbish! Love is love.'

Debora stopped, thought for a while and then continued: 'I am a terrible romantic. People say I live in a world of fantasy, but that is why I am alive. Which intelligent person would be able to survive in this horrible country? Now listen, you, whatever your name is. I am known as a loud mouth and they won't do anything to me; I mean, I can say anything. So don't bother to tell people at CADIS [the UNITA secret police]; they know everything that I say. You would just bore them.'

The dance went on. At some point the captain and Debora began to dance. They held each other tightly, like lovers. Hosi was confused. He wondered why Debora and the captain had been so quick to tell him about their private lives.

Later Hosi found that everyone was eager to tell him about their lives because they felt he was, as someone had called him, 'a political virgin'. He had not suffered as much as them. He was a *tabula rasa* – a blank sheet waiting to be filled in on the principles of the struggle. Perhaps they also thought he embodied some kind of purity: he was not ambitious and they did not expect him to rush to any CADIS officer to inform on them.

People were dancing to Michael Jackson. The captain was trying the 'Moonwalk', to the delight of the girls. Just then Sergeant Herculano stormed in, panting. When he saw Hosi, he stood with arms akimbo and said: 'I have found you at last. Let's go back. Never do this again.'

'Can't I bid the captain farewell?' Hosi asked.

The sergeant shook his head: 'Let's go back. No more talking.'

Hosi followed the sergeant and got into the Land-Cruiser that was waiting outside. As soon as the car started, Sergeant Herculano said: 'I will tell you something that you don't seem to know. Here we are organized. You were supposed to tell me and I was supposed to ask permission from the personnel department as to whether you could go to that party or not.'

Hosi slapped his chest and said: 'This is my country and I should be free to go wherever I want.'

Shaking his head the sergeant said: 'That is the problem with people that have just come from abroad. They are complete anarchists and have no notion of organization or discipline. Remember one thing – this is a war. Discipline is crucial.'

116

Hosi said: 'But I was with the captain. Surely he knows what he was doing?'

'That's not an excuse,' the sergeant retorted. 'He's a madman. The only time he sobers up is when he is painting.'

As soon as they entered the guesthouse the sergeant told Hosi never to go out again. Everything he did from now on was to be based on a programme determined by the competent authorities.

Hosi went to bed feeling sad. He thought of the captain and Debora. He wished he had spoken to her for longer; he would have asked about Osvaldo because he was sure that she must have known him. Then he thought of Sergeant Herculano. Hosi hated his talk of programmes and the like. Someone in the guesthouse yawned loudly.

14

The following morning Hosi found breakfast – strong black coffee with brownish biscuits – on the table. There was cheese on one of the plates. Sergeant Herculano joined him at the table and began to eat eagerly. 'Where is the cheese from?' said Hosi. 'France, Holland or Ireland?'

It was as if he had asked something very strange. The sergeant stopped eating and said: 'Another fact you will always have to remember about this place. Here we don't ask where our food comes from. We eat to stay alive and to please our stomachs.'

As the sergeant continued eating, a tall, dark man burst into the room. He was carrying with him three walkie-talkies. (Hosi later discovered that the more walkie-talkies an officer had, the more powerful he was.) The tall man stood before Hosi and said: 'Hosi Mbueti? Good. I am Kandalu – Colonel Kandalu. I am the political coordinator of this region. Welcome back to the motherland.'

Someone called the colonel on the walkie-talkie. It was obviously a high-ranking officer calling because the colonel sprang to attention at once and said: 'Yes, Mike. Kilo Lima over here. Yes, Mike. Yes, there should be no more Foxtrot Ultimo Charlie Kilo about. I understand. Oscar Kilo, Oscar Kilo.'

The colonel tucked the walkie-talkie into a holster that was fixed to his belt and said: 'Let's continue, young man. Yes, welcome to the motherland. We need all the people that are abroad to come back home. There was a time when our enemies went about saying it would not be long before we would be completely wiped out. They were right in a way. In 1975, when the transitional government had collapsed, we

118

were reduced to a few hundred men and women. Our enemies had, however, overlooked two things: our ability to survive and our leader. As you are aware, our leader is known all over the world. He has made the grandsons of Lenin and Stalin soil their pants.' The colonel burst out laughing. Hosi laughed too.

The colonel continued: 'Now, you should be taken around Jamba, the Bastion of the Resistance and the Last Hope of the Black Race, if not Africa. Certain African reactionaries would dispute that, but we should pay them no heed.'

There was another call on the walkie-talkie, and the colonel left. 'I have the programme ready for you,' said Sergeant Herculano. 'Two o'clock: meeting with an Alvorada representative. Three fifteen: visit to the secondary school. Four o'clock: visit to the hospital.'

At two o'clock the Alvorada representative, a short, dark girl who, Hosi concluded, was not older than twelve, arrived. Hosi took to her at once. He had never met a young girl with such confidence. She smiled and said: 'My name is Etosi. I belong to the Alvorada, which, as you might know, is the organization that looks after the needs of children. As our beloved leader says, children are . . .'

Hosi waved his hands and said: 'Just a minute. What did you say your name was?'

'Etosi.'

'Lovely name, not so?'

The girl giggled. Hosi grunted and said: 'And you have a lovely face too. Have you got any sisters?'

'Yes. I have three sisters,' she murmured, looking down. There was a momentary silence and then the girl said: 'But they've all got fiancés.'

Hosi hit the table and said: 'Ah, too bad.'

Still looking down the girl said: 'I haven't got a boyfriend.'

Where was this leading? thought Hosi. He shifted and said: 'Now, please continue. Tell me about Angolan children.'

The girl giggled and said: 'We are the leader's right hand. We are also his left hand. We are the future of the nation.'

Next was the visit to the secondary school. Sergeant

Herculano offered to take Hosi. They passed several reed houses on the way. Hosi could tell that these were the officers' quarters because they were very large.

Hosi had not been to the best Zambian secondary schools, such as the Kenneth Kaunda Secondary School or the Canisius College, but he felt he had been very privileged when he compared himself to the students in Jamba. They were all seated beneath huge trees, listening attentively to their teacher. They did not pay any attention to Hosi or the sergeant. As Hosi walked around he recalled how at the end of every year the final-year students at his Zambian secondary school had broken windows and blown the light bulbs to celebrate the end of their exams. He also recalled that most of them had skipped their lessons to go and drink. But here in Jamba he saw people who were thirsty for knowledge. He really believed that here was something that no one but Angolans had – the desire to learn and to advance, whatever the obstacles.

They came to a group of children having a Latin lesson beneath another tree. '*Labor*', the teacher – a lean man with a priestly collar – was saying, '*omnia vincit*'. Hosi turned to Sergeant Herculano and said: 'I can think of no other African nation where young people are being taught Latin under trees.'

Herculano beamed and said: 'We're great, my brother. Some people still do not believe that fact.'

After the school Hosi and the sergeant were taken to the hospital. The Jamba Central Hospital was composed of several reed edifices. The main building had been built as a bunker, to minimize the number of casualties in the event of an aerial attack. A diminutive girl who introduced herself as a laboratory assistant offered to take them round. She led them into a room in which young men and women were busy looking into microscopes, then she asked them to follow her into the wards.

The first they went into was for the war-wounded. It smelt of alcohol and the medicines used to cure wounds. A number of the patients – mostly teenagers – had had their legs amputated, at the ankle or at the knee. Hosi tried hard not to let his face show that he pitied them. The wounded had vacant expressions on their faces. One or two smiled and Hosi returned their smiles. In one bed there was a boy who had had both hands blown off. He lay next to another who had been blinded by an explosion.

When they came to the end of the ward the lab technician said: 'Those are the war-wounded. Journalists from all over the world often come over here with their television cameras to see them. Then they are able to show the world the valiance of the Angolan people.' As they walked to another ward, Hosi saw an amputee singing a lament and playing a tin guitar.

After the hospital Herculano insisted that Hosi visit the workshop where weapons were repaired. Hosi was amazed by the number of men busy working on different weapons. He turned to Sergeant Herculano and said: 'Have these people had some special training?'

'Training? This is a university, the people's university. Breathing here is learning. We all improve ourselves by the day.'

A bearded, corpulent, mulatto major who reminded Hosi of Junior came forward and said that the weapons before them were a testimony to the efficiency and power of the UNITA soldiers. The major began to explain to Hosi about the weapons, but Hosi could not help wondering how many people had been killed by them.

Herculano now said the tour was over and took Hosi back to the guesthouse. It was still daylight. Hosi felt unhappy with the guided tour. He wanted to explore Jamba on his own. Angola, he had said to himself repeatedly, was his motherland and nothing was going to prevent him from going wherever he wanted. He decided that he would wander about and see whatever he could. Were there parts of Jamba that he was not supposed to see? He dismissed the idea at once.

He walked out of the guesthouse and followed a gravel road. At one of the communal waterpipes several boys and girls were sitting and chatting. He stood for a while and watched them. He wondered what stories they had to tell. They had lived most of their lives in the forest and did not have the slightest clue what life was like in a town. Hosi felt fortunate:

at least he knew what Huambo had been like in the colonial period and he had seen the escalation of the war. For the boys and girls at the water pump, life had just been nothing but war.

That night Hosi spent most of his evening writing in the notebook he used to sketch plots for short stories and novels. At first he had simply wanted to make an entry describing what had happened to him that day, but he wrote on.

Met a representative of Alvorada. She must have been twelve. I think she's only twelve: her breasts are just about to come out. She has such eyes that will soon be sending revolutionaries running amok. She said her name was Etosi; I thought it was very euphonic. On the whole. I am not attracted to young girls or nymphets, like that middle-aged man in *Lolita*. I was thinking of writing an African version of that story. It would be the story of an old Zambian man who discovers that his son is not the father to his fourteen-year-old granddaughter. From there on, the old man begins to fancy the daughter. I should think of the end, or the epiphany, to be precise.

Then Herculano took me to the school. I did not spot any particularly beautiful girls but I was moved by the sight of the students attending lessons while seated beneath trees. I used to find lessons boring – especially when that rogue droned on about vectors and quadratic equations. But here these people are anxious to gobble down every word their teachers say. Herculano said Angolans are a great people. I agree. Well, I can be honest with my notebook; and if some curious cat pries into it, I don't give a fuck. Let me face the facts. I am no ordinary African; sometimes I feel I am not an ordinary human being. My mind is very complex. While people think of banal things, I concern myself with serious questions such as why men and women are so stupid.

Then we went to the hospital. It was a horrible sight. I wonder what is going on in the heads of those guys who have had their hands or legs amputated. The saddening fact is that the war will one day have to come to an end and those who shot at each other from trenches will have to shake hands. For there will simply be no more people to die. The war just has to come to an end. Whoever is responsible for this mess is a son of a bitch.

Then the workshop. I should very much like to work there someday. I have to come to an end. It is cold and the pen is not writing properly. I need a woman in my life. Someone to kiss and caress me; someone I can write sonnets for. The problem with Angolan girls is that only gunpowder turns them on. That is why the men go around carrying pistols (I should certainly get one) and grenades strapped to their waist. Herculano said he knew of a man who is only able to ejaculate by holding a grenade in his left hand. His wife ran away from him and he is at Kapakala getting mental treatment. My left armpit is itching; I might have a wet dream.

15

Hosi felt confused and tried hard not to think. He knew that sometimes confusion is more bearable than the truth. One question, however, kept popping into his head. He could no longer evade it. Why had he come back to Angola?

There was a facile answer: that he had returned to the motherland because he wanted to contribute, etc., etc. But there was a complex answer too and it kept thrusting itself into his mind.

Hosi had dreamt that he was at a base in the UNITA-controlled areas. A traditional dance was going on. A group of happy boys and girls were dancing to a folk song. Hosi recalled having heard the song as a child. He couldn't, however, remember the exact words for they had now been replaced with words from one of the Elder's speeches. When the dancing reached fever pitch, Hosi saw a group of loosely dressed women carrying a large black coffin. He looked closer and could see his parents seated by the fireside, warming to the drumming. His father had grown a beard, his mother looked younger and both were smiling at him. The drumming became louder. The coffin was opened. A man holding combat fatigues was dancing furiously before Hosi. Hosi was scared and refused to take the fatigues.

When Hosi woke up from the dream, he felt frightened. There and then the question of why he had returned surfaced. Facts unfurled before his mind. Hosi had returned to Angola because he was an Ovimbundu and because he was educated. He was part of the Umbundu élite and UNITA was the only party in the world in which he would be taken seriously. The MPLA was for the Kimbundus and the Bakongos. That was a fact, yet Angolans refused to acknowledge it in public.

Hosi was ambitious and he hoped to be sent abroad one day on a scholarship. He wanted to go to Britain, admiring everything English as he did. He thought America was vulgar and the Soviet Union totalitarian. Hosi hoped one day to attend a British university and to write impeccable English. He wanted to pen novels that would not only win literary prizes but put African writers of repute, such as Achebe, Ngugi and Laye, to shame. His novels would lay bare the core of the African soul to the world, would be part of school syllabuses and would encourage students the world over to delve into his life in order to understand his work.

Hosi's ambitions did not lean towards politics. He thought that politicians were vulgar and that their vocation consisted of no more than intrigue and the ability to survive. Any fool could be a politician. Hosi hoped to be an eminent thinker and often imagined the day when the world would mull over his pronouncements. He believed strongly that he was unique, a genius in a world of ignoramuses. He tried hard, although without great success, not to let these ambitions be known. Ambitions are often among the best-kept secrets. He had returned to Angola because he was ambitious.

Hosi sat down on the bed and rubbed his eyes. He was still thinking. Yes, ambition, that was what had brought him back to Angola. But he now realized that he would not be sent abroad. He would instead be sent for military training and then to the front line. That frightened him. He thought of the boys he had seen the previous day at the hospital. But then a voice inside him said a person could die anywhere. Indeed, the other day had he not heard on the BBC that several old women had died of cold in Surrey? There was not much to life, after all. Human breath, which people held so dear, was not that precious. Hosi held his heart and imagined a bullet ripping through him. He would fall and that would be the end of him. Another soul gone, just like that. And if he was lucky he would be buried, then rot, and make no mark on Angolan history.

Hosi's thoughts were disturbed by Herculano, who brought him a set of combat fatigues. This was it, the dream, Hosi said to himself. Herculano said: 'Here you are. No civilian clothes for a young Angolan man. This is a nation of fighters, of patriots. Put this on and you'll begin to feel like a real soldier.'

'A nation of fighters? Perhaps this country would be better off if it was a nation of cowards.'

'My friend, don't think that I am stupid,' Herculano replied. 'You talk of philosophy to me because you've read many books and you think that I will tremble. No way. My friend, it may be early in the morning but I could still discuss philosophy with you if I wanted.'

Hosi burst out laughing. Herculano said: 'I'd like to make a lot of money. I'd actually like to have several hotels in Huambo and Luanda. Please don't tell this to anyone.'

'Why?' Hosi asked.

'Because we are supposed to be fighting for the country, not ourselves.'

As Hosi dressed himself in the combat fatigues, Herculano looked at him admiringly and said: 'There you are, a real soldier. I am sure that you'll be an officer soon.'

'Herculano, sometimes you say things without thinking.' Hosi said.

'I know what I am talking about. A man with your brains should not be a sergeant like me. You should be an officer and do the thinking. You are the future of Angola.'

They were silent for a while and then Herculano said: 'I would like to make money. Not because I am greedy, but for my son. He is with his mother in Zaire. She won't let him see me until I become very rich.'

'That is very strange,' Hosi said. 'Herculano, are you really telling me the truth? Some of your tales are quite far-fetched.'

'Brother, believe me. I have a son. Now, when people see me they just say, there goes the fat sergeant. None of them knows that I am a father. Let me tell you the story.'

Herculano sat beside Hosi and began to recount his story: 'I used to be a dancer, a professional dancer under the Portuguese. I had never wanted to be one. I mean, I came from a proper family. We are Protestants from Allende mission and dancing was frowned upon. But I got employed at Kadumbu,

126

a club that was frequented by wealthy Portuguese, as a bartender. The reason I want to own hotels is that I have an idea of what is needed to run them. Anyway, that is beside the point. One day a white lady who was very drunk asked me for a dance. It was a slow, sentimental number playing. I squeezed the woman properly and she began to doze on my chest. No. I am not lying. Why would I tell a lie? The white men did not take this well. So from then on they began playing pop music. I was the only black present and everyone was drunk. They were playing something by James Brown. I can't remember the song's title but somewhere in the song he goes "yeeea-houuu kiriule, kiriompa!" Do you know it?'

Hosi shook his head. Herculano clapped his hands and continued: 'My friend, it was hell. They all sat down and began to applaud me. One of them bought me a bottle of champagne. Brother, that was paraffin to the fire. I wiggled my waist, waved my arms into the air, tossed my head like they had never seen before. Soon they were tossing bank notes at me. You won't believe this but I should tell you. One of the women was so amazed by my dancing that she took off her bra and threw it straight at me. It landed right on my face. I held it aloft, kissed it and inserted it in my back pocket. Bank notes were flying all over. My boss, Senhor Pinto, said from then on I would be the club's dancer. He devised a special show just for me. I became famous, a superstar. Then came the war. I fled to Zaire. I went to Kinshasa and lived in Matonge. I worked in a butchery owned by a Portuguese. Then I fell in love with a Zairean woman called Bernadette. She was not very beautiful but you know what Zairean women are like. In the dark they are all the same – fantastic.

'One day I had a quarrel with my Portuguese boss, so he sacked me. I went to Matonge and got drunk in a bar. They were playing Sam Manguana, Tabu Ley and the others. I started dancing. The Zaireans were dumbfounded. And you know that as far as rumba is concerned, Zaireans are the best dancers in the world. But there I was, wiggling, stomping, like they had never seen before. Bank notes were thrown at me. Others just looked at me, open-mouthed. Then I had an idea.

127

If I danced at Gengele market three times a day I would make a lot of money. I bought a cassette player and went to the market. There, my friend, I started playing one of those South African *sunguras*. Zairean women started throwing their shopping money at the little bowl that I had put in front of me. I'd go home with money every day. Bernadette loved me then, the way I love Angola now. Every evening when I'd get home, I'd find not only my meal ready but also the bath water. Bernadette would practically drag me to bed even if I was not willing. It was not easy my friend, but I managed.

'I told Bernadette that I worked in an office. I often went home with a pile of papers and in the evening I'd make a show of working on them. They were the same papers. Bernadette never bothered to look at them. She believed that they were genuine. Bernadette asked me where exactly in the city I worked. I told her that it was secret because I was the only person in Africa who knew the recipe for Coca-Cola.'

Hosi burst out laughing. Herculano said: 'Well, I had lied. All men lie when they are in love. Soon Bernadette noticed that most of my money was in small bank notes and that I seemed to have cash every day. I told her that I was so qualified that I was paid by the minute. She believed me, or at least I thought so.

'I kept on dancing. I even prepared a special costume. I got a pair of very torn trousers and a very dirty shirt as well as an awful-looking hat. I painted some of my front teeth black using a crayon. People thought it was wonderful. And then there was another attraction to my act: I began to wiggle my waist while standing on my head. Tourists took photographs of me.

'All along I kept telling Bernadette never to go to Gengele market. Not only was the place infested with thieves, drug dealers and deviants of all sorts but also it was very dirty. The flies from the meat and fish being sold there, I told her, were as deadly as tse-tse flies. My friend, she believed me. She loved me dearly, I know that very well. I know that as far as women are concerned there is no such thing as a handsome man; the pocket counts more. But I tell you, brother, this woman was crazy for me. I think one of the reasons she loved me was that she knew Zairean men are all crooks and terrible womanizers – they are a disgrace to the human race. We all like women, but to go about it like the Zaireans do is simply absurd. I was very different from the other men. In the evenings I'd simply come home and take my Skol or Tembo in peace and do what most Angolan refugees do abroad at night – listen to the news.

'Then I began to fall in love with Bernadette. At first she was just going to be a shelter but my heart started to itch and I convinced myself that I was going to live with this woman for the rest of my life. She must have given me that stuff – the love potion. But I was afraid that she would leave me if she found out about my dancing. So I began to think of other ways of making money. I began to think of starting a business. I had various ideas. Unfortunately, I come of a family that is not very lucky. I don't know, but everything we've done seems to have ended in disaster. Under the Portuguese, for instance, my father had tried a piggery. After a while, the pigs began to die mysteriously.

'So this time I consulted a witch doctor. Not a witch doctor in the ordinary sense – not the kind who gives you stuff to harm other people, just somebody who could give me a lucky charm. He was an Angolan called Sebastiao. Sebastiao da Cruz.

'My friend, it is a long story. I will make it brief. I went to see Sebastiao in Kingabwa. He lived somewhere near L'Avenue Tropicale. When I got to his house I found that there were people waiting. Most of them were Angolans. I was surprised to see Bakongos, Umbundus and Cabindans gathered there. The witch doctor had such a good reputation that he had made enough money to afford a second-hand Mercedes. I joined the other people who were sitting waiting in the room. I remember it very clearly. The television was playing. The comedian Mangobe was on. Anyway, after a while, it was my turn. I went in. Sebastiao was a short man with bulgy eyes. As soon as he saw me he said: "You're not a very lucky man, not so?" I said: "Yes, sir." As I was sitting down, I wondered how on earth this man knew about my problem.

'He played about with his cowrie shells, said a few incantations and then gave me some roots which, he said, I had to immerse in my bathwater every day. I went home and followed Sebastiao's instructions. They worked. After a week, people began to throw 100-zaire notes as I danced and one wealthy man even took off his gold watch after watching me for a while. Soon they began to hire me at dance functions. A man from *Elima* said he wanted to interview me. I agreed. My friend, that was a very foolish thing to do. In the interview, I said my dancing was a political gesture because I saw myself as the Angolan cultural ambassador. Relations between countries, I said, often paled into flowery rhetoric. I believed in concrete diplomacy. By dancing the *kazukuta* at Gengele market I was affirming that a specifically Angolan dance could be appreciated by Zaireans, thus bringing the dream of Pan-Africanism nearer to fruition. My friend, the reporter was open-mouthed. He just could not believe that such polished words were coming from the mouth of an Angolan. "*Citoyen*," he said, "*vous êtes très intelligent*." I said: "It is not intelligence, it is just that I am an Angolan."'

Hosi laughed and interrupted Herculano's story: 'Now I understand myself better. Part of the Angolan identity while abroad is to feel that one is more important than the indigenous people.'

Herculano slapped Hosi on the thigh and said: 'Listen. I have never told this story to anyone. Angolans are terrible listeners! Anyway, I was very pleased that my name was going to appear in *Elima*. People the world over would know that a certain Herculano Sachipangele was alive and well. Bernadette never read a lot. She could write letters to her parents and the like, but she certainly was not interested in politics or sport. She was the last person I would have expected to pick up a newspaper. But one night, after one of those exhilarating bouts, I lay by her side telling her of the good things that awaited her in a free Angola ruled by our leader. She said: "I hope I won't have to wait too long for a video player since your dancing pays so much."

'My brother, that was a shock to me. I could not control

myself: I released some bad air instantly. I said: "What do you mean?" She said: "I've read all about it in *Elima*." I was dumb for a while and then said to her that I had been found out at last and that there was nothing I could do. No. She did not leave me. Instead, she started demanding more money whenever I came home. And you won't believe this. She spent most of the money buying expensive wax materials, lipsticks and such rubbish! Now, just imagine, my friend. I was breaking my waist making money for this woman for her to spend on her lips. I know we are taught to believe that African women are oppressed. I agree that they are oppressed to an extent. I mean, there are hordes upon hordes of male beasts simply battering them whenever they feel like it. But there are also men who are suffering at the hands of women. The Zairean woman is another creature, my brother. When she starts sucking your money, she ends up sucking your very blood. Bernadette also started giving money to her relatives. I was now poor and went back to Sebastiao for help.

'He played about with his shells and said: "The spirits say that you will have a child – a baby boy for that matter. But you should not tell your wife that you intend to have a child." As I walked home, I said to myself: How on earth is that possible? I mean, how was I going to get Bernadette pregnant without her knowing of my intentions? My friend, as the Zaireans say, *Mokili est compliqué*, the world is complicated. I insisted that we made love regularly: in the morning, in the afternoon and in the evening. I'd tell Bernadette to join me in bed whenever I could. Sometimes, especially in the day, she refused. She said such a gigantic appetite for the act was due to the strong Zairean beer.

'Brother, I tell you she became pregnant. To make matters complicated, I began to see tiny men whenever I opened the tin in which I kept the roots Sebastiao had given me. I ran back to him and said things had just gone too far. He said the tiny men wanted a child for doing various jobs like robbing banks. Their work would get done properly only if they had a human sacrifice. In other words, I was supposed to kill my child as an offering to them. I said no way and went straight to

131

Bernadette. I told her the whole story. She left at once and wrote a letter saying I was a wizard. I was so disappointed that I decided to leave Zaire at once and came into the bush to help in the fight for the motherland. Once Angola is free and UNITA is in power, then I will ask for my son. If Bernadette refuses, I will involve the governments. If that does not work, then there will be a war. Don't tell this to anyone. I have told you because I trust you.'

Two weeks passed without Hosi being contacted. He would wake up in the morning, read, eat and sleep. He was bored stiff. Whenever he asked Herculano what was going on, Herculano would simply nod and say: 'I don't know. The movement's leadership knows best.'

'But don't they know that I am getting bored?' Hosi would ask.

'No. They don't,' Herculano would reply. 'They know, however, that the Angolan people are being oppressed.'

One morning Hosi was lying in bed thinking when Herculano handed him an envelope. It contained a letter. Hosi could not believe it. It was from Raul, who said he had heard that Hosi had come and he wanted him to pay a visit to Bionge. Hosi jumped from the bed and shouted: 'Herculano! Herculano!'

Herculano came in fuming. 'Now, my friend, this is too much. I am Sergeant Herculano; I was not given this post for nothing. By calling me Herculano you are not insulting me; you're insulting the Angolan people.'

'Sorry, sergeant. But I have good news for you.'

'No news is good for me,' the Sergeant interjected, 'unless it has to do with the joy of the Angolan people.'

'Well, it has to do with the joy of one Angolan person. A guy called Raul. He's a captain. When my parents died, I fled to Huambo. I had a fight with the first boy that I met. Then he became my friend. While I was in Zambia he must have been in the army. He's at Bionge.'

'Bionge?' said Herculano, surprised. 'That is where all the war-wounded are. Your friend must have lost a leg or something.

132

Fidel Castro will go to hell. He will never be forgiven for what he has done to the Angolan people.'

'But he could also be at the hospital as a medical assistant,' Hosi said. Herculano nodded.

Herculano said Hosi could not leave for Bionge without permission from the DEP (*Departamento do pessoal*, Personnel Department).

There was a long queue at the DEP building. Several girls who had been brought from central Angola were waiting to be seen. They were all dressed in tatters. Hosi was too embarrassed to look at them. The girls were to be posted as nannies, ending up as fourth or fifth wives of the officers. It was said that the less attractive the nanny, the better treatment she got from the lady boss. There were also several young men in the queue. Some were going to submit forms applying for marriage and others were asking to be allowed to go and pay visits to friends in other posts.

The queue moved slowly, but at last it was Hosi's turn. A man was standing behind the counter, flipping through a huge folder. After a while he turned to Hosi and said: 'What do you want?'

'I want to go to Bionge.'

'For what?'

'To see a friend.'

'Who?'

'Raul. Oh, Captain Raul.'

'The handicapped captain?'

'I suppose so.'

'Let me see your papers.'

'What papers?'

'I am in no mood for debate. Your pass.'

'I don't have any pass.'

'Right, then a letter from the coordinator of your section.'

'That too I do not have. I have been here for less than a month. I have just come from Zambia.'

'Anyone who steps into UNITA territory needs a document. How do we know whether you're an enemy? Your name, please!'

133

'Hosi Mbueti.'

The man went to pick up some folders, looked for some paper, nodded for a while and then said: 'Uhm. Now tell me, what are you going to see the captain for?'

'It's personal.'

The man looked straight at Hosi and said: 'My friend, I did not wake up well this morning. Answer my question: what do you want to see him for?'

'He's a friend.'

'We all have friends.'

'Well, we knew each other as children. I would like to see him. Surely a visit to a wounded man would brighten his day, not so?'

The man nodded and began to fill in a form. After a while he said: 'What is your grandmother's maiden name? I mean the one on your mother's side?'

'What do you want that for?'

The man heaved and said: 'Do you know or not?'

'I don't.'

'Good.'

The man wrote for a while and then passed the paper over to Hosi. It was the pass to go to Bionge. By this time there were no more people in the DEP office. Hosi looked around and said: 'Why all these files?'

'Organization,' the man answered.

'You won't defeat the Cubans by having mountains of papers containing the maiden names of grannies that are long dead,' said Hosi. Then he went home, hoping to leave for Bionge the following day.

Hosi was fast asleep when Herculano woke him up. He had been summoned by Colonel Bazooka, who headed the information office. As Hosi dressed himself, Herculano whispered: 'What have you done?'

Hosi shook his head. He sensed that Herculano was afraid for him. A day before, Hosi would not have been afraid, even if he had done something wrong. He knew that he was an intellectual and thought he was indispensable. But that afternoon Hosi had been told things that had shocked him. George Ornelas Sangumba, a man who had once been a UNITA foreign secretary, had been killed. For years foreign reporters had come to Jamba asking for him and had been told that he was somewhere in the north. Then there was Valdermar Pires Chindondo. He too had been killed, along with his followers – young students who had just come out of Huambo colleges. Then there was a man called Puscas. He had been shot dead after complaining that northerners were being mistreated in the UNITA-controlled area. Hosi had heard of all these people before. The names had appeared in books on UNITA and yet they had been shot long ago. Herculano told Hosi to keep his mouth shut because intellectuals were the very people the secret police were after.

It was a cold night. The wind was howling. Hosi knew why he had been called: the remarks he made about bureaucracy had been passed on. Several questions kept coming into his mind. Would he be sent to the infamous underground prison at Esquadra Piloto? Or would he be sent into internal exile in some remote area? Or would he simply be killed?

The information offices were a bunker with a grass roof and several newly cut branches on top. A lean, shy-looking soldier led Hosi into Colonel Bazooka's office. Colonel Bazooka was tall and light-skinned; had a long beard and spoke fluent English.

'Come in, gentleman,' he shouted to Hosi, who was standing at the door. The two exchanged pleasantries, then the colonel asked Hosi about Zambia. They spoke for a while about boxing; the colonel said he was a great follower of Muhammad Ali and Hosi said he supported Sugar Ray Leonard. Then the colonel stood abruptly and said: 'When you are carrying out an insurrection, you either bring it to an end – that is, to victory – or die. I think these words are from Lenin. Here we are carrying out an insurrection. We are dealing with life and death. As I am speaking, people are dying. Some of our brothers are in prisons; others have lost limbs; and others have not eaten anything for a long time. They are brave people. They deserve to be honoured. That is the duty of every Angolan.'

He coughed, then continued: 'Right. I have a report here. It says that this morning you went to the DEP wanting a pass to go and see Captain Raul, who you said was your childhood friend. The report says that you behaved arrogantly. Raul is an extraordinary man. He is a hero. Children are taught to be like him. If Angola had more men like him, we would be very far in our struggle. When the enemy had almost captured him, he destroyed all the vital documents. What you have done is a disgrace. You are the opposite of Raul. You think people have been here all these years waiting to be lectured by someone like you, who only came yesterday?'

The colonel was getting worked up. He threw down the book in which the report had been written and said: 'Nobody is above the law here. We've suffered to build this place and create whatever we have. We should be respected. You insulted us all. The problem is that we blacks do not respect each other. Had this been built by whites you would have accepted it and you would have never questioned the bureaucracy.'

At this point Hosi decided to interrupt him, and said: 'Well, the South Africans certainly have much to do with this.'

The colonel frowned and said: 'What do you mean?'

Hosi laughed nervously and said: 'It is a well-known fact.'

The colonel shook his head and said: 'I know that it is hard for someone like you, who has just come from abroad, to fit into this society. I understand also that it is not a proper society. We are trying to do two things at the same time: first, we are trying to annihilate the lackeys of the Kremlin in Luanda; and second, we are trying to create a new man, the man that will take Angola to the socialist revolution. I simply ask you to be very careful in everything that you say. Right?'

The captain then handed Hosi a little brochure, saying that he would understand the war better once he had read it.

As soon as Hosi arrived at the guesthouse, he began to read the brochure. It was written in English, and was entitled *UNITA – The Constitution and Statute of Internal Regulations*. Several passages in the booklet had been marked with a red pen. Hosi took note of them all. The first read: 'Our national and democratic revolution must be followed by a socialist revolution, the sole guarantee of the defence of our people.'

He flipped on to another marked passage. 'Art 46 – Capital punishment shall be the penalty for very serious offences.'

Hosi lay in bed thinking. He felt very confused. He asked himself whether UNITA was socialist or capitalist. From what he had read, it struck him that it was socialist. Hosi was not opposed to socialism but he did not trust it that much. Everyone knew that Ujamaa in Tanzania had got nowhere and that Nyerere had admitted failure. But perhaps Hosi's aversion to socialism went deeper. He had never known who killed his parents but people in Zambia kept saying that it must have been the MPLA. When he fled to Zambia all he heard about were the problems caused by socialism and communism. The elders kept talking of communist imperialism and the Lord was often invoked in prayer to deliver the people from socialism.

Hosi's distrust of Marxism, socialism and communism (he never bothered to learn the differences between them) was reinforced at school when he decided to study English literature. One of the set books had been Solzhenitsyn's *One Day in the Life of Ivan Denisovich*. It was the only book on the course not by an African author. At first Hosi had not been able to understand it, but when he did he found it frightening. He felt that he knew the people whose lives in the camp were being described. A voice in him kept saying that it was the Russians who had driven the tanks that had forced the Ovimbundu to flee to Angola. Then his teacher, a staunch Christian, had cleared his mind. Mr Vasco, an Indian from Goa, had told the class that although Solzhenitsyn wrote to describe the evils of Stalinism, the point he was actually making was that socialism as a whole was evil. It was then that Hosi had developed his hatred of socialism.

Hosi subscribed to UNITA because he was Ovimbundu, but he liked to think that part of the reason for his loyalty was ideological: the MPLA stood for communism, which was evil, while UNITA stood for democracy, which was good. Now, as he lay on the bed, he felt confused. He asked himself why the booklet went on about socialism. The MPLA talked of creating a new man – one who was revolutionary and versed in Marxism. UNITA too talked of creating a new man – one who was versed in socialism and in the Paramount Thought, for that was how the ideas of the Elder were described.

Angola, Hosi concluded, was as confused as he was. The best thing to do was to join in the mess. That way he would feel less confused. Indeed, as a friend of his had once told him: 'In a lunatic asylum, the only people who don't make sense are those who are slightly sane.'

16

The following morning Hosi prepared himself to go and see Raul. The road was sandy and the Land-Rover tore into it furiously. The driver was a taciturn man who stuck his tongue out whenever they came to a bump. After a while they reached the savannah. Hosi could see swans on the edges of little swamps. The Land-Rover came to a halt to allow several elephants to cross the road. This was the closest Hosi had ever come to elephants. He was awed by their size and noted how their tusks had a brownish hue to them. He had always thought that tusks were completely white. Hosi turned to the driver and said: 'These tusks are worth a fortune. I think there must be very few elephants left in Africa.'

The driver frowned and said: 'Good. If I had my way I would have shot them all.'

'Why?' Hosi asked, startled.

'Because they are a nuisance. I was once at a camp near Muie. There was a particular type of tree surrounding the camp which the elephants liked. They started eating them like mad. The only camouflage we had against enemy jets was destroyed. It was suggested that the elephants be killed but the camp commander – a major – insisted that they be allowed to roam freely. One morning the MiGs struck. It was hell. You don't know what it feels like to be under aerial attack.'

By now all the elephants had gone, so the Land-Rover went on. An impala ran across the road; the driver swerved and swore. It began to drizzle. They went through a thick forest that led to another savannah. There again Hosi saw several little swamps with birds around them and a number of flowers on the banks.

When several black impalas crossed the road, the driver said: 'Do you know that those are found only in Angola?'

139

Hosi gasped and said: 'I have heard so much about them. There are two things unique to Angola: a flower called *Welwhicha mirabilis* and these black impalas. I hope they will survive the war.'

As Hosi contemplated the scenery, part of him felt that the land belonged to him, but another part felt that in actual fact it belonged to the Elder, for he was the head of the party. It was the Elder who decided what could and could not be done. Indeed, Herculano had told him of two Catholic priests who had once criticized the Elder's poems and had been shot dead at once.

Eventually they came to an area with several huts. They stopped before the one which was the guards' post. Hosi jumped out of the van and asked where he would find Raul. The guard told him to walk past the main hospital building to a small hut at the end of the row. As Hosi walked, he noticed that each hut had flowers planted in front. It was now about ten o'clock in the morning. Apart from the guard, Hosi had not yet seen anyone. Then he suddenly saw many people beneath a huge shelter. Some had crutches; others were in wheelchairs. Hosi hated to see lame people. He was unable to conceal the fact that he pitied them and he had been told on several occasions that lame people hated to be pitied. None of them seemed interested in him. Hosi found this disconcerting. They looked at him like people tired of being watched.

At last he came to Raul's hut and knocked on the door. 'Come in,' said a voice.

Raul had not changed much. Hosi recognized the fierceness in his face that had been there when they first met. He was sitting in a wheelchair, reading a magazine. As soon as he saw Hosi, he clapped his hands and said: 'I have always known that I would meet you one day in a free Angola.'

'What a huge man you've grown into!' said Hosi. 'We have a world boxing champion here!'

Raul smiled and said: 'I am as helpless as a baby. I almost died, but more of that later. I dreamt that I had died and met you in heaven. Two days later someone told me that you were in Jamba. How strange!'

'Very strange,' Hosi answered as he sat down on Raul's bed. 'Angola is a very strange phenomenon. But tell me, what has been going on in your life?'

'War, my friend. We know nothing here apart from war. We have to fight for this wretched land. That is it.'

'Wretched land?'

'Sometimes I think it is. Just look at the misery around here. I mean, in other times all these young men would be in schools, messing about, enjoying their youth. Now, they are here, complete invalids.'

'Is that a proper thing to say?'

'Of course not, but who would bother to lock up someone like me? I am useless. They would be wasting their time. If I dropped dead right now, they would be more than pleased. It would be one less mouth to feed.'

'Raul, I don't want to offend you. What I will say might hurt you, please forgive me.'

'Come on,' Raul interjected. 'I hate to be spoken to as if I had lost my mother. Say what is in your heart.'

'These young people have sacrificed themselves for a price. They are a monument to the Angolan people's resistance against foreign domination.'

Raul said: 'I will soon be gone.'

Hosi banged the bed and said: 'Rubbish! Don't say that. You might live longer than some of the elephants I saw on my way here. Now tell me, have you got a wife or a girlfriend?'

'Yes,' Raul replied, 'but things are not going very well. Her name is Lila. We used to love each other but now things have soured. Maybe I should tell you my story.' Raul leaned back and spoke slowly.

17

Things were not going well in the 67th region. Lieutenant Raul got a message from the regional headquarters saying he was to intercept an enemy battalion that had settled at Kalonga on the banks of the Cutatu river. It was not very clear whether it was just one battalion. The enemy had been there for a month and it was suspected that several other companies had joined up during this period.

It had been quite a while since Raul had seen action and he was craving for it. He had risen through the ranks due to sheer bravery and daring, but he knew that he had to participate in several battles to keep commanding the respect of his men. That was why the attack at Kalonga was going to be vital.

The messages from the regional headquarters were handed over to him one afternoon while he was seated under a huge mulemba tree. The enemy, said the message, needed to be dislodged without fail or the supply routes to the north would be cut and Elavoko – a strategic camp – would come under threat. Raul folded the message, put it in his breast pocket and went to lie on the bed in his room. He called out to Ernesto, his aide-de-camp, who answered promptly and trotted into the hut.

'Go and call Lila,' Raul ordered.

Lila was Raul's fiancée. He loved her very much, not only because he thought she was very beautiful but because, as everyone kept saying, she was very politically sound. Some said she would eventually become the leader of the women's movement – the highest post a woman in the UNITA-controlled area could aspire to – or, under a UNITA government in Angola, a minister.

Lila was of medium height and a bit plump. Some said in

private that she had the sexiest body around, but no one said it in her hearing for she had a reputation of being ruthless. She believed that everything was political, including love. She kept telling younger girls that the ideal man for an Angolan woman was a brave man, a man who would not only adhere to the principles of the movement but who also believed in each and every word that had been said by the Elder. In fact, she was said to know great passages of the Elder's speeches down to the last comma.

Lila came into the hut and kissed Raul, who was by now dozing on the bed. He sat up and said: 'I think we might not see each other for a while.'

'What?'

'I will be going on an operation, at Kalonga. If I don't come back, remember that I loved you.'

'How many men are you taking with you?'

'Two companies.'

'Is that enough to dislodge a battalion?'

'That is the advantage of being guerrilla fighters. We are like ants. Once we get into the elephant's trunk, we can easily bring him down. You know what it is like. Anyway, remember this: you were gunpowder to my heart. The mere thought of you was enough to set off an explosion of love in me.'

Lila smiled and said: 'Sentimentalism, I hate it. I am not your typical Angolan girl who giggles at every flattering remark. In the ideal society that we are working for, love will be political. Girls will go to bed with men not because they are attractive but because they hold proper views, views that will advance the cause of the masses.'

'Listen,' Raul implored, 'you should know by now that there is on the one hand political rhetoric and on the other real life. They are not the same thing. For the moment, we lovers should put politics aside. Now come over here and let me listen to your heartbeat.'

Lila hung back and said: 'I know what that will lead to. Not at this time of the day, please. It would be foolish for us to be romancing while our enemies are planning how best to massacre us.'

143

Raul tried to grab her hand, but Lila freed herself and left. As she walked out, he wondered whether Lila was really the type of woman for him.

Two weeks later preparations were being made for the attack. By now Raul and his men had reached an area that was two days' march from Kalonga. Three men were sent off to spy enemy positions. They had all acquired MPLA uniforms and had had special identity cards forged for them. The three spies were expected to mix with MPLA soldiers and find out the exact number of men present and if they had any sophisticated weapons.

As they waited for the return of the three spies, Raul became increasingly worried. Kalonga was a settlement where his mother and his sister, Berta, lived. He felt a strong urge to do a most unprofessional thing – write a letter to his mother informing her that they would soon be attacking the settlement and that she should therefore move away. He knew that if the letter fell into the enemy's hands, he and his men would die, but he wanted to do everything that he could to protect his mother.

Raul had not seen his mother and sister for over eight years, though they had been in touch with each other through constant letters. At first his mother's letters had been short and terse, like telegrams. Eventually they became longer, but even so Raul concluded that his mother thought they would never see each other again. Then, in one of her letters she said that she had problems with her eyes and was about to go blind. There was nothing he could do for her.

He decided to write and warn his mother of the coming attack. He approached Corporal Big Bang, a fat fellow who liked tight-fitting trousers. He too was a spy and often wandered into the MPLA lines. He handed him the letter and said: 'I am going to ask you to do me a big favour. I want you to take this letter to my mother.'

Big Bang was startled and said: 'Come on, Comrade Lieutenant. This can't be done. How will I be able to get into Kalonga on my own at this time?'

Raul said: 'Calm, calm, brother. Let me explain. The prob-

144

lem is my mother. I want to tell her to leave Kalonga because we are soon going to attack it. She is an old woman and will soon die. But I think that she ought to enjoy the last days of her life.'

Big Bang stepped forward, patted Raul on the shoulders and said: 'Lieutenant, we all have mothers and we all wish that we could save them, but what is best for our mothers may not be best for the Angolan people.'

Raul laughed and said: 'Big Bang, you are my brother. I am not corrupt. All I want you to do is help save my mother. We are fighting this war because we believe in saving lives, not so?'

Big Bang nodded. Raul continued: 'Then if we can save one or two lives, I see nothing wrong in it.'

Big Bang took the envelope and walked out.

Kalonga was to be attacked in two days. On the way there, Raul and his colleagues tried to get some food from the villagers, who said they would exchange whatever food they had for Walkmans and radios. The villagers said many battalions had passed through the village and they had enough salt, sugar and blankets. Frantic negotiations ensued.

At some point the guerrillas became livid, saying that the villagers were not being realistic and were behaving as if they – the guerrillas – were enjoying the hardships. Not one of them, they contended, had taken to arms because he enjoyed it; rather, they wanted to liberate Angola.

The villagers said they had heard the same story over and over again from both the MPLA and UNITA soldiers. At last it was decided that the soldiers could exchange their radios and tape recorders for cassava tubers and sweet potatoes. There were a few murmurs as some of the guerrillas said that the villagers were not only pompous but also reactionary, but Raul said the people were always right.

The soldiers left the village early the following morning. During the time they stayed there they had made sure that no villager left to tell the enemy of their presence. They walked till midday, then they camped in a thick forest. By now the three spies who had been sent to Kalonga, including Big Bang, were back. Big Bang said he had handed the letter to Raul's mother without any problem.

A model of Kalonga was erected in the clearing. Raul stepped forward and began to describe the attack: 'We'll be in Kalonga at around four in the morning. We'll move from east to west.' Pointing his stick to an edifice he said: 'This is the building in which the weapons are being kept. We'll have to blow it apart. Our commandos will have to get to the officers' quarters to capture a Cuban or a Soviet. If we capture one of them then we can show him to the world. Remember this, white men take the lives of other white men seriously. Whites in this war are not supposed to be shot; they are supposed to be captured so that the world might know of the atrocities being committed against us.'

Raul continued by explaining how the attack would end. He said repeatedly that civilian casualties were to be avoided. As soon as he stopped talking a soldier began to chant a song. They all stomped and held their Kalashnikovs high.

On the journey to Kalonga the soldiers said very little to each other. When they did speak it was in whispers. The signal man, a short fellow called Kadimba, walked by Raul's side. He was listening out for any message that might come from headquarters.

The wind began to blow hard. Now and then the soldiers would come across a flock of impalas or a herd of elephants. None of them was allowed to shoot. They came to a marshland. The tracks created by the elephants here looked as though several tractors had been at work. They had to cross the marshland. Raul felt cold water seep into his boots. He hoped that no leech would work its way in. They were moving across in Indian file. The guerrillas hated the marshlands for there was no camouflage against aerial attack. After several hours, Raul told the men to rest. Orders were issued that no fires should be lit, for the enemy, who had obviously been sending out patrol squads, might learn of their position. Raul's body-guards came closer to him. If the commander fell, then the whole operation was doomed.

At around three in the morning they came to a point where

the final preparations were to be made. At this point someone was heard loading his rifle. Raul asked angrily who had made the noise. No one knew. It had come from some bushes not far away. Two men were sent to find out who it was, but they found no one. The soldiers remained silent, waiting for orders from Raul. Then someone reported that he had smelt a cigarette nearby. They knew now that the enemy was at hand.

Later, Raul remembered what happened next only vaguely. The first thing he heard was a thump. Then a soldier yelled out, '*Ha maim we ndifila nhe?*' – Mother, what am I dying for? And then bullets began to rattle all around. His soldiers did not panic. Single shots would have frightened them for they would have wondered where the snipers were, but now they knew for sure that they had been ambushed.

Raul fell to the ground. He felt cold and his legs ached. He looked around and saw several soldiers lying dead. Their guns had been taken. Raul summoned all the energy he could and stood up. He found it hard to walk because his legs were still aching, but he struggled on till sunset. Then he came across a tall, tough-looking villager. The man showed no surprise when he saw Raul.

Raul said: 'I am lost, father. Please help me.'

The man screwed up his face and said: 'Who are you?'

'Ask later. Now I need some water, please.'

The man gave Raul water and honey. Raul felt better at once. He turned to the man and said: 'You saved my life, father.'

The man shook his head and said: 'It was the power of God, my son. I always meet skeletons in the forest. It is hard to tell whether the soldier belongs to UNITA or the MPLA. They just lie there. The other day I met a boy who had been killed in some confrontation near Lombe. He was refusing to rot: grass had grown through him. How much more death are we going to see in this country?'

The man took Raul to the nearest UNITA base. The person in charge of the base, a sergeant, could not believe it when he saw Raul. He told him that he had already been added to the list of heroes, of patriots who had died for the motherland. The sergeant radioed regional headquarters about Raul's reappearance and a torrent of messages saluting Raul soon arrived.

Hosi had been listening attentively all along. Raul shrugged and said: 'That is my story, brother. Here I am now, an invalid, a hero confined to a wheelchair.'

Hosi smiled and said: 'But you are alive. That is the most important thing.'

Raul nodded and said: 'Alive and miserable. Please, Hosi, if ever you get to see Lila, tell her that I need my notebook. That is all that matters to me, my notebook. Please do everything to get it. If I die, please keep the notebook and try to have it published so that future generatons might read the thoughts of an Angolan patriot.'

Hosi said: 'Now tell me about the reasons that made Lila leave you.'

Raul smacked his lips and said: 'It's a long story. Where do I begin?'

18

At last it was clear that Hosi would go for military training. He felt relaxed. He no longer thought of being sent abroad but dreamt of battlefields, tanks and jet fighters.

One afternoon he was lying on his bed reading Clausewitz's *The Art of War*. Earlier in the morning Herculano had warned him to be wary of books. 'There is only one correct thought,' he had said, 'and that is the Elder's thought.' Hosi had paid no attention to him.

Yet Hosi could not concentrate on the book because there were too many things on his mind. He thought of Raul and his story. He admired Raul, admired his courage and faith in the cause, and he felt slightly inferior to Raul, because although he too had a story to tell, it was not as harrowing as Raul's. But there was also a part of him that did not admire Raul all that much and that part kept telling him that Raul and people like him had been sacrificed in vain. They were patriots and would be eulogized in political speeches, praised in poems written by the Elder and recited by beautiful girls, applauded but then forgotten. Hosi hated his own cynicism but it stuck in his mind.

According to the voice in him, all this applied not only to the people on the UNITA side but also to the people on the MPLA side. Only the other day he had heard a journalist say on the BBC that there were several young men in Huambo and Luanda who had had their legs amputated after stepping on landmines after an ambush. These too would be forgotten. And then there would be the final day when the fighting came to an end, the day when one side would have won. So many people would have died but the only solution would be to shake hands and hope for a better future.

Hosi's thoughts were interrupted by Herculano, who burst into the room, stood with arms akimbo and said: 'Tonight there will be hell in the pavilion.'

'Why?'

'It's the Elder's birthday. It's a national holiday. You are somewhere else. How can you call yourself an intellectual and a patriot if you do not know the date the Elder was born?'

'So what will happen?'

'Women, young women and girls, will be in abundance. Not only that. This is one of the few times of the year when the ordinary people of Angola are allowed to drink.'

Herculano asked Hosi to accompany him to the place where a special brew, made by fermenting a kind of juice supplied by the South African army, was being served. The brew was served from a water carrier that had been captured from a town under MPLA control. There were several men before the water carrier when Hosi and Herculano arrived. Each was holding a can and they had formed an orderly queue. There was a military policeman nearby. He held a baton in one hand and a can in the other. Since his return to Angola, Hosi did not remember having seen so many Angolans with genuine, hearty, beaming smiles on their faces.

The consumption of alcohol was frowned upon by the Elder. One of his closest aides was once heard saying that with blacks there was no moderation in drinking habits: either they became alcoholics or they remained teetotallers. The people had not taken this comment well and on the day this aide was demoted and sent to some remote area in the north, there was much rejoicing.

Petronella, a thin woman with very dark skin who did the brewing, walked majestically past the men. They all looked at her affectionately. She was smoking a cigarette the way washer-ladies used to under the Portuguese – that is, the lighted tip was burning in her mouth and the butt was pointing out. The men thought she was very sophisticated.

Herculano got his fill of the VA (Viva Angola) brew and the two walked back to the guesthouse. After a few cups, Herculano went on about the son he had left in Zaire. Then they

150

went to the pavilion, where speeches in praise of the Elder were being read. Most of the men had drunk some of Petronella's beverage and they were very happy. They clapped the speeches loudly and when they were ordered to cheer, they responded as though they expected UNITA to be in Luanda the next day.

People from all over the territory had gathered in the pavilion. Everyone was anxious to start dancing, but the dance would not begin until midnight – the exact moment the Elder was said to have been born.

Hosi began to take an interest in the girls. While in Zambia, he had never been attracted to Angolan girls, because they were kept secluded by the elders, who were worried that Zambian men would marry them. Also, Hosi and his contemporaries wanted Zambian citizenship and the only way to get it was to marry a Zambian girl. By marrying an Angolan girl, they would not only continue as refugees but also be unable to get work.

Soon the people in the pavilion began to divide themselves according to their position in the movement. There was a dais at one end of the pavilion. Members of the movement's leadership had not yet come, so it was empty, but there was a long table there with bottles of J & B whisky and plates of spicy meats. Next to the table sat the wives of the members of the movement's leadership.

Derogatory remarks were often made by members of the public about the wives of the movement's leadership. People said they were more interested in chiffon dresses than in seeing Angola free.

Next to the wives of the movement's leadership sat several attractive young girls. These were the official dancing partners of the leaders of the movement. Their relationship to the leaders of the movement was not confined to the dancing floor; it extended to bed. These girls were supplied with perfumes, chiffon dresses, hot combs to stretch out their hair and creams to smooth their skins. They were despised by low-ranking bachelors, who viewed them as snobs and opportunists, and by the official wives of the leaders of the

151

movement as prostitutes who would eventually snatch their husbands.

The cheerleader, a short, bearded man, walked forward and asked the people to join him in singing a song in praise of the Elder. The people responded lackadaisically. The cheerleader waved his arms and said: 'Nonsense! We are not going to celebrate the old man's birthday like this. Come on, inject some force into the singing. We should show the world that we are a blessed people. Come on . . ."If I had a child . . .".'

'"I'd name him after the Elder,"' the crowd chanted back.

At midnight fireworks were set off. People began to shout almost in a frenzy. The bands which were at one end of the pavilion belted out a deafening tune. Everyone was shouting that only the Elder could save the Angolan people.

Then the dancing began. The first songs were reserved for the leaders. Their official dancing partners would sidle up to the dais and pose. Then the members of the movement's leadership would take their pick. The soldiers were amazed by this. Most men had almost to go down on bended knees and beg to get a woman to dance. Not with the members of the movement's leadership: women posed for them instead. UNITA, they said, is great!

After seven songs the floor was opened to the public. There was pandemonium. All the soldiers rushed to the women and girls and pulled them on to the floor. Some of the girls refused to dance. This led to several heated arguments. The police came forward and told the soldiers to move on and find some other partners. There were foreign journalists around and it was important that the people behaved themselves. But Petronella's services were now having results and people's behaviour was not at its best. Two drunken men were dancing with each other. A policeman came and hit each of them on the head and said: 'Two men dancing with each other? What are you going to be up to next?'

Men were frantically asking for dances from women. One soldier was turned down three times. He walked over to Hosi, patted him on the back and said: 'Who the hell do those bitches think they are? I mean, Jamba is filled with girls that

152

have vowed not to dance with someone below the rank of captain. Bitches! Man, you know that we men scratch our balls to impotence crawling under enemy fire while these bitches are being fucked. And then they think they are too good for us!' Hosi shook his head in sympathy. The soldier moved on.

Hosi had two dances with a girl from the secondary school. As they danced, Hosi tried to strike up a conversation, without success. Then he was approached by a stout, attractive woman who exuded authority. She had been dancing with high-ranking officers. She stood in front of him and said: 'I am Lila. I hope that Raul told you about me.'

Hosi nodded and smiled. 'Come on, let's dance!' said Lila.

As they were dancing, Hosi said: 'Raul told me a lot about you. When are you getting married?'

Lila smiled and said: 'Oh, some day.'

They danced for a while without saying another word to each other. Then Lila said: 'What else did Raul tell you?'

'Everything. Why do you ask?'

'Because I think you are the only person he can trust.'

'You might be right.'

'I know it. You see, everyone here is contaminated. There are no political virgins here. We've been through so much. We believe that we are fighting for a just cause. People from abroad bring with them a degree of scepticism. They question things. We all wish in private that we could question things, but we can't. We've survived horrible bombardments. There is no other way about it. We just have to be right and we will also make sure that those that are making us suffer now will pay for it.'

Hosi was paying so much attention to what Lila was saying that he began to miss the dancing steps. A boy soldier wielding a Kalashnikov came over and said to Lila: 'Brigadier Quintao has sent for you.'

Lila turned to Hosi and said: 'I will be back soon. Don't vanish. I know the brigadier there wants to have a dance with me.' She excused herself and left. Hosi nodded. As she walked away, she swung her buttocks about as if she was listening to some secret rhythm inside her.

A slow number was playing. Hosi walked off the dance floor and sat on a bench. Men held the girls very tightly. The older women had all gone by now. Some of the men danced with closed eyes and had blissful expressions on their faces. The girls leant on to the men's chests, their eyes dreamy.

Lila came back. She asked Hosi to escort her to her house. Hosi accepted reluctantly. The night was very dark. Lila walked in front of him with a torch. He wanted to engage her in conversation but Lila said talking in the dark was not good because they could be overheard.

Hosi tried to make out what Lila was like. From what Raul had told him, Lila was supposed to be the new woman, one to whom nothing but the revolution mattered. And yet the woman before him came across not only as sensitive but also as overly cautious.

At last they got to Lila's house. It was made of reeds and was small, with a sitting room and a bedroom. Lila switched the lights on and Hosi saw a huge portrait of the Elder. Next to it was a smaller portrait of the Elder. Lila told Hosi to sit on the wooden chair. She went into the bedroom and came back with a bottle of whisky. She asked Hosi to join her but he refused.

'Now, don't be a hypocrite,' Lila said.

'I really can't. I wish that I could, but alcohol symbolizes something for me.'

'What?'

'Failure.'

'I agree. But you are an intellectual and you must know how to take it moderately.'

Hosi smiled. Lila sat opposite him and said: 'I have to tell you this, I won't have anything to do with Raul. He has been writing frantic letters asking for his notebook but I won't give it to him.'

'Notebook?' Hosi asked.

'Yes, when I found out that he was a traitor, I left him and stole his notebook. I thought it contained information that could be used by the authorities. But there is practically nothing in it.'

'I deplore what Raul did, but I think he deserves some compassion,' said Hosi. 'We have to understand that he is only human and, like you and me, capable of mistakes.'

Lila shrugged and said: 'You won't go far with that kind of reasoning. What we are dealing with are people's lives. The main question in our lives is whether we will become free or not. I am sure that some people on the other side have come to believe the MPLA propaganda and think that we are rebels. They think this is an insurrection. So we have to carry this battle to the very end or we'll die. We have to flush out the weaklings and traitors among us. Raul is as dangerous as a 2,000-kilo napalm bomb. You know what I called him when we last met?' Hosi shook his head. 'I called him a heap of flesh. And indeed that is what he is; he has no soul.'

'So you lied when you said you would marry him?'

'Spending the night in the same bed as a traitor is like spending a night with the devil. I walked away from him and I don't want anything to do with him. Any woman who involves herself with a traitor stains her life.'

Hosi frowned and said: 'Stain your life?'

Lila smiled and said: 'Yes, stain your life. You see, we are living in a kind of political paradise. Your standing is determined by your deeds and the people you associate yourself with. If you associate with evil, then people will start thinking that there is evil in you, however hard you try to distance yourself from it. I am in love with Brigadier Quintao because he is a very brave man.'

'I thought Brigadier Quintao was a married man?'

'So what?'

'Well, I am not very keen on polygamy.'

'But it is part of our African heritage. Just because we live in the modern age and we are trying to be modern does not mean that we have discarded our past. Quintao has three other wives. They all love him because he is a revolutionary. Reactionaries are never loved in this land. No romance for them. That is a fact.'

Hosi looked straight at Lila and said: 'This frightens me.'

Lila smiled and said: 'Why? Are you a reactionary?'

155

'No. I think the term reactionary is meaningless. In Africa a reactionary is one who has fallen out of grace with the ruling élite, or someone who challenges ideas that are considered sacred.'

Lila waved her arms and said: 'You're mistaken. A reactionary is someone who goes against the will of the people.'

'Ah, the people. I hear it all the time – the people, the masses, the public. It is all nonsense.'

'What do you mean?'

'There is no such thing as the people's will. At least in Africa.'

'Why not?'

'Because the people are there to be manipulated. The people are thick. That is it.'

Lila frowned and said: 'Am I talking to a reactionary? The people thick? Is that what you said?'

'Yes. In Africa the people are stupid. We still have a long way to go. Look at this. In some African countries when a regime is overthrown ministers are executed in public. After the shooting, the people – yes, the masses – go forward and begin to spit on the bodies of those who have been shot. A few years after there is another coup and the same people will be ready to go forward and spit again on the bodies of those who have been deposed. Yet these are the same people who go to airports and get heart attacks under the burning sun dancing for their dictators, the same people who confer life-presidencies on their dictators, the same people who applaud when they hear that their dictators have mansions in Europe and have sent their children to be educated abroad. They never stand up and say: "Right, we've had enough. Let's have stable governments and not rulers that become philosopher-kings as soon as they step into the state house."'

Lila shook her head and said: 'Honestly, you sound like some reactionary white South African.'

'How should I sound, then?'

'Like a revolutionary or a patriot, a Pan-Africanist. Like someone who has faith in the people. Have you heard of negritude? Try and understand it. I am sure that the whites would love to hear you say all this. It would confirm their prejudices about Africa and black race.'

Hosi hesitated for a while, then said: 'I really don't care what the whites think of us. They might think that we are primitive or that we are cultured in our own way. That is their business. What concerns me is what is happening to us. You shout at the whites and say: "Stop calling us primitive or we'll fix you." Very well, they'll shut up. And then they'll hear that there is another coup in Africa or that some dictator like Amin is eating his enemies. The whites will be laughing at us between their bedsheets while giving us the impression that they can see only positive aspects in us. Meanwhile, our prisons will be filling with reactionaries, as you call them, and our development will be retarded. That is it, my sister.'

Lila chuckled and said: 'I can't be your sister. Our views are kilometres apart. Anyway, who filled you with all these ideas?'

'Nobody. I just think for myself.'

'Listen to me. I am in love with Brigadier Quintao because he is a brave man. He does not fear to die for his people.'

Hosi smiled and said: 'I really don't believe in polygamy. I will have one wife – that is all.'

'Why?'

'Because I am a terrible romantic. I believe in love. In pure, poetic love as in the time of Plato. For all the rhetoric going around in the world, there is still that part of us that we are not able to understand, the part that inspires romance. Love will save the world. That is true, my sister.'

'I agree with you. Indeed, I am your sister. But it is not your type of love that will save the world. It is pure love. Love for the people, love for the movement, for the leader and for Africa.'

The two were silent for a while and then Lila said: 'Tell me, what would you do if you had a girl?'

'I'd read her some poetry. There are some Shakespeare sonnets that are just wonderful. Take this line: "Shall I compare thee to a summer's day?" Then I'd kiss her and give her a thousand orgasms in five minutes.'

Lila burst out laughing. Then she suddenly rushed into the

bedroom. She said she needed to listen to the news on the Voice of America. Hosi was surprised because he knew of no Portuguese news bulletin at that hour. Lila called out to him: 'I can't find the station. Come over here and help me find it.'

Hosi walked into the bedroom. In one corner was an AK47 rifle and a rucksack. Next to it was a box on which several books lay. Lila sat on one side of the bed, looking at the radio. Hosi walked past her to pick up the radio. She told him that the station she was looking for was on shortwave three. She then told him to put the radio down and sit by her side. The two sat still for an instant.

Hosi said: 'Lila, can you give me Raul's notebook?'

'No.'

'Why?'

'Well, I think Raul is a pseudo-intellectual. He has not understood the struggle. His so-called reflections are shallow and worthless.'

'But let me see them.'

'No. I don't want to be a purveyor of intellectual trash.'

It was then that Hosi smelled Lila's breath, a mixture of sweets and alcohol. He began to find her irresistible. She suddenly began to cry, rocking backwards and forwards and saying: 'I have no father, I have no mother, I am lonely and I have been through so much, so much.'

Hosi did not know how to react to this. He extended his arm and stroked her back. She began to cry again. Hosi felt sexually aroused but also embarrassed. Then Lila took his hand and placed it on her left breast. 'Squeeze it,' Lila said softly. He squeezed. Lila turned to him and said: 'Did you feel any scar on my breast?' Before he could respond, she smiled and said: 'That was caused by a fragment from a bomb. I almost died.' She turned around and pulled up her dress. She placed Hosi's hand on a spot next to her navel. He could feel that there was a scar there too. Lila said: 'That was a bullet from the enemy.' Then she said: 'What else did Raul tell you?'

'Everything. Why do you ask?' He wondered what she wanted from him. Was it sex or compassion? He settled on the latter and continued stroking Lila. She lay on the bed sobbing, talking of the many people she had once known who were now dead. She then got up, walked over to the sitting room and ordered Hosi to leave. 'Quintao might be coming,' she said.

Hosi kissed her and said: 'Please can you give me Raul's notebook?'

'Leave. Never ask me for the notebook again or I will call the military police.'

Hosi left at once.

19

The following day a parade was to be held at the infantry battalion stadium to celebrate the Elder's birthday. Early in the morning a man went round with a megaphone telling people that they were to gather at the stadium at nine o'clock. That actually meant that the programme would not start until twelve or one o'clock. He reminded everyone that as there would be foreign journalists present it was imperative that they all behave themselves properly.

Herculano told Hosi that a Land-Rover would come to take them to the stadium. It came just before eleven, by which time most people had already set off. When they got to the stadium Hosi could not believe his eyes: there were so many people, hundreds upon hundreds of them. He suddenly began to think that Lila had a valid point when she said that the UNITA cause was not only just but also noble. How could all these people have been misled? That was not possible. These were the people who had been oppressed and had come to join UNITA. They believed profoundly that UNITA would liberate them.

By eleven o'clock, the programme was ready to begin. Speech after speech was read. Then a group of traditional dancers came forward. Next a group of boys stepped up to recite chunks from the Elder's speeches. After that a girl recited one of his poems. A company of well-drilled soldiers came forward and did a marching routine. People were so impressed by their drill that they went on clapping for long after the marching had finished. The trousers of one of the commandos tore at the buttocks, but fortunately, none of the foreign journalists saw the incident.

Then the Elder himself came and gave a long speech. Several

tanks that had been captured from the enemy went past the dais. They were followed by a group of prisoners, dressed in grey trousers and black T-shirts. This was the closest Hosi had come to MPLA soliders. It struck him that not only were they black but also they looked like people he had known. He thought this was not so absurd after all: Osvaldo, his brother, was in the MPLA. Over the years he had heard so much about MPLA soldiers that he had begun to think of them almost as extra-terrestrial beings, but he suspected that there were Angolan patriots in the MPLA who thought the same of UNITA.

Once the prisoners had gone past the field, a football match was to be held. A team named after the Elder's birthday was going to play against a team named after his mother's birthday. It was at this point that Hosi decided to have a closer look at the prisoners. He thought that he would perhaps meet Osvaldo or someone who knew him. He wondered whether people were allowed to talk to them.

They had been herded into a clearing, where they sat on tree trunks with vacant expressions on their faces. They were surrounded by fierce-looking military policemen who had machine guns. Hosi walked over to the prisoners and asked a policeman for permission to talk to them. The man was startled and said that only his senior officer, who was standing nearby, could make such a decision. An old woman dressed in *chitengue* garments was having a heated argument with the police chief at that moment.

'I just want to talk to that boy. I know him,' the woman was saying angrily.

'But he is a prisoner,' the policeman retorted.

'I don't care. I know him. I was the midwife at that boy's birth.'

'He's not a boy. He was a lieutenant in the MPLA airforce. He was shot down at Kazombo. He is not normal.'

The old woman shook her head and said: 'I just have to talk to him. I have assisted at the birth of many people. Several of these people you now call brigadiers and colonels came into this world in these hands. I will tell you one thing. These

161

hands you see over here have assisted in the birth of four pairs of twins. They are all living. What are you telling me? I have been a midwife for thirty years. I really don't care about your silly politics. Now, that is a baby that came to these hands. I need to talk to him.'

The prisoner was looking at the old woman anxiously. She threw her arms into the air, thumped her chest, knelt down and even snorted to make her point. The policeman wiggled his index finger at Hosi, who stepped forward. The policeman said: 'Now, what do you want?'

'I want to talk to those guys,' Hosi said.

'You mean the prisoners?'

'Yes.'

'I can't understand this. How can you people come and say you want to talk to prisoners just like that? This is anarchy!'

The old woman said: 'Don't use such words with me. Just let me talk to that boy.'

The policeman scowled and said: 'None of you can talk to the prisoners. Off you go!'

'Either I talk to that boy or I will take off my clothes.'

The policeman began to sweat. Hosi was enjoying this. The old woman frowned and stood still. The policeman asked her to follow him. Hosi sidled up behind them. They were led to another high-ranking officer. The policeman explained to the officer what Hosi and the woman wanted to do and after thinking for a while, the officer said there was nothing wrong in letting them talk to the prisoners as long as it was done in the presence of the policeman. The old woman leapt with joy.

The three walked back to the prisoners, and the old woman went straight to the prisoner she wanted to talk to. She hugged him. He began to cry.

The old woman said: 'Who is your mother?'

'Marcelas Campos,' the prisoner answered.

'Campos? Where are you from?'

'Maquela do Zombo.'

'So you're Bakongo?'

'Yes.'

'I thought you were from Dondi. Don't worry. You look

162

exactly like Delfina's son. I am a midwife. Many babies have passed through these hands. Some of them are in the MPLA, others in UNITA. I don't care. They all passed through these hands.'

The prisoner kept nodding, tears in his eyes. The old woman looked at him straight and said: 'Do you believe in God?'

The prisoner nodded and said: 'Yes.'

The old woman smiled and nodded. The policeman said: 'That is enough. Now leave the man in peace. Please, mama, go away.'

The old woman turned to Hosi and said: 'And who are you?'

'Hosi Mbueti. I have just come from Zambia.'

'Come here with me. Tell me more about yourself.'

Hosi walked over to the old woman. She embraced him and asked him to have lunch with her. At first Hosi hesitated, but the old woman insisted so Hosi gave in. As they walked on, Hosi told her that he intended to become a writer some day. The old woman was very impressed by the idea.

The old woman's name was Teresa, and she was known by most people as Aunt Teresa. She lived near the Central Hospital because she was the best midwife in the UNITA-controlled area. If a woman about to give birth was told that Aunt Teresa would be present during her labour, she felt very secure. Many said that Aunt Teresa was in some respects better qualified than a doctor who had been to medical school. Nobody knew her age; bureaucrats who tried to find out were told to shut up at once. 'What is going on in the world?' old Teresa would ask. 'Little boys who came into my hands only yesterday asking how old I am. I won't tell you.'

Although she was careless with her mouth, Aunt Teresa was loved by everyone. She was also highly respected and children included her name in the lines they hummed while skipping. This had sparked off a fierce debate among the Jamba politicos. They said no person other than the Elder could be included in play-songs, otherwise little children would have no sense of direction. Others argued that since Teresa was such a loved, progressive figure, she deserved to be sung about. The song had been banned, but Teresa had threatened to strip herself naked if the decision was not revoked. It was scrapped at once.

It was very hot. There were several people on the road that led from the stadium to the hospital. As they walked, people would come and say a few words to Teresa. Some would joke with her; others would simply remark how beautiful her head-gear was, whereupon she would tell them at length how she had come by it: 'Oh. It was given to me by Marta. Now, Marta is the daughter of Eurico, who married Delfina. Now Delfina and I went to the same school. Beautiful woman. She married the teacher, Demosthenes – that man could sing. If you got him on tenor, Jeremias on the bass and Mateus on soprano, you'd look around and see people in the church in tears. Yes. Marta gave me this headgear.'

Teresa lived in a tent. She ordered Hosi to sit on a wooden chair. There were bundles and bundles of things all around, with no clue as to what they contained. There was a little kitchen outside. Teresa went out to light the fire, then came back and said it would not be long before lunch was ready.

Teresa sat on the bed and said: 'Tell me, son, what is going on in the world? They gave me a radio but I just can't understand the news. I asked someone to fix it on the Trans-world radio in Swaziland. They have services in Umbundu at night. Good people, they are giving us the word of God. I will never move the pointer from that because I survive on those services. Tell me, what is going on in the world?'

Hosi said: 'A lot, aunt. They are planning an offensive. But, as you know, it won't work.'

The old woman held her head and said: 'More blood, more blood. How much more blood are we going to spill?' She looked heavenwards and said 'Father, haven't we had enough?'

Just then a girl outside called: 'Grannie, what are you cook-ing?'

'Ah, Perola, I have a visitor from Zambia over here. Cook some good food.' Teresa turned to Hosi and said: 'That is Perola. She is the daughter of Amelia and Teodoro.'

164

Teresa fetched an old Bible. She flipped through it and stopped at a page, turned to Hosi and said: 'This is Matthew 24. Now listen to this: "And ye shall hear of wars and rumours of wars: see that ye be not troubled: for all these things must come to pass, but the end is not yet. For nation shall rise against nation, and kingdom against kingdom: and there shall be famines, and pestilences, and earthquakes, in divers places."'

Teresa closed the Bible and kissed it. She kissed it again and said: 'This is the truth. Son, there are many ideas going around in Angola. We hear of Marxism here and Maoism there. And now they are comparing our leader to Moses. What all these people have forgotten is that the truth can be found only in this book. Famines? Someone told me the other day that thousands of people have died of hunger somewhere in Africa. Has that not been foretold in this book?'

Hosi nodded. Teresa continued: 'The truth is that we are the chosen people. Yes, we the Ovimbundu. We are the chosen people. We are just like the Israelites. God is annoyed with us. I will tell you why. Under the Portuguese many of our people – that is, we the Ovimbundu – strayed from the proper path. The late Pastor Kangunga warned us, but we were too stubborn to take him seriously. People used to kill babies and bury them in their wheat fields in order to have large harvests. Married men used to sleep with other men's wives. People used to drink, including church elders. In the pulpit they would say to the people, don't drink moonshine because it is bad for your lungs. But at funerals or weddings they would get into a bedroom, close the door and treat themselves to Cinzano. God was watching! Now we are being punished for it. But it is too much – I mean the blood. I work at the hospital and sometimes I see lorries bringing young people who have been wounded. My heart bleeds. I often say to God, we've had enough. It is now their turn to suffer.'

'Whose turn?' Hosi asked.

'The northerners. God writes straight in crooked lines. I know that he has not forgotten us. The northerners are sinners. I am told that they believe in Karl Marx, who says there is no

God. They have bought MiGs to come and bomb us to death. The boys at the hospital tell me that they also have these helicopters which look like bees. They spill death. I was at Luangundu during the 1979 offensive. Only the devil could have done such a thing. We went for days without food. Many people died.'

Teresa wiped a tear from her right eye. They were silent for a while and then she continued: 'Mbueti, I must tell you that I will die very soon.'

'Why?' Hosi asked.

'I am old and I don't think I will survive this war. That is why I prefer to listen to Transworld radio. At least I am in touch with my creator.'

Perola came in with their lunch – corned beef and maize gruel. She was tall and very shy. She smiled at Hosi. Teresa said: 'Ah, Mama. Thank you very much for the meal. Make sure that you've put aside enough for yourself. Some of us have had enough in life and do not deserve to eat more. Now, don't just go without greeting your elder brother. Come on, greet him.'

Perola went forward and kissed Hosi on the cheeks. Teresa turned to her and said: 'Have you seen Grandpa Geronimo?'

'No. I think he is gone with Grandpa Kadimba,' Perola answered and then she left.

Hosi and Teresa began to eat. Teresa said: 'Geronimo is my husband. Things are not very fine, but I don't care. I love him and I know that he loves me too.'

'That is very good,' said Hosi. 'Love is important. But why aren't things fine?'

Teresa chuckled and said: 'It is a long story but I will tell you. My first husband, a teacher, Aurelio Kapingala, died in 1957, the year Abilio, my last son, was born. I loved him very much. I came to know him at Dondi. I was then at the MINS Institute. He used to work in the factory where religious tracts were produced. He died mysteriously. One morning he complained of chest pains; in the evening he was gone. Some people said it was witchcraft. What else could you expect from us? But I am a Christian and I said: "Well, the Lord called

166

him." Then one day Aurelio came to see me in a dream. He was dressed in a black suit and had a Bible in his left hand. He pointed his finger at Geronimo's house. Geronimo had just lost his wife, Emaculada. She had died of tuberculosis. I said to myself: what does this dream mean? I could not fathom the meaning. Some people would have rushed to the witch doctor. Not me. I sat down and prayed hard. I said to God: "Please give me the answer." Then the following morning Geronimo came to me and said he wanted to marry me. That was in 1963: I am sure that you were not yet born then.'

Hosi nodded.

Teresa continued: 'I said: "No." Geronimo said: "Teresa, you are a widow and I am a widower. We'll make a good couple." I said: "Please get this right. I do not love you. I have heard a lot of things about you, but I won't go into it." Geronimo said: "Tell me, or I will ask the church elders to convene a special meeting to discuss these allegations." I was frightened so I told Geronimo that some people had said that he had become wealthy due to a little snake which he sent to steal from Portuguese merchants. Geronimo was annoyed. He even threatened to beat me. I said: "Please, there will be a scandal. Don't do it." Geronimo left feeling very annoyed. The following day I wrote him a letter apologizing. He accepted my apology at once but still kept coming to ask me to marry him. He was a very understanding man and I also discovered that he was very religious. In the evening he would come and we'd chat for a long time. He seemed to know a lot of things. He was the only man I knew who knew the whole Book of Psalms by heart. I told you earlier that we the Ovimbundu had become sinners. I am no exception. The devil is powerful; he works in different ways. Soon I began to love Geronimo and he began to spend nights at my place. He showered me with presents.

'Now I was very close to Geronimo and people had become suspicious. The church elders were suspicious too. They suspected that something was going on between Geronimo and me. One of the most vocal church elders was Adao. He was as old as I am now, and half-deaf. May he rest in peace! Adao and his fellow elders met and said: "No, there is something fishy going on between Geronimo and Teresa." Adao said he would investigate our relationship. In those days the church had power. If it was found out that we were having an affair, Geronimo would have had serious problems. His name – and mine – would have been stained for ever.

'Adao decided that there was one way he could find out about our affair. He was going to climb the tree in front of my house late at night and observe Geronimo come in and out. The church elders, as I later came to discover, had said that it was better if this was done by a healthy, young man, but Adao had refused and insisted on doing it himself. You see, Ovimbundu men can be very stubborn, especially when they are old. So old Adao began climbing the huge mango tree in front of my house, hoping to catch Geronimo. After the fifth day, Adao was lucky. I was kissing Geronimo good night when I heard someone cry from the tree: "Geronimo, stop. I have caught you, stop." Geronimo began to tremble. I too began to tremble. Adao stared at us and said: "Ah, now I have caught you." Geronimo said: "Old Adao, you are an elder of not only the village but also the church. You've caught me. There is nothing we can do apart from prepare for tomorrow, when we can talk things over." Adao agreed.'

Teresa coughed and shifted position. She shook her head and then said: 'My son, the devil was at work. As soon as Adao left, Geronimo said to me that I must lie at the meeting that was going to be held the following day. He told me that I should say that it was actually the opposite that had happened – that is, I was supposed to say that it was Adao that had been after me and that Geronimo had come to my rescue. I agreed to do this. Indeed, the following morning in the meeting I said it was Adao who had been after me and that Geronimo had come to tell him to keep away from me. Now, Adao was a bit deaf and did not understand everything that was said in the meeting. Not only that. He was dozing for most of it. At the end of the meeting a prayer was said. It was said by Pastor Frei, the brother of Alvertina Sachipangele, who, I am now told, lost a leg after stepping on a landmine. God, Angola,

168

how much more blood? Anyway, Pastor Frei closed his eyes and said: "Lord, we are confused. We do not know what to believe. Only you know the truth."

'They later discovered that we had lied because Geronimo was found again in my house. We were both expelled from the church. It was very shameful. Geronimo decided to leave for Huambo and asked me to come with him. I refused. There was no midwife at the hospital and I felt I had to help the people. Geronimo went to marry a woman from the north. I asked to be forgiven. They refused at first. Then I threatened that I would convert to Catholicism, and they gave in and accepted me. That was it. From then on I heard very little of Geronimo.

'Then there was the war and we all came to the bush. That was when I met Geronimo again. He approached me and said: "Teresa, this time we must marry." I hesitated at first. Then, you won't believe this, my first husband came in a dream. He pointed again to the direction of Geronimo's house and nodded. Before he left I cried out to him. I said: "Can I marry this man?" The teacher nodded and said: "Yes." When Geronimo came again to ask for marriage I agreed. He was very pleased. There were, however, several problems with my sons and daughters. I have five and they all live in the UNITA-controlled area. Ezequiel, the eldest of them, was the most vocal. He said: "Mum, you're too old to marry again." I looked straight at him and said: "Mind your own business. If I am in love, I am in love." He said: "But, Mum, people are talking. They are laughing at you, saying: 'Look at those two old people who are in love.'" I looked straight at him again and said: "I am not living for people; I am living for God and myself." Ezequiel said: "Mum, don't embarrass us, please don't marry that Geronimo. If you marry him, I will never talk to you." Then he left.

'There was only one person who supported me. That was Mariana, my second daughter. She said: "Mum, don't pay any attention to these people who are saying that you're old. You should do what you think is best for yourself." But above all, I decided to consult the master himself – Jehovah. I prayed in the morning, in the evening and at night. He put it very loudly and clearly: Geronimo was the man for me!

'But there was another problem: Geronimo had a son, Kasinda. They call him by some funny name now.' Teresa opened the tent's door and shouted: 'Perola, what do they call Kasinda?'

'Gargarin,' Perola shouted back.

'Gargarin, that is it. He is said to be one of the best commanders of the MPLA now. I can't understand. I can't understand some of these young men. They know very well that an Ovimbundu has no place in the MPLA and yet they are prepared to be used by northerners. Yes, young men kept coming to me in secret saying: "Granny, the man you intend to marry is the father of one of the worst sons of Angola. At the battle front when people hear that the other side is commanded by Gargarin, they all start trembling." I told this to Geronimo, who simply shook his head and said: "Don't blame that boy; blame Angola. If you look carefully, the people who are dying most in this country are people from the south." I sympathized with him. In fact, Eurico Lombajo, the son of Celeste, is said to be a high-ranking man in their PIDE. I don't know what it is called.'

Hosi shifted and said: 'I think it is called DISA.'

'Ah, right, DISA. Eurico got into their hands and today he is on the devil's side. I understand Geronimo. So I accepted his proposal. Ah, we had a proper church service. I even wore a veil. Geronimo had a black suit. Many young people came to the service but they were all laughing at us. They have nothing in their heads, let alone in their hearts. If God was to descend on this land we are now living in, he would be very annoyed with us Ovimbundus, and especially with the young people. Almost all the young couples are living in sin. OK, they have their revolutionary marriages where an official comes and says some slogans. That is why their marriages don't last. I will tell you this, son, don't tell it to anyone else. There was a young man, I think his name is Raul. I knew his mother. He survived an enemy attack and then it was discovered that he was a traitor or something. His fiancée, a girl called Lila, was carrying his baby. When it was known that he was traitor, she went straight to the hospital and asked for an abortion. That was because her boyfriend was no longer a hero. In my time that was unheard of – a woman was supposed to stand by her man all the time, come what may. In those days our marriages were united by God and were sacred. My marriage to Geronimo is holy. Some people laugh at us but God up there is nodding. After I got married to Geronimo my sons refused to talk to me. I wept for nights and days. I said to God: "Please make my sons understand me. I love them very much, but I also love Geronimo." Still, my sons never came. Apparently they don't want to associate themselves with Gargarin. They want to be promoted.'

Just then Geronimo was heard outside. He came into the house and smiled as soon as he saw Hosi. He looked frail and old, and walked with a stoop. Still, Hosi noticed, he had a holster into which a revolver had been fitted. Hosi stood up at once and greeted Geronimo.

Teresa said: 'He is going to be a writer. His name is Hosi Mbueti. He has just come from Zambia.'

Geronimo smiled again and said: 'I knew your father. We were both civil servants. Those were the days. Under the Portuguese Angola was a proper country. Now it is ruled by semi-literate sergeants. They will get nowhere.'

'Papa, there goes your mouth again,' said Teresa. 'Learn to control it.'

After a while Hosi left.

20

Miguel Samuel Belshior was said to be a walking history textbook. He had been imprisoned by the Portuguese; had belonged to the MPLA; moved on to the FNLA and eventually ended up with UNITA. Whenever he was asked to talk about the war against the Portuguese, it was as though a valve in him had been loosened – a torrent of facts, including very trivial ones, would flow.

He was a tall, dark man and, despite his advanced age – nobody knew exactly how old he was – he affected a lord-of-the-earth swagger. His skin seemed to tell his life story: it had once been chapped and was now a mixture of roughness and softness. Although he was a major, he insisted on being called Uncle Belshior. When pressed he would say: 'A lot of children whom I saw crawling only yesterday are now brigadiers and colonels. No, I am not on the same footing as them. I am an old man, not a major.'

Part of Hosi's military training included attending Uncle Belshior's history lectures. Most of Hosi's fellow recruits were in their teens, had come from different villages all over Angola and were illiterate. This made him feel slightly uncomfortable. The senior officers insisted that he mingle with the peasants. This, they kept saying, was because 80 per cent of the Angolan population were peasants and Hosi, being young and a future leader, was supposed to know about them. What made Hosi slightly uneasy was that he could not speak Umbundu properly. And he also felt that he did not have a lot to learn from the peasants. He valued their experience and he also knew that they had the ability to survive conditions that he couldn't. But he thought that they had inferior minds.

The last notion frightened him, but he felt it was true. Hosi sought the company of people who would stimulate him, people with whom he could discuss the purpose of existence, poetry, the African identity and international politics. All this was important to him, but still he felt remorseful and hated himself.

One afternoon the recruits were sitting on wooden benches in a huge room made of grass, listening to Uncle Belshior's lecture. They found it was hard to distinguish fact from fiction and indeed Uncle Belshior had once been cautioned and told to teach facts, not his life story. 'Nonsense,' he had replied. 'I have lived through Angolan history. I know what I am talking about.'

Now Uncle Belshior cleared his throat and said: 'Second lecture, the beginning of the struggle. All of you here are my grandchildren. You've seen nothing. I will tell you. Years ago there was the colonialist from Portugal. That is why we have to speak this dreadful language, Portuguese. I suspect that some of you are not aware of the fact that this is not our language. The Portuguese was a horrible man; he was a beast. Now we have other white beasts around – the Cubans and the Soviets. It's now rumoured that there are Koreans too. We also have black beasts – get this right. In another lecture I will tell you about the evil men in the MPLA, FNLA and UNITA too. Yes, evil men in UNITA. I have just recovered from a backache that has taken years to heal. Someone has been trying to bewitch me.'

Uncle Belshior paced about. 'I said the Portuguese was evil. So we decided to overthrow him. There is a lot about him that I will tell you in the future. Meanwhile, I should tell you about UNITA, our party. As you know, it was formed in 1966 . . .'

Then Uncle Belshior explained what had led to the founding of UNITA and talked of the first battles, the first traitors, the first triumphs and the first defeats. The recruits listened attentively. Finally he asked if any of them wanted to ask questions.

Hosi stood up. 'Are we supposed to think of yours as the only correct version of Angolan history?' Hosi asked. Uncle

173

Belshior looked straight at him and began to nod. 'But a person who belongs to the FNLA or the MPLA would give another version of Angolan history. How am I to know which version is correct? Who holds the truth?' He sat down.

Uncle Belshior paced out again, his eyes looking down. He then turned to Hosi and said: 'The truth? The truth belongs to those who have suffered. The truth belongs to those who have stomachs that have moved at the sound of a MiG jet fighter. The truth belongs to the child who died of starvation. The truth belongs to the man who's had his balls squeezed by pliers held by a Soviet or a Cuban interrogator. The truth belongs to the brave man in the trench. He has not eaten anything for two days and when he eats, it will be a cupful of roasted maize. The truth belongs to the woman who is in the family way, being carried on a stretcher. The truth belongs to us. We are the people – and only the people can hold the truth. The truth belongs to UNITA. I have seen many young men come here and try to exercise their intellectual powers. This is not mathematics or logic. This is a war. Blood is flowing. People are being maimed. And there is only one truth – our truth.'

The recruits murmured. Uncle Belshior turned to Hosi, smiled and said: 'Understand, Mbueti?'

Hosi nodded. Uncle Belshior smiled again.

Once the lecture was over the recruits marched to their dormitories, huge adobe edifices with grass roofs. The beds were made of wood with grass for the mattress. As soon as he was in the room Hosi lay on his bed. Next to him slept a gawky fellow who stammered. His name was Joao. He was given to talking in his sleep; Hosi had never heard him but the others said that he went on about how much he missed his mother's sweet potatoes.

Sergeant Ngola, the training officer, came into the dormitory and everybody stood up – some awkwardly, to his obvious displeasure. The sergeant was short and stocky, with a protruding stomach that had split his shirt at the navel (he had replaced the button with a big silver pin). With a stick tucked under his arm he walked across the dormitory, pausing at

174

various recruits and looking at them as if trying to decipher something from their expressions.

'My brothers,' he began. 'I beg you to prepare yourselves. You are all chickens now. We will first turn you into women, and then into men. Understand?'

'Yes!' they answered in unison.

The sergeant nodded. He paced about and said: 'Think properly. If you have the heart of a donkey, please say so. Then we might arrange a proper place for you. There is a shortage of cooks in Jamba, by the way. But in Angola we do not need cooks; we need fighters, men who can defend the cause and the Angolan people. You will be woken at four in the morning every day and made to exercise. I know that most of you have come from the central province and are very thin and weak. I understand that there is very little food up north. But I also know that the Angolan peasant is very lazy. Our time here is not determined by the position of the sun; it is determined by the position of the hands on the clock. The food here is very good, but remember this: a stomach is like a child. You have to discipline it, otherwise it will give you problems. So you should teach it to take as much as you can when there is plenty and as little as possible when there is very little. Right?'

'Yes!'

The sergeant left, but the recruits had to stand up again because Lieutenant Raimundo, the political commissar, then entered the room. He was very handsome, so handsome that one of the recruits had said that if he was a woman he would have married him.

Lieutenant Raimundo said: 'Soon you people will be at the battle front. It is good that you are all young. Angola needs you. The fighting is being carried out by the youth, who will be the sole benefactors of the fruits of the revolution.'

A yawn came from the end of the dormitory and the lieutenant left. Hosi sat quietly on the bed, thinking about his life, till he was interrupted by Carlito, who patted him on the shoulder.

Hosi smiled and said: 'I am thinking about my brother.'

Carlito, who was lean and had a front tooth missing, said: 'I know what everybody else is thinking.'

'What?'

'They are thinking of death. None of us wants to die.'

'Not all people die in war.'

Carlito moved closer to Hosi and said: 'Listen, I have been told that men who have had too much sex are likely to be more cowardly than those who've had no sex. They know what they will be missing if they die. Have you been to bed with a woman?'

'Of course. You not?'

Carlito thumped his chest and said: 'Never. And I will never sleep with a woman.'

'Why?'

'I don't want to be a coward. Angola needs brave men. I will die for my country and make sure that I kill at least one Russian and four Cubans. Tell me, brother. Between a woman and your country, which of the two would you choose?'

Hosi was silent for a while and then said: 'Well, it depends on the woman. If she is an angel, I might choose the woman.' He laughed.

Carlito remained silent, then said: 'Brother, I have to tell you this. Your country is your country. You might be a traitor, a reactionary, a murderer – it is still your country. Your country is like your mother: she can never disown you. As for women, they rush to where their bread is buttered. If the MPLA and the Cubans work their way to Jamba today, they will shoot all the men and spare the women so that they can go and marry them. I will also tell you this. There is a man in Bionge. He was once considered a hero. As soon as it was discovered that he was not a hero, his girl left him. Your country is your country; women are women.'

Hosi said: 'But the country also belongs to women.'

'But they only cause problems! What have these women done to help the resistance? Nothing. They've just been giving men in charge of warehouses headaches. And that is not all. Do you know that the Angolan woman is the worst witch in the world? If you look carefully into the eyes of most Angolan women you will see that they resemble the devil. That is true.'

Hosi burst out laughing and said: 'Come on, who has been pumping all these ideas into you? I think women deserve more affection than the country. It is not love for the country that has made us recruits be trained to go and kill. Love for the country entails anger and intolerance. The more you love your country, the more you are prepared to kill for it. You become a maniac. But love for a woman creates the best in us.' Hosi held his heart: 'I mean poetic, pure love. If you love a woman, then you'll appreciate nature. For women are the breathing flowers of creation. If you love a woman, you will love life, and you will be able to love your country in a different way.'

Carlito shook his head and said: 'You are dangerous. I won't tell this to anyone. If all Angolans thought the way you do we would all be dead by now. Women above the country? No way!'

Carlito left. Hosi only hoped that he would keep silent.

At four in the morning the whistle blew. Groans were heard from all corners of the dormitory. The recruits dressed in the black shorts and T-shirts they had been given the previous night as quickly as they could.

Hosi was reminded of his days at the Zambian secondary school. The recruits were shouting and singing. The sun was not yet up and it was very cold. They had to do their exercises early, because by midday it would be too hot. Once the jogging and the exercises were over, the recruits were told to go and fetch breakfast. A huge shelter, already sooty black, served as the kitchen. In it there were three black drums from which the coffee was dispensed. Hosi stood in one of the three queues, holding a large cup, waiting for his coffee and biscuits.

Carlito was right behind him as they waited. He patted Hosi on the back and said: 'Say, is it true that those South African biscuits are actually meant for dogs?'

'I don't think so; otherwise we would be ill.'

'There is a guy who was heard barking the other night. The coffee also includes some stuff that makes you hate the Cubans more. I tell you, yesterday after coffee you should have been near the latrines. Everyone was grinning "Cuuubaan or Ruuus-siann" while shitting. You can never tell with the Cousins.'

'Cousins?' Hosi asked.

'Yes. That is what we call the South Africans. They are our cousins. It is like having a rich cousin who is a thief. You hate him for his acts but like him for his money.'

Hosi laughed. As the cooks were pouring the coffee and handing out the biscuits, the head cook, a tall, thin man who claimed that he had once cooked for Salazar himself, stood to one side, observing carefully to make sure no one took more than his fair share.

After breakfast the recruits were to be taught about the workings of the Kalashnikov by Second Lieutenant Kaputa, a slender fellow who lisped. Brandishing a rifle, he said: 'This is your mother, your father and your wife. If you are sad, cry to it. If you are happy, dance with it. And if you are frisky, well, do what you can with it. This is your life. This is your freedom and the freedom of your country. There is no louder voice than this. People will not listen to the wisest man on earth; but they will listen to this. Indeed, as the Elder says: "He who has power will rule; and he who has power will make history."'

Pires, the company cheer leader, stood up and said: 'He who has power?'

'Will rule!' they all answered in unison. Pires sat down, smiling.

After that the recruits were taken inside a T55 tank. The instructor said that although it looked harmless, it was actually a horrific machine, and that it was not unknown for soldiers to shit themselves when faced by it. But, he added, nothing would frighten a UNITA soldier.

Supper was served at five o'clock. After that the recruits normally went for lectures around the fire. They had had three lectures so far. One was about the danger of tuberculosis; after that the exchanging of cigarette butts was prohibited. Then there was a lecture about AIDS. The medical assistant said that as there were no condoms in the UNITA territory, the best solution for the soldiers was to abstain from sex. This had been met with several murmurs. One recruit was heard mumbling that the problem they were having was the absence of women, not AIDS.

This night there was no lecture and Hosi was lying in his cold bed. Outside the dormitory the recruits were gathered under a huge tree, talking. After a while they began to sing a very melodious song. It was as if all their sorrows had converged somewhere in their throats and were slowly being poured out.

Hosi left his bed and went to join the others by the fire. He sat on a log. Someone said to him: 'Hey, beware. Men are not supposed to sit on logs. Your bazooka will be rendered useless. See what I mean?' It was Pepeshe, a sly-looking man said to be an expert on herbs. Hosi left the log and sat on an adobe.

Pepeshe shook his head said: 'Now, Mbueti, come over here. Take my stool. You are an educated man. Where is Angola going if future leaders are made to sit on adobes while worthless people like myself sit on stools?'

Hosi declined his offer. Pepeshe said: 'Now, come on, for the sake of the motherland you have to accept this stool.'

Hosi accepted reluctantly, though he felt humiliated. He wanted the other recruits to treat him as an equal. He said: 'I am not the future leader of Angola. I hate politics.'

They all looked at him intently, and one recruit said: 'What do you want to be, then?'

'I want to be a writer, a novelist. I want to dissect the Angolan soul and have it bared to the world.'

They all laughed. Pepeshe said: 'But you can be a writer and a politician. In fact, it is easier to get published if you are a member of the Central Committee.'

'I don't admire politicians. Any fool can be a politician, but it is not anyone that can be a writer. I am told that a lot of the members of the MPLA Central Committee are semi-literate.'

Pepeshe said: 'Well, it is pointless to argue with people who have brains. You end up getting more confused. Just let me continue with what I was saying before you came. I was talking about Lumumba. He was a great man. I don't mean the Zairean Lumumba; but our Angolan Lumumba. He was

179

bullet-proof. Nobody knows the charm he used. When he was killed, he had to be axed to death because no bullet would go through him. I am told that he had once been chopped to pieces by an old Lunda man and cooked. That explains why he was bullet-proof.'

Then Pepeshe described the different herbs that would make a man bullet-proof. He also told the story of another officer who was said to be bullet-proof. Only syphilis had managed to take him away. At some point Pepeshe was interrupted by Bidu, a stout man who spoke infrequently. He said: 'Pepeshe, be careful. From the way you talk, it is as though using herbs in the war is positive. It isn't. Our enemies rely on science. The Russians don't have witch doctors. They have men that use mathematics and other scientific principles to get along.'

'You've got it wrong, my brother. The reason why we are not winning this war is because we want to fight it on their terms. Do you know why the Boers are that powerful? Don't tell me that it is because they are white. Not at all. They are powerful because they always go to battle with a black witch doctor. Take it from me. Where you get a South African battalion you are likely to find a Zulu herbalist.'

Bidu said: 'The problem with us is that we talk too much. Have you ever seen a Zulu witch doctor yourself?'

'Never. But I tell you that Benjamin, who has seen them in action, says they have a witch doctor. How else can you explain the fact that they make the Cubans shit their pants?'

Bidu said: 'If I had my way, I would have made a law here stating that anyone who talks too much should be hanged.'

At this point, several people came to Pepeshe's rescue. They said that if Bidu did not want to hear Pepeshe's story then he should go to sleep. Bidu went silent at once.

After a while, Hosi returned to bed. There he could not fall asleep. He began to think of the long and tortuous Angolan history. He also wondered whether many people before him had felt as sorry for the country as he was feeling. He wondered how many people on the MPLA side had braved cold nights for the love of Angola. He wondered how many MPLA

180

soldiers had walked long distances, believing that they were doing what was best for their country. Hosi thought of Osvaldo and wondered whether he still believed in communism and the equality of all Angolan people. He thought of Junior, who was now reputedly a high-ranking MPLA officer in Huambo.

Hosi's thoughts were painful, for whenever he remembered his childhood, Osvaldo and Junior always crept into his mind, yet now he was being trained to go and fight them. Well, they too had been trained – to fight him. There was no reasoning. Angola had been plunged into war and to be alive now was to believe in fighting.

Hosi thought of Aunt Laura and Kaluanda. He wondered what had happened to Old Pedro. He recalled his teacher, Xavier Ramos. He began to see them all together in his mind. Xavier Ramos, Junior and Osvaldo had aged. They were awaiting Hosi's arrival on a very bright, pleasant day. Some people were singing; others were talking. Kadinguilinha was also coming from Portugal to witness Hosi's arrival. He and several of his friends were to come in a helicopter. The sky was filled with swans. Angola was peaceful and beautiful. There were flowers everywhere. Then the helicopter landed and Hosi was about to greet Osvaldo when he felt something shake him. He started from his reverie. It was Carlito.

Hosi said: 'What do you want?'

'Between your mother and your country which of the two would you choose?'

Hosi shook his head and said: 'Please leave me in peace. I was having a very good dream.'

'Oh, sorry,' said Carlito. 'I will come for the answer tomorrow.'

21

It was rumoured that some of the recruits were to be selected for further training. This was the training that distinguished real soldiers from fighting men. Hosi had heard countless stories about what went on at the training camps. It was said, for instance, that the recruits slept through the day and did most of their training at night. It was so hard that many died from exhaustion or loss of heat.

But it was all still rumour and Hosi and his colleagues had been told on several occasions never to pay any attention to this sort of talk. A rumour monger, it was said, was as evil as a Cuban. Still, rumours kept circulating. One which Hosi found particularly chilling was about the PC7 aircraft, which was said to carry a deadly rocket-launcher. Soldiers would face a helicopter or even a MiG bomber calmly, but as soon as they could hear the PC7 they would all be seized with a fit of diarrhoea.

The news came at last. Hosi and several other recruits had been chosen to go for the special training. The names of those that had been picked were read out at the parade one afternoon. They were told to pack their belongings within thirty minutes and wait for the lorries that would take them away. As those who had been selected packed their belongings, the others came to bid them farewell. Hosi could see the sadness on their faces. They felt that they had been singled out as the weaklings of the group.

The lorries were due to arrive in the next thirty minutes, but Hosi called them the UNITA minutes: it could be fifteen minutes or three days. What was important, however, was to be ready. Hosi had all his things packed, but he had to pack his mind too. He had somehow become accustomed to the camp. He had also become fond of the other recruits. They admired him for his persistence in reading whenever he could and would gather round, asking him what the book was about. He had found it hard to talk to the other recruits. One day, however, they had insisted. 'Come on,' one of them said, 'don't be selfish. Tell us. What is this little book you've been reading?'

'Essays. A collection of essays by an English philosopher, Bertrand Russell.'

'What does he say? Tell us!'

'OK, I will tell you what is here,' Hosi said. 'He says you may tell people that if you need to boil water you have to put it in a fridge, and that if you want to cool it you put it on the fire. Do you all know what a fridge and a cooker are?'

One of them scratched his head. The others said quickly what they were. Hosi continued: 'Russell says that the people would believe it. But when they wanted to boil water they would go for the fire and when they wanted to cool it they would go for the fridge.'

They all looked at Hosi puzzled and one of them said: 'Is that what you've been reading?'

'Yes. But it is not as simple as that. He was actually talking about propaganda.'

One of them shook his head and said: 'Hosi, my brother, don't confuse yourself. I would expect a person like you with such an appetite for books to be reading the Elder's works. They are everywhere and they are books which deal with Angola. Our very destiny. But you waste your time with silly white men who go on about fridges, cookers, propaganda and all that lot. Come back to earth.'

At last, after three hours, the lorries arrived. Hosi, who had been lying on the bed, was asleep. Someone kicked him in the leg. It was Sergeant Kalei. Clenching his fist the sergeant said: 'Come on, you are a soldier, not someone about to give birth to twins. Get trotting. To the lorry!'

Hosi got his rucksack and jumped into the lorry. Made in Poland, it had been captured from the government forces. There were several such lorries which had been modified by

183

the UNITA mechanics. Hosi thought it looked ugly. The recruits squashed themselves in.

The lorry laboured its way through the southern Angolan sand. It began to drizzle and a cold breeze made the recruits huddle together. It was hard to believe that those who were shuddering with cold now would one day go out and send shivers down the spines of the enemy.

At last the lorry came to an area that had once been a swamp and was able to increase speed. It was now warmer. Hosi had been leaning on somebody's back. It was Benjamin, a boy who said little but was rumoured to cry often in private. Benjamin's back was wet. Hosi wondered whether this was because of the drizzle but actually it was from sweat. Hosi also noted the trickles of sweat oozing from Benjamin's hair and on to his neck. A blackish dot in one of the trickles stirred itself. Hosi realized that it was a louse. He closed his eyes and when he reopened them the louse had wandered back into Benjamin's hair. Just then Hosi felt something itch between his testicles. He put his hand into his trousers and pressed the part that had been itching hard. Lindo, a shy boy from Lobito, saw Hosi do this and smiled at him. Hosi smiled back.

The lorry was on sand again and reduced speed. Someone began to sing and others joined in. At first Hosi did not feel like singing. Most of the songs were praising the Elder and although Hosi felt that there was nothing wrong with praising the Elder – he was the leader and deserved all respect – he did think that the line had to be drawn somewhere.

Hosi joined the singing on 'Ndombua Kolela', 'Hold on, my bride'. As if they had practised before, some sang bass, others tenor and others soprano. Hosi found the song so beautiful that he had the feeling that the birds in the bush would soon join in:

> *Hold on, my bride,*
> *Keep to the house on your own.*
> *It is worthwhile,*
> *For this is the time of war.*

184

Hosi liked this chorus too:

> *He's greedy, really greedy,*
> *Really, he's greedy,*
> *My cousin,*
> *Really, he's greedy,*
> *I've not yet made the bed but he's*
> *already taken off his trousers.*
> *Greedy, he's really greedy.*

The lorry came to a halt at what was called an agricultural production centre. A rumour soon went round that this was a centre which had 500 women and eleven men. It was also said that the lorry was not working very well. The driver, a diminutive man who spoke with a lot of gestures, said to the recruits on top of the lorry: 'I have a problem with the gearbox. I will have to send for a mechanic. We don't have to be at the camp till tomorrow morning, so we might as well take a rest.'

The recruits yelled in unison: 'Viiiiiiivaaaahhhh.'

Before they wandered into the centre, the recruits had to be briefed by the centre's commander, Corporal Amadeu, a lean man who stammered. He ordered the recruits to follow him. When they had arrived at his headquarters – four adobe huts – the commander said: 'This is a very important centre. Most of the women here are married and their husbands are in battalions at the front. How should I put it? Well, those of you who are saying to yourselves, "Ah, tonight is the night," might as well forget it. Now, follow me and come and meet the people at the centre.'

As the recruits walked Hosi overheard a conversation behind him.

'Just because he does not function he thinks it is the same with everyone.'

'Shut up. This is the problem with us. We do most of our thinking between our legs, not in our heads.'

After the commander had given a long talk about what went on at the camp, the recruits were told that they could wander about and meet the people there. The women lived in mud huts. Hosi was impressed by the neatness of the surrounding areas. He noticed in particular a red petticoat and a white bra which were being dried on the roof of the pit latrine. He had a strong suspicion that all the recruits would notice them. The sight of these two garments had definitely enlivened his spirits. He felt he was back in a familiar place, a place where people were more concerned with what they were going to have for dinner that night than with memorizing the latest slogans to keep their patriotic fervour aflame.

He smelt fish being fried. (It later turned out to be a turtle.) His mouth watered. At this point he heard a voice from behind say: 'Hullo, brother, who are you?'

Hosi stammered a bit at first: 'Hosi Mbueti. We're passing through the camp. We're just having a rest. Our lorry has some problems.'

The woman was lean, of fair complexion, and had dimples which Hosi found particularly attractive. She smiled, but Hosi cursed himself for having told the woman that he was a recruit and that they were passing through the centre. He had not been taught this, but it was almost common knowledge that information should be disseminated only by the appropriate authorities. In war, as someone had told Hosi – he couldn't quite recall who it was – there was no such thing as trivial information; everything was important.

The woman, who said her name was Guida, told Hosi that there was to be a birthday party. 'It is Cristina's. I am sure you guys will celebrate with us, won't you?'

Hosi shook his head and said: 'I don't really know. I'm only a recruit. These things are decided upon by the officers.'

'Your Portuguese sounds strange. I suppose I shouldn't ask, but which part of Angola do you come from?'

'I have a slight accent. That is because I grew up in Zambia, where the official language is English.'

'So you speak English?'

'Yes.'

Guida turned round and shouted into the hut: 'Cristina. Come over here. There is someone who speaks English.'

186

Cristina came to the door, and said: 'All I know are English songs I hear on the radio. I know "What's love got to do, got to do with it". I also know "Don't play with my doodo. Don't play with my doodo."' Hosi laughed. From the way the women spoke Portuguese he could tell that they were literate. Their grammar was impeccable and they had no accents. The two women told Hosi that they were teachers and that their husbands were commanders at the battle front. They said there were many children of school-going age in the camp and there were also adults who needed to improve their reading and writing skills. The two women left Hosi and rushed over to the camp commander to convince him that a dance should be held for Cristina's birthday.

Hosi wandered on. He saw a group of women seated by a fire, roasting meat. They greeted him and invited him to drink *chisangua*. Hosi did not feel like drinking, but he remembered the many times he had been so thirsty that he had wished for someone to come to his rescue with a cup of *chisangua*. Also, refusing anything was not the done thing. The women would consider him a snob – well, not quite a snob. In this war, where on certain occasions intellectuals who knew books and books by heart were said to have gone down on their knees for a cassava tuber, snobbery had disappeared. Snobbery had turned into arrogance, which was quite another thing.

Hosi enjoyed the *chisangua* and asked for more. The women seemed pleased. After the second cup he said: 'Ah, after these two cups I am not the same. I have just been reminded that there are many good things in life which I've not yet tasted.'

The women burst out laughing. One of them said: 'Wait till the Cubans are out of the country. Then we will brew proper *chisangua*, a *chisangua* that will make unfaithful husbands confess after a cupful.' They laughed again.

Hosi decided to return to where the other recruits were assembled. A number had gathered around two recruits playing draughts. After a while Guida and Cristina came and said that they had been given permission to hold the dance. Everyone seemed pleased.

Soon it was dark and the cold wind blew hard. Wild animals

187

could be heard howling in the distance. As he sat beside the huge fire with the other recruits, Hosi felt that the centre had some special alluring qualities, qualities that made him feel like staying there for ever.

The recruits were summoned to the camp's pavilion, a large room with a grass roof named after the Elder. Several women were already present and after a while the room filled. The recruits chatted with the women as if they had known them for a long time. It was said repeatedly that most of the women were married and that their husbands were at the battle front. It was common knowledge that having a fling with the wife of someone at the front was a serious crime, so serious that all the soldiers would unanimously call for the offender to be executed at once. Such offenders were held to be worse than those who were captured and gave information to the enemy. At least they would have arguments with which to defend themselves: they could say that they had resisted till the East German interrogator worked on their balls with pliers for a while. But a man who slept with another man's wife could have no valid excuse. Still, there were countless stories of unfaithful women and reactionary men.

A tall, obese woman waved her hands, signalling everyone in the room to be silent. They all complied. The woman said: 'I am Ester Kulanda, the centre's social and cultural co-ordinator. We are happy to have you here today, which also happens to be the day Cristina Esteves, a teacher at this centre, is having her birthday. To begin the programme, I would like to call the commander to say some words.'

Corporal Amadeu stepped to the front. He had prepared a long speech. Hosi sighed as a few slogans praising the Elder were chanted before the corporal began his speech.

A diesel lamp was brought closer to Corporal Amadeu to help him read better. He cleared his throat and began: 'Distinguished guests gathered here tonight, I would like to welcome you in the name of our movement, our armed forces, our revolution, the peace-loving people of Angola and our most beloved leader, the dearest son of the land, the highest revolutionary poet, the commander of our valiant armed forces, political strategist of international calibre, the Elder . . .'

188

Corporal Amadeu was interrupted by a woman with a husky voice shouting: 'Viiiva Angola!'

'Viiiva,' they answered in unison.

'O, dear Elder!' the woman cried out tearfully.

'Speak! Speak! The world is listening to you.'

There were ululations and whistlings. The corporal wanted to continue but had forgotten his last sentence. When the woman had first shouted out he had had his finger marking the place, but then he had had to clench his fist like everybody else and now he was lost. He began to sweat. Hosi hoped that someone would tell the man to take it easy. The corporal searched again but still could not find the sentence. His crooked handwriting did not help much. He suddenly wished that he had asked someone with a more legible hand to write the speech for him.

Corporal Amadeu, who had once worked at an agricultural centre during colonial times, knew that the previous five years, during which he had been leading the women at the centre, were some kind of probation. The movement, he thought, was actually assessing how well suited he was for a higher post. Corporal Amadeu felt that he was more than qualified to be a regional agricultural officer or even the secretary for agriculture, and believed that the present secretary was simply there because he had attended the same school as the Elder. At least, that was what everybody said.

But, as the corporal often said to himself, the revolution cut straight through crooked lines and one day his hour would come. He was now convinced that the hour had come. The first sign was the appearance of the recruits. Many lorries taking recruits to the camp had passed through the centre, but none had ever stopped. Why was it that today this lorry had actually stopped? After careful thought Corporal Amadeu finally reached the answer – it was his promotion. These were not all recruits. The movement had actually sent some spies or investigators to test how politically sound he was. He needed to prove that politically he was as healthy as the movement's flag: never wavering and ever ready to defend the Elder's principles. So it was important that the speech was a success.

There were a few murmurings in the audience. Then there was silence, because Corporal Amadeu actually smiled – he had finally found his place. He continued with his speech, not mentioning Cristina once. At the end, people applauded and chanted more slogans. The corporal left.

The cassette recorder which was to play the dance music had broken down. There were angry shouts. 'There are many saboteurs around!' someone cried.

'Who says we cannot dance because there is no cassette player?' someone else shouted. 'Bring the drums. That is what we need. Let the drums burn.'

'We have a Jazz King,' a woman called out.

Jazz King was the brandname of a huge wooden radio cum record player that Angolans who went to South Africa as contract workers brought back with them. They were very old and highly respected. Hosi found it amazing that although people in the UNITA-controlled territory said they had had to run for their lives on many occasions, they had managed to flee with several Jazz Kings.

Batteries were very rare in the bush, so getting the Jazz King to work was difficult, but people had found a way round the problem. It had been discovered that the dynamo of a bicycle gave out nine volts when the tyre was rotated. So a bicycle would be turned upside down (that bicycles had been brought this far into the bush amazed Hosi too) and someone would sit on a chair and begin to turn the pedals with his hands. Two wires from the dynamo would be fixed to the battery terminals of the Jazz King. As long as the person kept turning the pedals the Jazz King would play as though new batteries had just been put into it.

After a while a Jazz King was brought in by a hefty youth, one of the small number of men who lived at the centre. A woman followed him with a bicycle whose front wheel had been taken off and the connection from the bicycle to the Jazz King was made. Records were brought in. The youth sat on a chair and began to pedal. Cristina insisted that they should play a song by Roberto Carlos, the Brazilian singer. The others objected.

'Come on. Get some *sunguras* there,' someone cried. *Sungura* was a word written on the label of some Kenyan records which had been very popular with villagers in the colonial days. The dance began. There was to be no holding of partners; everyone had to dance on his own. After two numbers the music stopped. The hefty youth who was pedalling said he would continue only if he was promised a plate full of sweet potatoes. He refused to resume pedalling, insisting that he should be given a gourd full of the choicest *chisangua* that could be found in the camp. The women told him to buzz off, saying that he was a glutton, so he took offence and walked out of the room.

One of the women took over the pedals and the sound suddenly improved. For the rest of the dance, the women took turns at the pedals. In the middle of it all the recruits had to reassemble. It was time to move on to the camp. They all rushed into the lorry, which had somehow been mended without the mechanic coming.

At last they got to their destination. The sun was about to come out and several large adobe dormitories with grass roofs could be seen in the distance. They depressed Hosi. All along, he had not considered what he was going to find. Dormitories meant to him a horrible lack of privacy.

The recruits were told that from now on each of them would be referred to by a number; Hosi's number was 105. All the recruits were pleased that in a few months they were going to be real soldiers, not just men in uniform. They all kept saying that there were many people in the UNITA-controlled area who went about saluting and walking as if they had just wrung a Cuban's neck while the same people would shit themselves at the sound of a MiG21. This was not going to be the case with them; they were going to be made into men and a half.

Hosi made his bed and decided to take a quick nap. He did not even take off his boots. As he began to fall asleep, he could hear the others talking, their voices receding slowly into some distant background. He felt peaceful.

He was woken up by a kick on his boots. A tall, dark recruit was shouting at him: 'Up, up, up! Time for parade.' Hosi forced himself up and trotted along with the others. Those who had already assembled were busy singing a song with a catchy tune that Hosi had never heard before. Like many others, the song praised the Elder.

As in Jamba, there were several instructors at the camp. One of them came forward with a sheet of paper and said: '254, 105 and 23, come forward.' Two recruits walked forward.

'105! Where is 105?' the instructor shouted.

Someone pushed Hosi from behind. He stepped forward, stumbling as he did so. The instructor, a corpulent man who kept trotting about with a stick tucked under his arm, looked straight at Hosi and said: 'Now, where were you? There was a group that had been chosen to go and gather firewood. You were included among them but you did not turn up when your number was called. What was going on?'

Hosi scratched his head and said: 'Should I tell the truth?'

'Truth or no truth, you will know what it is like to be a pansy in this camp. Now, tell me.'

Hosi coughed and said: 'Well, I was asleep. After yesterday's tiring journey I couldn't stand it any more. I just had to sleep. I am sorry, comrade instructor. There are times when biological necessity takes over.'

Pointing his stick at Hosi, the instructor said loudly, so that everyone could hear: 'We've had them before. Petit-bourgeois kids who think they will intimidate us with their Portuguese. No way! You can get away with big words in Luanda and Portugal, not here. He says he was asleep when his name was called!'

At this point someone from the crowd began to sing a song meant for traitors and other opponents of the revolution.

'One little person cannot hold back the struggle.'

'Yeah! Yeah! Yeah!' The others sang back together.

The instructor waved his stick furiously, telling the recruits to stop singing. He screwed up his face and said: 'You are really raw! Politically immature and lacking a thorough understanding of the struggle. Who told you that the Kamunukamosi

192

can be sung at will? 105 was sleeping when he was supposed to be awake. Now, that is really wrong, but it does not mean that he is as evil as, say, a Cuban or a Soviet. He is just mistaken.'

The instructor turned to Hosi and said: 'Fifty press-ups. Quick.'

Hosi fell down like a log – that was how it was supposed to be done. After thirty press-ups Hosi felt exhausted. The hot sand hurt his palms and the heat on his back made him feel very uncomfortable. At last he did the fiftieth then leapt up as vigorously as he could manage. The instructor was impressed. He wet his lips and said: 'We appreciate men who are tough and have brains. Those are the sort that are needed to defeat the enemy.'

Hosi nodded and marched back to the parade.

22

It was a Sunday afternoon. Most of the recruits had gone to play football – the only activity encouraged which was devoid of politics. Hosi did not like football. Instead, he used his free time to read and to listen to plays on the BBC World Service. He found a place in the shade of a tree.

The announcer on the BBC said the play was going to come on in an hour. In the news bulletin he heard of many who had burnt to death in Wales when a mental hospital caught fire. Hosi began to grieve for the people in that faraway land. He imagined them screaming as fire peeled their flesh. As he was listening, he was struck by the thought that most Angolans thought that their sorrows were the deepest in the world. This, he realized, was not entirely true. There was sorrow and grief all round the world.

Hosi began to read, but was disturbed by a shadow. He looked up and saw a tall man with a blotchy face. He had probably had smallpox as a child. He sat next to Hosi and said: 'My name is Raimundo. I know you are Hosi Mbueti. Strange name. Were you always called that?'

'No!' Hosi replied. 'I used to be Armindo Coelho Hosi Mbueti. I did away with the Armindo and the Coelho in Zambia, to make things easy.'

'Why?'

'Well, you see, Armindo and Coelho are Portuguese and that would make the Zambians think I was a foreigner. That can make things pretty hard.'

Raimundo took some tobacco leaves out of his pocket. They were not very dry but he treated them carefully, like a child who has just been given a toy. He turned to Hosi and said: 'My brother, we have to fight. In the old days of the colonial-

194

ists we had proper cigarettes. There was AC, Negrita and what have you. Cigarettes for all sorts of people – lawyers, mechanics, prostitutes. By the way, in the Angola that we are going to create, there will be no prostitutes.'

Raimundo tried to light the cigarette but failed. He shook his head: 'Imagine the new Angola that will be built. It will be like a house whose foundations have been mixed with the glorious blood of patriots or the best sons of UNITA. It will be a shame if there are prostitutes, Angolan beauties doing it for money. No way.'

Hosi had come across many people like Raimundo. He found it hard to fathom their remarks. If they were mad, then there was method in their madness. (Hosi had heard this expression at a beer hall in Zambia. A man and a woman who had been very drunk had been having a heated discussion about the holiness of the Pope. The woman, a Roman Catholic, had insisted that the Pope was indeed God's ambassador on earth. Gleaming with importance, the man had said: 'I understand the madness of you Romans. The problem is that there is method in your madness.' Hosi had been impressed. Method in your madness! He had remembered the phrase ever since.)

Hosi wanted to get rid of Raimundo. It was not long till the play began. But Raimundo showed no signs of wanting to leave. The cigarette was now alight and giving out a smoke which Hosi thought was mildly repulsive. Each time Raimundo inhaled, he would smile to himself.

Hosi said: 'Tell me, brother Raimundo.'

'Comrade Second Lieutenant Raimundo!' Raimundo corrected Hosi.

'Sorry. Yes, tell me, Comrade Second Lieutenant. Have you ever smoked marijuana?'

Raimundo tittered and then pulled a severe face. 'Marijuana? Not us. That is for the MPLA solidiers, the Cubans, the Soviets and all the dogs furthering Soviet imperialism. We may smoke rubbish because we don't have tobacco, but never marijuana. I was once so desperate that I had to smoke pumpkin leaves. Just imagine.' Raimundo hissed and said: 'The Russians are sons of bitches!'

195

They were silent for a while and then Raimundo went on: 'Do you know why there is so much confusion in the world?'

'I guess I do,' answered Hosi.

'I am not referring to the Paramount Thought. Sometimes I hate to talk about it. The Elder is so intelligent that when simple-minded people like myself talk about his thoughts we are likely to get completely confused. What I am telling you about is the way of this world; not the way of the thinkers, but the way of we who live in this world. There are two things that cause confusion in this world. Women and money. That is the truth. I don't have any brains, but I do have something up here, my brother. Women and money, that is it!'

'But how does that explain the Angolan conflict?'

Raimundo cleared his throat and said: 'This is just between us, the two of us. It should not go beyond us. If it does, then I will be demoted, beaten and all the rest of the shit they give to reactionaries. I am no reactionary. That is the truth. The only problem is that these people over here are too thick to understand me. Women and money, that's it. I tell this to trusted friends. They all fall about laughing. I just say OK, I will stick to my views. Then I sit down and think over it for a while. Two words keep coming to my mind – women and money, women and money!'

'I asked you to explain the Angolan war: that is, from the women and money angle,' Hosi said, impatiently.

'Right,' Raimundo began, 'once the Cubans, the Soviets and that lot are out, what will happen? We're going to move into Luanda. We might hold elections, which we'll win. Then what will remain to be done? The women and money will start clinging to us like flies. Even those mulattas in Luanda ...' Raimundo slapped Hosi on the back and went on: 'The mulattas, those are real creatures. Beautiful! I knew one mulatta in Lobito. She had the most beautiful body I've ever seen! Yes, all the women will be falling over us; so will the money. That is what we are fighting for, and that is what the lackeys on the other side are fighting for too.'

Hosi wanted to pursue this further but had to excuse himself, as he wanted to go somewhere quiet to hear the BBC

196

play. He bade Raimundo farewell and went into the dormitory.

At five sharp the whistle for supper blew. Although Hosi was dozing the whistle awoke him. By now, he slept with one of his senses alert either to the whistle or to his number being called.

Hosi got his plate and walked to the parade. The others were already gathered and singing. He did not know the song. Before they marched to the post where they would be given their food, an instructor came forward and said that he was going to read the names of the recruits who would act as night policemen. Hosi's number was read out with that of someone he did not know. As they marched to the kitchen, Hosi wondered what it was like to serve as a night policeman. He knew that they were supposed to take care of any problems arising during the night. Often one of the recruits would fall ill; or elephants would come into the middle of the camp; or a dormitory would catch fire. That was where the night policemen came in.

Supper was maize gruel with boiled salt fish. Each of the recruits was also given a cup with juice in it, not too much since the chief cook believed the recruits would use it to brew an alcoholic drink. Hosi still felt hungry as he trotted over to the shelter where the night policemen spent their nights. If there wasn't much to do, the two policemen would spend the time chatting or listening to the radio. Night policemen were given coffee, biscuits and peanut butter. The prospect cheered Hosi up as he saluted the captain who was seated inside the hut.

'In!' the captain shouted.

'105 over here. I am on duty tonight,' Hosi said.

'Where is the other bloke? Number 355. Where is he?'

'I don't know. I don't even know him.'

'What do you mean, don't know him?'

Hosi remained silent. The captain told him to sit down while they waited for 355. Hosi was delighted when it turned out to be Raimundo.

'I meant to tell you this afternoon that you and I would be

on duty,' said Raimundo. 'The problem is that I got carried away. You see, whenever I talk to an intellectual I feel great. I feel great because I can pour my thoughts out and I know that they won't be met with indifference.'

Hosi nodded and said: 'But I don't think I am a proper intellectual, I am a pseudo-intellectual – beautiful word, not so?'

'I know why you deny being an intellectual. No way, brother. You are an intellectual, that is it. But I understand that it is not a very safe thing to be. All the traitors we've had so far have been intellectuals. Name any of the traitors and you will see that each of them had been to secondary school or beyond. There are many intellectuals around but they are all in hiding, pretending that they are dunces like ourselves. With me it is clear. I did not go beyond primary four. I can say whatever I want and all the security men will say is, "Well, what else can you expect from such a dickhead?" Now, that is not the case with you. Every word you utter will be looked at closely. If it goes counter to the Paramount Thought, you are in for it – no promotion for five years. And when you want to marry, everything you've said will come under scrutiny. Do you have a bride in mind?'

'No.'

'Good. These women are bloody witches. Not only that, but they are crazy about corned beef and chiffon dresses. As I was saying, when you want to marry, you will have to apply to the department of personnel. They will check your file. If your political health is not sound, then you won't marry. Why is it that the few intellectuals we have have had to make do with peasant women while semi-literate majors have two or three black Portuguese ladies?'

It was time for the Portuguese news on Radio France International. Hosi and Raimundo listened to the Sony radio in silence. Raimundo grunted whenever a news item struck a chord with him, but there was nothing about Angola so Hosi went out to fetch a tin in which they could make some coffee.

As the water boiled Hosi turned to Raimundo and said: 'You said women are witches. I am sure if the leaders in the

Women's League heard you, they would insist that you be shot.'

Raimundo laughed and said: 'The top women in the Women's League are the expert witches. Africa is mysterious and backward. The whites have been to the moon. All we know is witchcraft. Well, we are not *that* far behind. Look at it this way: they have been to the moon but they know next to nothing about witchcraft. So we know something they don't know. I will tell you a story, my brother.' Raimundo made himself comfortable and began: 'I have never lived in Jamba for long. That is very good, because if you do you're likely to lose touch with reality; you forget that we are fighting a war. Every Tuesday the South Africans send meat, cheese and eggs. When I was there, I refused to eat them. My philosophy was this: if I am to eat anything from the devil, then I must just eat what will keep me alive, nothing more.'

'Please get to the story,' said Hosi.

'Right. I was in Jamba one time and the atmosphere was horrible. One morning, a man who had been badly wounded at the battle front was found lying unconscious metres away from the hospital, covered in human excrement. When he was asked what had happened to him he said two women had dragged him from the hospital at night and punished him severely. As if that was not enough, the Jamba witches began to attack the Elder's bodyguards. They all began to hear voices and see visions. Just imagine! Day in and day out thousands of people were dying and yet these women were busy practising witchcraft. The witches had formed their own liberated territory.

'In the end the leadership said no. This has gone too far. So they consulted a witch hunter, Mariano. I tell you, he was a man and a half. He would simply look at a woman, say she was a witch and she would admit it. Yes, the leaders turned to Mariano. He was the official witch-finder, a true revolutionary.

'Mariano was told to sift out all the witches. Man, you would not have believed it. Those women who speak difficult Portuguese were found with incredible things: human ribs, baby fingers, human thigh bones, hyenas, mermaids, bags of sugar – while everybody else has to do without sugar – and tins and tins of cooking oil. The leadership said: "No. This is just too much. What kind of society are we building?" There was only one solution – burning the witches.'

Hosi flinched.

Raimundo shook his head and continued: 'Burning the witches – that was the only proper solution. I think there has never been a better decision taken by the leadership.

'One morning the activists went about Jamba with their megaphones saying people were supposed to assemble at BI at six in the morning. We blacks have one big fault – we don't have a notion of time. So what this actually meant was that the programme was going to begin at ten, because people would get there by eight or nine. Anyway, by midday we were all assembled.

'At some point a number of people were sent to gather firewood. We did not know what was going to happen. Anyway, we all went and fetched the wood. Then the witches were brought in. Each of them had been shaved. Except for a small boy, who was a walking juju potion, all the witches were female. And they were all beautiful! Whenever I see a beautiful woman and my heart begins to throb I say to myself: "Wait a minute! The beauty before you could be the number one witch around." What was I saying?'

'The witches and the firewood.'

'Hah. The wood was lit and they were all placed in the fire. It was the most impressive thing I've ever seen. I have seen hundreds of men die, and I was at Kangamba where human flesh was as worthless as corned beef. By the way, is a tin of corned beef that expensive abroad?'

'I don't think so,' Hosi said.

'Hm. I ask because someone once told me that a tin of corned beef was more expensive than a grenade.'

'Carry on. I want to know what happened to the witches.'

'The burning began. They were surrounded by the police and began to burn. The smell of burning human flesh is actually sweet. It is not the kind of smell that brings saliva

200

into your mouth, not the kind you get when you roast beef. It has a strange kind of sweetness to it. I felt great; so did everybody else there, including the children. We saw evil die painfully and slowly. That night everybody slept peacefully. One of the witches almost jumped out of the fire but she saw there was no escape and sank back into the flames and in no time they were all gone and the liberated territory became peaceful once again.'

Hosi closed his eyes and contemplated the sight of poor witches burning in flames, surrounded by the public. There were things in the world that made him feel insignificant, things he knew he could not influence. This frightened him. There had been many times when Hosi wished he had not heard stories like the one Raimundo had just been telling him. He had heard about the burning of the witches in Jamba but he had confined the whole incident to the back of his mind. He had liked to think of it as fiction from some novel or film. He found it hard to think that such a thing had actually happened in Angola, caused by Angolans. Now that Raimundo had told him the story, there was nothing he could do about it. The witches kept wailing in his mind.

Raimundo said there might be something about Angola on the South African news so they tuned in. A UNITA communiqué was quoted saying that forty-two government soldiers had just been killed. 'Good,' said Raimundo. 'Serves the bastards right!'

Hosi turned to Raimundo and said: 'But why? And why did the witches have to be burnt? If we are fighting for justice, then we should try and start practising it right away. The burning of witches was a crime!'

'Heh! Heh! Intellectuals! You and your mouths! That is why you get in trouble.'

'I honestly think that you hate women. Not all women are the monsters you make them out to be.'

'You are wrong. I am not against all the women in the world. I just have reservations about Angolan women! Someone once told me that the Algerian airforce had the largest number of women pilots in Africa. I think Angola has the largest number of flying women – except that they don't fly in aeroplanes; they fly on magical things.'

Hosi interrupted Raimundo and said: 'There must be something wrong with you. Have you ever been jilted? I haven't met anyone like you before. There is an English word for a man like you: you are a misogynist.'

Raimundo pulled out a notebook and said: 'Say it again. I have to take that down.'

'But you don't know a word of English.'

'So what? Anyway, that isn't true. I have a book called *Essential English* and I have learned a lot of important words. Now, miso . . . what?'

Hosi told him. 'Answer my question. Have you ever been let down by a woman? Why is it that you are filled with so much hatred?'

'I have not only been let down by women; I have been betrayed, stabbed in the back. This has happened to me several times. Now the Angolan woman won't be able to mess with us men any more. They could toss the likes of me about because there were many men around at the time. Now there aren't enough. They are dying in their hundreds daily. In liberated Angola polygamy will be the only viable solution.'

'You've not yet answered my question,' said Hosi. 'Has a woman ever let you down?'

'I said several. But the one who hurt my heart most is a beautiful girl called Belita. I almost committed suicide that day. I loaded the Kalash and was about to fire off when I said to myself: "Look here. Your life is precious and the motherland is desperate for it. Why, then, would you let it go for the sake of a simple slut who's probably a witch too?" I unloaded the Kalash, drank some coffee, listened to music and decided to live on.'

'What had happened?'

'Patience! You're very impatient! Before learning to dance one should be able to crawl and then walk and then be able to relate to the rhythms. You cannot jump from the first stage to the last. That is a rule of life. So when I tell you something, you have to be patient, because I will tell you in bits.

202

'I will tell you about Belita. It all happened when I was
doing a stint at the Polivalente. One Saturday morning I was
taking a stroll when I saw a white man approaching me. He
was accompanied by a young black man. I said to myself: "Is
this a South African? Portuguese? Or what?" The man spoke
English very fast. It must have been very poor English. I often
listen to the news on the BBC and pick up some bits. This
man sounded as though he had a drilling machine in his
mouth. I couldn't understand a word of what he was saying.
The black man said the man wanted me to take part in a film.
He told me to follow him.

'As I walked behind the two, my heart soared. My mind
was working fast. Hundreds of ideas kept swirling around. It
was not for my personal glory – far from it. It was for the
glory of Angola, and, above all, the black man's glory. I know
that we blacks the world over have been taken for a ride. It
was said that we were morons, that we were repulsive, and so
on and so on. I was going to change all this. Now, get this
clear. I know that I am talking to an intellectual, not a peasant.
I want you to know that I'm not boasting. I'm just stating the
facts. I know that the whites in Europe enjoy seeing pictures
of naked Africans or ugly Africans with heads like ugly fishes.
Not this time. I am, let's face facts, fairly handsome.'

Hosi chuckled. Raimundo was startled and said: 'At least by
Angolan standards.' Hosi waved to make Raimundo continue
talking.

'So here I was – handsome and with a different kind of
intelligence. You see, there are two types of intelligence: one
that is acquired at school and by hard, hard work; and the
other which is natural and pure. That is what I have. Now,
the whites are used to seeing the educated black man – the
man who parrots their ideas. They say, "Well, not a bad
nigger." That was not the way I was going to come across in
the film. They were going to say: "Ah, now there is pure
African intelligence." In the television film, I thought, I
would come across as living proof of the vitality of the Angolan
soul.

'When we came to the other white men who were doing the

203

filming, I was in for a surprise. One of those surprises you can only dream of. I was told that I was going to get married. I said to myself: "Shit! If this is a dream then an outstanding witch must be behind everything!" I scratched myself. Truly, I wasn't dreaming. Inside myself, I gave out one of those loud laughs, the kind that tickles your throat. Someone was told to go and fetch me a black suit and proper black shoes.

'The ceremony was going to be held in a church. A church? The last time I had been in a church had been under the Portuguese. I hadn't taken the church we had in the bush seriously. I had also become very sceptical of religion. How could God allow the Cubans and the Soviets as well as their MPLA lackeys, who are evil incarnate, to have it their way while we God-fearing people had to take to the bush? I said to myself at one point: "There is no God. The only God is the God that would liberate Angola – Papa AK47." Now, I was going to get married. I began to think twice about God. "Could our troubles have been a way of testing how firm we were?" I asked myself. At that moment the answer was a clear yes. Let's listen to some music.'

Raimundo pulled out a small cassette recorder from his bag and inserted a cassette, which began to play at once. He nodded and said: 'That song is diamond. The fellow is singing sense.' The song was entitled 'I want to return to my Africa.' The singer said that he would like to return to the traditional Africa where he would play drums and confer with the elders. Raimundo closed his eyes and imagined himself holding a partner. He hissed and said: 'Shit! The Cubans should leave as soon as possible and leave us in Angola to do our own thing.'

Raimundo was about to resume his story when they were disturbed by a soldier at the post, panting and shirtless, who said: 'Night guard, you won't believe what I've seen.'

'What?' Hosi asked, agitated.

The soldier, who was sweating, rubbed his forehead and said: 'I woke up in the middle of the night because I wanted to go and piss. As soon as I lit my lamp I saw movements on the bed at one end of the dormitory. When I looked closer, what did I see? Two men on top of each other, or rather one on top of the other! I tried to look closer but the lamp went off. When I lit it again the men were no longer there; they had simply vanished. Incredible! This was something I had never dreamt could happen.'

'What is the problem, then?' Hosi asked.

The soldier screwed up his face and said: 'I see two wizards screwing each other and you say that there is no problem?'

Raimundo, who had all along been listening open-mouthed, said: 'I am Lieutenant Raimundo. I will come along with you and investigate.' Raimundo stood up and followed the soldier to the dormitory.

As the two disappeared into the night, Hosi turned to the thick report book in which other sentries before him had filed reports. Some of them had filled things in simply because they needed to write something, so they had included the most trivial things. But one entry caught his attention: 'The night was peaceful,' it began, 'but later became violent. A strange sound was heard coming from the forest. It was concluded that it must have been the howling of a hyena. At exactly four o'clock there was a thunderstorm.' Hosi continued leafing through.

He felt slightly frightened. The images of the burning witches were still flickering in his mind. He imagined he could hear them screaming from their inferno. He tried hard to forget about them, concentrating on the music the cassette player was playing instead. To his relief Raimundo came back and said: 'Where was I?'

'I can't remember,' Hosi answered.

'Come on, remember or I won't tell you what I've just seen. Incredible! Where is the black man going with his witchcraft? I wish I knew. Tell me, where was I?'

'I think you were on God. You were saying that you believed in God because you were suddenly going to have a wife.'

'Hah, right. I was given a black suit and a pair of shiny black shoes. There were several white people involved with the film. They took photographs of me and kept telling me to smile. I kept saying, "Why not," and flashed my African ivory with pleasure.' Raimundo laughed loudly and continued: 'After a while I was told to get into a Land-Cruiser and we drove to a church. At every bump I felt as though my heart was about to come into my mouth. I was really excited. At last we got to the church. They were all there: a choir, old Christians dressed to the nines, smiling girls and women and children. I said to myself: "You bloody-fucking son of a bitch, this is your day!" And then the bride was brought. I couldn't believe my eyes. She was so beautiful that the first question that came to my mind was: "Does this creature ever go to the toilet or fart?" She reminded me of Mary, the mother of Jesus. She was pure and a virgin.'

'How do you know she was a virgin?'

'Heh! Don't behave like the dog that wanted the bone it had in its mouth and the one it saw in its reflection in the river or you'll have nothing. Now, choose between these two: how to tell a virgin, which is a subject which might last all night, or how I have been let down by Angolan women? Which of the two do you find more interesting?'

'The last. Angolan women and you.'

'Right. You are on the way to becoming an enlightened cadre. Angolan women and me is certainly a more interesting subject because here I am, a fighter, a man who is prepared to give his own life for the motherland, and yet the women of the land have tried to take me for a ride.

'Anyway, the bride came. She found me in the church. As she walked into the church the people sang "*Ndombua weya*". I looked around, because I expected Abraham, Peter or Jesus to be at hand. It was complete paradise. There were two large cameras and they kept rolling as we came before the altar.

'The priest stepped forward and said a few things. He asked me whether I was going to accept the girl as my wife till death would us part. I said I would. The same question was posed to the girl, whose name, incidentally, was Belita. Belita said yes. And then our lips touched. It was electricity. At some point, we were made to sign papers. I wrote one of those frightening, important signatures – the kind which Portuguese governors used to sign death warrants. The white man who was filming

206

as I was signing could not believe it. I held the pen firmly and scribbled with the confidence of a clerk.

'After that we walked out of the church. I was holding Belita's hand and feeling great. The white men ran to the front of the church and their cameras began to click again. They asked us to kiss again. I was incredibly happy!

'We stood in front of the church for a while. Cameras kept rolling and clicking. Then a Land-Cruiser came to pick us up. As we were driven off, people were clapping and cheering. I tried to wave, but someone at my back told me not to. He said I was waving like the Elder.

'After the whites were gone, Belita took off her veil and bade us farewell. I said, "Come on, darling, you can't do that." She said, "Who are you calling darling?"

'I said, the first day of marriage is not easy, but we should try and understand each other. She burst out laughing; so did everybody else. I couldn't understand what was going on, but I kept my own counsel. Then someone said: "That was just a film. We hope you did not take it seriously."

'I said: "Shit!" Who the hell did those whites think I was? They just told me I was going to get married while in actual fact everything was just being put on for the English to watch. Somebody else said: "There was a couple that was going to get married. The problem was that the film-makers thought they looked too frail, and the bride was a masterpiece of ugliness, an improper representative of Angolan beauty."

'I said: "So we went through all that for nothing? No. I can't believe it. This girl is my wife." Belita burst out laughing and said she had a fiancé who was at the Mavinga front. When she mentioned him I wished for an instant that a Cuban, Soviet or MPLA sniper would fix a good one into the bastard's head.

'She laughed some more and said: "It was just a film, nothing more."

'I felt something swell in my throat. My mouth went dry. I felt a kind of wild anger swell in me – not the kind of anger you get when confronting Cubans; that kind of anger to the power of 100, mathematically speaking. Belita looked at me

207

and laughed some more. I was looking a complete fool. But I am no chicken. I gave Belita one of those punches reserved for tough men. She fell to the floor and was seized by convulsions. Her beautiful face swelled up and she looked as ugly as a gorilla. I felt great! I drew my pistol from the holster. Everybody who was around fled. Belita began to tremble and said: "Don't kill me." I spat in her face. She said: "Thank you." I left at once.

'I didn't get away with it. Five special commandos came for me. They manhandled me to the military police post. On the way, they managed to give me a few punches. But that was nothing compared to the pleasure I felt when I saw Belita with a swollen face!

'They handed me over to four policemen. There was no need for a trial. A note from one of the commanders said that I had assaulted a defenceless woman and deserved to be given a proper punishment. The guards told me to sit down while they ate sweet potatoes. After they had finished they told me to lie down. Each of them had a whip. They began to lash my back. At first it did not hurt. I was still feeling triumphant after the blow I had given Belita. The men kept lashing. Then it began to hurt. I began to cry like a baby. I cried out to my mother and to my grandmother. I pretended to faint at one point. The men continued with the lashing. I was crying like a child. I tell you, Hosi, there is nothing more pleasurable than crying like a child if you are an adult. As we grow older we learn to express our emotions in a specific way; we forget that basic and instinctive way of letting our feelings show – crying out loud.

'After the guards had finished with me they threw me into prison, a bunker which was very dark. I was the only person there. The following day I was taken out, demoted at once and sentenced to three months' imprisonment. After three weeks in prison I wrote a long letter asking for forgiveness. I said I had not only wronged Angola but also the whole of Africa and mankind. I asked to be forgiven and promised to contribute as much as was required to further the struggle. Well, I am sure the letter never got to the Elder. I was set free and given a long, severe warning.'

Hosi was silent. He was feeling uncomfortable. There was so much to Raimundo's life, horrible and fascinating – that is, if all that he had been telling him was true – that his own life seemed to be nothing in comparison. Raimundo was tired after his long story and now fell asleep.

Hosi was also about to start dozing when he heard someone running quickly towards the hut. He shook Raimundo, who gave out a prolonged sigh and continued dozing.

'What is it?' Hosi cried out.

'Night guard, the elephants. There is one right behind our dormitory. It will walk over the dormitory any time now.'

The policy was that the soldiers were supposed to be as friendly as possible to the elephants. If, however, one of them posed a threat to property, then it could be scared away with a shot fired into the air. Hosi loaded the AK47, thinking that he would have to fire to scare the elephant. He followed the soldier, a lean youth who had a brisk step and spoke very fast.

'There. I am sure it must be there,' said the soldier.

Hosi flashed the torch and saw the trunk of a large tree. When he flashed the torch lower he saw a silvery tin. Hosi walked forward and bent to see what was in the tin. He concluded that it was filled with urine. Hosi turned to the soldier and said: 'No elephant. You mistook the tree trunk for an elephant. And take that tin to the toilet. A soldier should not have a chamber pot. And stop disturbing us with your fantasies, right.'

The soldier disappeared into the dark. Raimundo remained asleep.

23

The training was getting harder. The instructors expected the soldiers to run, crawl and jump longer distances. Hosi had begun to enjoy it all by now. He no longer felt nervous when throwing a grenade. And that was not all. He and a few other soldiers had been selected to be trained on a new anti-tank missile that had just been introduced to the army. There were also lessons in topography and the theory of war.

Once in a while, however, he had arguments with the instructors. There was the time he had been asked to explain what camouflage was. Hosi had answered that it was basically the breaking of your shape; but instead of stopping there he had gone on about the different types of camouflage and at some point he began to talk about politics. The instructor took off his beret and threw it at Hosi. Hosi had remained silent after that.

There had also been an occasion when he disputed a point that was made about map-reading. The instructor, who had quickly become exasperated, stopped and said: 'Blood sucker! We are not here to show how smart we are. We are here to learn how to kill, because the people on the other side are now busy learning how to kill us. So shut up and let me do my job.' Hosi apologized and the lesson continued.

One Saturday afternoon Hosi was walking along the parade-ground when he saw Raimundo rolling a huge tyre. This was one of the punishments that was meted out to those who had broken the camp's rules, which were legion. Deviation from the Paramount Thought was also a serious offence.

Hosi sidled over to Raimundo and said: 'What on earth have you done to deserve this?'

Raimundo shrugged and said: 'They're bloody niggers; that

is why they'll never get anywhere.' Raimundo turned back to the wheel and continued rolling.

Hosi later discovered that Raimundo had been accused of gross deviation: he had told someone that he was writing poems in secret that would one day put all the poets – including the Elder – to shame. Someone also told Hosi later that Raimundo was a hopeless case and that only part of him – his courage – was useful; the rest was completely worthless.

By now Hosi felt that there was nothing to war that he did not know. For the first time he began to dream about it, particularly the glorious aspects: the thrill of planning and annihilating the enemy; the pleasure of taking the enemy by surprise; and the promotions. Hosi began to imagine himself as a Field Marshal, a Field Marshal not in the mould of Idi Amin or Bokassa or some other African dictator, who had conferred the rank upon himself, but a Field Marshal in the tradition of Lord Mountbatten. Hosi loved that name. He often said to himself that had he been born an Englishman he would have called himself Mountbatten.

By now Hosi had made a lot of friends. He liked listening to the stories of the other soldiers. One day he was approached by Tiago, a tall, handsome boy with a goatee. Hosi was seated beneath the tree where Raimundo had found him reading Clausewitz. Tiago sat beside Hosi now and said: 'I am told that you are very bright. I know that you are. Is it because of that little book?'

'Bright in what?'

'Bright in the whole business of war.'

'I am not that smart. That is why I am always having arguments with the instructors. Perhaps I may not make such a good soldier. Good soldiers don't think; they act.'

Tiago laughed and said: 'Soldiers are not supposed to think that much; but officers are supposed to think fast. Someone once told me that war is a kind of chess – one man at each end and the pawns on the board. What do you think?'

Hosi shrugged and said: 'It might be so . . .'

Tiago interrupted him: 'Let me tell you this. Do you know about the Katanguese? They are the people fighting the

211

Mobutu regime in Zaire. They are all very short and dark – typically African. Whoever has fought them has had severe headaches. Usually when they go to the battle front they walk with a naked woman who has an empty calabash on her head. When the enemy starts firing the bullets, they all end up in the woman's basket. I myself fought them in Luso. We eventually managed to defeat them.'

'How?' Hosi asked, open-mouthed.

'You won't believe this.'

'Please!'

'We ensured that a naked man with an erect cock passed in front of our battalion. That rendered the women's charms ineffective.'

'Really?'

'Anyway, all this is beside the point. I've come to see you about something different.'

'What is it?'

'People like you are definitely going to become leaders or commanders. You need some protection; you need to be bullet-proof.'

'How is that possible?'

'I've heard it said by several people that sometimes they feel you are white. The fact is that you've never been to Europe and even if you were to go, you'd still remain what you are, a black man.'

'What has all that got to do with this?'

'When I talk about protection I expect you to know what I mean. By protection I mean having a special charm that will render a bullet fired by a Cuban, Soviet or Angolan as useless as if you had been hit by a bean.'

'You are talking of witchcraft?'

'That is why people think you're trying to be white.'

Hosi frowned and said: 'Fire off, man! You sound like some man proposing to a girl. Get to it!'

'I have this charm. Once you have it you'll be bullet-proof.'

Tiago pulled out some powdery stuff that was wrapped in a cloth and showed it to Hosi. It had a strong smell.

'Do you want some?' Tiago asked.

'Yes.'

'Now, here comes the snag. This stuff will work only if you give me that book in return.'

'What? Clausewitz on war?'

'Yes. You've been reading all the stuff in there and know something about war. I know something about African charms, so I want to give you some in exchange for that book. Fair, not so?'

Hosi hesitated and then said: 'Fair!' He handed the copy to Tiago, who began to leaf through it at once, beaming. Tiago held the copy to his heart and said he would read nothing else in the coming weeks. He was about to go when Hosi said: 'Before you leave, tell me how I can get this working.'

'Shit! I almost forgot to tell you. Here are the rules. Never eat anything cooked by a woman during her period; never cross a fallen tree trunk; never shake hands before bathing; never eat okra; never fart in the presence of a woman; when urinating, never hold your apparatus with your left hand. I will tell you the rest later.'

The following day Hosi saw Tiago rolling the tyre. He had been caught out. During the parade the camp commander, a tall man who had developed a pot belly, came forward and said: 'I really can't understand some of you. Indeed, as the Elder says, man is a complicated being. We are here to train you to be soldiers, not sorcerers. That chap you see over there rolling the tyre was caught with a charm which he said could make a person bullet-proof. He's a quack, a complete charlatan. If our enemies were as foolish as he is, we'd be in Luanda by now. Our enemies are professionals. They have no time for roots or any such crap. They believe in their heads and their ability to think. That is why they are so effective.'

At this point one of the the activists clenched his fist and began to shout: 'Down with wizards!'

'Down,' they all answered in unison.

'Down with traitors!'

'Down.'

'The youth?'

'Is the president's right hand.'

213

'Viva Angola!'

'Viva!'

Hosi pitied Tiago, but he joined the others in chanting slogans denouncing him. The commander ordered Tiago to be brought forward. A bucketful of water was poured over his body and he was told to repent before the battalion. Then the activists began to sing songs reserved for traitors and other political aberrants. At last it was decided that Tiago should be punished. He was to wear what was called a bishop's hat for a week. One of the activists whose speciality was drawing portraits of the Elder went forward, got some cardboard and inscribed several things on it: 'I am a reactionary! I am ugly! I am a wizard! I fly at night! I am a disgrace to Angola!'

After the huge hat was placed on Tiago's head, everyone began to jeer him. Others came and made gestures at him, even his friends. When Hosi came to Tiago he heard him say: 'Do you want your book back?'

'Keep it!' Hosi shouted back. Tiago smiled. The others who were jeering him became annoyed. 'Keep your dirty teeth in your dirty mouth, you bloody traitor,' someone shouted.

It was strange how rumours circulated considering that the intelligence network was very effective and the intelligence officers were everywhere. It was 1985 and the offensive was on. It was said on the news that UNITA or the enemy had made certain advances or had suffered certain losses. But there was the other news: the talk of the PC7, the aircraft that spat bullets like rain; the talk of the MI25 helicopter; the talk of the BM21 rocket-launcher; and the talk of the T55 tank. These frightened Hosi, like everybody else, but it was a strange kind of fear. It was not the fear that Hosi had felt as a child. It was less strident, and yet somehow stronger. It was the kind of fear that was expressed in the fervour with which slogans were chanted; in the servile attitude that people had for the Elder; and in the way people were moved to memorize chunk upon chunk of his speeches.

Hosi felt that it was the kind of fear that made some wish they could be shot in the head and die a hero's death rather than carry on with it. It was an all-pervasive fear. There was fear of MiGs and fear of the sky at night: some of the stars were said to be Soviet satellites busy photographing UNITA posts. There was also the fear that the water in the stream had been poisoned. Then there was the fear of the intelligence officers too. Hosi felt that each word he uttered passed through the machinery of the Paramount Thought and that he was judged as to whether he had strayed too far or not.

Now and then Hosi would sit by himself and think hard. Many of the answers that he came up with made him sad. On one occasion he considered freedom, democracy and national sovereignty. He knew that although the MPLA claimed that theirs was the freest land, this was not so. He knew that the prisons which had held political prisoners in the time of the Portuguese were still full. And he knew that UNITA was no different. He knew that a number of prominent people had vanished for disagreeing with the Elder. He knew that if he was to give rein to the thoughts that were running in his head he would qualify as a traitor. He knew too that there were people on both sides who believed that they were fighting evil and died doing so. He closed his eyes and saw streams of blood flowing. When he opened them again, they were filled with tears.

Hosi began to hate himself. He felt that by now his training should have driven out all this sentimentality. He realized that what he actually needed was to go to the battle front, see death and become wiser. Perhaps then all these thoughts would stop tormenting him and things would be completely clear. Hosi remembered how someone had once told him that there were two main initiation ceremonies for an Angolan boy: the time he was circumcised and the time he fired his first bullet.

24

Like other people in the liberated territory, the soldiers cele-
brated any historic occasion with great zeal: they would gather
at a parade; the camp commander would make a long speech;
the Elder's poems would be recited and passages of his
speeches would be read out. But that was all; there was no
dancing. The soldiers had demanded that at such times women
from agricultural centres be brought in to entertain them or to
dance with them. The camp commander had rejected the
suggestion at once. He insisted that there was supposed to be a
difference between UNITA and government soldiers. The
government soldiers, it was said, went to battle not only with
their women and crates of whisky but also a nine-piece band
just in case they won and the need to celebrate arose. This, the
commander maintained, was a recipe for disaster. A true
revolutionary, he insisted, was supposed to draw a distinction
between pleasure and the struggle.

It was 13 March, a special day, the day on which UNITA
was founded. The camp commander and other officers had
travelled to Jamba to take part in the festivities there. After
the usual programme – speeches, poems and the like – there
was football, then nothing. The soldiers were bored. Hosi
decided to take a stroll around the other dormitories. The
soldiers in one looked so lively that he suspected that someone
had brewed some alcoholic drink in private. At one end of the
dormitory two soldiers were playing very old acoustic guitars.
Another was playing bongos. The soldiers were clapping and
singing along. The song, by Poera, was entitled '*O Chombo*',
'The Pig'. In it, Poera compares power to a pig that has run
amok; it will be recaptured and cooked by UNITA. The
soldiers could only imagine they were holding a female partner,

but then someone came up with an idea. Why couldn't they dance holding each other if each of them took a turn at dancing like a woman. Soon, several soldiers were putting on canvas shoes, wrapping themselves in bedsheets and pretending to be girls.

Hosi's mind was adrift when a soldier wrapped in a brown bedsheet came forward and asked him to dance. Hosi took his hand and tried a few steps; his partner soon picked them up. As they danced, Hosi noticed that his partner had slightly bowed legs, which kept hitting his as they danced. Hosi liked it. As the dance got faster, his partner flapped his elbows about and Hosi noted that the smell from his armpits had a sweet, womanish tinge to it. He bent over and whispered into his partner's ear: 'Do you use perfume?'

The soldier looked straight at Hosi and said: 'Of course not! I am not a woman.' They danced on. The soldier swung his crotch rhythmically and provocatively at Hosi, as though he had once been trained to turn men on. Hosi held him by the waist and changed the steps; the partner got into the new rhythm at once. The two guitars began to play a slow number. The soldiers clung to each other, taking in each other's breath with pleasure.

At some point the little band began to play a fast number. Two soldiers, one dressed as a woman, the other dressed normally, were holding each other tightly, gyrating their crotches vigorously. The others stopped dancing and cheered them on. They clapped, whistled, made lewd remarks and encouraged the band to play on. One of the guitarists, emboldened by the applause from the dancers, stood up, placed the guitar behind his neck and continued playing. The two dancers had by now let go of each other and were busy dancing on their own. Some soldiers were stomping, others were gyrating their crotches and others – the Chokues and Lundas – were dancing as they had been taught at circumcision camps.

Hosi tried to do the 'Moonwalk' *à la* Michael Jackson, but it did not fit in with the music. Soon the soldiers were dancing in a circle. One would come and challenge another to join him in the middle of the circle; once there the two would try to

217

out-dance each other. Hosi felt so happy that he began to shout in English: 'Let's get it on, brother, man. We gonna paint the bush red tonight. What you see is what you get.' Others, who could not make head nor tail of what he was saying, joined in the babble and shouted out whatever came into their heads.

At some point a political activist told them all to stop dancing. He sat on a bed and said: 'It is all very well if we dance. Angola is ours and we should be allowed to do what we want. But what is not right is that some of you are trying to dance the Elder's dance. You can dance in whatever way you want but never imitate the Elder. The struggle is a serious thing and we should respect the Elder all the time – even when we are having fun.'

There were a couple of yeses from the audience, then the dance continued. One of the guitar strings broke so the playing stopped for a while and someone shouted out: 'I know that as we are dancing some of you will be getting hard and will want to jerk off later. Please do not do it. Angola needs children. Too many people have already died so we should not waste the seeds of the nation. That is all I have to say!' This remark was met with murmurs of assent. When the dancing came to an end, each of the soldiers went to his dormitory.

Rumours about the offensive at Mavinga and the power of the government forces kept circulating. At the parades, the camp commander would tell the soldiers not to take what was said in the radio news bulletins seriously; UNITA was definitely going to win, come what may.

One fact, however, began to emerge. Most of the food was being diverted to the battle front: the coffee was sugarless and the portions of maize gruel were reduced. A number of the medical men had to leave. Sooner or later, it was whispered, Hosi and his colleagues would have to go and face the dreaded Cubans, Soviets, Bulgarians, East Germans, Koreans, Vietnamese and, of course, the MPLA lackeys.

There was no longer much training. The soldiers spent most of their time thatching the roofs of their dormitories. The routine was as follows: the whistle would blow early in the morning, the soldiers would race out into the plains nearby, gather grass and come back for breakfast. At around ten they would go into the forest to get logs for the roof. They would then spend the whole afternoon at work on the thatching. There were, naturally, a few who played truant, but these dwindled almost to nil when a larger tyre for punishment was brought!

Hosi had been having a pleasant dream. It was about a girl he had loved in Zambia called Mary. Mary had been a born-again Christian and abhorred any earthly pleasures. Hosi had loved her deeply and had once gone down on his knees to prove how deep his love was. The girl had spat on his face. Now, in the dream, Hosi had just been made a Field Marshal after a long, arduous struggle to defeat the lackeys of communist imperialism. In the dream Mary came to visit him in his mansion beside the Atlantic Ocean, on top of a hill between Lobito and Benguela. Hosi stepped forward and looked straight into Mary's eyes, which were transfixed by the epaulettes on his shoulders. Hosi told Mary in Spanish that he loved her, singing a Julio Iglesias song. (Later, Hosi was ashamed of this point in the dream because someone told him that Julio Iglesias had said he would never sing to Africans because they were monkeys and would not be able to understand his music.) Mary smiled and pointed to the bedroom. Hosi lifted her up and carried her in his arms into the room. Just then someone kicked him. He shrieked and woke up. The others, who by now were ready to go to the morning parade, began to laugh at him.

'Another dream?' someone asked.

'Yeahhh,' Hosi yawned.

Hosi dressed himself quickly and rushed to the parade. The instructor said this day was to be just like the others, so the soldiers divided themselves into groups of six and ran to the plains to fetch grass. This day Hosi was given the Kalashnikov rifle to protect the others. The main danger came from lions, who could hide in the brown grass and take their victims by surprise. Hosi felt slightly uneasy at the thought that he was responsible for the safety of the other five in the group.

The sun had only just begun to rise and the different shrubs

219

in the middle of the plains were indistinct. From their shapes, Hosi kept imagining all sorts of ferocious animals: hyenas, leopards, tigers (in Angola!), lions. But as the sun rose higher, everything became clearer. They walked on for a while. There was a lot of elephant excrement about. Hosi had once heard that it could be used as firewood, although he did not see how. One thing that struck him was the place where the elephant had urinated. The sand on the surface had hardened like some kind of cement there. Hosi had heard that elephant urine was a cure for something, but could not recall what.

They walked further. Over the past days people had been coming daily to fetch grass, so now the best grass for thatching could be found only some distance from the camp. The fresh morning breeze blew. Hosi felt happy. The others in the group were not speaking to each other; each of them was too engrossed in his own thoughts. Hosi imagined that perhaps in a free Angola he would eventually become a tourist guide. No, that was too lowly for him. The minister of tourism, that was better. He imagined a time when he would be entrusted with the duty of giving foreign dignitaries a tour of southern Angola or the UNITA-controlled territory. He would cough importantly, turn to the foreign dignitaries and say that only a few years ago he had been a trainee carrying bundles of grass on his head. Then the dignitaries would all nod with envy and say: 'Hah, the fella's come a long way!'

The other soldiers began to pick the grass while Hosi stood guard. After a while he said he wanted to go and relieve himself. The others said he could go only if he agreed to leave the rifle behind. Hosi said that he would not be long and would not go beyond the first bush he came to. The others said it was all right, all they needed was the rifle. Hosi replied that they were being irrational. If a lion was to attack them, they would be able to defend themselves by shouting; and anyway, the lion would not attack them because they were too many. But without a rifle, Hosi said, he himself was so vulnerable that a lion could kill and devour him easily.

'Egoist!' one of them thundered. 'Is one single life more valuable than the lives of others? These are some of the attitudes we'll have to wipe out in the Angola we are constructing.'

Hosi handed over the rifle and left. He walked for a while but could not find suitable shrubs. From some of them he heard strange noises and suspected that some snake or poisonous reptile might be lurking about. At last he found a proper place, some distance from where the others were working.

Having finished, Hosi walked back. To his astonishment, the others were not there. He looked out to the horizon but could not see them. He felt nervous; he was alone and not armed. He recalled what someone had once told him: 'The only disadvantage of being captured by wild animals is that they do not believe in keeping prisoners for propaganda purposes; they believe in eating them for dietary purposes.' This had once struck Hosi as a joke but now it seemed very real.

Eventually he got a grip on himself and decided that he was going to find his way home and report the other five for leaving him behind. He started walking along a path which he thought led to the camp. As he walked, he kept cursing the others. He knew precisely why they had treated him this way. It was his education. He had completed secondary school in Zambia and they hardly knew how to write properly. Their envy was pointless. He was a man made of finer stuff. Even if he had never stepped into a classroom he would still be thinking of the sorts of things that occupied his mind now.

Hosi banged into a stump on the path and swore loudly. He was angry with himself for being foolish. The more noise he made the more likelihood that he would attract lions. He continued cursing the others. They were reactionaries – worse than that. They were people who would not have second thoughts if someone were to offer them a million dollars to sell Angola out.

The sun was shining fiercely by now. Hosi had been walking for almost an hour and although he tried hard not to panic, he began to sweat and was feeling very uneasy. After three hours, he concluded that he was lost. He walked over to a huge tree, sat in the shade and began to weep. He remembered how Raimundo had said that there was an effective way of crying, the childlike sobbing meant to cleanse one's soul of everything. After a while, he stopped crying. He wondered whether anybody was watching him. If they were, then they must be laughing at him by now. He looked at the bright-blue sky and tried to spot the Soviet satellite. Someone had once told him that there were people with very powerful binoculars looking down at what was going on in the UNITA controlled territory. These Soviets, Hosi concluded, could be watching him, and laughing at him. He rubbed away his tears, put on a brave face and walked on.

He was feeling thirsty and hungry. He came to a small crater which had water in it but when he walked closer, he saw that the water was greenish and contained animal excrement. He decided that he was not that desperate and walked on. He listened for the sound of a vehicle but there was none. Although he had been trained in several aspects of war, Hosi knew next to nothing about survival. He had heard stories from the others about how people could live on wild honey and wild fruits, but they had been referring to the forests of central Angola, which teemed with vegetation, not the semi-desert in which he was now stranded. He hoped everything would soon be over.

There wasn't a single soul in sight. Hosi walked some more. There was only one being Hosi could turn to – God. As far as his faith was concerned, Hosi had been vacillating; in the past few days he had come to a firm conclusion that there was no God. Like a French philosopher he had once heard someone quote, he believed that God had been created by man. That was not all. If God was as merciful as Christians said he was, why had Africa seen so much misery: the famine in Ethiopia; apartheid; and the never-ending war in Angola? Why couldn't God have intervened and brought about peace, tranquillity and prosperity? Hosi had asked these questions several times and someone had once given him the answer. He had said that there was no God and that Africa would advance only when its people believed in outstanding men such as the Elder – 'Give

222

me seven Jehovahs to one Elder,' the man had said – who would deliver the continent from turmoil.

As Hosi continued walking, he began to address the God he hadn't believed in. He didn't care whether he was black, white, yellow, a Marxist or a capitalist. All that mattered to him was that God should listen to his plea and get him out of this mess. If only he could be forgiven for doubting God's existence and be shown the way to the camp, he would be forever grateful. God seemed to turn a deaf ear to his prayers.

Hosi then thought of his parents. He visualized his mother and father somewhere in heaven; his father would have stayed longer in purgatory. He began to speak to his father first. He was certainly aware of the tribulations that he had gone through – the school in Zambia, the tribalism, the hunger and the lack of clothes – and the determination with which he had pulled through. And now here he was, trying to help defeat those who had come to defile the motherland. He was sure that his father approved of his participation in the fight for the motherland. Could he, then, intervene with providence and get him out of his difficulty now? All he needed was to know the way to the camp or to find someone.

Hosi looked around. There was an eerie silence. He turned to his mother. The baby who had sucked from her breasts and then had the misfortune to see her dead had known very few days of happiness in his life. Now, as a grown-up soldier, he was lost deep in the Angolan semi-desert. Couldn't she help him just once more and get him to the camp, where a cool drink was waiting for him. Still nothing came into view.

Eventually Hosi became used to his surroundings and even began to enjoy his loneliness. He could say anything and insult anyone without being taken to task, because nobody would hear him. No, it was not that simple. There was still a danger. Suppose someone was hiding behind the shrubs or, as he had often suspected, the trees had been bugged? Many such thoughts flitted through his mind.

At last it was evening. Hosi had been walking the whole day. If he had been going in the opposite direction to the camp, then he was a long way away from it by now. The idea

223

of committing suicide had occurred to him more than once. He thought it would be the easiest solution. Instead of being attacked by a pride of famished lions and enduring a slow, painful death, Hosi felt he could save himself a lot of trouble by simply taking his own life. He wondered how he could do this. Maybe he would tie his belt to the branch of a tree, make a loop for his head and hang himself. But he still had so much energy left; he would climb a tree if he saw a lion and would turn to suicide only in the last resort. It was now almost six o'clock. Hosi wondered how he would spend the night. He did not know where the safest place to sleep was. He thought about a tree, but was worried that he would fall out once he was asleep.

He climbed a large tree to get an idea of the lie of the land. To his immense pleasure, he saw a fire. He heaved a sigh of relief and crossed himself. At last, he said to himself, he had found people who would lead him back to the camp.

The fire made Hosi regain all the hope and energy he had lost. He felt as if he had been lost for weeks. Though his stomach rumbled and his throat ached, the thought that water and food were at hand made all this seem insignificant. He began to walk with great vigour. The sounds coming every so often from behind the bushes no longer frightened him. He had come through the worst.

He had been walking for some time now without seeing the fire so he climbed a tree again to make sure that he was going in the right direction. At first he saw no sign of the fire, and he began to worry, but then he spotted it in the distance, beneath what looked like some huge trees. He climbed down and continued walking, making sure that he was heading straight for the fire.

After half an hour Hosi came near. He hid behind the bushes and tried to make out the figures he saw. He was surprised and also scared. He had not been expecting to see what now faced him. Three women and four men, each naked but for loincloths, were seated, warming themselves before the fire. Hosi trembled as a flurry of questions came to his mind. Was this some ritual gathering of the many wizards and

224

witches in the UNITA-controlled area? Would they kill him and cook him if he was captured? Hosi strained his ears, but could not understand what the people were saying. Eventually he realized that he had come before the Kamusekele, a nomadic tribe that wander around southern Angola and northern Namibia. He was relieved, but soon began to feel anxious again; how would the people before him react?

Then one of the men looked in Hosi's direction, wiggled his forefinger and said in Umbundu: 'Come here. We've seen you.' Hosi felt like a thief caught redhanded. He walked over to the fire and shook hands with the four Kamusekeles, who seemed not at all perturbed by his arrival. It was as if they had known him for a long time and were expecting him. Hosi sat down and began to explain his plight, switching between Portuguese and Umbundu every so often because he was nervous. One of the men said in imperfect Umbundu that someone who could speak not only Umbundu but also Portuguese would be coming soon to help Hosi.

Hosi asked for water. A woman went into a shelter – a collection of twigs placed against a tree – and brought him an animal-skin bag filled with water. Though the water gave off a smell Hosi found nauseating, he gulped it down enthusiastically. As Hosi drank, the others stared vacantly into the sky, whiling away time.

Now that he was feeling better, Hosi started to think about the Kamusekeles as he waited for the man who was coming to help him. He remembered having heard them as a child, and also of other peoples said to have strange customs. He had heard, for instance, of the Sele, who lived somewhere near Benguela and were said to be cannibals. He had heard countless stories of valiant Umbundu men who had defeated cannibals singlehanded, but he also recalled that while in Zambia a fellow Angolan refugee – a Chokue – had told a girl Hosi was after to beware of him, because like any Umbundu Hosi could be a cannibal. Hosi realized that as far as myths went in Angola, a cannibal was anyone who did not belong to your tribe.

Hosi also recalled that he had heard many positive things

about the Kamusekeles: they were said to be experts in finding their way through the forest; they were said to be good at detecting trees that contained enormous quantities of honey in their trunks; and they were said to be immune to almost all diseases. High blood pressure, mental depressions, diabetes and other ailments that afflicted town dwellers like the Umbundu were said to be absent among them.

Hosi was now wondering when his helper would come and was getting impatient. All he longed for was to be told how he could get back to the camp or the nearest track used by the lorries which would take him there. He continued with his ruminations about the Kamusekeles. He recalled that while at primary school in Zambia he had been taught that there were four main races in the world: Caucasian, Negroid, Mongoloid and Asiatic. In Africa, it was said, there were five different races: Hamites, Bantu, Nilotes, Negro and Hottentots. He looked at the Kamusekeles carefully and saw that their hair was short and their skins were lighter, though their features were rough. He concluded that the Kamusekeles certainly did not belong to the Bantu race. He promised himself that in a free Angola he would study them and write a long book.

At last the helper arrived. He was uncharacteristically tall, handsome and had the gait of a man who had once had authority. He said that his name was Njekwa. Hosi began to tell him his story. Njekwa kept nodding, as if he already knew what had happened to Hosi, and said that they often came across soldiers who had lost their way. He said they would take him to the camp in the morning.

A woman brought Hosi roasted meat and some fruit called mangongo. While he was eating – with the gusto of a starving man – Njekwa stood up, scratched his head and said: 'We're going somewhere near Rivungo tomorrow. We'll take you near the route used by the trucks.'

The other Kamusekeles disappeared into their huts to sleep. Hosi and Njekwa were left by the fireside. Njekwa said: 'Tell me about your life.'

Hosi hesitated at first and then poured out his life story. Njekwa listened attentively, moving only to add twigs to the

226

fire. After a while Hosi said: 'That is all I have to say. Now, what about you?'

Njekwa laughed, snapped his fingers and said: 'Each person has his story to tell. Some have terrible stories; some have funny stories; and others have stories which are simply incredible. That is our Angola.'

Hosi looked up, saw a shining object in the sky, turned to Njekwa and said: 'That must be a Soviet satellite. They must know that I am lost. Those Russians – they are powerful.'

'Forget about the Russians,' Njekwa began. 'Let me tell you about myself.'

Hosi was surprised. Njekwa had pronounced the word 'Russians' with such a Portuguese nuance that he doubted whether Njekwa was a Kamusekele. Indeed, as he soon discovered, he wasn't. Njekwa excused himself, saying that he was going to pick up his smoking pipe. He came back, sat down and lit the pipe. Each puff filled his face with the expression of a man about to have a life-long burden lifted from his back. Hosi stared at him silently. Although he was eager to hear Njekwa's story, what preoccupied him most was the desire to get back to the camp. He could not wait for the morning to come.

Njekwa began: 'Do you know that I am not a Kamusekele?'

'I suspected so.'

'Pity.'

'Why?'

'I don't want anyone except for the people I move with to know who I am. I am a Catholic priest. I have not been defrocked because I have been taken for dead. I knew your parents. They were, of course, much older than me. I have a feeling that I saw you as a baby. I am glad to see you now. I am not surprised at all. In the past few days I have been having the premonition that I would meet someone I had known years ago. I can tell that you're a soldier, perhaps a very loyal one, like most young men. I know that you might go back and report to your officers that you've met me.'

Hosi shifted and said: 'Who are you? What is your name?'

Njekwa continued without paying any attention to Hosi's

227

question. 'I have the feeling that since you've been brought up in Zambia you're not quite the same as the other soldiers.'

'How different am I?' Hosi asked.

'You're different because you've not suffered as much as the others. Suffering hardens people's hearts, unfortunately. You're likely to find more compassion among people who have three meals a day; among people who do not have to be constantly on the run for their lives; among people who have ample time for leisure. This might not be so apparent at the beginning. You might argue, for instance, that people who are suffering will do everything for each other. The truth is that all their moves will be calculated; they help the man in need so that he helps them when they are in need too. But at some point people who have suffered will want to give some kind of meaning to their suffering. Being involved in a noble cause is not enough. That is when sufferers need to see blood, but it has to be the blood of the fellow sufferers, the blood of their comrades-in-arms, spilled on orders from their commanders. Look at it this way: when a UNITA soldier sees the dead body of an MPLA soldier or that of a Cuban, he'll certainly rejoice, and will hold his Kalashnikov aloft and chant slogans. But when he sees the man he once ducked the enemies' bullets with in front of the firing squad, about to be shot for deviating from what I am told is the Paramount Thought, the war will gain a new dimension to him. It will be sanctified.'

Hosi waved his hands and said, 'No one gets shot in UNITA for that.'

Njekwa nodded his head and said: 'OK, not for that, but for something worse, such as contesting some of the decisions made by the leadership. Sorry for having digressed. You know that I am an exceptional Angolan?'

'Why?'

'Because I do not belong to a political party. That is why I am able to detach myself and look at everything objectively. What I've said about UNITA also applies to the MPLA. I am sure you've heard such terms as fractionism, coupism, reactionaries, etc., coming from that side?'

Hosi nodded.

228

Njekwa continued: 'Hundreds have gone after they were accused of those crimes. During the Portuguese rule, Sao Nicolau was filled with people the colonialists had perceived to be political aberrants. Now it is still filled, with people believed to be a threat to the communist system. We're all doomed.' Pointing to the huts in which the Kamusekeles were sleeping, Njekwa said: 'Those are the only free people. During Portuguese rule these people were living as they are living now. They kept wandering from place to place in search of food and water. The Portuguese thought they were too stupid to be civilized, so stupid that they did not even bother to teach them to read and write. When seen from afar these people might strike you as miserable and unhappy. They are never bothered by what goes on in the news; they pay no heed to the utopias the politicians on both sides keep harping on about; they are obsessed only with their daily survival. This is the reason I have walked hundreds of kilometres to come and live with them. There is something basic about them which gives them a degree of innocence no other tribe in Angola has. These are not people who are anxious to make their mark in the world: they are simply devoted to their existence. Spiritually, they are truly living in an Eden uncorrupted and untainted by man's smudge, as a fellow priest once wrote.'

Hosi interrupted and said: 'Can I say something?'

'What?'

'I don't agree entirely with what you've just said.'

'I don't expect you to. Why must people always agree with each other? This again is the result of authoritarian attitudes these politicos have imbibed from their masters abroad. But what do you disagree with precisely?'

'I think the Kamusekeles are a disgrace to Angola.'

Njekwa chuckled. Hosi continued: 'Europeans are disappointed when they come to Africa and find that we are not only articulate but that we can discuss philosophy and write poetry. What they actually expect to see are the Kamusekeles: they go about almost naked; they are nomadic; in a nutshell, they are primitive. Nothing pleases Europeans more than seeing lions, elephants, giraffes and other wild animals; and, of course, primitive Africans. Europeans would not see in the Kamusekeles human beings but some kind of wild animals that walk on two legs and can talk. In the future Angola – that is, in the Angola that will be built once UNITA comes to power – we'll make sure that these Kamusekeles not only go to school but start wearing proper trousers and shirts. Their women will have to start wearing petticoats, skirts and perfumes. We Africans cannot afford to have people like this around.'

Njekwa slapped his thigh and said: 'I know the point you're making. A year ago some UNITA officer took it upon himself to civilize the Kamusekeles. He took a number of them to Kaukuchi, near the Namibian border. He gave them proper clothes and tried to get them to eat pasta, tinned fish and the like. The Kamusekeles took it for a while but soon demanded their favourite diet – honey. Indeed, several drums of honey were brought to them. After a while, the Kamusekeles could stand it no more and fled back into the forest. The point is that what seems to us the most important thing in life is often not actually so important.'

Hosi appreciated why Njekwa had come to join the Kamusekeles. He felt that Njekwa was an independent thinker, a man whose views did not conform to the political fashion on either side of the conflict. He knew that there were others like Njekwa – men and women who tried to interpret everything individually. These would have to keep mum or their blood would be shed.

Njekwa coughed loudly and said: 'As I told you earlier, I am a Catholic priest. My real name is Artur Pereira. I am known as Father Pereira. They think I am dead; they might as well.'

'So you are trying to convert the Kamusekeles to Catholicism? How many are there in Angola?'

'Thousands,' said Njekwa. 'No. I am not trying to evangelize or anything of that sort. I am here because I want to remain sane. I want to put everything in its proper perspective. I have learned their language and I am sure that they'll accept me as one of their own soon.'

'Tell me about your notion of God, then,' Hosi said.

Njekwa laughed and said: 'It is a notion at which I arrived after much reflection. I believe that over the years there has been an increased attempt to personify God, to identify him with certain human traits such as nationality, race, etc. This is very limiting. True, as the Scripture says, he made us in his own image, but unfortunately we've not quite grasped what that means. It does not mean that because he made us in his image he is actually like one of us – far from it. It also does not mean that we should try and make him like us, let him share our prejudices, ambitions, and so on. Do you follow me?'

Hosi nodded.

Njekwa carried on: 'God is a principle that can be reduced to a mathematical formula. Nature and humanity are mere variables of this formula or principle. Our differences – political, philosophical, tribal or whatever – emanate from one and the same principle. I actually like to think of them as vectors of the force of existence. Back to God, anyway. What I am trying to say is that it is futile for the variable to try and speculate on the nature of the principle in the first place. Mathematically, we could put it this way: $A = X \times Y^2$. We may carry on with $X \times Y^2$, but at some point or other we will have to come back to A.'

Hosi laughed to himself. Angola, he thought, was a land filled with people who fancied themselves as politicians, heroes, patriots, revolutionaries, original thinkers and theoreticians. What these people had in common was a degree of insanity. That, indeed, was the reason he thought he and his fellow Angolans were a cut above other Africans.

Njekwa was now looking serious. He tossed his head back and said: 'I wish I could tell you more about my theory. But I have to tell you my life story. Where do I begin? All right. I will begin at the Cuando mission.'

'Are you really from there?' Hosi asked.

'Why would I lie?' Njekwa responded. 'I actually come from Kaluanda, which, as you probably know, is about a three-hour walk from Cuando mission. I was a very happy child. My father was one of the richest men in the area and he commanded the respect of everyone – including the local Portuguese traders. I did very well at school. I was expected to become a teacher or an administrator. I went along with that up to a point. Then I came under the influence of Father Amaral, a Portuguese who used to teach us morals.'

'Used to teach you what?' Hosi asked.

'Morals. Under the Portuguese all secondary school students studied morals. It was a mixture of Catholicism and philosophy. Father Amaral said a young man with my brains was fit only for one profession – serving God. I hesitated at first. Here was yet another man trying to dictate to me what to do with my life! I wanted to be free. I told him to buzz off and went on with my life. But the father would not let me alone. One day he came to me and said he had had a long dream the previous night. In it, he said, he had actually dreamt of a succession of black saints beside St Peter, St Paul and St Patrick up in heaven. Then the Virgin Mother herself had told him that Africa would produce a number of saints, one of which was going to come from Angola.

'At first I did not take him seriously, but later I felt something stir in me – something I am not quite able to explain. Then I understood everything: the time had come. I had to give myself to the Lord. I went to Father Amaral and told him that I was ready for the call. He was a short man with a long, white beard, dressed in a grey cassock and sandals – I can't remember now which order he belonged to.

'When I told him that I accepted the call and that I was prepared to become a priest, he almost jumped out of his chair. His face, which was usually solemn, immediately looked younger and livelier. Then tears rolled down his face. Shaking his head, he said: "Hah! At last my prayer has been answered." He kissed me on both cheeks and asked me to join him for dinner – a sumptuous dish cooked by a chap who is now a political commissar.

'When I told my parents about my decision, they were appalled. So were my friends. They could not understand why such a bright and virile young man like myself, who had made girls resort to rubbing tractor grease on to their legs to make

232

themselves attractive to him, had opted for a life of celibacy and poverty. Well, I knew that as a priest I would not be starving. As for women, I did not in the least care about them. As I was growing up, one fact was very clear in my head: I was not going to marry a local girl. I was not only too good for them – that is, intellectually, and, – let's face it, physically – but they all struck me as being irredeemably stupid. I am sure this will seem pompous to you. Well, it was; there was nothing I could do about it. I began to view our local girls as one does when one comes back from a city. True, I had gone to bed with one or two of them but that was only because I wanted to make sure that certain pipes were not blocked, as the saying goes. Of course, I often came across beautiful, intelligent girls at the student dances. I once even danced with the white Miss Huambo. In those days – the Portuguese were real bastards – two beauty competitions would be held annually: one for white girls and the other for non-whites. I was once invited to the competition and ended up dancing with the winner herself. Ask anyone from my time and they will tell you. I had made history.

'Though I was attracted to the town girls, I was very wary of them. I had a strong feeling that they thought of me as a country bumpkin. OK, out of compassion one of them might have said yes to my proposal, but deep in her she'd still see me as a mere villager, someone who had yet to be civilized. I wanted to preserve my dignity and avoided them. Then, of course, I met a few mulattas, but they didn't interest me.

'So Angola did not have any women that could send me crazy. My parents soon gave in. My mother then became so pro the idea that she began to claim that the Virgin Mother herself had appeared to her three times; but that is another story. I was ordained shortly before independence. Then there was the civil war. I was sent to Kaluanda. Though the villagers there were once staunch UNITA supporters, they all switched to the MPLA when UNITA fled into the forest. You know that people are like grass: they bend to whichever direction the wind is blowing.

'The MPLA party cadres who came into the village were

real zealots. Each of them thought of himself as Karl Marx reincarnated. Illiterate villagers began to be drilled in dialectical materialism in the name of progress. The point is not that philosophy is the preserve of town dwellers or the intelligentsia; far from it. The point is that the most important things should come first. The villagers needed to know about farming and health. Anyway, that was it. On the radio Cubans, Soviets and what have you were being thanked hourly for having helped in the defeat of the enemies of the Angolan people – the South Africans, American and British mercenaries and their Angolan lackeys, UNITA and the FNLA. Slogan-chanting became a way of life. Children became members of the Young Pioneers, which later became Agostinho Neto's pioneers. They were soon going about with Kalashnikovs. As for me, I was only allowed to see the people at night because they were supposed to be busy working in the fields during the day. Despite much opposition from the political commissar – a childhood friend of mine – I carried on. People came to see me whenever they could for their spiritual problems. Some of them had sons who had gone to the UNITA side and others had sons in the MPLA. They were torn between the two. They were always switching sides. Not so much because of the wind factor but because their sons had been conscripted by force. I tried my best to resolve their problems. It was at this time that both my parents died within months of each other. It was a terrible blow, but my heart was by now so calloused that however hard a tragedy it was, it did not unsettle me. And at this moment Arlinda came into my life – or rather, I came into hers. She was much younger than me, and I treated her as a little sister. Like every other girl from the area, she admired me. She told me that she was engaged to Ramillo Kalunsungu, a teacher. I was pleased to hear that because the young man was an acquaintance of mine. He had once wanted to be a seminarian. He was dedicated to his pupils and did all he could to help them read and write in spite of the continual interference from the political commissar, who wanted the children to master dialectical materialism before they could even write properly.

234

'One day, a jeep came and Ramillo was taken away. We learned in the news days after that he and several others had been charged with counter-revolutionary activities and that they were going to be tried in a people's court. Indeed, after a few days Ramillo and several others were tried. Two of the accused were sentenced to be executed in public at Huambo's main sports stadium. Ramillo himself was sentenced to two years' imprisonment with hard labour for having failed to report to the DISA authorities about the network of UNITA supporters he had belonged to.

'Soon after, Arlinda came to me crying. She said she was not sure whether Ramillo would ever come back. A lot of people, she said, had disappeared, never to be seen again. I tried to console her. As Ramillo was gone, I was asked by the political commissar to start teaching. I did so willingly. Arlinda too began to teach. We became very close. I found that though she was not that physically attractive, there was something that drew me to her. Occasionally we are drawn to women not because they have shapely bodies but because they have shapely souls. That is what Arlinda had. She had a virgin heart, a heart that gave forth pure, innocent emotions. I knew that she was grieving for her fiancé in earnest. The political commander tried to win her sexual favours by giving her sugar and cooking oil. He failed.'

Njekwa slapped his thigh, frowned and said: 'Shit! Cooking oil and sugar – that is what it takes to bribe a woman in the People's Republic of Angola. Where we are heading to?'

Hosi groaned in agreement.

Njekwa continued: 'But he never got anywhere. She turned down his sugar and came to me whenever she needed anything. She knew that I'd never let her down.

'Things were getting more complicated. More people kept disappearing. Arlinda and I became closer, so close that at one time she decided that she should become a nun. I objected, saying that Ramillo would soon be out of prison. Then Arlinda became pregnant. Rumour went around that the political commissar was the father of the baby. He seemed to be pleased to hear this; although he was a married man, he wanted to make

235

sure that people thought of him not only as a political heavy-weight but also as a sexual one.

'A year after the baby was born Ramillo came out of prison. Although Arlinda received him with open arms, she would not tell him who the father of the baby was. Ramillo came to see me. He said, "Father, help me. I am prepared to forgive Arlinda and love that child as though he were mine. Please, can you get her to tell me who the father of that child is?" I told him that that would not be possible and that I had already tried to worm it out of Arlinda but failed. The political commissar was transferred to another area and, along with other provincial bigwigs, was implicated in a diamond-smuggling ring. Things were fine for a while. Ramillo seemed to have accepted the fact that Arlinda was not going to tell him who the father of the baby was. Still, he often came to me and said what a wretched person he was. His years in prison had made him a marked man and he could not get a proper job.

'Then Arlinda's baby died. It was very painful for the whole village, but a kind of relief for me. For days afterwards, the villagers talked about the possible causes that had led to the baby's death. Needless to say, witchcraft featured high. A week after the baby's death Ramillo came to me and confessed that he had killed the baby. "I just can't help seeing the child," he said. A day after, Ramillo was found dead in my house, lying beside a gun fitted with a silencer.'

Hosi opened his mouth involuntarily and his eyes bulged. Struggling for words, he said: 'You shot him?'

Njekwa crossed himself. Hosi saw that there were tears in his eyes.

BOOK III

25

It was a rainy Saturday afternoon. Captain Junior of the Angolan Armed Forces was driving along a bumpy, muddy road. It was not a very safe thing to do. He knew that the forest was infested with UNITA bandits and the road heavily planted with landmines. He simply could not understand some of their actions. Years ago, for instance, a bomb had exploded in Canhe market near the Catholic church. Hundreds had died. And now they had taken to planting bombs where internationalist comrades – Russians, East Germans and Cubans – were housed.

The bandits, Junior felt, had sown hatred in the land. He distrusted servants so much that now he did not have one. What Junior failed to understand was that even people who seemed to have been enlightened – such as teachers, medical assistants and the like – supported the bandits in secret. In the two years that he had been regional head of the secret police, several rings of UNITA supporters had been uncovered. And to his disappointment, some of the people involved with it were very close to him.

Junior drove past Estufa. During the Portuguese rule, it had been a botanical garden. Now, nobody cared for it; people were too busy trying to survive. As he drove past the pool near the main market, Junior thought of the bandits again. He felt that they were out to spread divisions among the Angolan people. For instance, they moaned about northerners and mulattos. They kept saying that these two were wielding too much power in Angola. But all this was lies. If the bandits ever came to power, they would install a dictatorship and that would be the end of socialism for Angola.

Junior passed some dilapidated buildings. His heart sank,

and he swore. The bandits, he thought, were holding back the development of the motherland. If there had been no war, the buildings would have been properly repaired by now. He drove to an enclosed area near the railway station where he had an apartment. During the Portuguese rule, Huambo had been their pride. They had even named the city Nova Lisboa, after Lisbon. Now, Huambo was the symbol of Angolan despair: the hospitals were filled with people who had been affected by the war.

Junior went into his apartment and cooked himself dinner – fried eggs with bread. It was frugal by the standards of a party bigwig. He had a sitting room with a fridge and a television, a sofa and two chairs. These were all old.

Junior felt guilty as he sat down to eat. He knew that there were people who spent days and nights in queues trying to get food. He believed that because they had not had the proper ideological preparation, they would rush to conclude that socialism meant long queues and black market. High-ranking members of his party were just as bad: they had all betrayed the spirit of socialism, with their corruption.

Junior stopped eating and picked up a notebook. He leafed through it and came to a page he had marked with red asterisks. He noted a passage he had underlined:

There are two fighting against the will of the Angolan people: the UNITA bandits and their imperialist masters; and petit-bourgeois tendencies among our own cadres. Socialism won't be brought about by coloured video sets, big hi-fi equipment and all the rubbish the capitalists have produced to enslave us. I cry as I see my fellow cadres succumb to the false needs created by greedy entrepreneurs.

Later, when he was in bed, Junior was awoken by a loud knock. He walked over to the door and said: 'Who is it?'

'Mama!' came the reply.

Susana, a slender, light-skinned woman with an artificial leg (she had once stepped on a landmine), entered the house and sat on the sofa. 'It has taken two weeks to get here,' she said. 'That is because we can only travel in a military convoy. It is hell. When is this war going to be over?'

'Mother, I can't answer that question. This war will be over only when the bandits have vanished. We are being too soft on them. These people deserve no mercy.'

Susana rubbed her fingers and said: 'I understand you, Papa. But remember that those people in the bush are your cousins. Chimbika, for instance. He is a commander somewhere. Now, Chimbika is your cousin because his father, Mano Kadimba, is a direct cousin of mine.'

Junior thumped the chair and said: 'Mama, that is the problem with you people. You think in terms of cousins and brothers. You should think in terms of Angola. This thinking in terms of brothers, cousins and so on is a very southern thing. I will tell you something I was not supposed to have told you, Mama. There was a commander of the bandits that was supposed to have led an attack on Kalonga. Do you know it?'

Susana shifted and said: 'Ah. Kalonga? I know it very well. When Laureta got married in 1956 we had to go there to get the veil.'

'Yes, they were supposed to have attacked Kalonga. Then what does the fool do? He sends a letter to his mother telling her to go somewhere. The mother decided to tell her daughter, who was deeply in love with one of our commanders. She showed him the letter straightaway. The bandits were clobbered like hell. Now, that was a victory for the Angolan people. But suppose that that commander had been on our side? Many lives would have been lost just because he wanted to save his mother.'

Susana frowned and said: 'Well, my son, it is very hard to understand. To tell you the truth, Angola will send us all mad some day. Let it be. We know nothing.'

'Mama, you are the people – the backbone of the MPLA. All you have to do is be loyal and you'll be safe.'

Susana frowned again and said: 'Papa, we have big problems.'

Junior interrupted her and said: 'Problems are supposed to be dealt with by the social services department, not me.'

'This is serious. It is a problem and you will have to help us.'

'What is it?'

'Emaculada is in prison.'

Junior hit the chair hard and said: 'What the hell has she done?'

'Listen first. There is hunger where I have come from. We were moved from our houses to a settlement near Cuando, as you know. They wanted to keep us away from UNITA. We protested at the beginning but then gave in. After a while we decided to cultivate some fields. Emaculada planted a very large maize field because she was a very hard-working woman. Then people began to steal from her maize field. So Emaculada started living in a hut next to her field. At night she would wait for the thieves and chase them away. One day, she decided to take a hoe to chase the thief. The thief was a woman called Evalina. Emaculada hit her head so hard that she chopped it off.'

Junior shook his head in horror.

Susana continued: 'Nobody knew exactly what had happened. Emaculada became frightened and buried the corpse somewhere. One day, a dog was seen with a decomposing human hand in its mouth, and Evalina's body was discovered. When she was arrested Emaculada was asked the reason she had killed Evalina. She said she had been possessed by the devil. The commissar did not accept this. He said Emaculada should be sent for trial at the people's court in Huambo.'

Junior said: 'So what do you want me to do?'

'We want you to convince the people involved with the court that she was under the influence of the devil. I tell you, son, that Old Pedro – he has a problem too which I will come to later! – has certified that Evalina was indeed under the influence of an evil spirit. Now, as you know, Old Pedro is a prophet. He knows what he is talking about.'

Junior said: 'You are confusing things, Mama. My job is not to influence the course of justice. I believe in the People's

242

Republic of Angola and I believe that our institutions should be firm. When you ask me to intervene with the judicial process, you are asking me to tamper with your own rights.'

Susana shook her head and said: 'There you go as usual. Big, big words. You sound like everybody else. When are you people going to start talking sense? They said, "*O mbalundo vutima.*" You probably don't understand. I will try and explain to you in Portuguese. It means that wherever you go, whatever you do and whoever you are with, never let the place of your birth slip from your mind.'

'The problem with proverbs is that they are reactionary. I once suggested that people at the National Institute of Languages in Luanda should come up with several revolutionary proverbs. Proverbs that will stir people to act and not limit their horizons to their kin.'

Susana slapped her thighs and said: 'O my son, listen to me, please. I don't know why you are avoiding listening. Emaculada was under the influence of the spirits. Please help her.'

'Well, all I can do is get a psychiatrist to examine her and tell the court that she ought to be in a mental asylum and not a prison.'

Susana smiled and said: 'Thank you, Papa. Please do all you can. God will reward you. I know you young people don't believe in God – you are all materialists, as you call yourselves. Don't worry. We are praying for you daily.'

Junior smiled. Susana said: 'Now we come to the second problem. It is about Old Pedro. He too is in detention. It is a long story, but I will make it short. Old Pedro has a nephew called Casumiro. He is a UNITA soldier. He often used to come and see him at night. What Casumiro actually wanted was to take Graca with him into the bush. Now, as you know, Brito, the vice-commissar, wanted Graca too. When he got wind of the story that Casumiro was making secret forays into the settlement at night, he ordered the arrest of Old Pedro.'

Junior said: 'I can't help you there, Mama.'

Susana said: 'Dear son, do something. I only wish that you knew what Old Pedro had to go through for me: he prayed for my maize to grow properly, and I ended up getting three bags of maize. I was once troubled with a pain which would begin at my forehead, come all the way down to my waist and go out by my left foot. Old Pedro prayed for me: the pain disappeared. He's not only done a lot for me; he's done a lot for our people too. One day he told everyone that there would be something very strange happening. What did we see? A helicopter flew past the settlement and then exploded in mid-air.'

Junior said: 'What do you want me to do, then?'

'I want you to tell the officers to release him because he might pray and God will punish all of you.'

Junior chuckled.

Susana said: 'This is true. When he was arrested, Old Pedro was heard saying, "I curse the MPLA and its soldiers in the name of Abraham." I felt for you, my son. I went home, sat down and said to God that you had nothing to do with Old Pedro's arrest.'

Junior chuckled again and said: 'The problem with God is that he causes so much anguish on earth. People spend most of their time worrying about how he thinks of them and not worrying about how they can improve their lives.'

Susana clapped her hands and said: 'Thank you, Lord. Now, Junior, you're saying that God causes people anguish. At least you believe that he exists.'

'I know that he exists in people's minds. The fact is, Mama, there is no God.'

Susana shook her head and said: 'We've been through this before. But I will tell you one thing. The whites believe in God. And they have been to the moon. The whites believe in God and they made the aeroplane. What have we made to say there is no God?'

'I will tell you about another great white man – Karl Marx. He said there is no God, and the principles he formulated are now taking over the world. The Soviets are white and yet most of them maintain that there is no God. But that is beside the point. The fact is that you should stop thinking that just because a white man says something, then it is true.'

Susana looked straight at Junior and said: 'I will tell you

something. Did you know that Israel and the Soviet Union will one day go to war and that Israel will emerge as the victor?'

'Who's been putting that into your head, Mama?'

Susana said she was going to show Junior a pamphlet which was in one of her bundles. She went out of the room and came back after a while. She showed Junior the passage where the war between the Soviet Union and Israel was predicted.

Junior said: 'This is reactionary propaganda. I am sure that this has come straight from the CIA.'

'Don't talk like that about the word of God.'

'How did you get this?'

'Old Pedro. He gave it to me one day. It contains so much truth.'

'So this man sees a UNITA bandit and distributes CIA propaganda. And you want me to help free him. Mama, don't you realize he is a danger to Angola? Jomo Kenyatta was a reactionary, but he said something that makes sense to me. He said the whites came and asked the people to close their eyes in prayer. When they opened their eyes the whites had taken the land. These people are spreading Christian pamphlets now. When you open your eyes, you'll find that Angola will be gone. Your diamonds and land will no longer be under your control.'

Susana shook her head and said: 'Listen, son. I have another problem. It is about Miguel, Feliciana's son. He has all along managed to avoid military service by hiding in banana trees and under his mother's bed. Now they have caught up with him. The point is that the boy is epileptic. Those people in the army won't understand. We want you to do something.'

Junior threw his arms in the air and said: 'You want me to change the world. I tell you that there is only one way that I am able to help the people – by working with the MPLA, the vanguard of the masses.'

Susana chuckled and said: 'The problem with you, Papa, is that you talk to me as though I am not your mother. You talk to me the way politicians talk at rallies.'

'You are offended because I speak the truth.'

245

Susana looked straight at Junior and said: 'God bless you, my son. I have to go to bed.'

People at the Victoria settlement had had high hopes when they sent Susana to go and lobby her son. She returned with the sad news that he had refused to help them. Susana remained in her house for days. Some said she was weeping; others that she was praying.

'Surely, how can that boy turn us down?' said Kabinga to Americo as the two old men sat one afternoon beneath a huge mango tree.

Americo puffed at his pipe and said: 'He's a mulatto. That is the problem with him. That boy is confused. Like most mulattos, he has his stomach in Angola but his heart in Portugal.'

Americo passed on the pipe to Kabinga, who gave two energetic puffs and said: 'The poor woman. I would not have tolerated such treatment. I mean, this is what makes some people bewitch their own children.'

'Witchcraft does not work that well with mulattos. In the future we will tell them all to pack. You just wait. The reason the MPLA killed Nito Alves was that he said that if Angola is free, why, then, must the mulattos be the bosses? The mulattos called upon the Cubans and the Russians and ordered them to kill him.'

Kabinga leaned closer to Americo and whispered: 'But the man survived for a while.'

'But he was finally caught on top of a coconut tree. That is because he was a northerner. You see, they are all used to being cooks, servants and the like. So they can't survive in the forest. Had he been from the south, I am sure he would have survived.'

Kabinga smiled and said: 'That is why they are going to lose this war. Have you ever heard of a war won by the descendants of shoe-shining boys? We are the warriors. They know it. Shsh, be silent. I can hear the sound of a Land-Rover. I hope nobody has been listening to us! Nowadays even the chickens have ears!'

★

246

The Land-Rover that Kabinga and Americo had heard was Junior on his way to see his mother. This time he had several bodyguards with him.

'Can I come in?' Junior shouted at the door to his mother's house.

'Please, Papa!'

The house was very humble, with two rooms. One was Susana's bedroom. She lay on a wooden bed and had covered herself with a blue blanket. Junior sat on the chair beside his mother's bed. At one end of the bed was a basin containing several roots. Junior decided not to ask what they were.

Susana turned to Junior and said: 'I am dying. I have this strange pain. I am sure Old Pedro is not pleased with the way you are behaving. If only you could help get him out of prison, he would pray for me and I'd get better.'

'But, Mother, he's a traitor.'

Susana waved her hand and said: 'We've been through that already. Let it be. I will die and I know that I will go to heaven. There is no doubt about that. Only yesterday, I said to God, "Father, you see everything."'

'But, Mama, what do you really want? I don't see how the freeing of prisoners will help this?'

Susana said: 'It is the church. We belong to the same church – the Church of Zion. Old Pedro was our prophet. Now he is in prison. We have Prophetess Laura and she's now running the church. God appeared to her in a dream and said that there was only one person who could help the situation – that is me.'

'How?'

'By forcing those people that are holding Old Pedro. They say you have the power – and God knows it. You have put me in terrible shame, my son. Now they all look at me and say: "She did not give birth to a human." They are praying quite all right, but they feel I am the key to the problem.'

'But I *can't*.'

'You can. We had the case of Sabaka, for instance. He was let off because he had a nephew in the police.'

'What had Sabaka done?'

'You don't even follow what happens to your people now.'

247

'Mama, you know very well that I am a busy person. There are far more important issues that I have to pay attention to, such as the country.'

Susana smiled and said: 'We will all die. The country will still be there. Listen, my dear son, if you die today or if you get into trouble, who will be shedding genuine tears? Me. Nobody else. All those people with whom you use all those big Portuguese words will only say: "What a pity, he was a good man." But your people and I will be shedding tears that will be coming from the bottom of our hearts.'

Junior smiled and said: 'You don't have to tell me that. I know that you love me very much.'

'But you have to remember this. They are saying a lot of things. They are saying, for instance, that the reason you can't understand us is that you are a mulatto.'

'Now, Mama, you see the reason why anyone who is involved with the UNITA bandits should be locked up?'

'No. I don't.'

'Because these bandits believe in hatred. They believe in dividing us. By saying first that there are the mulattos and then the northerners and then we southerners, they are dividing the nation and ensuring that the war goes on. Mama, if you look closely at the MPLA history you will find that we've never believed in racial or any kind of division. The bandits say that we are dominated by northerners. That is not true. We are the people's party.'

Susana was seized by a coughing fit. After it was over she said: 'Are you going to help Old Pedro to be freed? He is a prophet, a man of God.'

'Mama, you've not been listening. Old Pedro is a traitor. He deserves to go to prison. But I will do one thing: I will go and see him and ask him to write a letter to the Central Committee, asking to be forgiven.'

Susana's face brightened. She smiled and said: 'Did you say that you will see him?'

'Yes!'

'My prayers are being answered. When you see him, please tell him that we are all praying for him.'

248

As Junior was about to drive away two men approached him: Kabinga and Americo. They shook hands and Kabinga said: 'Tell us, Comrade, how is the struggle against the UNITA bandits going?'

Junior smiled and said: 'They will soon know what it is to play with the Angolan people. They have the backing of the capitalists, who, as you know, are very powerful. But things will turn against them soon.'

Then Kabinga said: 'Comrade, we have this problem. Old Pedro is in detention. We are not quite sure whether he'll be able to cope. We just thought that some decision could be taken to have him put under house-arrest or something less severe.'

Junior said: 'We are looking into that.'

'Then there is also the case of this woman who is accused of having murdered someone. The truth is that she is mad. Her grandfather, Samuel Pulukua, took off his clothes in front of a missionary. They are all mad. Please do something.'

'That too is being looked into,' Junior answered.

'Oh, thank you!' Kabinga said.

They all shook hands again and Junior left for the prison.

The boy lay in bed at one end of the ward, surrounded by guards. The guards were bored; they did not know the reason they were guarding him. They also did not know why they had to accompany the boy whenever he went to the toilet. Instead of using the WC, the boy used a chamberpot and his mess was then taken away by members of the secret police. Now and then they had tried to whisper to him, asking why they had been assigned to guard him. The boy would simply shake his head.

The other patients in the ward did not have the slightest interest in the boy. They had seen so much in their lives that nothing excited them any more. Although the nurses tried hard to keep the beds in the hospital clean, so many people were coming to it that it was not possible. The sheets on the bed had turned brown. People kept coming to the hospital every day. There were those who had been injured in a bomb attack or those who had contracted some incurable disease. There was a lot of noise in the hospital for there was a ward full of children who had stepped on landmines and had had their legs amputated.

The boy had had several coughing fits. As soon as they came to an end he would spit into a shining metal chamberpot by the bedside. Every time he spat the guards would look at him. Then, after another coughing bout, they heard the boy spit what sounded to them like a stone. They bent over and looked into the chamberpot: it was a diamond. They all breathed a sigh of relief. The boy smiled and spoke for the first time in two days. 'Finished, this is it!' he said.

The guards were confused. They could not understand why he seemed so calm, even when he was going to be punished severely. Diamond smugglers – they were called *kamanguistas* – were said to be some of the worst enemies of the people. There had just been a trial which went out live on national radio. It was said repeatedly in political speeches that diamonds were the communal health, and that what the smuggler was actually doing was depriving the Angolan people of better schools, better hospitals and better education. The speeches were, of course, applauded but in practice many people still engaged in trafficking. It was rumoured that some of the authorities – some said it was those who were shouting loudest – had cronies involved in the smuggling. Angolans who had once lived in Zaire were blamed for smuggling and other illegal activities. It was often said that Angolans were by nature slightly sheepish and did not believe in dangerous schemes, while Zaireans had a taste for capitalism and saw smuggling as a reasonable thing to do.

Two officers came and took the boy away in a Toyota van. It was then that the other patients in the hospital noticed him and wondered what he had done.

Second Lieutenant Osvaldo Mbueti of the Angolan Armed Forces was said to be one of the brightest young men of his generation. He often remembered the time when he had been unable to recite the multiplication table. That had all vanished after his trip to Cuba. In Angola, on both the MPLA and UNITA sides, to be described as bright actually meant that one was in the good books of the party. Some of his enemies – and there were several – disputed the assertion that Osvaldo had any brains, but the party and the army trusted him and he was marked for a very high post in Huambo province. Some maintained that, considering his ability, the reason he had achieved so much was that he was Captain Junior's protégé. And who, they kept asking, would not have thrived with the blessing of the provincial head of the security police?

Osvaldo was actually a disappointed man. Angola did not mean much to him. His private wish was to get a passport and flee to Portugal or some other European country. It did not matter to him whether he ended up doing a menial job: all he wanted was to get away from Angola. He knew that his frustration dated back to his days in Cuba, but it had crystallized at Kalonga.

Second Lieutenant Osvaldo Mbueti belonged to the Intelligence Battalion of the Fifth Brigade. The government forces were planning to carry out an offensive against the UNITA rebels in the south, so the forces had to mass at Kalonga. Osvaldo was as excited as the other officers. All along they had been waiting for this moment. They even felt that the government had been delaying. They knew that a lot of war material had been supplied by the Soviet Union and that once this was deployed against the rebels, they would have no chance of resisting. They knew that the South Africans would not allow their puppets to be crushed out of existence, but they knew that things down south were not that fine. It was a well-known fact that South Africa would soon be plunged into revolution. Indeed, as Osvaldo had heard someone say, South Africa was the only country in the world where a true Marxist revolution could take place. This was because it was the only country that had a proletariat in the truest sense of the word. Osvaldo and his fellow officers could not understand why the commanders were taking so long to order the start of the offensive.

It was at Kalonga that Osvaldo had his first affair with a girl who, he felt, was truly in love with him. He did not love her. Osvaldo's heart had become calloused, as he often put it, after an affair with a girl called Jiji, from Luanda. Osvaldo had loved her very much. At first she had pretended that she loved him too. When Jiji became pregnant, Osvado was very excited. He had been wondering in private whether he was capable of fathering a child. In the past he had had several girlfriends. Sometimes he would use condoms – they were now being given freely since the advent of AIDS – but if he ran out of them, even though he would promise to come outside the girl, many times he came inside her. They would worry that the girl might be pregnant, but she never was and then Osvaldo would worry again. Angola, he kept saying to himself, was running short of people and any man worth his salt was supposed to leave someone who looked like him before he died.

Then Jiji had a baby. To Osvaldo's horror, it turned out to be a mulatto. At first Jiji refused to reveal who the father was, but when Osvaldo pressed her further she told him that it was an East German who had had sex with her in exchange for a bottle of perfume. Osvaldo had decided then that he would never love another woman.

Osvaldo met Berta at a dance at the Kalonga party head-quarters. At the beginning of the dance, revolutionary Angolan music was played. Then, as the night wore on and people became progressively drunk, Kassav and Zairean rumba was played more frequently. Then they began to play sentimental Brazilian music. Most of the songs were by Roberto Carlos. The dancers held each other tightly and exchanged kisses. Suppressed moans were heard as well as whispers.

Then, after the dance, Berta asked Osvaldo to escort her home. She said it was too dark and one could never tell where a Kwacha – that was how UNITA soldiers were referred to – might be hiding.

Osvaldo accepted at once. As they walked home, Osvaldo asked Berta to tell him more about herself.

'I live with my mother. She is very old and she has eye problems. I want to go to Luanda and study; I am sure that I could make it and become a doctor,' Berta said.

'Have you got any brothers and sisters?' Osvaldo asked.

'One brother. His name is Raul. I am told that he is a bigwig among the bandits. I hope he doesn't die.'

'I too have a brother who has chosen the wrong path. He fled to Zambia with some people in 1975. People from there tell me that he has joined the bandits. I just can't understand some of these people. It is clear that UNITA has allied itself with the worst government in the world – South Africa. It is also clear to them that UNITA kills and maims innocent people. Huambo is filled with children whose legs have been amputated by landmines planted by these rebels, and yet people still join them.'

Berta hissed in distress and said: 'My brother should be

forgiven. He was very young when he joined UNITA. He did not know what he was doing.'

They talked for a while and then Osvaldo said: 'Are you involved with someone? I mean, have you got a boyfriend?'

Berta smiled and said: 'No. There are no men here of my type.'

'What is your type?'

'Well, I know that as a revolutionary I am not supposed to be a snob. That is, it does not matter if I start going out with an illiterate peasant. The problem is that the peasants here are not my type. Most men in Kalonga are peasants or just a little above that.'

'You haven't answered my question. What is your type?'

'Oh, a romantic man, a man who knows how to love. That is not all. I need a revolutionary, someone who has understood the struggle and has some notion of dialectical materialism.'

Osvaldo burst out laughing and said: 'What you want is a boring man! A *Jornal de Angola*, not so?'

Then Berta kissed Osvaldo on the cheek and the two bid each other farewell. After that they saw each other frequently and when Osvaldo proposed to Berta, she accepted at once.

One evening Osvaldo and Berta lay in bed listening to Cananito Alexandre's '*Diga por favor*'. Berta turned over to Osvaldo and said: 'Take that horrible stuff off. Let's have Djavan or Milton Nascimento. Or what about that cassette of Fafa de Belem? Do you still have it?'

Osvaldo said: 'Who says the Americans are imperialists? The real imperialists in the Portuguese-speaking world are the Brazilians. Just look at the way we're all hooked on their music. Some Angolan girls cannot have orgasms without Roberto Carlos's voice in the background!'

Berta slapped him on the leg and said: 'Don't talk to me like that. I hate that kind of language; it's disgusting!'

'Not as disgusting as some of the things we get up to.'

Berta hit Osvaldo again. She then held his chin and said: 'Now, listen, you big head, I have some news for you. The Kwachas will be here in two weeks.'

'How do you know?'

254

'Well, as I told you the first time we met, I have a brother who is a commander. He has written to my mother and me, telling us to move away from here because they will be coming to attack Kalonga in two weeks.'

Osvaldo was excited. Information from the enemy lines was very hard to come by. There had been several attempts to infiltrate them but they had all proved fruitless. The guerrillas found it easy to spot a spy in their midst. This was not the case among the government forces.

Osvaldo got dressed, then said he had an urgent meeting to attend. He went straight to the signals men and asked them to pass the message to regional intelligence headquarters about the impending UNITA attack. He then went to the brigade commander and gave them the information too. The commander asked how he had come by the information. Osvaldo said he had somehow managed to plant a spy in the enemy lines. The commander was so excited that he felt he could get the details at some future date. They were all very pleased with Osvaldo.

Preparations were made and a whole battalion was sent to ambush the enemy. The operation apparently proved successful. According to reports sent to the national radio and the news agency, a complete unit of the bandits was annihilated.

Yet in truth the offensive was a failure. The commanders had underestimated the power of the South African Airforce. However, Osvaldo emerged a hero. When the regional commander came to address the battalions involved in the offensive, his name was mentioned. Soon he was promoted to lieutenant. But it was discovered that he had come across the information about the battalion not by planting a spy but because he was seeing a girl whose mother had received a letter giving details of the attack. This discovery had discredited Osvaldo, both with his colleagues but also with the commanders. And that was when he began to have second thoughts about the war. He began to hate himself for questioning the war, for he was actually questioning the cause for which many had sacrificed their arms, their legs, their very lives.

Osvaldo was quizzed about the information that he had

given to the officials. He confessed at once and asked to be forgiven. It was decided that from then on, Osvaldo would no longer work in the intelligence department; instead, he would go to the logistics section. He suspected that the reason he had been shifted was that he was a southerner. Junior told him not to worry.

It was then that Osvaldo met Xavier Ramos, the teacher. Like most high-ranking FNLA leaders, Xavier Ramos had fled to Zaire in 1975, when the MPLA had come to power. Then the government issued a communiqué that all those who had belonged to any political party other than the MPLA and wanted to return were free to do so as long as they started supporting the MPLA. Xavier Ramos had taken advantage of this.

One day Osvaldo had gone to the wedding of a fellow officer. After a while a man came up, tapped him on the back and said:

'Haven't I seen you somewhere before?'

'I think so. Are you Xavier Ramos, the teacher?'

'Indeed, I am. Right, you are Nataniel Mbueti's son. What happened to him?'

'Oh, he died. They both died in 1975, during the horrible confrontations.'

Xavier Ramos shook his head and said: 'So much blood has been spilt in this land! Where is my favourite pupil? He was called Hosi, not so?'

'He's in Zambia. I hope that he does not join the bandits; I believe that they have some following among young people there.'

Xavier Ramos asked Osvaldo when they could meet again. Osvaldo said on a Sunday, so on a sunny Sunday afternoon Xavier Ramos called, bringing with him a bottle of whisky. Osvaldo and Berta lived in a house at Kapango. That afternoon Osvaldo asked her to cook the chicken she had got by bartering bars of soap on the black market.

Xavier Ramos and Osvaldo sat together on an old sofa filled with holes. Xavier Ramos hit the sofa and said: 'You deserve to have something better than this.'

Osvaldo smiled and said: 'I am only a second lieutenant. I

am far behind in the queue when it comes to handing out goods.'

'You are joking. You are the people getting fat on the fruits of the revolution. Now, listen to this. I am your teacher and I hold you as dear as I would hold a son of the same blood as me. I am going to put a proposal to you. If you accept it, fine. If you don't, please keep it to yourself or my life will be in danger.'

Osvaldo began to sweat. He passed his hand over his forehead and said: 'Teacher, whatever I say to you, let it be between ourselves, or the two of us will be in danger, as you know very well.'

'I wasn't born yesterday. Remember, not only did I survive PIDE, but I have also survived our own DISA. The thing is this: there are a few beans that I have come across. If only they could be got into Portugal, we would make ourselves incredible money. I need your help. Of course, you'll be given some good stuff to keep your mouth shut.'

Diamond-smuggling in the People's Republic of Angola was an offence second only to treason. Osvaldo was reluctant to involve himself in such activities. He knew that if he was caught he would suffer. He shook his head and said: 'Teacher, I would very much have liked to work with you, but I can't. These people have a very sophisticated network. They'd soon catch up with me. For someone as trusted as I am to be involved in these activities would be a big disgrace. Teacher, I would also advise you to give up the whole operation. You will end up rotting in prison. Some of our brightest minds are in prison. We should not try and send more away.'

Xavier Ramos patted Osvaldo on the shoulder and said: 'It is not that I like to be involved in this; not at all. I am a noble man at heart, that is the truth. The reason I am involved with this – and please, dear son, don't denounce me – is that I feel that there is no justice. Yes, there is no justice in Angola.

'Let's look at it carefully. There is, on the one hand, the people's shops and on the other, the leaders' shops. What do you get in the people's shops? Practically nothing, really nothing. What do you get in the leaders' shops? Whisky, like this, perfumes, peanuts, razors, fridges and other luxuries. Now, who in the world does not like to live well? It is not only the Internationalists – the Cubans, Soviets and the like – who enjoy having good fridges and videos. We too would like to benefit from the fruits of our land. Honestly, sometimes I think this is worse than Portuguese colonialism. All right, the Portuguese used to call us niggers and give us a raw deal. But at least there were plenty of sausages around. If one morning you woke up and found that you had enough money, you could walk to a showroom and buy a car. Now, only the party bigwigs have them. But who the hell is prepared to keep on licking their boots so that you are admitted into the party, promoted after a few years and then get in a better position to get a car or a house? I tell you this: there are a few households in this land where people breakfast on champagne and caviar, then go and preach the virtues of Marxism to the proletariat!'

Osvaldo shrugged and said: 'Well, that is certainly wrong. Petit-bourgeois tendencies are hampering the revolution.'

'Petit-bourgeois tendencies? I hear and see that phrase all over. I hear it on the radio, on television; it is written on almost every pamphlet in the land. Petit-bourgeois tendencies! What the hell do people mean by that? Our politicians are behaving exactly like some Christians I have known in the past. They go on about sin all the time, and yet as soon as the sun goes down they do precisely the things that they preach against. We are often told that the socialist revolution will lead to communism. Nonsense. I am your teacher and I would never tell you something false. The truth is that there will never be communism here. We are Africans.'

Xavier Ramos leaned over and continued almost in a whisper: 'I tell you the truth, there is no better capitalist than the African. Oh yes! Take the Kuanhamas, for instance. You do not have to quote Ronald Reagan or whoever to know that having cattle is good. They know it, it is part of their culture. Mbueti, you should go to Zaire. There you'll see women criss-crossing Africa in search of business.'

Osvaldo said: 'I understand your point. But Zaire does not show African capitalism at its best. Men there send their women to sleep with other men in order to make money.'

Xavier Ramos scratched his head and said: 'Maybe Zaire is not a proper example. But you must understand my point. I was once a Marxist. Junior, this mulatto boy that is sending shivers down the spines of people, was once my pupil. I taught that boy to read and write, and he convinced me to become a Marxist. I believed him for a while. Then Mingo, my cousin – well, he was a bit of a tribalist – convinced me to turn to the FNLA. I understand that you feel there should be an equal distribution of wealth. The thing, son, is that there should first be wealth to distribute. How can you distribute wealth in the first place if there is no wealth?'

'Rome was not built in a day,' said Osvaldo. 'The Russians had their revolution in 1917; they have not yet achieved the final aim of the revolution.'

Xavier Ramos smiled and said: 'There will never be communism in the world. I just don't know why people can't get that into their heads. What does a peasant in Mongolia have in common with an Angolan peasant? The answer is, they are both greedy! Well, perhaps greedy is not the proper word. The truth is that the two want to live better; they want to have radios, ploughs, a good life. Let the Russians wait for ever for their communism; that is their business. We should get on with our life. What we need is wealth. How does that come about? Capitalism is the answer. I am not saying that 300 people should control the wealth of 7 million people. What I am saying is that everyone should have the chance of drinking champagne at least once in his life; everyone should have the chance of sending his child to the best school in the land if he works hard, and that a person should be able to wake up in the morning and be assured of getting a loaf of bread without too much hassle.'

Osvaldo interrupted Xavier Ramos and said: 'But surely that is the aim of the party. This is just a transitional period. To judge everything by basing it on the way things are now is to miss the point.'

Xavier Ramos shook his head and said: 'My son, if you are trying to propose to a woman and you are thinking about her beauty, you consider her as she is at present. You should

259

never think that she will become pretty in the future. So it is with the country. I can see you shaking your head; I know that you do not agree with me. Look at Angola, the way it is now. In Luanda, there is a school reserved for the children of the party leaders. It is called Sao Jose de Cluny. The party leaders also have special hospitals and other perks. It is nauseating!'

Berta brought in the chicken on a plate and left the men alone again. Xavier Ramos and Osvaldo began to eat. After a while Xavier Ramos said: 'We've drifted from the main reason that brought me here – the beans. You might sweat or even die for this country under this party and yet you'll never be rewarded, apart from being mentioned in passing in a political speech. But if you have American dollars, then you'll have your future secured. After all, what are we in this world for? Breaking our backs for a future that we'll never see, or having as much as we can get of what this world can offer? The lifespan of a man is small when compared to an elephant. I heard on the radio the other day that the life expectancy of an Angolan male is forty-five. What is forty-five years? Nothing! That is why, son, I advise you to think of the present, and the future. Join me in this operation.'

'I will have to think this over. Give me a week.'

Xavier Ramos smiled and said: 'Think with your brain, not your heart. The heart often does not want to know what is best for the stomach!'

During that week Osvaldo could not stop thinking about Xavier Ramos's offer. He agreed with a lot of things that the teacher had told him. Osvaldo also felt that he had no future in the army. Although he had been trained in Cuba and had gone to the Soviet Union and East Germany for intensive courses, he had not been promoted very high. He felt that fools had risen faster than him just because they had mastered Marxist terminology. That was not all. Osvaldo had an uneasy feeling that the MPLA cadres would have a poor future. He knew that if the UNITA rebels were not crushed, then the only solution would be a negotiation. And this would mean sharing posts with people with whom they had been fighting recently. As he mulled over the question, Osvaldo kept hearing

Xavier Ramos's voice: 'They are all doing it! They are all doing it!'

After a while, Osvaldo decided that he would indeed take part in the operation. If it failed and he came under the investigation of the police, he had devised a quick way out: he would shoot himself. He had wanted to do so many times in the past but had always stepped back from the idea.

That Sunday Xavier Ramos came again. He was delighted when Osvaldo told him that he had accepted the offer. Xavier Ramos began at once to give the details of the operation: 'We need someone like you who is known to have belonged to the intelligence department to go and bring the beans from Lunda. Once they've been brought here we will prepare everything and have a boy take the diamonds to Portugal. There, he will meet Madame Esmeralda. She will fix everything and we over here will receive the dollars.'

Osvaldo frowned and said: 'What about the boy? Who is he?'

'That is another story,' Xavier Ramos said. 'He is in hiding and will do anything to get out of Angola.'

Osvaldo shrugged and said: 'I am prepared to be involved in the operation but everything must be done to make sure we hurt nobody. You say the boy is in hiding. What guarantee have I got that he is not being blackmailed?'

'Listen, please! The boy and a friend of his dodged military service. So they decided to build a raft and flee to Portugal. Well, there was someone who had done it, so they felt that they too could. After building the raft the two were caught. One was sent to prison; the other, Silva, somehow managed to escape and has been in hiding for the past six months. We want to save the boy. So a false passport has been arranged for him. All he will have to do is pass through the airport in Luanda with the diamonds – we know how to arrange that – and then hand them over to the Madame in Lisbon and that is it. He'll be given a reward.'

They spent the whole afternoon going over the details of the operation.

*

After two weeks Osvaldo drove to Lunda and came back with the diamonds. He said he had gone to visit a friend of his. Xavier Ramos was happy with things so far, and Osvaldo felt very pleased with himself. He awaited the day Xavier Ramos would come with the dollars.

A week later, Xavier Ramos came panting to see Osvaldo. As soon as the two sat down, Xavier Ramos said: 'We are in trouble. Everything was going according to plan. A new passport had been found and the boy was made to swallow the beans, which were in a special container that would not harm him. But what does the fool do? He turned himself in to the authorities. He thinks they will forgive him if he turns himself in.'

'Shit! This is the end of me. I will shoot myself.'

Xavier Ramos said: 'Shoot yourself? Don't be so cowardly! I am sure that they are now interrogating the boy. And as I know those people, they will soon get to me – and you. There is only one way we can escape – by joining UNITA. We must go to the settlement where Old Pedro, Laura and the others are, I can get in touch with the UNITA soldiers and cross over.'

'I will never join those bandits. They are a disgrace to Angola. I'd rather be dead, or perhaps in a prison, than join them.'

Xavier Ramos said: 'I am going right away to the settlement. It won't be long before I meet some UNITA men. You talk as though you are referring to extra-terrestrial beings. Most of the UNITA soldiers are ordinary people just like you and me. In fact, I taught some of the UNITA commanders. They all knew me. I am leaving for the settlement. Please come and join me.' At that point Xavier Ramos left the house.

Osvaldo felt helpless. Once again, he began to think of ways of killing himself. He thought of drinking acid from his car's battery, then he thought of the sharp kitchen knife. He did not believe that killing himself would be cowardice. In fact, he felt it was a sign of bravery and valour. Many people, he kept saying to himself, wished to depart from the wretched world but were too afraid, imagining their relatives weeping for them, so they continued leading their horrible lives.

'Something is wrong!' Osvaldo heard Berta say behind him.

Osvaldo turned round, pulled out a pistol from his holster and shot Berta several times. She opened her mouth, tried to scream but could not, and collapsed.

Osvaldo turned the pistol to himself and pulled the trigger. There was no bullet. He walked over to a drawer in a cabinet that was next to the dining table. There were no bullets there either. He knelt down and began to cry.

27

It was a dark night, so dark it looked as if it would rain. Prophetess Laura and her followers had gathered in the adobe church. She was stout, with white headgear and a white soutane. There were cardboard boxes in each corner of the church, and small paraffin lamps rested on top of each one.

Prophetess Laura sat on a wooden chair. Next to her stood a tall, light-skinned man: Prophet Zachariah. He was giving a sermon. The twenty-five members of the church gathered there were listening attentively. He thumped his chest and said: 'We, the followers of the true Church – the Church of Zion – shall never be wrong. Why? Because we preach love. Why? Because we believe in the truth. Why? Because the holy spirit is with us.'

'Amen! Amen!' the congregation answered.

Prophet Zachariah continued: 'They say they have the truth. We say fine. But when you challenge their truth they lock you up. Right now they have our father, Prophet Pedro, in prison. They say that he has been giving food to UNITA. He has not denied it. That is because the Prophet believes in love. He believes in feeding the hungry. The truth? And yet you need tanks to make people believe in it. The truth? And yet you need spies all over. We don't have prisons for those who disagree with our truth. We don't have spies for truth. We don't need tanks for our truth. We don't need commissars for our truth. We don't need the party for our truth. Our truth is love. Our truth is compassion. Our truth can defeat tanks. Our truth can shoot down MiG23s. Our truth can render land-mines ineffective. Our truth is above politics. Our truth is love. And love is power.'

The congregation began to clap. Women began to yell.

Some of them were seized by the spirit at once and fell to the floor.

This was how the Church of Zion began. It was said that one day Old Pedro was in the forest looking for wild honey. He came across a green cloth (no member of the Zion church is allowed to wear anything green) which began to transmit to him the voice of God. God told Old Pedro that he had been chosen to deliver Angola from evil – in this case, godless Marxism – and cleanse the land of the dirt that Satan had spread all over. Old Pedro came back to the settlement and told the people. They thought he was mad, but that evening there were several thunderstorms even though the season was not rainy. Then Old Pedro predicted that in a few days something out of the ordinary would happen in the village. Indeed, two days later a T55 tank drove near the settlement and suddenly caught fire. Then Old Pedro went straight to some women and singled them out as witches. They confessed at once. A woman who had had a chronic backache since the time of Portuguese rule said she was suddenly cured when Old Pedro had prayed for her.

People began to believe that Old Pedro was indeed a prophet, and from then on began to call him one. Aunt Laura came from Huambo to be treated: she said that she had a thorn in her throat. It was soon cured. Then Old Pedro dreamt that God wanted her to become his second wife. She did not hesitate before the divine order.

At first the authorities tolerated the Zion church. But some provincial political officials stirred after it was noticed that most people at the settlement would rather go and listen to Prophet Pedro than attend the political rallies, which were quite frequent. Methodists, Baptists and other such Christians could be tolerated because their views were very well known and their churches were frequented by respectable individuals such as teachers and medical assistants. But little cults like this one were not to be tolerated, for this was where reactionary ideas were likely to ferment fast. The party officials were worried about Prophet Pedro's movement because they felt that its ideals were close to those of the Jehovah's Witnesses, who believed that their loyalty was first of all to God, and not to the state, the flag, the party or the country.

A spy was seconded to Prophet Pedro's church, a man called Eurico. When asked to give reports on the Church of Zion, Eurico said that he was still investigating and was waiting to get into the thick of the doctrines that were being peddled by the old man. Then one day, in the middle of a stirring sermon by Prophet Pedro, Eurico rose and confessed that he was a spy. He asked to be prayed for and forgiven. It was then that the authorities began to take the Church of Zion very seriously indeed.

Prophet Pedro was sent for and interrogated. He insisted on the story of the green cloth. His interrogators, however, asked whether he was not working for UNITA. He said the only political party on earth that he would work for was that led by God. What did he think of Angola, then? Prophet Pedro said at once that he thought that Angola had come under the hands of the devil and that soon God would empower him and his fellow believers to cleanse the country of all evil. At that point the interrogators decided to let him go because they believed there was something seriously wrong with his head.

Then Prophet Pedro went with a number of his followers to a UNITA base to pray for people and tell them about the message he had received from God. The people he met at the UNITA base were polite to him, but they too thought that he was not normal. When government authorities got wind of the fact that Prophet Pedro had gone to the base, they put him in prison at once. It was then that the members of the Church of Zion prayed hard and asked Susana to tell her son Junior to intervene with the authorities.

He eventually did so and Prophet Pedro was released. Two weeks after his release he died in his sleep. Rumour had it that on the day he died three pairs of twins were born in the settlement. Prophet Pedro had predicted his own death. In his last sermon, remembered by his followers long after, Old Pedro had foretold that the war would continue for a few more years and more blood would be shed. He had also said that he was going to plead his followers' case before God. Then he said that God had demanded that his rightful successor be Prophetess Laura. From then on, Prophetess Laura had begun to pray for people and make predictions. Her assistant was to be Prophet Zachariah, who was now talking: 'Now, I call upon our mother, Prophetess Laura, to come forward and feed us with words of love.'

Prophetess Laura stood up and walked forward. She was holding a wooden rod in her left hand. She closed her eyes and howled loudly: she had been seized by the holy spirit. She then calmed herself and said: 'Listen, people. Listen to the word of God. Let's worry about this world, for indeed we have a special place being prepared for us up there. Make no mistakes, brothers, make no mistakes, sisters. We are the chosen few. Angolans today are filled with hatred. People are killing each other day and night. Just listen to the radio: twenty more bandits killed, five more puppets killed. Yes, as though the young men are cows. And yet they are sons of their mothers. Yes, and yet they sucked from someone's breasts, someone who will cry for them. No one but us talks of love. Indeed, we are the chosen people. Some say Christians connived with the Portuguese. I agree. Yes, many churches are concerned with worldly power: they preach love in the day and sup with the devil at night. Today in Angola it is the church leaders who are preaching Marxism – the religion of the devil himself. Yes, these leaders believe in the God who rewards them with sugar. The God who rewards them with cooking oil. The God who rewards them with scholarships for their sons. The God who rewards them with government posts. The God who makes them join the secret police and spy on their kin. We at the Church of Zion do not believe in that God. We believe in the God of Abraham, the God of Moses. No way, Pharaoh won't intimidate us. He may use big Portuguese words, we won't budge. Hallelujah!'

'Aaaamen!' the congregation thundered back.

Prophetess Laura continued: 'There are no reactionaries in the kingdom of our God. There are no traitors. There are no enemies of the people. There are no agents of international exploitative capitalism. As far as our God is concerned, there are only sinners and the saved. The saved will go to Zion and the sinners to hell. A year ago a man called Kapangele came to preach Marxism. He said that we at the Church of Zion were mistaken. Where is Kapangele now? Dead! Who killed him? His God – the government of the People's Republic of Angola. So Pharaoh eats his own children? O yes, he does. Our God forgives!'

Prophetess Laura gave out another loud howl and then went to sit on her chair. Prophet Zachariah stood up and said: 'We are a happy people. We believe in rejoicing in the Lord. Now, to prove to our God that we love him, we should dance. Brother Abraham, get the drums playing. Everybody, let's dance to the Lord!'

Everybody stood up and started to chant. Two stocky men began to play drums and the congregation danced wildly. Prophetess Laura got up from her chair and began to dance too.

Several people came to see Prophetess Laura. Housewives in Huambo who had problems with their marriages came to her asking for special concoctions to make their husbands love them again. Men who expected to be promoted at work came to see her too. As a fee Prophetess Laura would ask only for a blanket, a chicken, or a pig in very difficult cases. Her enemies said she had become a witch doctor. She countered that by saying that God had invested certain roots with certain properties, just as He had given people certain talents. By telling a barren woman that by taking certain roots she would eventually conceive, what she was actually doing, Prophetess Laura would argue, was showing how the world was charged with the grandeur of God.

One day, Prophetess Laura was sitting in front of her adobe house when a nervous-looking man came up to her. It was Xavier Ramos. Prophetess Laura said: 'Is this teacher Ramos before me?'

'Indeed, Dona Laura.'

'Where have you been, my son?'

'All over Angola. I am in trouble, I must tell you.'

'You've been involved in the trafficking of diamonds.'

'How do you know?'

'God knows and sees everything! I am a prophetess.'

'Can we go inside? I am sure that they'll soon be hunting for me.'

Xavier Ramos and Prophetess Laura went into the sitting room. Xavier Ramos spoke very fast: 'Dona Laura,' he began, 'I am told that you've helped a lot of people get over their problems. Can you help me?'

'How?'

'By making these people forget about me or something. Just by preventing me from getting into prison.'

'No, I can't.'

'Why?'

'Because you believe in another God. It is only when you begin to believe in my God, the true God of Abraham, that you will be saved. Now, when you start believing in the true God, it won't matter whether they take you to prison or not, because you will have his protection.'

Prophetess Laura held Xavier Ramos's hands and said: 'Now, let's close our eyes and pray.'

Xavier Ramos complied.

28

Captain Junior could not believe the report before him. He could think of no reason why Osvaldo should shoot dead his girlfriend. According to the report, it was discovered that he had shot Berta only when he did not turn up for work for three days. Neighbours had also noticed a horrible smell coming from the house. Nobody knew where Osvaldo had fled to, but it was suspected that he – like several people who had committed crimes – had gone to the bush to join UNITA.

In the past months Junior had been dealing with the case of a Catholic priest, Njekwa. He had shot dead a man for no apparent reason and had vanished into the forest. There were some similarities between Father Njekwa's crime and Osvaldo's. Both were reasonable people and one would not have expected them to act like this on the spur of the moment. But everything now in Angola had become unpredictable.

Just then Officer Barros, a stout man with three chins, came in with another file. It contained details of a foiled attempt by one of the many underworld groups in Angola to smuggle diamonds. Junior read the reports quickly while Barros sat on the chair opposite him, awaiting his comments.

A boy, said the report, had been made to swallow a special container with the diamonds in. He was to board a plane going to Portugal. The boy, whose only crime was to have attempted to escape from Angola in a raft (the report had attributed this to youthful indiscretion), alerted the authorities at once. Now they were after the spirit behind the operation: Xavier Ramos. Nobody knew where he could be, but the possibility that he had crossed over to UNITA was ruled out because he did not have friends there, having been a member of the FNLA.

Junior heaved a sigh and said to Barros: 'In my darkest

moments I often think that socialism will never succeed in Africa. How can it succeed if the backbone of the revolution, the enlightened, behave in this way?'

They were silent for a while, then Barros said: 'The problem with us Africans is that we lack the patience and determination that is needed to carry out a socialist revolution. Look at Mozambique. They have completely strayed fom the true path, the path that would have led them to communism. They are now supping with the devil himself – South Africa.'

Junior banged the desk and said: 'If the Soviets made sacrifices, why can't we Africans make sacrifices too? If during the struggle against the Portuguese we said that none of us wanted to suffer or die, our people would still be under the yoke of colonialism. Yes, socialism is not a joke. It is hard to come by, but it is the best.'

Barros nodded with a slight frown on his face. Junior banged the desk again and said: 'As far as Africa is concerned, there is only one true way to success – Marxism-Leninism. Where are the African socialists now? Nyerere and his brand of socialism? Nowhere! Yes, we should make sacrifices to bring about communism. The cadres should be ruthless, for the ends justify the means.'

Barros nodded again. Junior looked at the reports once more, shook his head and said: 'I know the people in these reports. Osvaldo Mbueti is almost a brother to me. Xavier Ramos was my teacher – he taught me to read and write. Now, if I was a reactionary, I would be thinking of ways to save them. But I won't. I love Angola too much to trade it for anything else. I tell you, Barros: I don't care if it is my mother; if she goes against the revolution, I will make sure that she goes to prison. I shall never forget the bandit that warned his mother that they were about to carry out an operation. We got the information and did away with his battalion. War is war and a revolution is a revolution. There are no compromises.'

'That is how a true revolutionary is supposed to be, Commander!'

'One of the problems we have is that our men are

271

ideologically raw. What puzzles me is that some of them have been having political lessons since they were old enough to talk. A lot of these diamond smugglers and black marketeers were Young Pioneers. Take Osvaldo Mbueti. He has shot his wife! A true revolutionary does not behave like a savage. Yet Osvaldo went to Cuba as a boy and has made several trips to the Soviet Union! People like him should be shot at once!'

Barros nodded and said: 'Indeed, Commander!' Junior banged the desk, looked straight at Barros and said: 'Now Barros, get me Aires! I am going to track all of these guys down and bring them to court. No one can play with the revolution in this way!'

'Yes, Commander!' Barros saluted and walked out.

BOOK IV

29

When Hosi finally got to the camp he found that the others were packing their belongings. He rushed to the personnel department and found that his name was listed in the column for the dead. The personnel officer was busy trying to work out how many people he could dispatch to the front: the main 1985 offensive was on.

Hosi said: 'I got lost two days ago. Why should I appear in the column of the dead?'

The personnel officer stood up, walked up to the wall and struck Hosi's name off the column of the dead. Hosi was still not satisfied. He shook his head and said: 'Why did you write my name among the dead?'

The officer said: 'Don't trouble me. You came here and said you were not dead, so I struck you out. What else do you want?'

Hosi walked out of the office feeling very depressed. Was his life so worthless? Hosi Mbueti was simply a name that could be put on and struck out, like the price of a pig in a butcher's!

Someone came rushing to Hosi and told him to go quickly to the armoury. There he found a long queue: several soldiers were waiting to be issued with bullets and grenades. At last it was Hosi's turn. He was given an AK47 rifle, two grenades and three cartridges full of bullets.

Everything was moving fast. In no time a Magiruz lorry came into the camp and Hosi was ushered into it. They moved towards Mavinga. Hosi could read fear in the faces of the other soldiers. They suppressed this by singing, but whatever song they sang, a streak of sorrow would work its way in. The political activists tried to cheer up the soldiers by singing more loudly than them. Still, they all knew that in the coming hours some of them would die. Hosi recalled the time he had come under fire while training. He and his fellow recruits had not taken it seriously for they knew that the likelihood of their being caught by a bullet was remote. Now, they were going to face the enemy, and his main aim was to ensure that the bullets killed as many people as possible.

They arrived at the battle front late one night. As soon as the Magiruz came to a halt, they heard groans from soldiers who had been injured. Hosi thought that he could smell blood in the air. Once again, he regretted having returned to Angola. By now he could have been somewhere in Zambia, living the slightly shameful life of a refugee, but safe.

It had been raining and the soil was very cold. Hosi's boots were slightly wet. The soldiers said nothing to each other: they were awaiting instructions from the commanders. A Land-Cruiser came and stopped nearby. Two soldiers at the back were talking excitedly. Hosi could not help eavesdropping.

'They say they have Jagas with them. He is horrible.'

'Not as horrible as Seteka! That man knows the art of war!'

'Ah, but they are all peanuts when compared to our men – we have Tick-tock around. He'll make them shit!'

Then the car left.

A tall, thin man came and said: 'Now, you guys who've just come to the camp, be patient. We'll be coming to you soon. Don't fall asleep. This is the front line and we should be awake at all times.'

Hosi looked at his rifle. He felt depressed to think that he would soon be using it to kill somebody's son. Well, he said to himself, somebody's son was also waiting to kill him. This was war! For once Hosi thought of God. He prayed that God would receive him in his kingdom if a bullet were to kill him. Just then someone tapped him on the back. It was Carlito. Hosi could see his white teeth in the dark. Carlito said almost in a whisper: 'Do you know what it is like to die from a bullet?'

Hosi said: 'No, I don't!'

'I am told that it is not that painful. It is like having a tooth pulled out – one sharp pain and then you fall asleep.'

'Who told you that?'

'I know it!' Carlito answered as he walked away.

Hosi hoped that it would soon be morning.

At eight the soldiers had coffee. It was distributed in a make-shift kitchen. Rumours were flying around already: that at the front the MPLA were using PC7 spotter planes and the dreaded MI25 helicopter, mainly piloted by the Cubans. The MI25 was a machine that spilled death. Although the authorities made several attempts to thwart the spread of rumours because they dented the morale of the soldiers, these always proved futile.

It was now about ten in the morning. Hosi and his colleagues had been told to assemble at a point from where they would proceed to the front line. Just then Hosi noted a very old man sitting beneath a tree. He was playing a soot-covered accordion. It was said that he had just moved over from the MPLA side and was about to be taken to Jamba. The old man played and smiled to himself. A group of soldiers stopped and looked at him. The old man grinned and said: 'It is my birthday today. I am sixty-two today. I never thought I would live so long.' Then he resumed playing.

At last Hosi and his colleagues were at the battle front. The smell of gunpowder was all about. Now and then rockets fired from the enemies' cannon would fall nearby. Then the UNITA soldiers would respond too. Then there was a torrent of rockets and everyone lay down. A BM21 was being fired. This Soviet-made rocket-launcher was said to be able to launch twenty missiles at once.

Hosi heard a voice from behind say: 'Let's move forward. Let's get them.'

When Hosi looked to his side his colleagues were already racing to the front in a stooping position. His rifle was heavy. He felt as if he had been shot more than once already. Then they came to a point where the enemy could be seen distinctly. Hosi saw several men hiding behind the bushes.

277

'Fire!' the commander thundered from behind.

Hosi pulled the trigger. He had not loaded the rifle. He summoned all the strength he could and managed to load the rifle. He pulled the trigger again, but failed to fire; the safety catch was on. Hosi concluded that the rifle he was holding did not work and that he was going to die. He pulled the trigger again; it still did not fire. Then he pressed the safety catch. He had forgotten everything that he had been taught.

Bullets were flying all over. Most of them hit the trees with a stubbing sound. Hosi could hear some of his colleagues shouting insults at the enemy: 'Son of a bitch! Go fuck shit!'

He pulled the trigger. This time it fired. Hosi pointed at where he thought the enemy was. He clenched his teeth and pulled the trigger hard again. Then he saw someone throw a rifle up and cry out loudly: 'Oh mother!'

Now Hosi heard himself say: 'Son of a bitch! Go fuck shit!' He pulled the trigger hard; the rifle rattled.

Just then a very loud droning was heard. It was as if the soil was trembling. Hosi felt that it was the end of the world. He looked around. Everyone lay still on the ground, as if they were dead. A huge MI25 helicopter was hovering above, its wings tearing the branches of the tree apart. Hosi closed his eyes for a while. The helicopter was still droning. He was being covered in dust and felt unable to breathe; the helicopter was right above him. Then it disappeared. Hosi looked around. He saw Carlito lying on his back. Hosi trotted over to where he lay. There was a huge bloody opening in his body. Officer Kapulo was kneeling nearby. Waving his hands at Hosi, he said: 'If he's gone just get his rifle!'

Hosi took the rifle and covered Carlito's face with a cap. The soldiers were running to an area where they could find cover, for it was said that the MiGs were about to come. Hosi raced behind them. He found a hole and squeezed himself in. The foxhole was the sole succour of the guerrilla. Almost everyone knew that it had rendered the B52 American bombers worthless in Vietnam.

Indeed, after a while several MiGs began to bomb the area, continuing for almost an hour. Then the UNITA anti-aircraft

278

guns began to answer. Soon, a MiG was seen emitting smoke up in the sky. The pilot ejected himself and began to parachute down. The soldiers trained their rifles on him and began to fire bullets while hurling insults too.

The commander kept shouting: 'Don't fire! We need that man for information. Please stop the fire!'

The soldiers got carried away, though. They kept firing. Hosi said with a grin to someone kneeling beside him: 'It is against the Geneva Convention to kill a man coming down on a parachute!'

The soldier looked at Hosi and said: 'Geneva! Geneva! Stop that crap or I will Geneva you. Where was your bloody Geneva when that bastard was dropping bombs on us?'

Hosi remained silent. The pilot of the MiG plane was captured. Two soldiers helped him to his feet and led him to the command post amid insults from the soldiers. Hosi heard someone say: 'Shit! I only wish that he was a Russian. We would have turned him into corned beef!'

Hosi received orders that he was supposed to join the logistics section. Their position was twenty minutes away from where he was. He and three other people had been walking for a while and then they came to something Hosi could not believe: a human skull was hanging on a wooden fork. The other soldiers saluted and laughed. One of them said: 'That guy was an MPLA lieutenant. Good afternoon, sir!' Hosi could not look at the skull again.

They continued walking but lost their way and came to a swamp. Several MPLA tanks were trying to cross it. Hosi and his colleagues fled into a nearby forest. Then Hosi heard several loud bombs explode. He closed his eyes. When he opened them he was by himself. He began to cry. He was lost again. He felt like turning the rifle on himself, pulling the trigger and ending his life.

After a while, he decided to walk in the direction of the logistics point. It was very hard in the forest to tell which way one was going and Hosi only hoped that he was not moving towards the enemy. He went on for a while, then he heard a voice behind say: 'Drop your rifle or you are dead!'

Hosi dropped his rifle and held both hands up high. Soon, he was surrounded by four hefty soldiers. One, the shortest of them, hit him hard in the groin and said: 'Bloody Kwacha! Identify yourself!'

'Hosi Mbueti. I was in Zambia and I came back to Angola recently.'

The short soldier was going to hit Hosi again but his colleagues told him not to. Hosi began to cry. He remembered Raimundo and what he had said about crying. Hosi turned to the MPLA soldiers and said: 'Please don't kill me!'

This time the short soldier punched Hosi on the chin and said: 'Do you think we are killers? Is that what your racist masters have been pumping into your heads?'

Hosi wet his trousers. The short soldier hit Hosi with the butt of his rifle. Hosi sobbed.

30

The four MPLA soldiers blindfolded Hosi and tied his hands
behind his back. They then ordered him to walk in front of
them. Although he was blindfolded, Hosi felt he could see
everything. The short soldier's rifle had cut him on the forehead. He began to sob. He saw himself in prison or before a
firing squad. He saw himself being interrogated by intelligence
officers. And he saw himself being beaten. He regretted having
been born an Angolan and African. He wished that he had
been born in Europe or somewhere in America. Then he could
have spent his whole life concerned with motorbikes and
things that were good in life. And he would have been bothered
about his rights too. But he was an Angolan. Angola to him
made no sense! He did not feel a patriot in any sense. If at the
moment the whole of Angola was to be engulfed by the
Atlantic Ocean, he would not have minded.

He said to his captors: 'Please, brothers, do me a favour.
Just shoot me right away.'

The short soldier hit Hosi on the back with the butt of his
rifle and said: 'Your mouth. If you don't shut up I will cut off
your balls and make you eat them!'

They walked for almost six hours. It was now getting dark.
Hosi could feel that the soil had cooled. They halted at some
point. They removed the cloth that had covered Hosi's eyes.
He noted that his captors looked worried and were talking fast
among themselves in whispers as they did not want him to
hear what they were saying.

The short soldier was talking loudly now: 'How can you do
this, Figueredo. We have a prize of a prisoner. This guy is not
a peasant: he's an intellectual. I am sure that he must have
learned his English while being trained by the South Africans.

281

This guy has a lot to say. You get him on the national radio and everybody will know of the atrocities being committed against us! We'll be three intelligence men that captured a man with vital information!'

'There you go again. Patience. We've lost our way. First we should try and locate our position!'

They decided to continue walking. Suddenly there was an explosion and Nando, the short soldier who was in front, screamed out loud. They all rushed over to him. He had stepped on a landmine. They wrapped his leg in an old blanket and tied it with fibres. They untied Hosi and ordered him to carry Nando on his back. Hosi complied at once. Nando groaned and cried out for his mother.

Hosi said to him: 'You'll be fine, brother. You'll be fine.'

Nando groaned and said: 'These people will try and leave me. Please don't leave me behind. I know I will survive. I will see my mother. OK, I know that I will have no leg. But that is not a problem. All I want is to see my mother again.'

Hosi said: 'You'll be fine!'

They came to a point where it was decided that they should spend the night. Figueredo went and defecated beneath a tree. Little ants began to be attracted by the smell of his faeces. He picked them up and took them to Nando, who ate them with much gusto. Hosi began to sob.

Nando turned to Hosi and said: 'Please don't leave me behind, brother!'

Hosi said: 'I won't.'

'If I die, please bury me, brother, please bury me. Pray for me if you can. Bury me deep or some hyena will come eat me. Brother, never forget me.'

Hosi said: 'You're not going to die.'

The others were busy with a compass and a map, trying to locate where they were. Nando looked at Hosi and said: 'If I die, salute before my grave, my brother. I am a true patriot. I love Angola. I really do love my country!'

Hosi forced a smile and said: 'I will salute you. But the truth is that you're not going to die.'

Nando nodded.

They tried to sleep but could not. Nando kept groaning. Then the groans became faint and it was as if Nando had gone to sleep. They all fell asleep. When they woke up in the morning they found that Nando was dead. Hosi began to cry. The others said it was time to move on. Hosi said he had to dig a grave in which to bury Nando.

Figueredo said: 'Angola is filled with patriots that have not been buried. Just leave him under those bushes and then the soil will take care of him. The soil will bury him.'

Hosi saluted the dead body. The others were surprised. They walked towards the west for most of the morning and said very little to each other. Then Figueredo said to Hosi: 'You seem to have liked Nando. He kicked you when he was alive. Aren't you happy that he is dead?'

Hosi said: 'It doesn't matter whether I liked him, dead or not. What matters is his mother or his sister or his girlfriend.'

The other two MPLA soldiers were Manuel and Filipe. They listened to Hosi in silence. Figueredo said: 'Our lives are cheap. The politicians decide; we die. I am sure that both the MPLA and UNITA leaders have a lot in common.'

Hosi said: 'I agree. Just as there is no difference between the MPLA soldier and the UNITA soldier. We are all patriots. We all love Angola and we are prepared to die for it in our way.'

Figueredo grunted and said: 'What is good is that very soon there will be very few patriots left, so that the politicians will have no other option than finding a solution to this bloody war.'

'I am not sure about that. There are wars in Africa that have been going on for the past twenty or thirty years. Take the Eritrean war, for instance. Millions of Ethiopians are dying, but the Ethiopians continue buying MiG fighters.'

'I think we are different,' said Filipe.

Hosi said: 'The problem with Angolans is that they always think they are different from other Africans when in actual fact they have so much in common. I have been hearing it said all my life that they are the best black people on earth. The truth is that we are no better than anybody else. In fact, I often think that we are the worst. Any people that can go on killing each other the way we are doing deserves no admiration.'

They came to a tree that bore mangongo fruits. Filipe climbed up and threw several down. They ate till they could eat no more, then they walked on for a while. They came to a little lake. They were very thirsty, but they had to look for marks of recent animal footprints, because they were afraid of landmines. There had been people living in some houses near the lake, but they were now deserted.

After the mangongo fruit and water they laughed and began to tell stories – mostly about food – to each other. Then they came across a villager who was so afraid of them that he stammered and was incomprehensible. The villager told them that the next town was a day's walk going east.

Hosi had never walked that far in his life.

31

Osvaldo came to Prophetess Laura in tears. He said he had killed his girlfriend and had involved himself in diamond smuggling. Prophetess Laura prayed hard for him and insisted that things would work out well in the end. Xavier Ramos too stayed at Prophetess Laura's settlement, waiting for the secret police to come and pick him up.

Hosi and the MPLA soldiers became very friendly. As they walked on, they shared all the little food they found. They even asked Hosi to give them English lessons. Hosi was amazed by the quickness with which the soldiers learned the few expressions that he taught them. They escorted him up to the settlement where Prophetess Laura was. She prayed for him and took him to see Osvaldo. The two brothers cried when they saw each other. Xavier Ramos cried too when he saw Hosi. They spent two days recalling the good old days.

They kept scrutinizing the features in each other that had changed over the years. Smiling shyly, Osvaldo said to Hosi: 'Have you made any children?'

Hosi shook his head and said: 'None. How about you?'

'I don't know.'

Hosi said: 'I used to think that Angola was horrible. Not after having travelled across it. I think ours is the most beautiful country on earth. Some day it will be great. Some day when enough blood has been shed.'

Osvaldo smiled and said: 'I can't believe this coming from someone in UNITA. Are you people over there patriots? All you have been doing over the years is planting landmines and making sure that the economy of the People's Republic remains dormant.'

'People's Republic? Nonsense. This People's Republic that

has to be sustained by the secret police and public executions? Who are you trying to fool? This is a bloody dictatorship run by the Soviets and Cubans. The sooner it is overthrown, the better!'

Osvaldo shook his head and said: 'Pity, Radio Kwacha seems to have broken loose some people's nerves. The MPLA is the people's party. It has made mistakes, yes, but it remains the only party capable of answering the people's aspirations.'

This conversation was interrupted by Xavier Ramos, who said: 'Stop praising all these murderers. It's time that you two believed in your Aunt Laura and in the holy ghost.'

Then one day Junior and the secret police came to the settlement. Osvaldo and Xavier Ramos gave themselves up: They said they would rather perish in prison than become involved with UNITA.

After three days with Prophetess Laura, Hosi got in contact with the nearest UNITA camp. One morning several soldiers came for him. Aunt Laura put her hand on her heart, shook her head, sobbed and said: 'O Father, how much more do we have to cry?'

As he kissed Aunt Laura goodbye he thought of Osvaldo. Although they disagreed on many things, there was one point they were agreed on – they all loved Angola. Yes, they were all patriots!

Raul's Notebook

Reflections

I am a bit depressed today. I know it is silly, because what has depressed me is the death of two babies. One was Brigadier Mbeu's; the other was Joel's, the cook. Brigadier Mbeu's baby died of asphyxiation and excessive heat: his mother had piled him with several thick blankets, making it hard for him to breathe. Joel's baby died of pneumonia. There is no absolute equality on earth, but we should strive to bring about as much as we can.

It has just struck me that death is a balancing factor in the world. Death is important, and no one can evade it. Brigadier Mbeu's wife was worried that her baby would catch pneumonia if it was not covered with enough blankets; her efforts to that end cost the baby's life. Joel's wife, on the other hand, must have been looking for blankets. She had just come from the central province and our people there are finding it really hard. I saw a very beautiful girl the other day dressed in tattered clothes, her feet covered with jiggers. When I saw her I felt something clot in my throat. It will only melt the day I shoot a Cuban, the sons of bitches who have brought all this suffering to our land.

I heard a harrowing story the other day. Maybe harrowing is not the proper word; a soldier like myself should avoid such emotive words. The motherland is so dear that even if the swamps are to be filled with blood we, the sons, will have to be ready to fall too. Anyway, the story. A boy from Silva Porto, which the lackeys of the Soviets have now named Kuito, said he once saw a man carrying a bag containing the head of a Cuban. The man, said the boy, opened the sack, pulled out the Cuban's head and held it aloft by the hair, the red flesh of his neck dangling. I asked myself: was this cruel?

287

The answer is no. Suppose I go today to fight in Mongolia and help crush the people's will – that is, help in the installation of an unpopular regime. And then I am captured by the resistance of this regime. They might as well turn me to mincemeat and offer me to the lions or whatever animals they have over there that eat humans. The fact is that I did not have the right to be there in the first place.

This brings me to the point that our enemies are always harping on about internationalism. Internationalism and imperialism are synonymous. As the Elder said the other day, the Soviet Union is an empire that has the desire to expand engraved on its very soul. They will see their dreams come to fruition only over our dead bodies. We are the heirs of the spirit of Kapalandanda. The Portuguese came with their message of civilization. Kapalandanda did not listen to them; he told them to return to their land. And then they turned to force. He said, 'Right, I too will show you what I am made of.' So a heavy battle was fought. This is history, not the stuff the lackeys in Luanda keep broadcasting on their radio. The Soviets and the Cubans are behaving like the Portuguese. In the name of the advancement of communism they are killing our people. But they know that we are not just ordinary people; we are brave. They will see. They will soon flee or we'll force them to eat shit. Bastards!

I have not touched this book for the past three weeks. Not that I have not been reflecting. Many things have been flitting through my mind, but I think they are trivial, and as we are mainly concerned with the motherland – that is, life and death – I feel that this book should not be used to record any of my trivial thoughts.

Although this might seem trivial, it isn't in actual fact. The point is Pilartes, my personal assistant. As an unmarried officer, there are certain things I cannot do because I am too busy thinking of ways of saving the motherland. I cannot cook for myself, wash my clothes, polish my shoes, send messages. That is why the movement has assigned me a personal assistant. I like him and treat him very well. Although he is much older than me, I treat him with a lot of respect, and whenever occasions to have him admonished arise, I do it with consideration. Although the movement has conferred certain ranks on us, we should never forget our African culture: elders must be respected.

There is, however, one problem with Pilartes: nothing pleases him more than frying. Whenever we are given meat or dried fish, he pours the cooking oil into the pot and sits besides the fire seeing the food fry. I don't like fried food; I like cooked food. I told this to Pilartes. He became annoyed.

'Why, then, do they send us cooking oil, sir?' he asked.

'To cook,' I said to him. 'But that is not the prime reason. We should try to economize. Every time you eat anything here in the bush, you should remember that you are doing so because somebody has given his life.'

Pilartes promised that he would lessen the frying. He didn't. I took him to task again. He said that the frying reminded him of the days he worked as a cook for the Portuguese merchant in Kalukembe, where he comes from. I asked him why he should be so obsessed with the past, especially such a shameful one as colonialism. And then he held forth on why he looked back to the days of Senhor Fadario, his Portuguese master, with so much nostalgia. He said Fadario's wife had taught him to cook the best Portuguese dishes and now, if it had not been for the Cubans, he would have been a great chef in some hotel. He said he had known Sergeant Quality, who had gained fame for having been the Elder's cook at the beginning of the resistance, and he was much better than him. I shook my head and was about to tell Pilartes how wrong he was when he said one of the other reasons he kept frying things was vitamins. 'Do you know why it takes four bullets to kill a white man?'

'I don't,' I said.

'It is vitamins. We have few vitamins, so one bullet is enough to do away with us. Not so with the Cubans or the cousins.'

'Which cousins?' I asked him.

'Our cousins, of course, the South Africans.'

'Oh. I see.'

'Where South Africans and Cubans meet it is as if two lions

289

are meeting. What is actually working are the vitamins, not the men. How do they get so many vitamins? By frying. Just frying will do.'

I discern two things in Pilartes's attitude: longing for colonialism and ambition. The first is despicable. These people are just stupid. The Elder has been preaching for ages about the iniquities of colonialism: how we blacks were humiliated; how our wealth was plundered; how our sisters were raped. And yet there are some who long for those days. Man, as the Elder says, is a complicated being. I agree with him completely. There are some girls who spend the afternoons listening to tangos and boleros from the colonial times. These people are mad. The movement has given them cassette recorders, hoping that they will listen to the Elder's speeches or revolutionary songs by our own musicians. Not with them. They whistle along to useless songs. One might understand such attitudes on the part of the peasants. Let's face it: if you give a peasant bread and you tell him that you've given him democracy, he will believe you. But these people who listen to honky colonial tunes are intellectuals!

Lila, my sweetheart, came across this notebook. She says what I've written above are not reflections. I don't remember the Portuguese word she used to describe what it is. The revolution will make new men of us. I am already a new man. In other parts of the world men would not stand being treated the way Lila treats me. She not only corrects my Portuguese grammar in front of Pilartes, of all people, but she also ruffles her feathers whenever it seems as if I am about to deviate from the Paramount Thought formulated by the Elder. Indeed, no one should deviate from the Paramount Thought, otherwise we will all die. However, there are times when we can go round the Paramount Thought to make a point which will converge with the Paramount Thought at some point. It is sad but some of our cadres do not understand this.

Lately I have been thinking of poetry. I often feel like writing some poetry myself. In fact, I wrote several poems which I

290

lost somewhere in the 17th region. But I shouldn't write poems. I have been thinking of the reason. Well, we have the highest revolutionary poet: that is, our leader, the Elder. He is undoubtedly the best poet on earth. This is not an exaggeration. Gill, who escorts journalists whenever they come to pay us visits, says they are simply flabbergasted by the quality of the Elder's poems. Why, then, should I, or any other budding poet, write?

Eugenio Kapingala is dead. I am sure he'll join the other heroes who have gone before him. I wonder what will happen to Stella, his wife. I am sure she'll soon be married.

I have been thinking of polygamy. It is not only important that we should preserve our culture – that is, the habits of our forebears – but we should also be realistic. Let's face it, there are more women than men in Angola. That is a fact. The probability of a man dying is higher than that of a woman. Women need men, so the logical solution is that one man – especially if he is high-ranking – can have more than one wife. There is nothing wrong with that. I heard a group of women complain the other day that young girls were after their husbands. What the self-loving viragos forgot is that if they had been in the young girls' position they would have been all for polygamy.

Personally, I might not marry more than one woman. Lila says she's prepared to share anything with anyone except her man. I respect the wishes of Angolan women, so monogamy will be the only way for me. I have just acquired a Portuguese dictionary in exchange for a pair of boots. Well, the fellow who had the dictionary is illiterate; that made things easier. I have been browsing through the pages and my vocabulary has improved tremendously. Weeks ago I would not have known what monogamy or polygamy meant.

I have not made love to any girl for the past two years and I have made no efforts to make love to any. That is how a true revolutionary must be: a slave to the cause and not a slave of

291

his flesh. This afternoon, just before I went to see Colonel Mbalunduvutima, I saw Fatima, Lieutenant Ndalu's daughter. She has grown very fast. She was wearing a miniskirt and I could not help seeing her thighs. Of course, being a normal man certain bolts in me were loosened. I think such dresses should be banned from this part of Angola. Colonel Mbalunduvutima tells me that in Europe and other parts of the world we African men are considered chauvinists; that is, we are too protective of our wives. Honestly, what is wrong with that? He also told me that in France, where he lived for a while, people made love in the streets and called that progress. Who are they fooling? That is complete regression. It is a return to the barbaric ways of their ancestors. No minis in Angola. What we want is peace and progress. Time for the eight o'clock news.

Who is a true patriot? Of course, the number-one patriots are the Elders, and all those who aspire to be true patriots should emulate them. Many people have tried to write poetry, for instance. Because they were not true patriots their poems were pure rubbish. The other day David, the signalsman, showed me a couple of his poems. There was one about the black sable, which he told me is only to be found in Angola; and there was another about the mulemba tree. Nothing wrong in that. However, I was appalled when he showed me one about Fatima. Those thighs are going to slow down the struggle. When men see them they think of nothing else. David told me that he loves her secretly. He is not a patriot. When people were dying, starving and undergoing the worst men could possibly endure, David took his pen and wrote Fatima a poem. Now, that is not what the Elders do. They love Angola so much. How I wish that we could all love Angola as much as they do!

FOR THE BEST IN PAPERBACKS, LOOK FOR THE 🐧

PENGUIN INTERNATIONAL WRITERS

Gamal Al-Ghitany	**Zayni Barakat**
Wang Anyi	**Baotown**
Joseph Brodsky	**Marbles: A Play in Three Acts**
Shusaku Endo	**The Samurai**
	Scandal
	Wonderful Fool
Ida Fink	**A Scrap of Time**
Miklós Haraszti	**The Velvet Prison**
Ivan Klíma	**My First Loves**
	A Summer Affair
Jean Levi	**The Chinese Emperor**
Harry Mulisch	**Last Call**
Cees Nooteboom	**A Song of Truth and Semblance**
Luise Rinser	**Prison Journal**
Anton Shammas	**Arabesques**
Josef Škvorecký	**The Cowards**
Tatyana Tolstoya	**On the Golden Porch and Other Stories**
Elie Wiesel	**Twilight**
Zhang Xianliang	**Half of Man is Woman**